Where Outlaws Roam
Royal Wade Kimes

This book is a work of fiction. Names, characters, places and incidents are either products of the author's imagination or are used fictitiously. Any resemblance to actual events or locales or persons, living or dead, is entirely coincidental.

ISBN 978-1-943276-28-8 (pbk)

ISBN 978-1-943275-54-0 (e-book)

Flaming Light Publishing - A Division of Wonderment Records.

Copyright © 2015

All Rights Reserved.

Where Outlaws Roam
Royal Wade Kimes

About The Author

Royal Wade Kimes is an uncommon and fascinating award winning writer known to his public as "The Gentleman Outlaw" after his appearance on the cover of True West Magazine. He is a recipient of the Will Rogers Award for his musical talents as well as his writing abilities. He is said by his peers to be the "outlaw of outlaws" because of his determination and will to go against the status quo and succeed. He is a class act individual, and a rare author that actually came from a family tree of notorious outlaws.

Where Outlaws Roam
Royal Wade Kimes

Acknowledgements

Thanks to my editor Betty Ford, Debbie Brooks cover graphics, T. L. Conklin back cover photo and special thanks to Don Gregory for use of his likeness.

Where Outlaws Roam
Royal Wade Kimes

Prelude

Banished from his country, an embarrassment to his family and the Queen of Great Britain, Tucker Shaw laid in the bottom of a ship for weeks on his way to America. His disregard for law and order in his homeland called for severe punishment, but because his family had ties to the Queen he was given a most unusual sentence. He was to be discarded on the shores where outlaws roam.

Though Tucker was shocked and saddened at being exiled from his homeland, he was somewhat excited about having the chance to see and rub shoulders with notorious outlaws. The idea of seeing Dodge City, Kansas and other lawless towns appealed to him. But when he was dumped ashore what he found was anything but outlaws and Wild West towns. He was in the middle of swamps infested with alligators, and his first encounter with people was a Cajun family with ruthless ways and a tyrant by the name of Reed Fletcher. Imprisoned by the swamp and Fletcher he wondered if he would ever see the heart of outlaw country.

Tucker finds himself walking a fine line between outlaw and lawman, but sooner or later he would have to be one or the other. The West demands it.

Meanwhile the beautiful Cajun, Macie, whom he met in the swamps, would haunt him while he took on the law and evaded Reed Fletcher at the same time. Circumstances surrounding an old lawman dictated what Tucker would do next. He was a young and carefree flamboyant man until he met the old lawman. In order to help out his new found friend he was made to wear a badge. Tucker had read and wondered what it would be like to live in the Wild West, and he was fast finding out. He was a young carefree flamboyant man until he was left where outlaws roam… until he unknowingly fell in love with the beautiful dark eyed Macie.

No one could be trusted and no one or anything was safe. Though wearing a badge, Tucker would be forced to make another hard decision, take Macie and run or let her be taken to jail for a murder she swore she didn't commit. The hell of it was, all the evidence pointed at her, and her motive… protect Tucker Shaw.

Where Outlaws Roam
Royal Wade Kimes

Where Outlaws Roam
Royal Wade Kimes

Chapter 1

For weeks Tucker Shaw had listened to the sea splash against the hull of the ship he lay in the bottom of. He was fed once a day, which consisted of one piece of bread and a cut of salt pork sized for a child, certainly not a full grown man. He was brought up twice a day and once at night to relieve himself, and even then he was blind folded. Even though he was on a ship at sea with no land visible, he was not allowed to see anything. The only thing he was given enough of, was fresh water. His senses had dulled to the continuous splashing of the waves hitting the side of the ship, but something was now different.

"Open."

He listened. The splashing had stopped. The ship was not moving. It was anchored. He rose up from the floor on his hands and knees. He tried to look up, but found it too difficult. The light from the portal was blinding. He listened and heard footsteps coming down the stepladder.

"Get up! You're home."

A foot kicked him in the side knocking the air out of his stomach. He rolled over in a fetal position. His legs were shackled in chains as well as his wrists. His ankles were bloody and blue and so were the wrists. His clothes were dingy white colored rags, nearly brown from grime and dirt.

"I said get up!"

Another man joined the one that kicked him. He was much bigger and with ease, reached down and pulled him to his feet.

Tucker looked at him with dull eyes. "I'm up." He mustered a smile through his misery.

"Tucker, boy, you might be from a family of wealth and fame in the Mother Country, but out here on this ship you're just meat for the fish and birds. You're family isn't here to save your sorry ass now."

"One must keep a positive outlook. My family didn't want me; maybe the fish and birds won't have me either."

The big man slung him towards the ladder. "Climb!"

Tucker waited for the blindfold. He turned to them. "What, no blindfold?"

"Not this time, you're home."

He turned and feebly made his way up the ladder. When he crawled out onto the deck and his eyes adjusted to the light, he could see many pairs of freshly shined black boots standing side by side.

He was suddenly yanked to his feet. In the boots were men in uniforms standing at attention, rifles by their sides. He was then turned from them to face two officers, a Captain Ross and a Major Parker. As he stood there his vision began to clear even more. He could hardly see when looking up from the deck. Then he saw a familiar face. It was Admiral Robert Fetter, an old friend of the Tucker family. Tucker smiled as he watched him approach the other two officers. It was the first time he had felt he had any chance to survive his ordeal. He was sure what had happened to him was an intentional lesson arranged by his family. He kept thinking of what great lengths they had gone to, to break him of his disregard of law and instruction, not to mention insubordination, and philandering.

"Robert."

The big man that had picked him up drove his fist into his stomach. He gasped for air as he went to his knees. Then he felt the man pick him up and stand him to his feet.

"You speak when spoken to."

Tucker looked at Admiral Fetter while trying to breathe. The admiral acted as if he didn't know anything was happening to him. He then slowly looked around him. The ship was lined with men the whole way around. He cut his eyes back to the admiral. He decided they were carrying the lesson to the limit, and it was time to end it. He would tell them what they needed and wanted to hear.

"Look, Admiral Fetter, the joke has gone far enough... I mean the lesson, it has surely worked. I'm terribly sorry for my actions, my lawlessness. I apologize to my caring, heartless family for embarrassing them... and."

Again the big man drove his fist into his stomach. Again he was without air. This time though, he felt his stomach was tremendously sore from the last two or three blows.

Captain Ross unrolled a scroll as Tucker was carried by the big

Where Outlaws Roam
Royal Wade Kimes

man on one arm and a smaller man on the other. He was made to stand before the three officers.

Tucker stared at Admiral Fetter, waiting for him to look at him. He didn't. He kept looking straight ahead as the Captain began to read aloud. Every man on the ship could hear the words.

On the Lord's Day of July 25th[th] 1880, under orders of the Queen of Great Britain and direction of Admiral Fetter, I declare and make it known to all under the sound of my voice, a judgment set forth against one Tucker Barthelme Shaw. I do hereby proclaim the Queen has decreed that said subject is to be banished from the Mother Land known as Great Britain forevermore. It is the wish of the Shaw Family that the aforementioned soul be spared the penalty of death. Mr. Ira Shaw, father of the guilty and shamed individual was given three choices of punishment for his son. The first was hanging. The second was the removal of one offending hand, one offending foot and both offending testicles. The last was banishment, to never be seen or heard from again. Because the Shaw Family Name is well respected in Britain, all effort has been made and engaged upon to put closure to this matter diplomatically. Tucker Shaw being the nephew of the Queen... has been spared death by hanging, and may continue to live his life, wretched as it is. The name Tucker Shaw shall never be spoken in Great Britain from this day forth.

Tucker was the nephew of the Queen on his mother's side, and because his mother and the Queen were very close he was not put to death, anyone else would have been. He was spared.

Captain Ross rolled the scroll up. Then Admiral Fetter slowly unrolled another that was handed to him by Major Parker. He stared at it for the longest time. He looked up from the scroll and into the eyes of Tucker. The admiral's eyes were glassy and burned as he stared at the lad he had bounced on his knee when he was but a baby. Ira Shaw, Tucker's father and he were friends, which came about through the Queen and Tucker's mother. He was present the day Tucker was born. Today was the first time he saw confusion and a touch of fear in Tucker's eyes. If there was one thing Admiral Fetter admired about him, it was his fearlessness. He was courageous in battle and afraid of no man. His only enemy was himself. He was extremely good looking at six feet with his dark hair and blue eyes. He had a chin that looked to be chiseled from stone. Until this trip he always stood straight and dressed like a prince. He could ride a horse better than all the warriors of England and could out shoot the most of them. He was somewhat bent now, holding his stomach. He looked at him and thought… what a waste and what a disgrace.

He looked back at the scroll."Tucker Barthelme Shaw, you are to be banished not only from the Mother Land's shores to never set foot upon her again, but if you were to make your way back, you will be hanged immediately by the neck until dead. You have chosen loose lawless ways your lot in life, and therefore you are to be put ashore… where outlaws roam… America, the West. You should and will be with your kind.

America is known for outlaws of the west, such names as the James Gang, the Dalton's and more. You are to be given one single shot rifle with twenty-four shells, signifying one year of your life, one shell per year you have lived. You will have one long blade knife, two days rations and one canteen of water." He paused for an emotional second. "May God have mercy on your soul."

Tucker fought the lump in his throat as realization set in that this wasn't a joke or a reprimand. His eyes were watering and stinging, but he was determined not to shed a tear. He gathered his self and weighed his options. He saw none. So why yield and fold up now. "May I speak?"

Admiral Fetter nodded his head.

"First, I'd like to say I'm sorry for putting you to all this trouble, having to bring me all this way. I know you'd rather be doing something else." He paused for a breath. "Me being the way I am, slipping around in the dark I stumble onto things unseen by most eyes. It's not any accident you're the one hauling me away like common cargo… because you can be trusted not to throw me overboard. Has it not occurred to you that maybe I know you and my mother have a thing going when my ole poppa is not around? Admiral, you've made my mother happy, something dear ole poppa couldn't do. But then he's so busy tapping Bessie

Where Outlaws Roam
Royal Wade Kimes

Brown our maid, how could he satisfy mother? Who would have guessed such scandalous acts happening under the roof of the great Ira Shaw? Myself I hope you and mother don't get caught. The Queen will be so disappointed in you and mother, though I doubt she'd give a damn about poppa." He smiled and stared at Admiral Fetter.

There was a chuckle or two from the enlisted men standing at attention, but it was hushed before anyone saw who it was.

"Isn't it funny how it all works? Me, I'm open with my loose ways, you hide yours and I'm the one that walks the plank." He smiled again. "I'm the one being honest, not trying to hide my dealings. You sneak around in the dark like me and get off free as a bird. Now don't get me wrong, I'm pleased that mother has someone she can confide in and be made over. Mother deserves some kind of affection. It's poppa and Bessie Brown that puzzles me. She's a looker and poppa, well he's twice her age and he's anything but handsome. But Bessie Brown rides him like a race horse on a mile race." This time the ranks across both sides of the ship laughed, but quickly drew the laughter in.

"The upper crust does have its hidden sins... doesn't it, Admiral?" I'm betting it catches up with you. To be more serious, I hope it doesn't. I like you Admiral Fetter, Robert, always did, always will." He paused and looked around him for a moment. "Admiral, could I ask a favor? Would you please be so kind as to tell my folks I said I'm sorry I shamed them and didn't take time to learn how to hide all my dirty dealings like they have? Tell them I appreciate their sparing my life, that was just great big of them. Tell my ole poppa to lay off the corn liquor some and to stop tapping the maid. One or the other is going to kill him. Aren't we all just one big happy family?"

Tucker looked around at all the service men. "Hell, I thought poppa was going to kill ole Bessie Brown. I heard her hollering one night when mom was gone, I thought sure he was killing her." He grinned when the men broke out into laughter. "My old man is hung like a stud horse." Again they boomed with laughter.

Major Parker called them to attention immediately. Once it was quiet again, Tucker turned to the admiral. "You can tell the

Where Outlaws Roam
Royal Wade Kimes

Queen I said she better hope I don't come back. I'll expose her dirty laundry before she can get me hung in spite of hell." He cut his eyes to the big man that had hit him in the stomach. "Can this big ape unlock these chains so I can be on my way?"

The admiral was red faced with embarrassment. Tucker had exposed his private dealings in front of his men. He understood his anger, but still, to disregard the rank of an officer and friend. He nodded to unlock the chains. Though Tucker had embarrassed him he was still amused at the fact, even now, as dire as it looked and was for him, he was still standing tall to it. That part of him he had to respect. He would have made a tremendous military man had he applied himself. He served in the Queen's Guard for a short time, but instead of following orders, he chased and bedded women in high and low places, one was even a decorated general's wife. He out foxed all of the Royal Commanders one way or another in every way and in everything possible. They could do nothing with him. He was booted from service and from there he began his role as the Robin Hood of Britain. He embarrassed the Queen more than once, not to mention his own family, and he made fools out of law officers and military personnel alike. He was arrested twice and escaped both times. He killed two of the Queen's Guards in a gunfight at the Royal Kings Tavern. Tucker claimed self-defense and maybe it was. He had robbed, stolen, disrupted business and flow of money to the point it didn't much matter if he was guilty or not of killing the guards. He had to pay and pay he was. He had done too much to be forgiven any longer.

The big man turned and unlocked the wrists and then got down on one knee to unlock the ankles.

Tucker looked around at everyone smiling as his leg chains were being loosed. Once done, he came down across the back of the big man's head with both fists. He drove the man's face into the deck, and then he kicked him full in the face with his right foot. Blood immediately splattered. He broke the man's nose and knocked out two front teeth. He got him one more time in the face before they could subdue him. The big man was knocked unconscious and began to bleed from the ears. The medic on the ship checked him over and then stood.

Where Outlaws Roam
Royal Wade Kimes

"Admiral, you best get Tucker off the ship and this man lying here into a bed. I doubt he makes it. I think his nose has been driven into his brain."

Admiral Fetter cut his flaming eyes at Tucker. "I should have you hung, but I can't. My orders are to see you set ashore in America under any and all circumstances. You always beat the system… don't you?"

"Robert, it's a fixed and sorry system you and your kind have set up." He looked out towards the land called America. "Maybe this is where I belong, where outlaws roam… my kind. At least they're honest about who and what they are."

Major Parker handed him his rifle, shells, and his rations in a cloth sack. He nodded, smiled and then whispered. "John Mason was the big chap's name. He deserved what you gave him." He turned back to the admiral and saluted.

Tucker turned to Admiral Fetter. "I know I've always called you Robert, because we've always been friends, but today, for you, and for your men." He took a breath and saluted. "Admiral Fetter, you are one of the good guys, keep the wind to your back and in your sails."

Admiral Fetter was given orders not to show any respect of any kind to the prisoner, and positively do not salute him if the situation was to arise. The authorities knew enough about Tucker Shaw to know he might salute his superiors in an exhibit of flash and disrespect. He was known to flaunt his triumphs openly. Still, Admiral Fetter saluted him because of his sheer unwillingness to break and bow. He watched as he walked the bridge to land. Once on shore he turned, waved and disappeared into the brush.

Chapter 2

For the next two days he walked and slept in a total wilderness. He didn't have any idea where the ship had dropped him. What he did know, there was swamps, alligators and snakes big enough to swallow a man. He hadn't seen a soul, not even a track of a human being. His rations were dwindling and his spirit was too. He did manage to kill a squirrel and cook it. There was a tin box with matches in his rations sack. He smiled when he found it, because it belonged to Admiral Fetter.

Tucker was just sure he would pop out into the open and see cowboys riding grand looking horses on trails heading west. It hadn't happened. Where were the cattle he had read about, the big herds, the fights and shoot outs in saloons? All he had seen was mosquitos big enough to shoot out of the air and black mud so sticky thick he could hardly walk at times.

He lay down on a bank overlooking a small stream where the last of the evening sun could hit him in the face. He had dozed off when he heard a racket. He turned his head ever so slowly to his left. There were a half dozen ducks swimming across the small stream. He very slowly raised his rifle. He picked out the one swimming along behind the rest and squeezed the trigger. He saw the bullet make a tremendous splash a good foot behind the duck.

"Damn it!" He watched as they flew away, and he then looked at his rifle, and began to talk to himself. "I killed a squirrel yesterday, must have just gotten lucky. I shot while it jumped through the trees, no time to aim. I'd bet the Queen's purse ole John Mason knocked these sites off for me special like. I must thank him when I see him again." He smiled despite his pitiful situation.

"No luck I see!"

He whirled around with rifle cocked. There was a man standing back by a tree just a few feet up stream.

"You fired your shot. You'd have to reload to take one at me." He laughed. "Look, if you're hungry, follow me. I've got a camp just over this little hump of dirt here." He turned and disappeared.

Where Outlaws Roam
Royal Wade Kimes

Tucker lowered his gun and cautiously followed. When he entered the camp there were others sitting around, three men and five women. The four older women didn't look at him, but the young one did, and she kept looking, though her face was somewhat covered with long black hair. The other three men sized him up and went back to eating. The man who invited him to camp smiled showing very yellow teeth, and pointed at a rock by the fire.

"Make yourself at home, that's what we done when we got here. There's some hog meat on the stick there. Cut yourself off a hunk. It's damn tasty."

Tucker pulled his long bladed knife and cut a nice size piece. He tore off a bite as his eyes took in everyone once more.

"My name is Cook, Morrell Cook. These ole boys is my brothers, Dick, Sal, and Hon." All three nodded.

"I'm Tucker Shaw, pleased to meet you."

Morrell smiled. "You talk with an uncommon accent. You're not from these parts are you?"

"No, I'm sorry ole Chap, but I'm afraid I'm not from... these parts." He smiled at his host. He liked the way he talked. Though he found his speech to be amusing, he wasn't sure if the rest of him was as charming.

Morrell handed him a jar with liquid in it. "Try a snort. It'll tickle your innards and make that hog meat go down better. I'm not going to tell you how much hair it'll put on a man's chest, but it's a right smart."

Tucker decided he didn't like Morrell. In fact he was becoming a bit uneasy with him and his brothers. They sat eating and staring at him the whole time Morrell talked. He surveyed the camp again to see if there was anyone he might have missed in the little group. He was about to look over at Morrell when he saw something that stopped him in mid chew of his meat. If he wasn't mistaken, there was a bare foot sticking out of the brush over by and behind the three brothers.

"Boy, you got a lot to learn if you plan to make it in these parts. I seen you spot the previous owner of this here camp. That lone tent yonder was his and that red mule tied by the horses was his too. He didn't have but ten dollars on him… sum total. Times has been tough since the war." He shook his head as he drew his pistol and cocked it. "Like I say, you got a lot to learn if you're going to make it in these here parts. You didn't reload that one shot rifle of yours… bad mistake. Man wants to be loaded and ready to go to shootin' in this Louisiana swamp."

Tucker smiled.

Morrell cut his eyes to the other three. "Ain't he the fine haired one? He can smile not knowing if he has a next minute." He looked back at him. "What do you find funny there, Tucker? You did say, Tucker?"

"I did. Well, what I smiled about was… I didn't know where I was until you said Louisiana. I was pleased to have an idea of which way to strike out from here. According to the maps I studied of America, due north and maybe a little west, I should end up in one or the other of your states, Arkansas or Oklahoma. From there I could journey to Kansas. I would surely love to see Dodge City." He grinned rather largely. That's said to be a rip snorting town."

Morrell could hardly believe his ears. "Tucker, you may either be the dumbest sonofabitch I ever met, or you are putting on one hell of an act. I'm standing here with a gun on you, yet you act like Sunday School just let out and we're all going for Sunday dinner. Well, no matter, brains don't play into this."

Tucker laid his meat down on a small rock. "Well, I figure if a man offers another man some of his food, he can't be all bad." He knew he had big trouble staring him in the face.

Dick, Sal, and Hon started laughing. Hon threw the rest of his meat in the fire and drew his gun. "Morrell, I think you hit it. This boy is just plain damn dumb… but with that said and maybe known, he is a well put together lad. He's got good bone, square chin, near six feet I judge."

Dick stood and drew his pistol. "Yeah, I guess him twenty-five years. He's got good eyes, blue, and his shoulders are plenty broad enough." He looked down at Sal who was still eating. "What do you think, Sal? This is a family matter, speak up."

Sal stood and drew his gun. "Well, I'd say he'll more than do. It comes to me we're mighty lucky to come on to something like

Where Outlaws Roam
Royal Wade Kimes

this one. Hell, it's nearly like going to the town gathering and winning the prize bull, ya just don't expect to win it."

Hon laughed. "By God you're right! I figured all we'd find was a damn swamp rat... trapping beaver and muskrat." Hon eyeballed Tucker. "We done went and found the prize bull is what we've done!"

Morrell laughed. "We have, we shore have!" He looked at the four women. "Ma, what do you think? I noticed Macie eyeing him good, maybe like she could take a shine."

The older woman of the three elderly women looked up. She cut her eyes to Morrell and then back to Tucker. "He'll do. If Macie likes him, we all like him. It's the end result we're after, nothing more."

"Excuse me, but I feel like I'm at a sale or something. I think I better be going. I have a long travel ahead of me if I plan to see the great Wild West."

Morrell laughed. "I don't know how much West we have here, but you're in the wild already. It don't get any wilder than these damn swamps and the people in it." He grinned and then looked serious. "Now here's the skinny. Damn near everyone in this swamp country was wiped out by a damn plague of some kind. We all be kin here. Those three are my brothers as I said, and Macie is my daughter. We all got wives, but Macie there, she has no man and the prospects of getting one ain't so good. She's now nineteen and needing a mate bad, another month or two and she'll be out of hand in heat." He grinned real big. "So you've been picked."

"I've what?" He wasn't sure he heard right, for surely he didn't. No one could be that backward or barbaric.

"Macie is needin' bred and you been picked. If you was to take a shine to her afterwards... well, we might work out something where the two of you could be man and woman, otherwise you can just service her." He looked around at everyone. "We might be a little crude in our ways, but we don't go in for no breeding amongst ourselves. It ain't right and proper, Bible talks again it, and we'll not be guilty of it. You got to give us that. We try to hold above that kind of thing." He smiled. "You've been chosen fairly." He laughed. "Well, you didn't have any competition. She's yours if the two of you say it that way afterwards."

"My good man, just because I speak differently doesn't mean I'm an idiot."

"Didn't say it did. The little one won't talk like you anyway. Right now all you need worry on is being the stud Macie needs."

"The hell you say?" Tucker was astonished.

"Didn't say nothing 'bout hell."

"It'll be interesting to see what her pup will be named... her matin' up with a dude from some other place and all."

"What does that have to do with anything?"

Morrell smiled as he eyed his brothers. "Well, you take ole Hon there. He come by that name because he was a honey with women in his sparking days. The name Hon just kind of stayed on even after he took him a woman. Hon had his choice to pick from." Morrell glanced at Dick. This'en here is the older of us boys. Dick's real name is Buck. I don't have to tell you why we call him Dick. Before the damn plague it wasn't nothing to see women following him around like bitches in heat." Us Cooks are real men. Ole Sal is probably the more sensible and modest one of us. Pa Cook thought the name Sal was fittin' for a sound thinker. Sal don't take on airs about his manhood like maybe the rest of us do. We've always been a family that liked to brag a little."

Tucker's eyes were wide with amazement. "You folks might be the damn-dest thing I've ever encountered. God save the Queen, and I don't even like the bitch, but I'll not be participating in anything like this! I've done some outrageous and even scandalous things in my life, and I find myself a little embarrassed to be upstaged by a family of degenerate swamp rats."

Morrell's smile left him immediately. "Did you just insult our good name? We may appear ignorant, but we're anything but." All three of the brothers holstered their guns. Then they all four converged on him. He short jabbed Hon causing him to fall like a rock. He then swung hard at Morrell and landed a hard right to the jaw. He went sailing backwards as Dick landed a hard left to Tucker's jaw. He didn't go down, but he was dazed for a second. He saw the next fist coming and ducked. He short jabbed Dick

Where Outlaws Roam
Royal Wade Kimes

twice in the stomach and then upper cut him. He went down and out. Sal came from behind and broke a bottle over his head. He saw a brief moment of stars and thereafter was out.

Sal looked around at his three brothers who were all on the ground. He helped them up one by one.

Morrell was smiling as he rubbed his jaw. "He'll do for shore. He hits hard."

Hon was looking at a jaw tooth he had lost in the fight. He glanced at Macie. "By damn girly, you better ride the hell out of him. Your old uncle lost a good tooth in the damn doing for you."

She smiled as she stood by the tent. The four Cook Brothers carried Tucker to the tent, tied his arms apart and stripped him of his clothes except for his underclothes. They came out smiling and left Macie with him.

When Tucker awoke he was staring at the dark eyed swamp girl called Macie. He hadn't gotten a real good look at her before. She kept her head bowed and her hair was so long he couldn't see her face well. He wasn't having any trouble now. She had candles burning in the tent and was sitting on bent knees before him. She was completely naked. She looked like a wild beautiful animal of the wilderness that no one could think of taming. Her skin was a cream color and her eyes were black as lava rock. The candle light danced in the center of them making her even more sensual. Her hair hung all the way down to the palm of her back. He noticed the perfect curvature of her lips and the remarkable facial features. He wondered at her. How could anyone in this God forsaken place be that beautiful? Then he thought of her father and uncles.

"Macie."

"Yes."

He was relieved. She could actually talk. She hadn't thus far. "What are the chances of you untying me?"

"Will you make love to me if I do?"

He had seen the time he would have made love to something like her as many days and times as she wanted. This wasn't one of those times. She had a clan outside the tent he wanted to get away from. He looked at her. "Macie, it wouldn't be right."

"It's right if I am okay with it, is it not?"

"Yes, well, yes, but no. It sounded to me like Pa Cook wants a grandchild. He wants you pregnant and married."

"No, no, just bred. He told you the truth about the population of the swamp people. They are all but wiped out. I am the only girl to live through it. All the boys mine and your age died. I am in need and you are here. I think you were sent here for me."

"Oh… honey, you have no idea what it took to get me here, and it wasn't so I'd be with you, trust me."

She smiled. "You confirm what I'm saying. You come out of nowhere, and no one like you has ever been seen in these swamps. You say there was great effort for you to be here, you make my point."

"You know for you to be kin to those four outside, you're smart, you speak well."

"I had schooling. There was a lady brought in twice a week by small boat to teach the swamp kids."

"I see."

"Enough talk, Tucker."

When she said his name his thoughts went from escaping, to the way she said Tucker. There was something about it he liked. Nonetheless he needed to get loose.

Macie leaned over and slid on top of him. She ran her long slender fingers across his chest to each nipple and then she put her tongue on them. She moved up further.

"No, I won't do this. It has to be under my terms when I make love."

"Do you always get your way?" She smiled and it was both devilish and sexy.

He thought about that for a moment. He almost smiled, because he realized he pretty much had gotten his way all his life. "What if I do?"

"Well, that will change today." She put a powder like substance over his face and he knew nothing more. He was out like a baby.

Hon, Dick and Sal were looking at the silhouette the candlelight shown of Macie on the side of the tent, until Morrell came back from relieving himself. "You three mind your damn selves."

Where Outlaws Roam
Royal Wade Kimes

They turned and immediately walked away. They went to their women folk and bedded down, all but Dick. Seeing Macie's naked image put him in another state of mind. He took his woman just outside of the camping area, pulled her worn out dress up and roughly treated her.

Chapter 3

Tucker awoke to all kinds of swamp sounds. Darkness had invaded the bayou and night time creatures were on the move. He opened the fold on the tent and looked out. The camp was empty. He checked the body he had seen in the bushes before he was made captive. He wondered what else he had been made to do while out. There was an old piece of a shovel lying beside the dead man. He figured the Cooks left it for him to bury the man. He looked around him. His gun was leaning against a tree and his sack was full of things to eat. He had more rifle shells than he had before, and they had left him a map and marked where he was at. They gave him a way out of the swamp. He smiled. His next thought was of Macie. He wondered if anything happened between them. She was probably the most sensual woman he had ever seen... but Lord, to be mixed up with the Cooks would be worse than being mixed up with the Shaw's. He laughed, and then yelled. "America! You haven't shown me your greatness yet, only the poor and misguided."

The following day he came out of the swampy glades onto a sandy road. There were watermelons across the narrow road in a nice size field. He was both hungry and thirsty and a watermelon would take care of both. He ran to the first one and rolled it over. It had turned a yellow cast on the bottom indicating it was ripe. He cut it open with his big bladed knife and began to eat the juicy red fruit. He had eaten one whole half of the melon when he saw three men coming. They had two big black and red looking hounds with them. They were carrying rifles and as they drew closer they leveled them at him. One of the men was a giant of a black man and one of the white men was nearly as big. The one in the middle was slender, but tall. It didn't take long to find out he was the boss.

"I'm Reed Fletcher. This is my field of melons. The one you've ate is or was mine. It now belongs to you without offer of payment before being eaten. What that means is... you are a damn thief. Around here thieves are dealt with in a hurry."

"Sir, I assure you I'm not a thief per say. I've been lost in that

Where Outlaws Roam
Royal Wade Kimes

God awful swamp for several days. I was near to starved and needing water. I didn't figure a man would miss one melon when he had so many."

The slender man smiled and then sneered at him. "That's what you figured is it? Well stranger, if I let every damn stray that come by eat my melons I wouldn't have so damn many, now would I?"

"I suppose not, and let me say I am truly sorry for taking liberties. I can give you my rifle in trade of the melon."

Reed looked at his rifle. "I got no use for a single shot piece of iron rifle like that. I'm holding a repeater. No, we got ways for you to pay." He cut his eyes to the big black man. "Lester, bring him along."

"Wait! Now wait a minute! Bring me along where?"

Reed seemed agitated suddenly. "Boy, you're going to work that melon off. One melon is two weeks work picking cotton."

"Now wait a damn minute!"

Lester stepped forward to get him by the arm. He outweighed him by at least seventy-five pounds. Tucker sidestepped and caught him in the side of the head. He went to his knees and shook his head. He tried to get up, but Tucker short jabbed him with the butt of his gun. He went backwards and out.

Reed yelled at the other man with him. "Briggs, get that sonofabitch!"

Briggs rushed him and was met with a roundhouse swing of the rifle. He tried to back up, but the sand under his feet wouldn't let him. The rifle caught him across the nose and cheek. He went down and rolled over twice. He got to his hands and knees and then stood. Tucker was rushing in for the kill when a shot was fired.

"Boy, you take one more step and it'll be in eternal hell. Now, throw that damn rifle down before I blow a hole in you I can see through."

Tucker grinned. "Whatever you say." He threw the rifle at Briggs and hit him in the back of the head. He flattened out like a buffalo hit with a fifty caliber. The dust from the sandy roadway had boiled up all around them.

Where Outlaws Roam
Royal Wade Kimes

Reed fired his gun at Tucker's feet. "You're one of them."

"What's one of them?"

"You got one of those iron will's."

Lester began to make an effort to stand. Once he was upright he sauntered over to Briggs. "Can ya gets up, Briggs?" He waited until he saw him move, and then he lifted him to his feet. Lester gathered their guns and waited for orders.

Reed's eyes kept going from his men to Tucker. "Lester, put this sonofabitch to picking cotton. When he comes in from the fields, put him to cutting weeds. Get one of the Negro women to carry a lantern for him to see by. He misses one weed, he gets half supper ration the following night."

"I's will do-er Boss."

"Briggs."

"Yeah Boss?"

"If this dumb bastard tries to escape... kill 'em."

He looked at Tucker and grinned. "It would be a pleasure."

Reed pulled a cigar from inside his rose colored vest. "Boy, for resisting arrest, you'll serve another month on top of the two weeks. That work for you?"

"The name is Tucker, Tucker Shaw, and no it doesn't work for me. In Britain you wouldn't think of pushing a Shaw around."

"Sonny... you ain't in Britain. You're in Reed Fletcher country. What I say goes."

Lester swung his big fist and hit him in the side of the head. He was out cold.

Tucker woke up looking at several pair of big wide black eyes. They were all Negro people, and all but two of them were young boys and girls, ranging from eight to maybe thirteen.

The older one spoke up when he saw him awake. "You done went and done it, Mister. Lester and Briggs gots it in for you."

Tucker chuckled. "Is that all? You had me worried for a minute." He felt his jaw and checked his teeth. "Well, I didn't lose anything." He looked around at the building they were in. There weren't any chairs or beds anywhere. There was a little straw and a few pillows. It looked like an old barn made into a half done living quarters. He walked to the door with some effort as

Where Outlaws Roam
Royal Wade Kimes

he dragged a chain and ball along behind him. He found the door locked from the outside. There were some dirty white pots setting over by the far wall to relieve ones' self in.

"Mister, we got a potato and a piece of cornbread. There's water in that bucket hanging on a nail yonder. We all have to share the dipper."

"My name is Tucker, what's yours?"

The older boy smiled. "Angel Hound."

Tucker was staring off until he heard the name. "Where'd a name like that come from?"

"Mama called me Angel. Before I gots here I was on a plantation. The war freed me for this here job." He sniggered. "I been here six months. I tried to escape three times. Ole Reed Fletcher run me hard with those two hounds you seed today. He said I can run might near as fast as his dogs. Since that time, everyone calls me Angel Hound."

"What did a boy like you do to cause his self to be here six months?"

"I was on my way to Arkansas and took a short cut cross his land. He gots me for trespassing, and give me two months for it. I back talked him and got an extra month. He said ain't no nigger talking up to him. Then I stole a biscuit from the Fletcher kitchen cause I be hungry. That lands me more time."

Tucker realized he was a prisoner and if he didn't play along, he could possibly be one for a long time. He grinned as he gave thought to it. When did he ever play along with anyone?

He turned over on his side and closed his eyes. He opened them when a girl of about sixteen nudged him. "Mister, here's a pillow." He reached and took it. "I appreciate it. What's your name?"

"Pixy."

"Nice name. You have folks?"

"A mama. Me and Angel Hound have same mama, different daddy."

"I see. So... I guess you and Angel Hound were headed to Arkansas to find her?"

"All of us were."

"What?" Tucker rose up on an elbow. "Explain."

"The rest of these kids lost their parents. We couldn't leave them behind."

He looked at all the kids lying around the room. "I think you and Angel Hound have overloaded your wagon."

"We don't have no wagon. We has a mama and she'll know whats to do."

"How did you get separated from your mama?"

"The war. I was maybe one year old. Daddy died last year. Angel Hound and me decided to leave. His daddy was killed in the war. Angel Hound is near eighteen now." She smiled and half turned. "Well, goodnight."

"Goodnight." He watched as she walked back to her small bed in the straw and curled up. He couldn't imagine the kind of life she had lived.

Along about midnight shots were fired, hounds began running and loud voices were heard. Horses raced out of the corrals across from where Tucker and the other condemned were. It quieted down some and then more shots. This time they were further away. The hounds hushed and the shooting stopped. Thirty to forty-five minutes passed and horses could be heard coming back. Tucker dragged his chain and ball over to the wall near the activity. He peered through a crack in the boards.

"I be damned."

Angel Hound crowded in beside him. "What? Let me see."

"Old friends."

"Who?" Angel Hound looked through the crack when Tucker turned and leaned his back against the wall. "You know those people? They look worse than we do."

"I know them alright."

Suddenly a new noise. He turned around and moved Angel Hound over. He looked through the crack. There were six or eight lanterns lit and burning bright to give light to the event at hand. Reed was using a bullwhip on someone and he wasn't holding back. After the fifteenth lash the man cried out just a little. The next one he cried out a little more. Then one of the others cursed Reed. He was immediately slugged in the stomach and slapped to

Where Outlaws Roam
Royal Wade Kimes

the ground by Briggs. The whipping stopped at forty lashes. Then the man on the ground was stripped of his shirt and was whipped. They added ten lashes for his cursing. There was one left, but he was hardly able to stand. They tied him to the post anyway and Reed began to cut the meat off his back. He stopped at forty and the man never made a sound the whole time. Tucker didn't know if he was unconscious while being whipped or he was that tough. He also wondered something else. There were four Cook brothers, but three was all that was whipped. He would know the answer to all his questions soon enough.

The door to the prisoner's quarters opened and three men were drug in and dropped. Lester cut his eyes over to Tucker. "I's be real happy when you messes up and I sees you hanging on that whipping post. I hope Reed lets me do the honors."

"That might be the shortest whipping on record. I doubt you can count past two." He started across the room when Reed entered. "Lester! Leave him be. You and the boys go to bed. We have a lot of work lined up for tomorrow."

Tucker blew him a kiss and laughed as he left the room.

Angel Hound waited until they were gone and then knelt down beside him. "You be crazy, and you ain't long for this world you keeps that up."

He chuckled. "One half of winning a battle is to keep your opponent off balance a little. Ole Lester angers quickly. A man that can't handle his temper, I can beat every time."

"Well, you'll be having to, that be shore."

"Angel Hound, how many guards are there during the day?"

"Twenty guards, Lester and Briggs. If you count Reed Fletcher there would be twenty-three total sum."

"Is that all?"

"Ain't that enough?" He looked at Tucker with great curiosity.

"It's not enough to hold the likes of me and you is it?"

Angel Hound laughed. "I shore like you. I don't think you will lives long, but I shore like you."

Tucker's eyes darted over towards the three men when he heard one of them groan. In a few minutes Sal sat up. He looked around him trying to focus his eyes. He sat still for a moment.

And then put his hand on Dick. "Wake up." He waited. "Wake up, Dick."

"What?" Dick slowly sat up and winced from pain while doing it. "That bastard tried to kill us with his damn whip." His head turned towards his other brother lying beside him. "Morrell, you okay? Wake up. We done stepped in it. We got us a roof over our heads, but our neighbors over at the big house aren't the friendly sorts."

Sal leaned over and listened to Morrell breathing. He sat back up. "Dick, Morrell is dead."

"Morrell, dead?" He crawled over to him. "Morrell, wake up now! This here ain't no time to check out. We're in a damn pickle. It'll take all of us to break out of here. Morrell, wake the hell up!"

He didn't move. Tucker decided it was time he let them know he was in the barn. "I'm afraid Morrell is dead like Sal said. It looks like Reed Fletcher whipped a dead man." He now knew why the third man never made a sound.

Sal squinted trying to see through the lantern light hanging on the post between him and Tucker. "Dick, look here, that's Macie's man."

"I be damned." Dick glanced at him, but then returned his attention to Morrell. "Sal, I'm going to have to kill that man with the whip."

Sal kept looking at Tucker, but spoke to Dick. "In case you don't know, we're in a hell of a fix. We can't run with these chains on our ankles, and our backs will be so damn sore before long we'll be hard pressed to move at all. "

Dick put Morrell's hat over his face. "What we going to do?"

"Nothing till we heal."

Tucker laughed.

Sal cocked his head to one side. "Lover boy, what do you find so funny?"

Tucker heard what he said and immediately went back to the night in the tent. Did he actually make love to Macie or was it all a hoax? He eyed the both of them.

"I find it funny you two think you're going to heal up. I doubt anyone gets to heal or live very long in here. Morrell has already cashed in."

Dick turned to Sal. "He might be right, Sal. Morrell took a bullet. I found a small hole just under his arm... 'bout the size of a thirty-two."

Sal got to his feet, but it wasn't easy. He made it to the dipper and bucket. He took a full dipper and drank it down."Angel Hound spoke up. "Mister, we're allowed a half a dipper, no more."

"Nigger, that may be for you, but not for me. I drank your half... and mine. How's that?"

Tucker got up and walked to the bucket. He held his hand out for the dipper. As Sal handed it to him he punched him dead on the chin, knocking him unconscious. Dick made a feeble attempt to stand but went back down.

"I'll kill you for that. I don't give a damn if you did breed Macie."

"You tell Sal when he wakes up that he'll treat everyone in here with respect. I'll beat him to death if he doesn't. Do we understand each other... Dick?"

Dick had anger across his face but held himself in check. "We do for now."

"Good. Now listen to me. We're all going to have to work together to get shed of this place, so let us try and get along until then. Once we're free of it, then you, me, and Sal can go to it. I welcome the event. I would like nothing better than to beat your damn faces to pulps."

"They ain't been the man born that can whip a pair of Cooks. It can't be done."

Tucker laughed and then lay down. He smiled as he closed his eyes. So far America had been one big ole disappointment. Things had to pick up soon. He was almost asleep when Sal woke.

"Dick, what happened?"

"Macie's lover man caught you with one of his damn little short jabs and you thumped the ground like a head shot coon out of a tall cottonwood."

Tucker sat up on his elbow and stared at the two brothers. "Sal, speaking of Macie and the women folks... and I guess Hon, where are they at?"

"Macie's mother was killed outright. She took a bullet to the head. Dick's woman was shot, don't know how bad. The only one of the women I know positive wasn't hurt was Macie. They got away. Hon took 'em into the swamp like a bee to a hive."

Tucker lay back down and then sat up abruptly. He realized he was concerned about Macie. He shook his head to see if he could hear it rattle. It didn't, so he lay back down and drifted off to sleep.

Where Outlaws Roam
Royal Wade Kimes

Chapter 4

Before the sun was up Macie was tending bullet wounds. Dick's wife had passed during the night, and Edith, Sal's wife was hurt badly. Hon and his woman had escaped without any wounds. Macie counted herself lucky she wasn't lying back at the farm where all the shooting took place. She heard the bullet that hit her mother and she heard several more whiz by her.

Hon walked over and sat down on a rock by her. "How is she?" He was looking at Edith who was unconscious.

Macie shook her head slowly and whispered. "If she lives till noon I'll be surprised."

"Well, do what you can."

"Hon, all I can do is make her comfortable. She's bleeding inside."

"I'm going to kill ever damn one of those sonofabitches. They have Sal, Dick, and Morrell."

She cut her dark eyes to Hon. "I doubt they have Morrell. I heard a thud and I saw his body jerk. I'm afraid he got hurt bad."

"Morrell's okay, you'll see. All we wanted was a few melons and a place to sleep. There wasn't anyone using that tobacco barn anyway."

She looked at Edith when she moaned. "I've heard of Reed Fletcher. I heard you and the rest talk about him several times. You always stayed clear of him. Why did you go there? I don't understand it."

"Morrell thought we might cabbage on to a cow or two. Ain't no one else got much around here that we know of. You'd have to travel several hours to just find someone that could afford a damn pussy cat since reconstruction. Hell, we was fair nice people 'fore the war."

"Hon, I love you, but we ain't been nice people long as there has been Cooks. Ma was good and I've tried to be, but none of the Cook men have been worth spit, including you and you know it. I'm plum sick of the way ma and me have had to live. At least she's out of it now."

"You hush that talk." Hon looked away from her.

"Truth stings doesn't it?"

Where Outlaws Roam
Royal Wade Kimes

He turned and stared at her. "If you feel that way, why don't you just crawfish away from me and mine? When Sal and Dick gets back, we'll take us a vote as to whether or not you can stay. You got high and mighty after sleeping with that unusual feller. I wouldn't have thought screwing the man would have messed with your damn brain."

"Hon, there just ain't no reaching you is there?"

"Macie, you're stepping off in a gator hole."

Edith moaned and turned her head slightly towards Macie. She smiled, took a short quick breathe and passed.

Tucker watched as everyone took their cotton sacks and headed out into the fields. It had been daylight for only an hour at best. They were fed slop called oatmeal with bugs in it. Two guards were all that was out at the field. They sat on two good horses, the best he had seen in some time. He eased over by Angel Hound.

"Is this all the guards that watch the fields?"

"Nope. Normally there are four on horses and six to ten on foot. The rest are watching the house or other fields. Reed has melons, tobacco, cotton, and corn fields."

"Then he doesn't have enough men to watch us all properly. Where do you reckon the rest of the guards are today?"

"I seed them take the dogs and head out into the swamp. I reckon they going to try and catch the rest of the ones that got away. They be laughing and carryin' on 'bout it all. Boss had his so called experts with him, Raff Thibodeaux and a couple others. They be killers I hear. He only takes them on killin' trips."

"I see." He surveyed the landscape again. "Angel Hound, is that a riverbank I'm looking at about a half a mile due west?"

"It is for shore. It's where Boss Fletcher keeps his steamboat."

"Steamboat? Then the river is deep. How big is that boat?"

"Big enough Boss Fletcher have parties with lots of people, and floats it up and down the river half the night. He have a party least once a month. He even have them big shots law makers." He smiled real big at being able to tell what he knew.

Tucker became excited. He used to navigate the Queen's steamboat from time to time. That was the one thing he loved to do. He owned a sailboat at one time as well. "Where is this steamboat located on the river?"

"It be upstream towards the house."

"These parties, how many normally come out to them?"

"Thirty, maybe more I guess. What you be thinking?"

"I'm thinking we're leaving here before Reed Fletcher gets back." He glanced at one of the guards. He was smoking a cigarette with his left leg out of the stirrup and around the saddle horn. He looked to his right. The other guard signaled he was going to ride into the bushes to relieve his self. Tucker couldn't believe his luck. He eased over to the sore backed Sal and Dick.

Dick drew back a fist. "You get away from me."

"You lack brains of an idiot. Look around you... one guard. The other one rode off into the bushes. You two beat it over there. When he comes out, jump him. I'll have this one subdued by the time he comes out."

Dick looked at Tucker very skeptical like. "What the hell does sub... doo mean?"

"Harnessed."

"Oh." Suddenly Dick brightened up. He and Sal took off as fast as they could, which was about the speed of a large snapping turtle. The ball and chain along with the raw backs had slowed them considerably.

Tucker eased his way to within thirty feet of the guard. "I sure could use a bush to empty the ole bladder."

The guard looked him over and motioned with his head and pointed at a bush out in front of him. It was at least forty feet away. He eased in front of the horse and then suddenly grabbed the bridle bit. He pulled back hard causing the horse to jump and run backwards. The guard fell from the horse head first. He tried to get around with his gun, but he was somewhat dazed and slow. Tucker kicked him square under the chin causing him to fall violently backwards. His neck snapped from the force of the boot and he never moved again. He took the key to the shackles off the guard and sat down.

"Angel Hound, gather all the kids and beat it to the boat! We're getting out of here! I'm going ahead and get it ready to leave the dock." He unlocked his shackles and gave Angel Hound the key. He then mounted the guard's bay horse and rode like the wind towards the house. He rode to within view and then turned towards the river. He cut and weaved through tall cottonwood and willow. He saw the boat and waited to make sure it was clear to board. He didn't see any guards, so he touched the bay with his heel and loped across to it. He bailed off and ran onto the deck. The captain of the steamer was asleep with his hat pulled down over his eyes. He tapped him on the shoulder and when he roused up he hit him hard on the chin. He slumped from his seat at the wheel onto the floor. He then tied him up quickly with a cotton rope lying handy as if it were there just for the task. He hurriedly slipped below to the boiler and found three men below.

The big one of the three came towards him. "Who are you?"

"I'm the man that has stolen this steamer. I have five men with rifles above, you so much as stick your head out and you're a dead man. If you take us where we need to go, you will be paid handsomely."

"Oh, I don't think so." He started to take a swing, but the other two jumped him from behind. They knocked him out with a shovel. One of the men was a black man and well put together.

"Mister, me and this boy here with me be prisoners of this place. You be stealing a steamboat... we be interested in being stealed with it. We be running this here tug for a year now."

"Then fire this thing up and let's get away from here."

"We be firing her, Captain."

They tied the man up lying on the floor and began getting the boiler up to speed. Meanwhile he went back to check on the real captain and see if Angel Hound had made it yet. This wasn't his first time to steal a steamboat. He had stolen the Queen's boat once and took it for a nice ride after midnight. It happened to be his birthday after midnight... so why not? It wasn't his fault the fog made the lighting poor that night. It sank not a hundred yards from dock.

Angel Hound came into view with the rest of the kids just as Tucker came topside. He dragged the captain to shore and waited until everyone was on board before taking the rope loose

Where Outlaws Roam
Royal Wade Kimes

from the dock. He then pulled the anchor to its secure position. He helped Angel Hound find a place to seat the two smallest children and then called down to the boiler room. Within seconds they were shoving off.

They were half way out in the river when he saw Sal and Dick waving their arms for him to come back. He waved to them and then looked up river to navigate.

Angel Hound tapped him on the arm and pointed. One of the guards was racing up behind Sal and Dick. He pulled his pistol and fired no more than ten feet from them. Dick took the bullet full in the chest. Sal tried to run, but to no avail. He was gunned down with three bullets to the back. The guard then took chase down the riverbank. He was gaining ground as Tucker and his shipmate Angel Hound floated along.

"Angel Hound, take the wheel."

"Sir?"

"Take it. I've got to go down below to the captain's quarters." He left the wheel with him and soon returned with a long barreled rifle.

Angel Hound smiled. "How did you know there would be a gun aboard?"

"Reed Fletcher is a gator hunter as well as a party man. Makes sense he'd keep a nice gun on board." He laid the barrel across the side rail of the ship and took full bead, and aimed a little high. It was at least a hundred yards. He squeezed off the round. He stood and waited. The guard tumbled from the horse and rolled across open ground.

"Mister Tucker, that was a fine shot you be making."

Tucker looked up river, the boat was sitting and floating center of it. "Angel Hound, keep this old girl in the middle of the river and watch for drift logs. If you see any before I come topside, turn a little left or right to miss them."

"Okay, but you hurry." He had a wide eyed worried look. He felt honored to be asked to guide the boat up river, but he didn't want the responsibility of the boat to himself.

Tucker went below and began going through things. He opened a cabinet that had fine wine and whiskey in it. He took a bottle of the wine and continued to pilfer. He was looking for something more and found it. In a closet hung the best looking holster rig and side iron his eyes had ever seen. The holster was dark rich leather with twenty bullet loops in the belt. The gun was a forty-five with a six inch barrel. He checked the cylinder and found it loaded. There was a box of shells lying on a short narrow board on the wall. He strapped the rig on and stepped in front of a full length mirror mounted on the cabinet door. He smiled and drew the gun.

"America, only in America… I have arrived. And now as I have read about the West… I am heeled." He drew the gun again with ease and aimed. It had a good feel and a fine balance. He was no stranger to weapons. Unlike the Shaw Family Tree, he preferred pistols to rifles. He liked close contact when facing an enemy… or lover.

"Sir."

Tucker turned to see one of the men from the boiler standing there. "Something wrong?"

"I just needs to tell you I dumped the boiler man overboard. Seems we hit him a little hard. He be dead."

Tucker smiled. "Well then… carry on."

"Yes sir!" He turned and went below with enthusiasm.

Hon was the first to hear hounds in the distance. He held his hand up for his wife and Macie to be quiet. "Dogs! They ain't hunting rabbits either. Them there are trained for runaways… like what runs off from the Fletcher Farm. You two get your belongings; we got to get deeper into the swamp."

Fear struck deep within Macie. She looked in the direction of the bawling hounds and it was almost like a moment of divination came to her. She was certain those blood curdling sounds were confirmation of the coming end to the Cook Clan. Hon was the only male left if Reed Fletcher executed the others. Morrell had said in times past the Fletcher farm was your last stop on earth if you happened to get caught on the place. She was the only other one with Cook blood, a female. The extinction to a whole name line of people, be they good or bad was about to take place if Hon didn't make good on getting away. Her

Where Outlaws Roam
Royal Wade Kimes

offspring would have Cook blood but not the name.

"Damn, Macie, what are you looking at? Get yourself moving. We got to get from here. We have this one mule and horse. I'm putting my woman on the mule... I guess you walk along behind."

She stared at him. What she said earlier about the Cook name had not set well with Hon, especially since his three brothers were in such a bad spot, possibly dead. That was why he would make her walk. She also knew he would sacrifice her before anything happened to him or his wife. She smiled at him. "I'm ready when you are."

She looked up at Hon's wife who stared straight ahead, because she knew what the score was. Macie was not needed and anything or anyone 'not needed', with a Cook... was always disposed of.

She looked back after they had weaved through and around several swamps. The dogs were getting closer. She watched as Hon picked his way very carefully through the bayou. He was watching for alligators and poisonous snakes. He stopped and listened.

"We're going to have to chance swimming this marsh ahead. We got to lose them damn dogs."

She stared at him. "Do I ride behind on the mule?"

He smiled. "I'm afraid not, Macie. Anything could go wrong out there. The mule has a load with my woman and our camp sack. You're a fair swimmer as I recall. You'll make out. Just catch hold of my horse's tail. He'll pull you along."

"Yes, but aren't you leading the way?"

"What of it?"

"If something was to happen, the mule might take me under, coming from behind me like he will be."

"Suit yourself... mule or gator. If I wasn't riding I'd want to be between the mule and horse. You worry me, Macie. Grab hold of the tail of my horse when we get to the next marsh and shut the hell up!"

They trotted for another quarter before reaching the marsh. It was big and dangerous looking. She knew Hon was desperate by even thinking of trying it. She looked out across it and gave thought to her situation. She had always been kind of an independent thinker, and this was a time she felt she had to look to herself. It was time to break away from Hon. Even if they made it her life was going to be one of misery and hell. What kind of life could she possibly have living with her Uncle Hon and his wife? On top of that he would never let go of what she said about the Cook name. The longer his three brothers stayed gone the worse it would be on her. She had to change that, and she had to do it now.

They were about to enter the marsh when she spoke up.

"Hon."

"Yeah?" He turned and looked back.

"Good luck. I hope you make it. I probably will never see you again either way. Goodbye."

"Where the hell are you going?" He turned his horse to face her.

She turned and started walking due north. As she walked she answered him. "I'm walking in the direction of freedom! You best be moving before those dogs get here."

"Girly, you ain't nothin' but gator bait in this swamp without me!"

She raised her hand goodbye but didn't look back. "You crazy bitch! Get back here!" He grunted at her and then eased into the swamp water that became deep quickly.

Macie walked for a hundred yards and climbed a tree. She climbed to the top and bent it towards another tree. She stretched as far as she could and caught hold of the limb. She successfully swung her legs over to the tree and held on. Then she made her way around to the other side of it. There was a limb below her that went straight out and almost touched the next tree over. She made her way down to the limb and then began walking it very slowly like a high wire. The limb was going out over a bog with two alligators lying on the edge of it. They too saw her. She was almost to the other tree when she slipped and fell.

Hon was half way across the marsh when he spotted an alligator making his way towards them. He was at least ten feet

Where Outlaws Roam
Royal Wade Kimes

long. He was big, too big. He pulled his pistol and shot at it. The bullet splashed about three feet away and the alligator immediately sank under the water. He knew he was in trouble.

"Hon!"

"Woman, stay a straddle of that mule! We'll make it!"

Suddenly his horse jumped as much as he could sideways. Hon spotted the alligator and fired three times straight down. Blood came to the surface and the alligator flipped several times over and over as he died.

He turned and looked back at his wife, but she wasn't there. The mule was trailing fine but she wasn't on him. Then he spotted her ole ragged hat and blood in the water twenty feet back. He knew she had panicked and tried to swim her way to the bank. It was then he knew her death was keeping the other alligators off of him. That wouldn't last long. He had to get moving as he spotted several more out a ways.

Reed Fletcher watched as Hon's wife was taken into a death roll by a large alligator. She came up and over several times extremely fast. The alligator had her by the shoulder and neck area. Lester's eyes widened at the awful sight, but Briggs smiled. Raff Thibodeaux and his two friends, Neely Law and Devo Wells who were considered experts at their trade... which was killing... watched in awe. The alligator kept twirling over and over in the water with its potential kill. The rest of the men couldn't watch.

Reed dismounted and took his custom made rifle out of its carrying case. He walked to the edge of the swampy marsh and laid the gun barrel between a forked limb of a young willow sampling. He ran the tip of a bullet through his hair and inserted the shell into the chamber. He then waited for Hon to reach the bank on the other side. While he waited he glanced at Raff, Neely, and Devo.

"You boys remember the shot I made on that gator from my steamboat awhile back? He had one of my calves. I shot the sonofabitch through the damn eyes. I'm bettin' I shoot that Cajun center of the heart from here. I estimate it seventy yards."

Raff laughed. "Hell, Reed, that's no shot. Think back, I shot that black buck last year between the shoulder blades at a hundred and fifty yards and him running."

Neely laughed. "That was a hell of a shot. Why is it you get all the best kills?"

Raff sniggered. "I'm in the right place at the right time. I stay close to ole Reed." They all laughed and passed a half pint of whiskey around.

Lester walked over by Reed. "Boss, you be going to kill that man after he thinks he free from us?"

"I am. Killing a man is easy… but killing him and him being surprised by it, well, that doesn't happen just every day."

Lester looked at him and then gazed across the marsh. "Boss, he done lost family, now his wife… in an awful way." He paused. "Maybe we let's him go this time?"

Reed looked around at him. "You gone soft on me, Boy?"

"I just thinks he done paid a heavy price already is all."

"Well, some men have to pay more than others." He pulled the trigger. The rifle echoed in the swamp and birds flew from everywhere.

Hon Cook was hit in the left shoulder and knocked from his horse. He was dismayed at the sudden opening in his body. He struggled to his feet, stood and looked around him. He had made it to the other side of the swamp. What had gone wrong? He looked across the way and saw the hounds. Reed Fletcher was standing there taking aim again. He pulled his pistol just as a bullet splatted a leaf and grazed his head, knocking him flat to the ground. He didn't move again. He knew not to. He was done anyway. His head was bleeding badly and the hole in his shoulder was a horrible sight to look at. He whispered to himself. "The rotten bastard has killed us all." He tried to breathe normally as his heart raced out of control. He knew not to panic. A man could do some things if he didn't panic. He looked at the trees blocking out most of the light in the swamp. He smiled and wondered why he could smell alligator meat cooking. He hadn't built a fire. If he had to die this was the place to do it. He would lie quiet and just bleed out. Was the swamp always this dark? He reckoned not.

Reed smiled as he put his fancy rifle back in its case. "Boys, let's go home. It's been a successful hunt." He cut his eyes to

Where Outlaws Roam
Royal Wade Kimes

Briggs. "Take two men with you and ride around this damn marsh. I want that horse and mule. I saw them heading north after I shot the Cajun."

"I'll do it."

Suddenly one of the hounds bawled out. Reed turned his horse hard in the direction the hounds took off in. "Lester, bring the men, this hunt may not be over. We may have us another thief to hunt down. Raff, you get this shot."

"Now were talking!" They took off in a lope hunting a woman they didn't know by the name of Macie Cook.

Chapter 5

Macie had fallen while trying to walk the limb across the bog and was lucky enough to catch hold of it as she fell. She hung there as the alligators moved into the shallow water below her. She swung her long cream colored leg on top of the limb and managed to get back up on top of it again.

She was trying one more time when she heard a very loud rifle echo through the everglades. She knew by that Fletcher had caught up with Hon. She made it to the other tree and climbed across to another one that grew right beside it. She did that several times until she found a vine that was long enough to let her swing out to solid ground below. It would be soft boggy black dirt, making the odds of getting hurt a lot less. She was applying all her childhood knowledge and tricks in helping her stay alive. Playing in trees and swinging on grapevines was something her and all her friends did as children in the Louisiana Bayou. She held her breath and let go. She swung out nearly fifty feet and at her lowest point to the ground she let go. She rolled across the ground and stopped just before rolling into a wet boggy place. She stood, examined herself and then plodded on. She had covered at least eighty yards by walking limbs and swinging from the vine. She felt it was enough to lose the dogs. She would soon know, because she wasn't hearing any more rifle reports. She thought she heard a hound bawl out, so she began to trot. As she picked up the pace she looked to heaven in hopes God would help her out.

Three weeks later

United States Marshal Walt Sanders picked up a prisoner in Fort Smith, Arkansas and was about to head to Dye, Kansas with him, some eighty miles west of Coffeeville. His prisoner was a thief and murderer by the name of Simon Lick Tubbs. Simon Lick as he liked to be called was anything but handsome. He was slender built and rather tall with boney shoulders. He had mean black eyes and rust from head to toe from months of not bathing.

Where Outlaws Roam
Royal Wade Kimes

Marshal Sanders was a well-dressed handsome sort, and known throughout Kansas as a gentleman. He was older than most of the marshals and savvy from years gone by. He was edgy today. Simon Lick had killed a sheriff and deputy in Melt, Kansas, and then killed a woman in an attempted bank holdup in Dye. He was a man not to take your eye off of.

"Marshal, we been riding for three hours, my bony ass is beginning to hurt some. This saddle and foundered horse you gave me is not much on travel, least not comfortable."

Marshal Sanders was leading his prisoner's horse and had him tied to the saddle, both feet and hands. He wasn't taking any chances with him. His prisoner was right about the horse being foundered. He used the horse to transport prisoners if the ride wasn't too far. The horse was good for one good trip and then he had to have rest for a few weeks. Because he was foundered, he didn't have much speed, so trying to get away was foolish. The saddle was the worst thing to ride Marshal Sanders had ever tried to sit. He kept the saddle for prisoners because it was so miserable to ride. He looked back and pulled up.

"Any pain you might have doesn't concern me in the least. The fact is we've only been in the saddle an hour, not three. We're not even out of Fort Smith good. I do need to rest your horse though. He can't take much." He looked around him. "Looks like a good place to rest them right here." He eased over to a sweet gum tree and dismounted. He then walked over and sat down in the shade and took a drink of water from his canteen. The Arkansas River was only a couple hundred yards to the west of them. He planned to catch a ferryboat across it soon.

"What the hell... Marshal, ain't you goin' to get me down off this nag?"

"Wasn't planning on it. The horse can rest with you on him."

Simon Lick stared at him. "Don't you turn your back on me, I'll kill you shore."

"I appreciate the reminder." He stood up, drew his gun and walked over to his prisoner. He loosed the ropes on his feet and then put handcuffs on his wrists. He then untied the ropes that were already around his wrists, which also had him tied to the horse. He backed away and watched as he dismounted.

"Careful sonofabitch ain't you?"

"Try to be."

He sat down under the shade of the tree and stared at the marshal. "I'd like a drink of water."

"Where you're going you'll need lots of water."

"Oh, you're one of them God Almighty Believers are you? You think they's a hot hell waitin' for fellers like me." He laughed. "Tell me, Marshal, you reckon Jesus could do anything with me? You think he could save me from that eternal burning hell, turn me around and cause me to be the salt of the earth?" He laughed again, except this time it had a haunting sound to it, almost evil. "Hell Marshal, me and the devil have partnered up, if indeed that's who the sonofabitch is that has caused me to do the terrible things I have. All you civilized do goods make me sick. I take what I want, when I want, and from who I want. Life don't get any damn better than that."

Marshal Sanders shook his head. "I can't even feel sorry for you."

"Oh, come on Marshal, get down on them knees of yours and pray for ole Simon Lick. Hell, if you really are a Believer, then you got to look on me as a man God made. You can't do for the Lord… and turn your heart cold to me. Hell, Marshal, you don't know… I might be your test to see if you're fit to enter in." He cackled out. "I've put you in a hard place ain't I, Marshal? You might miss the pearly gates just on the count of judging and turning your back on me… a pilgrim asking for prayer… needin' saved from Lucifer himself. Hell, you might make a difference in the world by getting me to the altar. You might save other folks from dyin' if you could do that."

"Simon Lick, there won't be any more dying caused by you. Your days are numbered."

"My ole mama used to say that no man knows the hour in which the Lord shall come. She believed in that Bible… me, I never seen nothing in it or out of it. But I do believe no man knows when his day has come." He stared and then smiled. "You think you know when my time is at hand. Don't be so sure. The devil has powers too. He might free me in the night, or maybe

Where Outlaws Roam
Royal Wade Kimes

along the trail. He might spook that bay you're ridin' and you'd snap your neck."

"There will be a neck snapped, but a rope will do it. You'll be on the end of it."

Tucker Shaw had been in Fort Smith, Arkansas for four days and had already watched a hanging carried out by the court of Judge Isaac Parker. He hadn't been in America long, but long enough to know things weren't as rosy as he had read in newspapers and novels back home. The outlaw had a hard way it looked to him. He smiled as he thought about his encounter in Louisiana. The Cooks ran their string out too. He come to the conclusion the Cooks were outlaws, but of a different sort. They seemed more 'at home outlaws' than the flamboyant gun slinging types he had read and heard about. Those were the ones he wanted to see, and the towns they lived in were something he was excited about as well.

All that had been put on hold while he helped Angel Hound and Pixy find their mother. He hoped Pixy was right and her mother would know what to do with all the children. It turned out to be more than he had hoped for. Angel Hound's mother worked for a Mission and Shelter connected with the Saint Mary Convent and Cathedral. Arch Bishop Emanuel Ortega was the presiding head of the organization. Angel Hound and Pixy were reunited with their mother, whose name was Ina Brown. All of the kids were taken in as well. Tucker thought Angel Hound Brown had a nice ring to it, and Bishop Ortega saw a great need for him and his sister Pixy. They were shorthanded and he immediately asked them if they were interested in working for the Mission. The pay was low, but the food and beds were good. Once they were settled in he said his goodbyes, but not until Angel Hound got alone with him.

"Mister Tucker."

"Yes?" He eyed Angel Hound closely.

"I wants you to know I appreciate whats you done for me and Pixy... and the others. You took on a big problem you didn't have to takes on. You have a good heart, Mister Tucker." While standing in front of him he kept making lines in the sand with his shoe. He finally looked up. "Mister Tucker, if it be where you can I sure would likes to work for you... I mean if it ever comes where you could use a good man."

"Well... Angel Hound, if it ever does come I need a good man, I'll get hold of you and you come a running." He smiled when he saw him light up.

"You mean it?"

"I said it, and Tucker Shaw doesn't say anything he doesn't mean. The fact is, back home that's what kept me in hot water. I was always saying something the bosses of that world didn't like."

"Well, I don't knows who the bosses were, but they don't seem like much to me if'n they didn't like what you had to say. You're a good man, Mister Tucker."

He stared at him. He couldn't remember anyone telling him that. It had always been the opposite. Except for his mother... everyone else including Poppa Ira Shaw and the Queen's Command thought him anything but a good man. However, he was a bit brash and strong minded for such an elite bunch of snobs. He smiled at the thought.

"Mister Tucker, I need to get to work I guess. I want to make a good showing for the Bishop. Oh, and before I forget, mama wants to sees you before you go."

"Please tell her I'm available right now. I will wait here in front of the Mission."

"I will tell her. Thanks again for what you done."

"It was my pleasure."

In a few minutes Ina opened the door to the Mission and stepped outside. She had a sack with food in it and a Bible. "Mister Tucker."

"Please, call me Tucker." He smiled as he saw the tears rolling down her cheeks. Mama Ina was a nice looking lady. She had kept herself in somewhat good shape.

"I's can't thanks you enough for bringing my world together. I's thought my babies was lost to me forever. I's was in Mississippi when Angel was hatched, and was in Louisiana when Pixy came. The war was awful bad on me. I's was taken down to a big farm to works for a month. When I's gets back no one is left. The

Where Outlaws Roam
Royal Wade Kimes

plantation is gone, the livestock and the people. I's lost Angel and Pixy that day. It left me broken hearted. I's was freed not too long afterwards and searched for my babies but without any lucks. Then I's was offered a job here. Mister Tucker... I's was starving. That be the only reason I's came. Once I's was here, didn't have no way back, and didn't know where to get back to. I's been feelin' mighty lost for a long time." She caught her breath as she almost broke into crying.

"Ina, you don't have to explain to me. I don't judge you and I for sure understand circumstances. I've had a few myself over the last couple years, still do I guess. I'm just glad I was able to help you and Angel Hound out."

She smiled. "Where'd that boy get that name Angel Hound at?"

"I think he might need to tell you about that. I can say you raised a boy that is fast on his feet."

"I's see." She giggled. "Mister Tucker, does you have money? I's not being pry full. I's got a little put back money in case you needs a stake."

"No, not at all, I sold a boat and it brought a nice little sum."

"That be good. A man oughts to be havin' some foldin' money."

He smiled, kissed Ina on the cheek and walked down the street to the Rim and Bow Livery.

"Can I help ya young fellow?"

Tucker was looking at the oldest man alive. There wasn't a place on the man's face that didn't have a wrinkle or brown spot on it. His hands were callused and his fingers were somewhat crooked from arthritis, which was brought on by hard work most likely.

"Yes, I'm looking for a horse. He needs to have the ability to stride and have a walking gait of ease. His jog must be smooth and he must have a head full of sense. If he has any spook in him, leave him in the barn."

The old man stood there with his hands on his hips eyeing Tucker over. "You don't say? He has to stride does he? Needs to walk at an ease. You say he needs to have a head full of sense?

The jog needs to be smooth. Well, I've seen me some winners in my time, but you take top honors." He turned and walked back into the livery. Tucker followed.

"Sir?"

The old man turned. "You still here?"

"Yes of course. I'm here to buy a horse and saddle. I was serious and am willing to pay top dollar for the right one."

"My name is Tib... and I don't have the right one. I've got some dang good horses, but nothing you described. My horses can run, lope in a tea cup and turn on a dime. I don't have one that won't see a bugger once in a great while, and if anyone says they got one that won't... then he's a dead one." Tib stopped and grabbed a breath. "Besides all that, you need to work on getting rid of that damn accent you have. It's irritatin' me to death already."

Tucker laughed. "Of course you are right. I apologize. Let me ask then, can I take a look at your fine livestock?"

Tib smiled. "Come with me." They walked out back of the livery where Tucker climbed upon the fence and looked them over. The bay was nice but pigeon toed. There was two sorrels, one showed signs of a light founder. The other one had an old cut on the top side of his hock. It might not bother him, but he wasn't chancing it. There was a black that was nice enough, but he was not more than a two year old and had too much to learn. There was one more, a gray, and he too wouldn't do. He was roman nosed and somewhat sway backed.

"Tib, I'm not trying to be difficult here, but these won't do."

He laughed. "I show these ole boys to every buyer that comes in here."

"Why?"

"I learn right fast what the man knows about hoss flesh. Come around here on the other side of the livery. I have something that might just be what you're looking for."

When Tucker saw the three horses standing in the corral before him he smiled immediately. They were all three young mares, but put together right.

"This is more like it."

"Well, young fellow, you kept saying you wanted a gelding. So I figured to show you my cull geldings. I don't have any good

Where Outlaws Roam
Royal Wade Kimes

geldings right now, but any one of these three mares will do what you want."

There was a black, a blood red bay, and an unusual bronze colored bay with a white sock on the left hind leg. She was something to look at. She was just over fourteen hands and had good eyes, meaning she wasn't a fool. She didn't show the whites in them. He bought the mare and rigging to go with her for a hundred and fifty dollars. He was set to head for Dodge City where it was wide open country and the town was known for rough and readies. He had purchased a new hat, clothes, duster, and camping supplies. He figured to leave early morning. For now though, he had another need. He walked down the street to Candy's Gentleman Club.

He was met by a big busted lady more than glad to see him.

"Good evening."

He smiled at her. He was no stranger to Candy's kind of establishment. He frequented them quite often back home. He did it to keep the turmoil going for the Shaw's and their precious high society friends. Since he didn't know anyone in Fort Smith and wasn't planning to stay around, he decided to partake of the oldest profession in the world.

"I'm looking for a lady."

Candy smiled. "I have ten. You pick her."

Ten of the prettiest women he might have remembered seeing walked out into the room. But it was then that he suddenly realized something wasn't right. What was wrong with him? None of them pleased him. Why? He had always found one easy enough to please him in the past. He almost panicked. Was something wrong with him? He looked at them closer and decided he would pick one whether he wanted to or not. Something was wrong and he had to overcome it.

"This one." He pointed at a cute little dark eyed brunette.

"Lila, looks like you're it."

She took him by the hand and led him down the hall, smiling as she went. They were in there all of five minutes when he came out in a rush. He stopped and stuck a fifty dollar bill in Candy's cleavage and asked where the nearest saloon was.

Where Outlaws Roam
Royal Wade Kimes

Lila came out and stood with her breast completely showing and her hands on her hips. She cut her eyes over to Candy. "That man has a problem and it isn't his ability. I had him ready to go and he just up and flips me over, throws on his pants and beats it out of the room."

Candy looked towards the door he went through leaving the establishment. "Do you reckon he knows what his problem is?"

Lila smiled. "Don't you mean who?"

Where Outlaws Roam
Royal Wade Kimes

Chapter 6

Marshal Sanders had not made as good of time on the trail as he had hoped for. The horse Simon Lick was riding was playing out and had to be rested more often than normal. He realized two things. This was the gelding's last trip. It was time to retire him to pasture, and the second thing... he was going to have to make camp.

He was hoping to make it to Evansville before dark and lock his prisoner up there. The jail wasn't much, but it was more than he had. He wasn't even close to Evansville yet. It was going to be a long trip.

"Marshal, you may be the lamest lawman I've met. You have me out here on a horse that can't cut the mustard, he's slowing you up." He laughed. "I don't guess I have to tell you the longer it takes to get me to Dye, Kansas, the more likely I'm going to get away."

"About the only thing that's going to run off about you is your mouth. You talk a lot. In my profession a man in your position that talks too much is usually scared."

"Is that right?" Simon Lick's eyes narrowed as he glared at him.

After he dismounted he unloaded his prisoner and tied his arms around a tree. He then went about taking care of the horses. He watered them from a spring and fed them a portion of grain he carried in one of his saddlebags.

"Marshal, you ain't leaving me here all night like this are you?"

"We'll see." He smiled and then built a fire. He set about making coffee and heated a can of beans. He turned and looked at his prisoner. "I hope you like beans, it's what we got. Don't make any remarks about my coffee either. I make it like I like it, strong and black."

"The only remark I'm making is that I'm going to put a bullet in you... wait and see."

"Dead men don't shoot."

"Go to hell, Marshal."

He poured a cup of coffee and sat back against the trunk of a tree. "Good coffee."

"What about me?"

"You? Oh, well I thought I'd let you do without until those handcuffs and the position you are in becomes unbearable. Once it starts to be hell, then I thought you could have some. Since you're telling me to go to hell, I thought maybe you needed to see who was already there."

"You sonofabitch."

"You talk a lot."

Tucker walked into the Border Saloon just off Garrison Avenue in Fort Smith and ordered a double whiskey. He drank it down like it was nothing. He stared straight ahead as he ordered another just like it. The barkeeper looked at him with curiosity.

"You alright?"

"I am… why do you ask?"

"I don't have many customers come in here ordering doubles and drink them down like you are."

Tucker smiled. "No, I suspect not." He paused and looked around the room. "Barkeep, what would you say if I told you it was a woman that has me in such a tizzy?"

"I'd say you and every man I know has that happen to him sometime along the way." He laughed and walked down to the other end of the bar as two tough looking men walked in.

The big man ordered a whiskey and laid a short double barreled shotgun up on the bar in front of him. Tucker recognized the voice and he turned his back to him. He hoped his new clothes and hat would disguise him enough to go unnoticed. There was one problem and he was about to find out what that was.

"Hey you! Turn around! That rig you're wearing, that belongs to Reed Fletcher."

He turned and looked Briggs dead in the eye. He didn't know the man with him. "Correction, it was Fletcher's rig… it's mine now. I took it as payment for his taking me prisoner without due process of law."

"Dude, Reed Fletcher is the law. Where's his steamboat? Reed sent me up here to find it… and you. I'm to bring the boat and you back. The boat is to be in good condition, you however he has left to my discretion."

Where Outlaws Roam
Royal Wade Kimes

Tucker smiled. "Well Briggs, I'm afraid the boat is no longer with me, and as for my wellbeing... if it's all the same to you, I'll continue to take charge of that." Tucker's eyes became cold. His expression changed. "Briggs, the only way you're going to get me back to Louisiana is after I'm dead." He slung his double shot of whiskey down and stepped away from the bar. The rest of the men in the saloon scattered.

Briggs cut his eyes down at the shotgun. The other man was wearing a fairly nice side iron. "Do you think you can take us both?"

With a flare he answered. "I've been taking chaps like you for a while now." He smiled and waited. The saloon was quitter than prayer at a supper table.

Briggs let his hand lay on top of the shotgun. The longer he stood there the more nervous he became. He finally grabbed the gun, but was too slow and awkward. Tucker drew and shot him dead in the heart, and fired his second shot as the other man drew and fired. Tucker heard the man's bullet make a dreadful spatting sound in the wood at his feet. The man that fired the shot caught Tucker's bullet in the chest. He staggered backwards and then tried to turn. He fell hard into a table and crashed to the floor. Briggs was down on his knees with his hand still clutched to the bar.

The barkeeper walked around to where Briggs was at. He examined him and then looked up and over at Tucker. "He may be holding to the bar here... but he's dead as Boot Hill Cemetery."

A marshal by the name of Galt came to the saloon ten minutes later to arrest a murderer if indeed that was what it turned out to be. He asked the barkeeper who did what. Then he walked to the table where Tucker was sitting.

"You killed these men in self-defense?"

"I did."

"What was it about?"

"It's a long story."

"I've got time." He smiled and sat down.

Tucker started at the beginning and brought him up to present time. The only thing he forgot to tell him about was being brought to America an exiled prisoner, and Reed Fletcher's boat being sold. Those two things he felt were unnecessary to talk about.

Marshal Galt smiled and took a piece of peppermint candy out of a small tin can. He offered Tucker a piece but he graciously declined. "That's quite the story. Let me give you some good advice. Take that gun off. It invites trouble. You said you bought a horse... be on him at daylight tomorrow and get out of Fort Smith. My life, your life, and everyone around will probably be better for it."

"Yes sir, I was planning to leave early morning anyway."

"The gun?"

Tucker smiled. "I'm leaving town, but I'm not leaving my gun behind. I appreciate your concern."

Marshal Galt said goodbye and Tucker headed for his hotel. The drinks and gunplay had made him forget why he was in the saloon in the first place. As he walked towards the hotel he grinned. He stopped and looked around at all the buildings. He was in the Wild West, and he had played a part in adding to its wildness. He had actually shot it out in a saloon in Fort Smith, Arkansas. It could only get better.

Where Outlaws Roam
Royal Wade Kimes

Chapter 7

Reed Fletcher received news that two of his men had been killed in Fort Smith, Arkansas by a lone gunman. It was self-defense by all accounts and the bodies were being buried in the Fort Smith Cemetery.

Reed became insane with anger. In three generations nothing like this had ever happened on the Fletcher Farm. He had a black mark, a blemish on his reputation. He would not hold with that. He called in Raff, Neely, and Devo, all born marksmen. Raff was excellent with side arms and rifle, Neely was outstanding with a rifle and Devo was good with any kind of gun or knife. Reed gathered provisions for a journey and prepared to leave. He gave Lester instructions on running the farm while he was away. Reed Fletcher was going hunting… man hunting.

Tucker had just gotten off to sleep when someone knocked. He cocked his pistol and answered. "Who is it?"

"Marshal Galt."

"Marshal, my dear fellow, it's late. Can we not speak in the morning? I'm sure you plan to see me off anyway."

"Well, that's what I need to talk to you about. It looks like you won't be leaving in the morning."

"And why not?" He opened the door.

The Marshal was standing there with a wide grin and a stick of peppermint in his mouth. "A wire came from that Reed Fletcher you told me about. It seems you stole his boat and I suspect… sold it." He grinned again. "Would you like a peppermint?"

"No, I'll pass for the moment. Marshal, the boat was me and that passel of poor kids only option for a getaway. It was the only way to escape."

"Well, to tell you the truth I don't have any problem with that part of your story. What has me in a stupor is why you left out the part about selling the boat you made your escape in?"

"Did I say I sold it?"

Marshal Galt chuckled and slapped his leg. "You didn't say you didn't either. That's what I like about youth. It's daring… kind of dumb, but daring just the same." The smile left his face. "I'm afraid I'm going to have to take you in."

Tucker was standing with his gun in hand and the hammer back. He glanced at the gun and then back to Marshal Galt. "Do they hang people for wounding marshals?"

"Oh, probably not, but I'd probably kill the sonofabitch that shot me. If I was the man what shot me... I'd damn shore want to make it count. I'd shoot to kill."

"That's what I like about marshals, they're fearless, kind of dumb, but fearless just the same." Marshal Galt's smile vanished. Tucker motioned him on into the room with the barrel of his pistol. Once in he had him sit in a small chair over from him.

"Marshal, we have a dilemma. There's positively no way I'm letting Reed Fletcher have another shot at me of any kind. He'd love to have me locked up somewhere, or shoot me dead. You already know he has his men searching all of creation for me. Briggs and that other fellow worked for him, you know that. Now you're willing to let him have me sent to prison, for escaping his self-proclaimed prison farm."

"That's not true. I'm only concerned about the sale of property that wasn't yours. It wasn't me that sold the boat. I would have had better sense." He smiled and licked his peppermint.

Tucker smiled as he thought about that. "Yeah, I suppose you would have. I've never been one to use good sense. I've always been... daring." He laughed. Then he walked over by the marshal. "I don't guess you would change your mind?"

"Well, I'd shore like to, but I'm afraid I can't. I'm the law... and the law is the law."

"So... if I knocked you out with my pistol... I'd probably have to do time, is that right?"

"I'd say so. I'd say a year."

"What if, let's say you just woke up in my room and I was gone?"

"Well I don't plan to sleep here, so that won't happen. But if I did just wake up here and no harm from foul play occurred, I'd guess you'd be free as a bird."

Tucker smiled. "Marshal, you wait right here I'll be right back!"

"Son, I'm not following you and I'm not waiting here. I'm still taking you in."

Where Outlaws Roam
Royal Wade Kimes

"Well, if you're not going to cooperate." He walked to the closet while keeping an eye on the marshal, and pulled out a small piece of cotton rope that had been left in the small room. He then tied his hands behind his back. "I sure didn't want to have to tie you up. I'll be right back to untie you, I promise." He laughed. "Marshal, you haven't any way of knowing how funny that is. Where I'm from I've never kept a promise. I went out of my way to break them. America, it changes a man doesn't it?"

"Well I was born here, I wouldn't know. I suspect it could." He eyed him over pretty good. "You are an unusual duck, I'll say that."

"Now Marshal, don't you go anywhere." He turned and bound through the door. He locked it and left in a hurry.

"Come back here! You can't leave me here like this!"

Tucker was back within twenty minutes with a bottle and cotton in his hand.

"What the hell is that?"

"That's my get away medicine. I don't want to hurt you. I like you and you said I could do time for it. So, I'm going to let you sleep here in my bed. The room is paid for, and the bed is soft. I think you'll like it."

"You can't do that. There's probably a law against it... maybe obstructing justice, willful flight from the law... something. You've already broken the law by tying me up."

"Yes, but a slap of the hand at best is what that would be." He poured ether onto the cotton and proceeded in the direction of Marshal Galt. "This won't hurt a bit. You'll wake up a new man. Sweet dreams."

He tried to dart his head away from the ether, but to no avail. In just a few seconds he was sleeping like a baby. Tucker untied his hands and took his boots off. He then unstrapped his gun rig and hung it on the bedpost. He placed his head on the pillow and gave him one more good shot of the ether. He had used ether before when pulling some of his stunts on the Queen and her Merry Men. He once stole her whole wardrobe while she slept, well, while her Merry Men slept down the hall, out in the court yard and at the main gate. He smiled when he thought about that. He dressed every harlot in the red light district in royalty clothing that night. It was quite the show. In fact, it was quite the headline the following day.

He left the room, saddled his mare and rode out of Fort Smith in a hurry. How much trouble he was in he wasn't sure, but if he stayed around and waited on Reed Fletcher it was going to be a whole lot more. He was leaving in the night and riding for Kansas. If he was going to be banished to a country where outlaws roam, he wanted to be in the thick of them. From Fort Smith, Arkansas through the Oklahoma Territory to Kansas, he would be. At least that was what he had read and heard ever since childhood. What an exciting life it all sounded... and was turning out to be.

He pulled his bronze colored mare up as he got to the edge of town and looked back. He smiled and then spoke to her. "What am I'm thinking. Here I am on the run from some crazy man out of Louisiana for selling his stolen property... that I used to regain freedom, and I have a Fort Smith Marshal under ether while I get away. I've already had a gun fight in a saloon and have been told to lose my six gun because it attracts trouble. Little mare, it seems to me I don't have to look any further for outlaws, lawmen, and excitement than right here in this saddle." He grinned. "Now I see why there are so many outlaws in these parts. It's damned easy to be made one. Did you hear that? I'm starting to get the lingo. I said in 'these parts,' just like a westerner, a range cowboy. I may be a little green yet, but this country is changing that fast." He clucked to the mare and rode on out.

Where Outlaws Roam
Royal Wade Kimes

Chapter 8

"Simon Lick, wake up. Breakfast is ready."

Marshal Sanders took the handcuffs off of his prisoner long enough to get them from a round a small persimmon tree. He then fastened them back. He gave him a tin plate with bacon and griddlecakes.

"You're a damn cook."

"Shut up and eat. I want to be riding before the sun comes up."

"Where's my coffee?"

"I only have the one cup. You'll have to wait until I've had mine."

"Well ain't that a lick? I got to wait on the law dog." He grinned. "You ever wonder how I came by my name, Lick?"

"Never have."

"Well, I'll tell you anyway. You see when I robbed a place, I always made a lick. I made it count. I always got around to finding out when the money was there in its biggest pile."

"Looks like it's sure paid off for you… sitting there cuffed and wearing rags."

"Marshal, don't go to getting high and mighty with me. Hell, I robbed one place of five thousand and spent a thousand of it in one night on three little gals. I got 'em drunk and naked and spent the whole night with 'em. It was a real time."

"That's your idea of success?"

Simon Lick smiled. "I guess everyone has their own idea of success."

"Well, as crazy as that is, you finally said something intelligent."

"Marshal, I've got to relieve myself. Can I go over there behind my persimmon tree and take care of business? You'll be able to see me."

He eyed his prisoner as he gave it thought. "I reckon it'll be okay. You do anything that looks like it ain't an act of nature, and you'll be a dead man with your pants down around your knees."

"Now that would be pure-de embarrassing wouldn't it?"

What Marshal Sanders didn't know was that Simon Lick had spent all night working on a small limb on the backside of the tree. He stretched his neck and head around enough to use his teeth to bite the end of it off. He then would clamp down over the limb and run his teeth along the limb until he had it whittled down to a sharp point. All he had to do now was break it loose from the tree. The Marshal took his handcuffs off and then backed away as he held a gun on him.

"I'll be right over here watching you."

"Damn, can't I even take a nature call in privacy?" "I'm afraid not. I will be packing up the dishes, but one eye will be on you." He smiled. "I'd like for you to make a move. I'd like nothing better than to end this trip right here."

"Marshal, you worry me with the way you feel. I'm almost sure you're going to miss those Pearly Gates and split hell wide open, and all because of me."

He squatted down behind the persimmon tree and while the marshal packed up the dishes, he watched for his chance to break the limb off. It came when he dropped the coffee pot. He took his eyes off of him for just a split second, and that was all Simon Lick needed. The limb was only five to six inches long and easy to hide. He stood and buttoned his pants.

"Marshal, can I ease down there?"

"Come on." He kept his pistol on him as he approached. He had the cuffs in one hand and his gun in the other. When he reached out with the cuffs, Simon Lick suddenly came up with his right hand. Marshal Sanders felt a sharp stab deep between his abdomen and chest. Blood spurted immediately. Simon Lick charged in on top of him and they went crashing to the ground. Marshal Galt fired his pistol and hit him in the left shoulder. The shock of the bullet stopped his aggression immediately.

He waited to make sure his prisoner wasn't going to try anything else, and then gave attention to the stick protruding out of his chest. Blood was everywhere and still coming. There was a stick one half inch in diameter sticking out of his chest approximately two inches. He knew it was bad and he was in deep trouble.

"That don't look good, Marshal. In fact it looks real mean to me. I'd say you ain't got long if we don't find you a doctor."

"We?" Marshal Sanders was becoming desperate and irritated

at the same time. "Shut your damn mouth before I decide to finish you off."

He sniggered and examined his own shoulder. The bullet hit him high and had gone clean through. He was bleeding but not as bad as Marshal Sanders. He started to get up but stopped immediately when a bullet dug up the dirt by his legs.

"You make one move that's not ordered by me… and I'll break your damn legs with bullets."

"Marshal, you're like a damn bear when you get wounded, ain't you?"

"You don't hear good, do you?" Marshal Sanders became more steady as he leaned back against his saddle. He aimed and shot the left ear almost off of Simon Lick.

He yelled and grabbed it. "You sonofabitch! You could have killed me!"

"Yeah… could have." He looked down at the stick in his chest again. He would pull it out, but the thought occurred to him it might cause the wound to bleed more. He looked around him trying to think of what to do. He was growing weak. That meant he needed to get the horses saddled and get mounted quickly. He would have to make his prisoner do the work.

"Saddle the horses!"

He sneered at him. "You saddle the horses. It's not my damn job. Your job is to get me to Dye, Kansas and my job is to see that you don't."

Suddenly Simon Lick didn't have a right ear. "You bastard, you shot my ear clean off! My left one is all but gone… you sorry no good bastard!" He was holding both ears. Blood was running out over his hand from the right ear. "You're a sorry excuse for a law man… shooting an unarmed prisoner. My looks are ruined for life! You've shot my ears off!"

"I'll shoot something else off… you crow eating bastard." It was getting harder to breath. "You won't be able to stick that pecker of yours in any girl, let alone three." He took the deepest breath he could. "Now, get those horses saddled!" He watched as Simon Lick saddled the two horses. He then cuffed him and made him mount up. He led his own horse over to a low spot in the terrain, and after a couple of tries he managed to get his foot in the stirrup. He swung his leg over and sat hunched over for a second. He could see his prisoner thinking of jumping him again. "Come on you worthless hard looking bastard. I'll blow your damn head clean off." He coughed for the first time and the pain was severe. "Get moving!"

"I'm moving, but you don't look so good. Marshal, I swear you have a damn wooden peg sticking out of you!"

"Shut up and ride, damn you!"

Tucker Shaw held his mare up when he saw the campfire at the bottom of a long gentle slope. It was odd so much smoke and no one around. "Mare, what do you think? Shall we go investigate?" He clucked to her and rode in at a walk. He dismounted and found the coffee turned over, but the pot still had about a half cup in it. He went to his saddlebags and retrieved his cup. He poured the coffee and took a drink. It was good. He then noticed blood on one of the rocks around the fire. He walked over to where the horses had been standing and found lots of blood. There was even more a few feet from the smoldering fire. He cut his eyes over to his mount.

"Mare, I think someone is in trouble, big trouble." He mounted up and eased out on the trail of two horses. There were drops of blood alongside both horses, but one had a heavier blood trail than the other. "Mare, this horse to our left is carrying someone hurt badly." The mare flicked her ears back to Tucker every time he spoke. "You understand me don't you?" Again she flicked her ears.

He rode for two miles before he drew up. Ahead of him was open ground. He could see two horses and riders nearly across it. One of the riders was hunched over in the saddle as he rode. Suddenly the rider to the right whirled his horse and charged the wounded rider. There was a gunshot.

Tucker urged his mare on. He was coming full stride when he jumped from his horse knocking Simon Lick on his back. He was holding a rock high over his head intending to bash Marshal Sander's head in. Tucker rolled clear and drew his gun. That was when he saw the handcuffs.

Where Outlaws Roam
Royal Wade Kimes

"Halt! Mister, I don't know who you are and don't care. You got a pair of bracelets on, says plenty to me." Suddenly he laughed.

Simon Lick was sitting on his bottom in a sandy spot staring at Tucker, the interfering stranger. "What the hell is so funny?"

"Your ears. You haven't much in the line of ears do you?"

"This sorry bastard shot 'em off. I'm his prisoner and he used me for target practice this morning. I had to stick him to put a stop to it. I've been railroaded by this sonofabitch and the town he's from."

"Is that right?" Tucker eyed the wounded marshal. "Go on. Tell me what this law man done to you."

Simon Lick thought he might have just struck gold with his tale. "Well, the truth of the matter is I was riding through his town, there was a bank robbery and I was the one accused of it. Me being a drifter I was the perfect one to lay the blame on. Hell, I'd bet my last dollar this old reprobate marshal and the town mayor was the ones what stolt the money. I figure that banker in on it, too."

Tucker eyed the lawman. "What about that, Marshal?"

"This man's name is Simon Lick Tubbs. I'm taking him to Dye, Kansas for murder. He killed a woman while robbing the bank. He's not just wanted in Dye. He is also wanted in Melt, Kansas. He killed a sheriff and his deputy there. I'm from Dye. Melt doesn't have any law at the present to chase down stink meat like him. That falls to a marshal. He'll be... tried in Dye first. If the verdict comes in guilty... then we'll hang him. If it doesn't, then Melt wants him. One way or another the man will hang."

Tucker's eyes drifted back to the prisoner. "I don't mind a man having a little fun, but killing a woman and lawmen. That's a bad thing and you've gotten on my bad side, too. I hate liars, always have." He aimed and squeezed off a round.

The bullet cut the rest of Simon Lick's left ear off. "Now they match."

He grabbed the side of his head. "You bastard!"

Tucker looked from Simon Lick to the wounded marshal. "My name is Tucker Shaw."

"I'm Marshal Sanders." His grip relaxed and he dropped his six gun. He was too weak to hold it. Tucker picked it up and stuck it in his belt. He then examined the wound. It was bad, but he had seen bad before.

"My dear Marshal, this isn't good... you know that?"

"Yeah... well, all my senses are saying it ain't. I guess you're con... confirming."

"I am, but I'm not letting you die without a fair fight."

Marshal Sanders looked at him with dull fading eyes. "What does that mean?"

"It means it's up to me to get you to a doctor somewhere. A good doctor could go in there and sew the rupture up."

"I'm afraid I'm done then."

"Why?"

"The nearest doctor is back in Fort Smith."

"Is there not a farm around here close?"

Marshal Sanders thought. "Yeah, come to think of it. The Martin place is a mile due east of here. This trail forks about a quarter on up. The right hand fork will take you there."

"Okay then. I'll ride to the farm and get a wagon. First let me see something." He started to holster his gun, but then thought better of it. He cut his eyes to Simon Lick. "I bet you'd like me to drop my guard wouldn't you?"

"You damn right I would."

"Well, because of that I've got to do something I dearly hate doing."

"What's that?" He had a smile and a half sneer on his face until Tucker took two steps and knocked him out with a long hard right. He then went back to Marshal Sanders.

"Now, let me see something here." He lifted him to a sitting position. The blood immediately slowed. "Marshal, you've got to stay sitting. I don't know what's going on inside you, but the blood slowed when I lifted you upright. It could be the wound is able to bleed more freely when lying down. If the stick went in at a downward angle, it could be making it harder to bleed because of it. I'm betting that's the case." He put him up against a White Oak tree and left him a canteen of water. He then handcuffed

Where Outlaws Roam
Royal Wade Kimes

Simon Lick to a smaller Red Oak.

"Marshal, you hang in there."

All he could do was smile. He hoped this young Tucker Shaw could make it in time. He didn't hold out much hope.

Tucker made it to the Martin place without a hitch and brought both Mister Martin and his wife back with him. He left Marshal Sanders in their hands as he rode hard for a doctor in Fort Smith. He left instructions to keep him sitting up. He handcuffed the prisoner to a weight bearing post inside the Martin's barn and tied his feet with a well rope. He wasn't taking any chances with the likes of him.

Marshal Galt woke up late morning. Tucker had given him a little too much ether, but not enough to kill him. He was terribly sluggish. He just couldn't get his body to wake up. Deputy Nelson helped him to his office when he found him walking barefooted up Garrison Avenue.

Doctor Morton was examining him while Deputy Nelson looked on. "Well, Marshal, you're going to live. I'm somewhat amazed at this."

Marshal Galt was sitting in his chair behind his desk. "How so?"

"Well, the man that put you under. He knew just how much to give you to get far away from here and at the same time not kill you. He could have easily killed you. In fact I don't know anyone else that wouldn't have. It would have been purely accidental, but you would be dead just the same." The doctor shook his head. "No, the young man that drugged you knows a little something about ether, maybe medicine in general."

"Well, let me tell you something I know. I'm going after that peckerwood and I'm throwing him in jail."

Doctor Morton put his instruments in his bag and then turned to Marshal Galt. "My business is doctoring, but I am curious as to what charge you plan to bring him in on?"

He hesitated in answering. "Well, hell Doc, I can't bring him in. I'm all talk." He smiled and looked at both Deputy Nelson and Doctor Morton. "The last thing I want is for this town to get wind I was put under an induced sleep by some... some greenhorn dude. Not only that, you know it would come out that he took my damn boots off, hung my gun rig on the bedpost and laid my damn head on a nice fluffy pillow... and, and tucked me in. No, that's not happening."

Deputy Nelson was nearly in the floor with laughter. "He did all that?"

"Nelson, you can shut that trap."

"Yes sir... Sleeping Beauty." He and the Doctor laughed some more.

"You two go right on and laugh. See what I mean? The whole damn town would be laughing." He pulled out a cigar and lit it. He took a draw and then glanced at the two men. "With that said, he best not show his self in Fort Smith again. I'll arrest him for something." He eyed the Doctor. "Maybe I could arrest him for stealing medicine from your office?"

"Yes, well, I am missing one bottle of ether. However, I'm not pressing charges."

"And why the hell not?"

"It's been well worth the price of a bottle of ether to hear and see the results of its disappearance." Again laughter broke out. It ended rather quickly however when, speak of the devil, Tucker Shaw walked through the door.

"Marshal, Deputy, good morning. You boys don't make any sudden moves now. My gun is holstered and I mean no harm to anyone, but I need a doctor."

His eyes left Marshal Galt and trailed over to Doctor Morton. "Doc, I got a man that needs attention immediately or he's not going to be around long. He'll be pushing up daisies by this time tomorrow if you don't come with me." He grinned and looked over at the marshal. "That 'pushing up daisies' is cowboy. I'm starting to get the hang of this cowboy lingo."

Marshal Galt turned red all over. "Son, what you've really got the hang of is breaking the law. You put me to sleep, stole medicine from Doc Morton, sold property that weren't yours, and no telling what else."

"It does look bad, but it isn't all that bad. By the way, did you enjoy your rest?"

"Hell no! And just how bad does it have to look to be bad, I'd

Where Outlaws Roam
Royal Wade Kimes

like to know?"

Tucker cut his eyes over to Doctor Morton. "I guess we better go." He looked back at the two lawmen. "Do I have your word you won't follow us?"

Marshal Galt was baffled to say the least. "Hell no... you don't have no such a damn thing! You're all but kidnapping Doc Morton here!"

Doctor Morton interjected. "That's not so, Marshal. This young man has brought news of someone needing my services. It is my duty to see to the man."

"Well, if that's not a fine howdy do." He glared at Tucker. "You're under arrest for selling stolen property, and you're to stand trial for it."

"You mean Reed Fletcher's steamboat? Marshal, trust me that'll work its self out. Besides, it was nothing but a tub anyway and I didn't steal it, I used it for a getaway vessel."

"Well, while it is working its self out you'll be in jail."

"Marshal, we have a dilemma. How can I be in two places at one time? I'd like to accommodate you, but it just physically isn't possible."

Deputy Nelson started to draw his gun until he saw how fast Tucker could draw his. "Marshal, please tell your dutiful deputy to leave go. I don't want to hurt anyone... but me and the doctor are leaving. Now if I can't have your word you won't follow me, bad as I hate to, I'll have to lock you up."

"That tares it. You lock me up in my own cell and I'll run your young ass to the edge of the world."

"I guess that means you're not going to corporate?"

Doctor Morton turned and grabbed the door handle to leave. "I've not heard anything in here and I haven't seen anything in here." He left the jail and waited outside.

Tucker motioned for Marshal Galt and Deputy Nelson to step inside one of the cells. There was a prisoner in one of the other cells across from where he put the two lawmen. He was snoring fairly loud. Tucker smiled. "You two might try that, you know, catch up on a little sleep."

Marshal Galt grabbed hold of the bars and stared at him. "I

already caught up thanks to you. Up till now you hadn't riled me. If you leave me in here things is bound to change in my feelings towards you."

"Marshal, you're only in here because of your obstinacy."

"My what?"

"Stubbornness." He smiled and threw the keys to the cell over on the desk. "Marshal, please take notice I didn't take your guns. It's not like I disarmed you. It's not like some hardened criminal came in, took your guns and worked you over."

He turned and left the jail. Marshal Galt pulled his gun but didn't cock the hammer. He couldn't shoot a man in the back, and he might be killing someone else if he shot Tucker Shaw. He had no choice but to let him take Doc Morton to wherever and whoever it was that was critically wounded.

Doctor Morton was waiting outside. "Young man, you seem to have a knack for getting into trouble. Marshal Galt is an easy going type, but you may have exceeded his limitation."

"Doctor, I'm afraid I may have. I sure hope not, I like the man. I do find him a bit serious regarding his work."

"Speaking of work, where is this man that's critically hurt?"

"I guess that horse and buggy standing there is yours?"

"It is."

"Then follow me."

Chapter 9

Reed Fletcher and his three expert gunmen were a half a day's ride out of Fort Smith when they stopped at a nice farm. The owner and two of his workers greeted them.

"Afternoon... my name is Short Benson, you boys passing through to Fort Smith?"

Reed tipped his hat. "We are. I'm Reed Fletcher from Louisiana. These gentlemen are Neely Law, Raff Thibodeaux, and Devo Wells. I have a rather large farm in Louisiana. I plant just about anything that grows."

"I see. I'm always glad to meet a fellow farmer."

"The same here. I don't see many hands in the fields. It looks like you have a good corn crop."

"We do. I've had a good year. Those fine horses you're riding look tuckered out. You're welcome to lay over here if you like."

"I appreciate that."

"We have a guest house that will accommodate the four of you. My wife will have supper at six. You boys be washed up and you're invited to sit to supper with us."

Reed smiled and dismounted.

Short noticed the guns the four were wearing and what looked to be a fancy case two different rifles was in. "Ah, what brings you up this way?"

Reed glanced at his men and then smiled at Short. "We're on a hunting trip."

Short tried not to show his confusion at the answer. "I see. Well, the hunting is okay, but I'd think Louisiana would be just as good if not better."

"Oh, it's probably better. We have a lot of everything down there. By the way, would it be possible to site our guns in while here?"

"I don't see why not. I have a tree I site mine in with now and then."

"That'll do fine."

Short rubbed his earlobe softly. "You never said what you was a hunting up this way."

Reed smiled. "We're man hunting."

Short started to smile but withdrew it immediately. "What'd this man do?"

"He stole my property and sold it. He also killed some of my workers."

"He sounds like a mean one. Have you notified the authorities?"

"I have. The man was last seen in Fort Smith."

"Well, I hope you catch him. Like I say, make yourselves at home. Be washed up around six, we'd be pleased to have you for supper."

"Thank you for your hospitality."

Short turned and walked to the house. Reed turned to his men.

"We need to check these rifles. We bumped two of them kind hard coming through some of that timber. I think we stick to the trail from now on... no more short cuts." He turned and walked out away from his men looking north. He was getting closer to Tucker Shaw each day.

Tucker and Doctor Morton arrived at the Martin place just before dark. Marshal Sanders was still hanging on, but he was terribly weak. He had lost a considerable amount of blood.

Tucker went to the barn to check on the prisoner. He lit a match and found a lantern. He lit it and walked over to Simon Lick.

"You bastards left me handcuffed here damn near all day. I've wet myself twice and need to do more than that. I'm damn near dead from lack of water."

"You're not as bad off as Marshal Sanders. He must be a good man."

"Why is that?"

"I'd a killed you. He didn't. I figure he's a good man." Tucker studied the prisoner. "You wouldn't have any idea what I'm even talking about would you?"

"I don't give a damn what you're talking about. All I want is these cuffs taken off from around this post. I've got to relieve myself and I got to have water. If this keeps up, I might be better off dead. You two make living a damn chore."

Tucker took the key to the cuffs and unlocked them from the

Where Outlaws Roam
Royal Wade Kimes

post. He then locked them back to both wrists.

It was very difficult for Simon Lick to stand. Once he did, it was even more difficult for him to take a step. His legs were stiff from sitting all day in one position and his shoulder was stiff from the bullet wound. It too would need tended. He was one pitiful sight. He had no ears, his shoulder was bloody and he limped when he walked from lack of blood circulation through his legs. As Tucker followed him to the outhouse he offered a comment.

"If I were you I'd think twice about attacking another lawman. You look like hell over it. I bet before you did that you was being treated fair. Bad decisions like that create pure hell don't they?"

"Mister, I don't know who you are, but you're saddled with one smart mouth."

"Tucker Shaw." He chuckled. "My folks and half of Great Britain would agree with you on my mouth."

The prisoner held his wrists up to take the cuffs off so he could enter the outhouse and take care of nature's calling. Tucker stuck the key in, but before he turned it. "I'm not Marshal Sanders. I haven't taken an oath. I don't like you, and that makes killing you easier than it might normally be. You make one move, breathe wrong and I'll blow holes in you from head to chest." He turned the key.

Simon Lick was looking direct into Tucker's eyes. He saw the certainty of what he was saying. He then turned and went inside the little outhouse. Tucker backed away from the little building to where he could see all sides of it. He was watching it closely and had for several minutes. Then he saw a weed move a few inches to the left. He raced up to the outhouse and cocked his pistol.

"Come up and out of there!"

Simon Lick was lying on his back in a deep drain off from the outhouse. The grass and weeds were so high the prisoner was nearly free before he saw him.

He crawled out from under the toilet and stood. He had dung all over him and smelled to high heaven. Tucker very carefully handed the handcuffs to him.

"Put these on, I'm not touching you."

"And if I won't?"

"Your choice." He aimed at his foot. "Put those cuffs on or I'll blow a hole in your left foot. I told you, I'm not under an oath to do right by you. I don't care if you live or die. I don't care if you make it to Dye, Kansas for trial or not. I don't care if you hang or get shot. I just don't give a damn about you at all. Marshal Sanders in there fighting for his life is a different story. He's a good man, and in my opinion was too good to you.

"You and that old bastard lawman will get yours."

"I'd be real careful threatening me. I might shoot you for name calling. It seems to me you aren't getting the hang of what I'm saying. How many parts of the body will sustain damage before you catch on?"

"You better get the doctor out here. I'm bleeding from my shoulder some."

"You can bleed to death for all I care. Marshal Sanders is being operated on. Once he's done with him, then we'll see about you. I know a little about the medicine field, and I am almost certain those wounds you have will set up infection after crawling around in human waste. That would be one terrible way to die. You be a good boy and I'll make sure Doctor Morton tends your wounds, disinfects and puts a bandage on your sorry ass."

Doctor Morton asked Mrs. Martin for a tub and Tucker filled it with well water. It was cold but he didn't care. The water was for the prisoner. He was just too filthy to be tended to. The doctor said the cold water would be good for any wounds he might have. When he poured the last bucket of water under lantern light, he once again took the handcuffs off the prisoner and stepped back away from him.

He and Doctor Morton were the only two out in the yard. The Martins were asked to stay inside and watch Marshal Sanders. Doctor Morton laid his hand on top of Tucker's shoulder as the prisoner undressed.

"What happened to his ears?"

Tucker grinned. "They're missing aren't they?"

"That's what I mean." He looked at Tucker with curiosity.

"Marshal Sanders shot them nearly off trying to get his

Where Outlaws Roam
Royal Wade Kimes

attention you might say. I cleaned them up a little afterwards."

"I see. Well, I've got to get him cleaned up or he'll set up infection and die."

"That would be too bad."

The following day at near noon Marshal Sanders asked for Tucker. Doctor Morton went to the front door and found him lying asleep on the floor of the screened in porch.

"Tucker."

He turned over on his side, but didn't rise.

"Tucker, wake up."

This time he sprung up with gun in hand. Doctor Morton was surprised. He hadn't noticed the gun being in his hand.

"Doctor, it's you? I was dreaming and it wasn't going so good for me. I dreamed I was in a big ship and they were taking me back home to face the Queen, and then I was to be hung. You woke me just before they dropped the trap."

"Well, you might say I saved your life then."

"Yes, and I shall be indebted to you forever."

"Well, never mind that, Marshal Sanders wants to talk to you."

"Oh?" He stood up and straightened his shirt. "Okay then." He walked into the house and was shown to where he was lying.

"Son." He looked at Tucker with tired eyes. You've probably saved my life, if nothing don't happen in the healing process. Doctor Morton is watching for infection of the lungs. I guess that projectile Simon Lick stuck in me was mighty dirty."

"Marshal, you'll be fine. You have lots of living to do yet."

"Yeah, and that's what I want to talk to you about." He stopped to get a better breath. "If I pull through I'm getting out of this game. I'd like to swear you in as temporary Deputy Marshal of Dye, Kansas if you'll take the job. Your first task would be to get Simon Lick Tubbs to Dye."

A rush of thoughts come racing across and through Tucker's mind. He was banished to America, he had been shot at, chased, and was wanted by the law, he'd had a shootout in a saloon, met the wildest sensual woman on earth and now was being asked to be a deputy marshal. He thought he was going to see lawmen and outlaws by being here. Somehow the Wild West made you one or the other whether you wanted to be or not, and in some cases... both. "Only in America."

"What'd you say?" Marshal Sanders had almost dozed off waiting on Tucker to respond. The medicine Doctor Morton was giving him made him drowsy.

"Marshal, you don't even know me."

"I know you saved my life. I saw how you handled my prisoner. I also seen you could handle that pistol you wear."

Tucker looked down at his gun rig. "Marshal, this rig is not even mine."

"I don't care. You know how to use it." He took two good breaths. "Well, how 'bout it? Will you do it? I'll write out the paper and Doc Morton can witness. I have a badge in my saddlebags. You'll be running the town of Dye until I get on my feet. I'll ride there and make it permanent if you take to it. I'm through. I think I'll ride on up into Pueblo, Colorado and live peaceable. I have my eye on a piece of ground there... and a lady I met I've been writing to. Might turn into something."

Tucker smiled. "Marshal, if my family and the Queen knew of this they'd have to bury half of them from heart failure. I accept."

"I'd shake your hand, but I'm just too weak."

"Get some rest and we'll talk again later." He left the room numb and excited.

Where Outlaws Roam
Royal Wade Kimes

Chapter 10

Angel Hound had been down to Garrison Avenue on an errand for his mother Ina. He was walking back towards the Mission when he spotted Reed and three of his men. They spotted him at the same time. He took off in a dead run. Reed spurred his horse in pursuit. Raff turned down a side street and Devo followed. Neely Law fell in behind Reed.

Raff turned sharply down an alley and came out dead in front of Angel Hound, who slid to a stop. He started to run but a rope suddenly appeared around his waist. Raff had roped him and then jerked him down.

"Here he is Reed, roped and ready!" He began to laugh at him.

Reed brought his horse to a halt and dismounted. "Hello, Angel Hound. We've missed you, boy. What do you mean running off like you did? It might have not hurt me so bad, but you took all those others with you and fell in with a bad man. I've surely been sick with worry about you." He slapped him across the face as Raff held the rope tight. "That's just a taste of what's coming if you don't spit out the right answers from this point on. I'd hate to have to take you down on the Arkansas and put you're nappy head under until you were made to see your mistakes... or stop breathing."

Angel Hound was shaking and his eyes were large with fright. "Boss Fletcher, why don't you leave us be?"

"Boy, what the hell do you mean? You owe me. You owe me three more months of work, to work off the fine you kept accumulating. I'm teaching you right from wrong, and being proper on paying what's owed."

"I don't owes you nothing. I gets it paid but you adds to."

"Are you challenging me, Boy?" He slapped him again.

"I'll not be taking any sass from a damn Negro smart mouth. I've already added a year for your running off. I'm adding another two months for back talking me."

Angel Hound all of a sudden began to smile. Reed thought he was looking at him, but he was looking past him. Ina was taking long fast steps towards them. Marshal Galt and two other men wearing badges were just ahead of her. Ina had seen Angel

Hound running for his life. She beat it to the Fort Smith Marshals Office and discovered Marshal Galt locked in his own cell in the back of the jail. She let them out and they came with her to rescue her son.

Marshal Galt drew his gun. "Hold up right there! Get your rope off that man, and don't anyone move sudden."

Reed turned to face him. "Marshal, this... man as you called him is my prison worker. He's a runaway."

Ina walked past Marshal Galt and right up to Reed Fletcher. She slapped him so hard he lost his balance and took two steps backwards. "You don't own Angel! You must not have heard down in Louisiana how the war done freed us Negros?" She took a step towards him, causing him to back up another step. Her eyes were wide with anger and daring him to press her.

Marshal Galt had to chuckle. "I'm guessing by Ina saying you're from Louisiana, that you're Reed Fletcher. You're the one pressing charges over stolen property being sold here in Fort Smith."

"Not only that, but when we get Tucker Shaw back to Louisiana he'll face murder charges as well. Two of my prison guards were killed in the escape."

"Forgive me, Mister Fletcher, but this prison you speak of... is it a state or federal penitentiary?"

He looked over at his men. "It's neither. It's my own. When people break the law, trespass and other things, I make them work it off."

Marshal Galt stared at him. "You mean to say you hold people against their will without court orders?"

"I'm law on my farm."

"Well, you're not on your farm up here. Angel is free to come and go as he pleases. You won't be taking him or anyone else back with you."

Angel Hound grinned real big.

"Now see here. I have pressed charges against this Tucker Shaw and I aim to see he gets his just due."

"Tucker Shaw may be another matter, but you stay away from the kids he brought here."

Reed stepped to his horse and mounted. "Where is Tucker

Where Outlaws Roam
Royal Wade Kimes

Shaw?"

"That's a good question."

Reed looked perplexed. "He is in town?"

"No, I'm afraid he's not. He and Doctor Morton left town on a mission to help someone critically wounded."

"I don't doubt that. It seems people end up that way around Tucker Shaw. Tell me, Marshal, how is it he was able to leave town with a doctor?"

Marshal Galt smiled. "Now that would be a long story if it was any of your business, since it's not, I'll not bore you with it." He turned to Ina. "You and Angel head on back. I'll take care of everything here."

Ina smiled and then glared at Reed. "You stay clear of me and mine Reed Fletcher, you hear me?"

Marshal Galt holstered his gun as did his deputies. "Reed, follow me down to the Marshals Office. I would like to discuss the Tucker Shaw case with you."

He smiled at his men. "Lead the way, Marshal."

Tucker decided to get started with his prisoner. He was sworn in as Deputy Marshal of Dye, Kansas, and papers were written and signed by Marshal Sanders. Doctor Morton signed as witness to legality. It was two o'clock in the afternoon and he wanted to get started, but before he could go Marshal Sanders asked to see him again. He walked in his room and found him awake. He looked pale and weak, but he was breathing.

"Deputy Shaw, there's one thing I forgot to tell you about Simon Lick Tubbs. He has a small gang. I think there are maybe three men that rode with him. I've not seen any sign of them along the way, but I'm not along the way too far. Keep a good eye out. Watch your back trail, gullies, and high rims. The three he rode with are mean ones."

"I appreciate you telling me. I don't guess it occurred to you to tell me that before I was sworn in?"

"It did, but I didn't." That was the first smile Tucker had seen from Marshal Sanders.

"Well, I'll keep my eyes peeled for trouble."

"You'll do fine."

"Marshal, get well. I'll see you in Dye."

"It may be a while. I've got a right smart of blood to build back."

"I'll hold the fort until you get there."

"I'm hoping you'll want to stay on when I do."

"We'll see. Take care of yourself."

He turned and left the room. He walked out to the barn and took the cuffs off of his prisoner, but not before he put him almost asleep with ether. Doctor Morton gave him a fresh bottle. He asked Tucker how he got so good at using the stuff. He informed him that he trained in the Queen's Army in usage of anesthesia. He also informed him that he was a hand to hand soldier for a short time. He didn't go any further as to why a short time.

"Doctor, it has been a pleasure meeting you. I thank you for the fresh bottle of ether. He cut his eyes over to the prisoner. "I have an idea I'll be using a lot of it."

"Well, he's your prisoner. You can handle him however you see fit."

"Well Doc, take care."

"Watch yourself, Tucker."

He waved to Mr. and Mrs. Martin and rode out leading his prisoner on a foundered horse. It would be slow going until he found a ranch or town with horses for sale. He was planning to leave the foundered horse and get a good one.

He rode for two hours at a slow walk and was nearly bored to tears. He kept searching along the way for farms or ranches, but none were on the trail thus far. He made a bend around a bluff of black slate rock and before him was the greenest wide open meadow he had seen anywhere. About a half mile across to the other side was a blue stream of water and cattle grazing. He spotted a ranch house in the distance and decided to ride to it.

He rode up in front of the house and saw five good looking horses in a corral by the barn. A man came out of the barn and walked up behind him.

"Can I help you boys?"

Tucker turned in the saddle. "I'm the Deputy Marshal of Dye, Kansas. I'm in need of a good horse. Would you have one I could

Where Outlaws Roam
Royal Wade Kimes

purchase?"

"Well, normally I have some for sale, but the State of Kansas isn't too good about sending me my money for stock at any great speed."

Tucker laughed. "I understand. You won't have to worry this time. I'll be buying him for my own use. I have cash."

"Well, in that case, step down and let me show you what I have."

Tucker glanced at his prisoner who was still sleepy eyed. He stepped down and led the two horses to a hitching rail by the barn. He tied them and then he put a loop around one of his prisoner's boots and ran it under the horse. He made another loop and drew it up tight around that boot. He then went with the owner of the ranch.

"My name is Thaddeus Post." He glanced at Tucker. "Your prisoner... he's a hard looker."

"Thaddeus, glad to meet you. Yes, he has endured some hardship brought on of his own doing. I'm transporting him from Fort Smith to Dye, Kansas. It's exceedingly painful leading that old foundered horse he's riding."

"I imagine so." They walked in a corral where five geldings stood. He looked at Tucker before he spoke. "These boys in here range from four to seven years old. That big bay is seven. The sorrel roan is five and has lots of heart."

Tucker wasn't listening or evening looking at the two horses he spoke about. His eyes were on a deep liver colored chestnut with a perfect blaze down his face. He had a good saddle back and four good straight corners under him. His girth line was deep and his hips were high. They also arched up at the back and then gently sloped forever. He was the best horse he'd seen since being in America.

"That one, what's his story?"

Thaddeus laughed. "He's five years old and has a lot of spirit and power. He's not been rode just yet. Pace, my buster tried him, but he didn't last long."

Tucker walked over to him and gave him his elbow to smell. The horse forked both ears forward and smelled him, and then blew softly.

"Can you saddle him?"

"I can, it's your call."

"I like him."

"So do we, but we can't ride him."

Thaddeus saddled the chestnut and some of the hands appeared out of nowhere. It didn't take long to find out a stranger on the ranch was about to get piled. They all collected on the fence.

Tucker walked to him as two ranch hands held him. He let the horse smell him again, and then he stepped up into the saddle. The boys holding him let go and backed away. The horse stood perfectly still for a minute and then broke into a buck. He got higher with each launch. Tucker took his hat off and whipped his backend as it came up. The cowboys began hollering for the stranger to hang on. The horse made two more rather large stiff legged jumps and then bucked smoothly to a stop. Tucker touched him with his spur and he walked off, but he gave to the spur somewhat sideways as he did. He snorted and forked an ear down towards where the spur touched him. Tucker laughed.

"You don't know what that is, do you boy? You'll catch on." He thought about that. Ole boy, you have a name... Catcher. I'm calling you Catcher."

He walked him to the gate and dismounted. He stood there by him a few seconds and then easy and slowly put a foot in the stirrup. The chestnut stood. He put some weight in it and still he stood. He stepped up and let his leg come over easy. The horse stood as if asking what's the big deal, why are you moving so slow?

Tucker turned him back and forth in the corral several times and then rode him around it a couple of times more and dismounted. "It'll take a while to get him reining, but how much?"

Thaddeus smiled. "Two hundred." I would have asked three, but you did part of my job. He's a beauty. I think he'll make a good horse."

"I have a question. Why have you waited so long to break this ole boy?"

Where Outlaws Roam
Royal Wade Kimes

"Well, I have a big ranch here. Until this year, he'd always get away from us. He's got a mind of his own."

"So he's hard to catch?"

"Has been for me. He may not be for you. He seems to act differently with you."

"He's all horse that's sure."

Tucker bought a saddle that fit him and saddled him up. He transferred Simon Lick to the bronze colored mare while Thaddeus turned the foundered horse out on the range to live out his life.

Tucker said his goodbyes and left the ranch after being offered a job busting colts. By the time he had ridden near to ten miles the gelding was learning how to travel a little. It would take a day or two for him to find his balance with a rider atop him. Tucker was keeping a close eye on him because he wasn't shod. Thaddeus said he never had been which made his feet tough as a buffalo horn.

Tucker watched his back trail and paid close attention when crossing gullies, high rocks and canyon rims. He kept a wary eye on them for reflections and movement. It paid off. He came into a rockier terrain and detected three horses with riders hurrying around a rock slide about two hundred yards ahead.

Marshal Galt sat behind his desk facing Reed Fletcher and his three men. "I guess what I would like to know from you Mister Fletcher, is what your intentions are?"

"Regarding?"

"Tucker Shaw for one thing... and your stolen property for another."

"I want my property back, and I want Tucker hung by the neck or shot dead, it doesn't matter which."

"Well, here in Fort Smith it does. It's the law's job to bring in criminals up here. Maybe where you're from, it's left to the citizenry. I'll be going out looking for him. I best not see you and your men anywhere around. Now, as for Tucker Shaw being brought to Louisiana for trial, I doubt that happening."

"And why the hell not?!" Reed was sitting down and nearly came out of his seat. "The man's a murderer!"

"Not to hear him tell it." He paused. "The fact is Tucker has a passel of witnesses to support his side of the story. Your man was trying to stop Tucker and the kids and he had to shoot him, because he was afraid one of the man's bullets might hit one of the kids."

"That's outrageous!"

"Whatever it is… it clears Tucker Shaw. Now where he's not clear at is the sale of your property and obstruction of justice."

Reed was very disturbed. "I don't know anything about obstruction of justice, but I do know about my damn steamboat! It's gone, he took it and I want it back!"

"Well, like I say, I'll be going after him soon enough. Meanwhile, you and your… your gunmen here better get a hotel and settle in until I bring him back. Like I say, if I catch you boys out there on the trail I'm not going to be happy."

"Marshal, it's a damn free country last I checked. I go where I please."

"That's fine, and yes it is a free country. But if you break the law in my district your freedom will be negated for quite some time. Do we understand one another?"

"Oh, you bet we do, you bet we do." He got up and stormed out of the room with his men following closely behind. He wasn't hearing at all what he thought he would from the Fort Smith Marshals Office."

Where Outlaws Roam
Royal Wade Kimes

Chapter 11

Tucker eased the reins back on Catcher and stopped. He watched the gelding's ears. They were pointed straight ahead. He cut his eyes to the bronze mare. She too was looking straight ahead.

"What's wrong, Deputy? Did you see a ghost?"

"I see you're awake. You sure like to sleep a lot."

"You bastard, you put me out."

"I did you a favor. You don't feel pain when you're out. I'm about to do it again if you don't shut your mouth."

"I don't have ears because of you bastards. You're not worrying on my pain."

Tucker pulled his rifle and eased Catcher ahead. The trail crooked around through chalk like rock and between small scrub bushes. He dismounted and tied his horse to one of the small bushes. He then looked at his prisoner who was grinning.

"Simon Lick, you're just trouble. You don't know it, but you're my pay back for all the trouble I caused where I'm from. However, I wasn't killing lawmen and women." He walked back to him and looked up. "Well, here are your choices. I can hit you with the butt of this rifle and put you to sleep while I deal with what's waiting up ahead, or I can use the ether. What will it be?"

"You serious?"

He smiled at his prisoner.

When he realized he was, he rolled his eyes and looked towards the sky. "Could we do this on my word of honor?"

Tucker chuckled and then stared.

"Ether... damn it all."

"Ether it is then." He went to his saddlebags and brought back the bottle and a large cotton ball. "Bend down here and breathe this stuff."

Simon Lick was sleeping like a newborn in just a few seconds. He slumped forward in the saddle and then Tucker pulled him off the mare. He handcuffed him with another set of handcuffs to a sapling. "Now, you don't go anywhere, I'll be right back." He smiled as he took off, knowing his prisoner didn't hear a word he said.

Where Outlaws Roam
Royal Wade Kimes

He climbed a dusty hillside and eased up to the top. Unlike the side of the hill, there was grass, which was thick and green on top. He laid down in it and crawled across to the other side. He was rewarded for his efforts. Three men were sitting in ambush behind an array of flint stone. They had their rifles lying on the rocks and all three of them were aiming down the barrels. He eased the hammer back on his rifle, and grinned. When he pulled the trigger the man in the middle grabbed his backside. Tucker shot him in the behind. He levered another shell and nailed the one to his right the same way. The third man whirled and threw as many rounds up the hill as he could.

Tucker was laughing as he returned to his horses and prisoner. Simon Lick was still out for the most part. He was drowsy and trying to talk. His words were slurred and he really didn't know what was going on.

"Simon Lick, your friends are probably having some hard thoughts about now."

"What, what about my friends?"

"I think I'm a pain in their ass." He loaded his prisoner and started down the trail.

"Deputy Marshal."

"Yeah."

"I'll play along with you... if anything else should come along. I'm not liking this ether much, makes me feel bad. I can work with you."

"That's real nice of you... would we be having a change of heart?"

"Not so much that. Have you taken a real good look at me? Hell, I'm beat up and chewed up worse than a loser in a dog fight. I can't take much more. I'm all in."

"Whoa." Tucker pulled up and looked back at his prisoner. He smiled at him. "Yeah, you do look a little rough."

"A little? Deputy, what would a man have to look like to be looking terrible rough to you?"

"He'd have to be skinned."

Simon Lick's eyes widened as his mind processed what was said to him. "We ain't using no knife on me."

"Then mind your manners." He paused and smiled. "You know

Where Outlaws Roam
Royal Wade Kimes

something Simon Lick. You may welcome hanging before we get to Dye, Kansas."

"I'm damn near there now."

Tucker moved on, but not before he checked his back trail.

Doctor Morton made it back to Fort Smith and went straight to the Marshals Office. "Marshal Galt."

"Doctor, I see you're back. I'm saddled and waiting to leave. I was just waiting on you. Who was it needing a doctor and where is Tucker?"

"Do you know Marshal Sanders?"

"I do. What about him?"

"It was him that was badly wounded. It seems his prisoner nearly killed him. I'll have to go back out and check on him tomorrow. I think he'll pull through, but he's weak and lost a considerable amount of blood."

"I hate to hear that. Where is he at?"

"He's at the Jeff Martin place."

"And his prisoner, is he alive?"

"He's on his way to Dye, Kansas."

"Who the hell is taking him?" Marshal Galt was baffled.

"Tucker Shaw. Marshal Sanders swore him in as Deputy Marshal. Tucker saved his life. He did a good job handling Simon Lick as well."

"The hell you say, that British... dude?" Marshal Galt walked back and forth behind his desk. He stopped and stared at Doctor Morton. "It doesn't make any difference. There's a man in town by the name of Reed Fletcher that has brought charges against him. He's sworn out a warrant for his arrest. I've got to serve it."

"Well, you have to do your duty. I wouldn't want your job though, on two counts."

He looked at the doctor inquisitively. "What would that be?"

"Well first, he's a good man. The second thing is he can handle himself rather well. I think you'll have your hands full serving a warrant on him."

"Is that right?" He stared at Doctor Morton for a second. "Why does everything have to be hard?"

"It's the way life is."

Marshal Galt picked his rifle up off the desk. "Well, nonetheless I have to do it." He motioned for two of his deputies to follow him. They went outside and mounted up. Doctor Morton walked out and waved goodbye as the lawmen tipped their hats to him.

Reed Fletcher and his men were standing in the lobby of the River Valley Hotel across Garrison Avenue from the Marshals Office. He watched as Marshal Galt and his deputies rode out.

"Boys, let's get our horses. Marshal Galt doesn't know it, but he's going to lead us to Tucker Shaw."

They beat it down to the stable and mounted up. Reed had the stable boy saddle their horses as soon as he saw Doctor Morton pull up to his office. He knew he would put away his bag and then go see Marshal Galt.

They mounted their horses and left in a lope. When they were in sight of the lawmen they pulled up. Reed looked behind him at his men. "We best not get too close." He looked back up the trail from the way they come. "Boys, have you noticed anything or anyone behind us?"

Raff glanced at the others. "I haven't, have you boys?"

Devo shook his head negatively, Neely however kept looking back. "I ain't seen anything, but the hair on my neck is standing up... something's back there."

Reed kept looking. He saw nothing. He glanced at Neely. "What do you think?"

Neely shrugged his shoulders in lack of an answer. Raff eased his horse over by Reed. "Maybe I'll let you boys go on ahead. I'll pull off into these post oak bushes and see what follows."

"That's not a bad idea. It might be nothing." He stared back up the trail again. "I guess it could be Angel Hound."

"What or whoever it is I'll take care of it."

"Okay then. Boys, let's ride."

Reed and his two men left in a short lope. Raff rode up on the bank of the wagon road and hid in among the post oak scrub trees. The ground was poor and full of small sand rocks. It was hot sitting in one spot where air couldn't get into very easy. He was beginning to sweat and so was his horse. Horseflies finally

Where Outlaws Roam
Royal Wade Kimes

found the horse and were attacking from beneath and on the rump of the gelding.

Raff Thibodeaux a man who had killed men and lived on the edge of the law his whole life, would never have thought an insect like a horsefly would be what got him killed. His horse kept stamping his hooves in an effort to ward off flies and gave Raff's position away. He never heard or saw it, but he felt it. Six inches of steel was thrown and stuck between his shoulder blades. He caught his breath and sat his horse with a blank stare. He teetered to the right and then the left. He straightened and then fell forward over the left shoulder of his horse.

He was lying face down until the knife was removed and he was turned over. He stared at his killer. "Do I know you?" He closed his eyes and drew his last breath of life. Ten minutes later his horse left with a new rider.

Reed pulled his horse up and looked back across a long wide open space they had crossed. They had been riding at a slow walk for quite some time.

"Raff should have caught up with us by now."

Devo frowned as he looked at Neely and then to Reed. "Something happened. I can feel it. Raff, he's not one to fool around."

"I think you're right. Boys, we better keep a sharp eye behind us. There's someone on our trail."

Neely turned in the saddle to look back. "Who?"

"Angel Hound's mother warned us to stay clear of her. Maybe she's taken it upon herself to take revenge on me." Devo chuckled. "Reed, that woman ain't riding any horse after us."

Reed laughed. "From the way she was stepping the last time I seen her, she wouldn't need a horse."

Devo laughed but then became serious. "We're laughing, but whoever it is, they aren't to be taken lightly if they done Raff in."

Reed shook his head in agreement. "Let's ride." They loped off looking back every now and then for the first half mile. When the trail went into big timber they slowed down and paid attention to what might lie ahead.

Where Outlaws Roam
Royal Wade Kimes

Marshal Galt was riding at a fair jog, and had been for quite a while. He finally pulled up. They were within a mile of the Martin place. He was on a mission he didn't like. Marshal Sanders and he had known each other for twenty years, and if he had enough faith in Tucker Shaw to make him a Deputy Marshal, that had to say a hell of a lot about the man.

"Farley."

"Yeah, Marshal?"

"When we get to the Martin place you station yourself in the barn loft. Best I remember they have one. You'll be able to see good from that advantage point. We don't want anyone slipping in on us."

Deputy Farley looked over at Deputy Nelson, and then he zeroed in on Marshal Galt. "Marshal, who are we worrying about sneaking up on us? I thought we were the ones doing the sneaking and hunting."

"Yeah, well, I don't trust that damn Louisiana Cajun."

"Reed Fletcher?"

"Yeah, he seems a little head strong and gun happy. I saw the guns they were toting. I think we'll just take precautions and watch our backdoor." He looked at Deputy Nelson. "You stay near the horses. Keep your rifle in hand."

"Marshal, I've known you ten years and you've never taken so many precautions. What's up here?"

"I've been around men like Reed Fletcher and they're not to be taken lightly. They keep coming." He paused and then smiled. "To be damned honest they ain't like the rest of the population on this earth. They have no quit and don't give a damn for anything."

"That's good enough. I'll be ready if anything happens."

"Okay, let's ride."

A few minutes later they rode into the Martin place slow and easy and were met at the front gate. "Hello, Mister Martin."

"Marshal Galt, what a nice surprise! Get down and come in! I suppose you're here to see Marshal Sanders?"

"I am. I'm also on the trail of Tucker Shaw."

"Tucker? What on earth for? The man is on our side. He saved Marshal Sander's life and took care of that hardened criminal like

Where Outlaws Roam
Royal Wade Kimes

an old hand."

"I heard." He dismounted and followed him inside the house. He was then led to where Marshal Sanders was lying.

"Galt!"

"Marshal Sanders, what have you gone and done?" He took a chair beside his bed.

He ducked his eyes down. "I let Simon Lick Tubbs jump me. The bastard had a persimmon projectile he drove up into my chest." He reached over on a small oval shaped cherry table and picked up the persimmon stick. "The bastard used his teeth to sharpen it, fine piece of work. The man is an artist."

"He's also a damn killer." He eyed his old friend over.

"You getting better?"

"Hell, Galt, it'll take more than a persimmon sprout to kill an ole bull like me."

"That's good, that's real good." He hesitated and Marshal Sanders realized something was on his mind.

"What's wrong?"

"Well, I've got a disagreeable, uncomfortable task ahead of me. That boy, the man you swore in as Deputy Marshal... I've got to arrest him."

"What the hell for?" Marshal Sanders tried to sit up more but was too weak.

"Now don't overdo yourself here. I don't mean to upset you... but I would like to know what you know about this lad."

"Not a whole hell of a lot, and maybe I should know from what you're saying. He saved my life, I know that. Galt, I was a goner. Hell, I didn't have any hopes of making it. That boy leaned me up against a tree and made me stay like that until he could get back with help. Then he rode like hell to Fort Smith and came back with Doctor Morton. I was delirious part of the time, but the next thing I knowed there was a doctor and hope. The man is okay, Galt. I don't know what this is all about, but I can tell you he's alright."

"Yeah, that's what I'm thinking. Now with you vouching for him it makes it even harder to go after him." He looked away. "The law is the law... ain't it?"

"It is. What's this boy done?"

"It's a long damn story. One thing he done was lock me up in my own jail. I can't even hold that against him. He did that to save an old friend's life."

"Yes he did save my life… but we can't very well skirt around the law either."

Mrs. Martin came in to check on Marshal Sanders. She took one look and knew he was exhausted. "Boys, you two will have time to play when Marshal Sanders gets well. I think he's had enough."

Marshal Galt stood. "Yes ma'am, I reckon so. I'll be leaving."

She smiled and left the room.

Marshal Galt looked into his old friend's tired eyes. "I reckon I'll be moving along. Sometimes I hate this job."

"I know what you mean. Ah, Galt."

"Yeah?"

"I'm quitting. When I get to where I can ride, I'm riding to Dye. If that Tucker Shaw is still there acting as the law, then I'm swearing him in as the Dye, Kansas Marshal, and wiring the Kansas Governor of the fact. He can send papers when he wants to. I'm done. If Tucker isn't there, then I'll have to find someone. I'm through either way. I'm getting too old and I'd like to live some calmer days."

Marshal Galt was both pleased and sad. "I don't blame you. On the other hand I'm going to miss you."

"Hell, it ain't the end. I'll be where you can come see me."

"I'll do just that, too." He reached down and half shook his hand. "Be seeing you."

"Watch your back, Galt." He smiled and closed his eyes. He had spent all his energy for now.

Marshal Galt and his deputies rode out after watering their horses. Deputy Nelson kept looking back and Galt noticed him being a little nervous acting.

"What are you looking at?"

"Nothing… and it bothers me."

He chuckled at him.

"You can laugh if you want to. I don't know what it is, but I've started getting a bad feeling about this here little trip."

    Marshal Galt didn't say anything, but he did steal a quick glance back behind him, for he too had been having odd sensations when looking back. He suspected the Louisiana bunch was back there somewhere, but it was more than that. It was uneasiness about the whole mission. He rode on in silence.

Where Outlaws Roam
Royal Wade Kimes

Chapter 12

The town of Dye, Kansas was a nice looking little town. Buildings lined both sides of Front Street and there were at least two streets on the east and west side of the town. The jail was smack dab in the middle of it with an alley way on both sides. Behind the jail was a solid high board fence, but Tucker could see part of the gallows it housed from the top of his horse. The street was busy with people; wagons of all types lined both sides. Children were running and playing while their mothers shopped and looked at fabric out in front of two of the stores. As he passed by each group of folks they would stop what they were doing and follow along behind him. He turned his head slightly to gauge their intent. He decided they were curious as to who he and his prisoner were.

"Whoa Catcher." He pulled up to the hitching rail in front of the jail and stepped down. Simon Lick watched as the people approached.

"Deputy, get me off this horse and in jail. I don't know what these people got on their minds."

"I know what I'd have on mine. I'd drag you off that mare and string you up." He untied the ropes, pulled him from the mare and marched him inside the jail. He found the cells, four all together, and then locked him up. "I'll be back in a short while. I'll see how you get fed."

"You better. I'm so damn hungry I could eat your horse."

He walked out on the steps of the jail that sat about two feet above the boardwalk on Front Street. He surveyed the crowd and estimated nearly a hundred people. They just stood there staring.

"I suppose you good people would like to know who I am?"

A big man in baggy pants and suspenders spoke up with a big man's voice. It was rather deep and calm. "We'd like that, yes."

"Yes sir. Well, I'm Deputy Marshal Tucker Shaw. Marshal Sanders swore me in after he was critically wounded. Now don't get ahead of the wagon here." He saw the people suddenly go to talking among themselves. "He will pull through. He needed someone to bring the prisoner he was transferring from Fort

Where Outlaws Roam
Royal Wade Kimes

Smith, Arkansas to Dye. I have paperwork if you need to see it. For now, I'm the law in Dye, Kansas."

A rather heavy looking woman spoke up. She had a kid under each arm standing by her. One girl and one boy the best he could tell. If the one was a boy, he needed a haircut.

"Deputy, is that the man that killed Ruby Centers?"

"Well, I didn't know her name, but he is the one accused of killing a woman while robbing the bank."

"I saw the man leaving the bank, but he don't look the same."

"Ma'am, he lost a couple ears along the way."

The crowd laughed. Then the big man spoke again. "I don't suppose you'd be in for letting us string the bastard up right now would you?"

"I'm afraid not. He is entitled to due process of law."

A murmur ran through the crowd. "Folks, if you could quieten down just a little." They hushed and stared up at him. "I need to see the town leaders in my office and the person or persons that prepare the prisoners meals."

Another lady spoke up. She was small and attractive. "That would be me and my sisters. We have a place of business three doors up called Sisters." She smiled. "Deputy, you sure do talk pretty with that accent you seem to be stuck with."

The crowd bellowed out. Tucker himself laughed. "Ah, yes my lady, I am seemingly stuck with it. However, I am picking up things like 'these parts, loaded for bear, and fine haired one'."

The town roared. They liked the new Deputy Marshal. He turned and went inside and was followed by two men and the small attractive lady. They all gathered around in front of the desk sitting back towards the wall. Tucker sat on top of it and twirled a pencil around his fingers for a few seconds.

"Might I ask you to introduce yourselves?"

The tallest very distinguished looking man with a silver mustache started first. "I am Thomas Penn, Mayor, of this fair town. The short dumpy man dressed in an armor of dry goods clothing was next. "I'm Toe Clements, head councilman and serve as chief officer on the planning commission. I own the store across the street, the Front Street Dry Goods Store." Then the attractive lady spoke. Tucker found it interesting that the men went first. Was it because women were second class or did they have some rule in place regarding men in office, that they were to be given a certain respect?

"I'm Connie Sway. I have two sisters, Kathy and Billie, one older by one year and one younger by one year. We own an eatery establishment called Sisters. It is a very nice place and on Friday and Saturday nights we have a fine supper with wine and candlelight. You may bring your wife or significant other and be assured you will find nothing better in Kansas City, Fort Smith, or Saint Louis."

Tucker smiled as he thought he just caught her fishing for information as to his eligibility. "Well, it's nice to meet you and know your names. First I would like to address Mrs. Sway."

"Miss Sway." She smiled.

"Oh?" He smiled back at her. "Well, Miss Sway, in feeding the prisoners I would like to feed flat tray, no dishes. Water to be served with meal in a tin cup. You can bring it in and sit it on my desk. If I'm here I will feed the prisoners. If I'm not... I'll feed them when I get back."

"Deputy Shaw, that's inhumane." She was visibly disturbed.

"It was inhumane to kill Ruby Centers and drive a projectile into the chest of Marshal Sanders too." He waited for a comeback but got none. Instead she stared at him and then turned her eyes to the floor. His point was made.

"There's one other thing. The prisoner I have locked up back there is a mean dangerous man, and from time to time I suspect I'll have more like him. I would like you to never go further inside this jail than my desk. Is that agreeable?"

"It is." She never raised her eyes and spoke rather low.

"Are you okay, Miss Sway?"

"I'm fine... and you can call me Connie."

"Okay then, Connie." He turned to Thomas Penn. "Mayor, I don't know how Marshal Sanders did things here and I'm hoping you can shed some light on that for me."

"In what way?" The man had a very nice speaking voice and held himself straight as an arrow.

"Did he allow guns? Did he have a curfew? That sort of a thing is what I'm looking for."

"He allowed guns except on Saturday nights. He also had a curfew on that night."

"I see. Well, that sounds fair enough."

Thomas was surprised. "I was sure you were going to make big unwanted changes. New lawmen always do."

"Well, I'm not here to change what he has set up. It stays as is unless something happens that warrants a change."

He glanced at Toe Clements. "Is there anything planned regarding building, streets, roads, and is there any appropriated monies laid aside for anything? If so, what for and who is in charge of it?"

Toe beamed from the volley of questions. "Sir, you're not any ordinary United States Deputy Marshal. You've asked questions that put you in the know in almost every situation that could come up." His eyes made a half moon turn to Thomas who was much taller than him. "Deputy, another street is planned and work starts next week. The street runs north and south and will be our first full street running in that direction. It will be on the west side of town."

Tucker smiled. "The same side the bank is on."

"Why, yes it is." He was surprised Deputy Tucker knew that. It was evident to Toe and Thomas that Deputy Tucker Shaw was observant.

"Anything else?"

"Well, the only other thing of importance would be the ten thousand dollars set aside to build a new school. However, that will not start until next year. School takes up in a couple of months when harvest season has come and gone."

"Where do you keep this money?"

Toe looked around at Thomas as if asking if he should answer the question. Thomas answered for him.

"We keep it in the bank drawing interest. Why would you ask that?"

"I'm a lawman. I like to know where things are and why they're there. I once worked rather high up in government dealings and I learned how things operate, why they do and who makes it so."

"Indeed." Mayor Thomas seemed unconvinced and was somewhat skeptical.

Tucker smiled. "Don't worry, Mayor, I'm the law, not an outlaw."

He turned to Connie. "Would it be out of order to ask you to bring the prisoner's meal in about an hour, and maybe bring me something as well? I have some things I have to do and don't have time to see your wonderful establishment just yet."

"That's fine. Yes, I'll have it right over."

He smiled and looked each one of them in the eyes. "I appreciate you bringing me up to date with the town and giving me an idea of how things work. A good understanding helps when problems arise. Well, I guess that concludes our little meeting. I look forward to working with you."

When they left Tucker checked on his prisoner and then took his horses down to the Lemon Drop Livery. The place was run by a woman of about fifty years of age who also sold lemonade out front of the business. She was quite the lady.

"Before you ask... the United States Government has a contract with me to stable your horses. You're allowed two and I see that's what you... you got. She hesitated as she spoke about the horses. They were so well put together and beautiful she forgot herself. "Mister, you got a couple nice horses there." She patted Catcher on the rump and then looked the bronze mare over. "My name is Bet, Bet Price. I own this joint such as it is. Would you sell either one of those two?"

"I'm afraid not. I appreciate the offer though."

"I'll trade you, pay you cash boot and throw in a month's supply of lemonade."

"You drive a hard bargain. The lemonade is hard to turn down... but I guess I have to say no."

She laughed. "Well... that's okay. You get a free glass anyways when you board your horses here. It's kind of an appreciation thing."

"That's just real nice." He thought for a second about that. "What do you do when it turns off cold?"

She stared for a minute wondering if he was serious. "You're not the brightest lamp in the room are you? Coffee." She laughed

Where Outlaws Roam
Royal Wade Kimes

and went about her business as Tucker smiled at her. She was savvy and had just made fun of him.

He turned his horses loose in the corral and was assured they would be hayed and grained later in the evening. He then made his way back down to the jail. He stepped up on the porch and looked the town over. He hadn't been in America any time at all and already he was a deputy marshal. He hoped it was enough. The ten thousand dollars for the school loomed large in his mind. But then there was Marshal Sanders. He liked him. He decided he could be a lawman same as he could be an outlaw. Maybe fate had chosen lawman for him. He thought sure he would be joining the ranks and likes of some of the famous outlaws already come and gone in America, but no longer. He saw one go by way of the hangman's rope in Fort Smith. Being a law man might be the better end of things. He smiled and went inside.

Chapter 13

Three men rode into Dye at six in the evening. Tucker was sitting out on the front porch of the jail as they rode by. Two of the men were sitting to one side of their saddles. They rode all the way to the other end of town where Doctor Bates office was. He waited until they dismounted and went inside before he stood up. He slowly walked in that direction. He leaned up against a big oak tree and waited by their horses. He found blood on two of the saddles, and the horses were needing water and feed in the worse way.

The door to the doctor's office opened and the one who wasn't bleeding came out. He saw Tucker standing by the horses and stopped.

"Who the hell are you?"

"I'm the pain in both of your partner's backsides."

The man had a look of danger in his dark eyes. He went for his gun and dove to his left as he fired. Tucker levered his rifle twice, hitting the man both times. The gunman's bullet went way wide of its mark. He waited for the other two. When the door opened it was Doctor Bates.

"I'm afraid you'll have a long wait if you're waiting for the two inside. I had to sedate one of them to remove a bullet. The other one died from loss of blood."

Tucker walked to where the doctor was standing. "When you get him patched up, let me know. He goes to jail."

"What did he do?"

"He was lying in ambush for me. He's one of Simon Lick Tubbs gang. Marshal Sanders said they're wanted all over the state of Kansas."

"I'll let you know as soon as the man can be moved. What about the one lying over there you just shot?"

"Doctor... he is past needing anyone but an undertaker."

"I surmised. Well, Carl Tines is the Dye Undertaker. He'll be along. Somehow he always shows up where gunfire takes place." He smiled and went back inside.

Tucker untied the three horses and saw to their needs.

Where Outlaws Roam
Royal Wade Kimes

Reed and his men made camp about a half day's ride out of Dye. They were being extra careful not to get too close while tracking and following Marshal Galt and his deputies. Neely came back from checking the horses and sat down on a smooth rock.

"The horses are fine." He glanced at Devo and then stared into the fire. "Reed."

"Yeah."

"The hair on my neck stands up every time I think about Raff. It's a mystery to me what happened to him, but something damn sure did."

Reed sipped on a cup of coffee. "It bothers me too... not knowing what happened, or who it is that might have done him. I don't like it much that I might be standing right next to the bastard unbeknown to me."

Neely poured a cup of coffee. "You think maybe we ought not to of come off up here? We're out of our element. We hunt gators and crawfish. We drink and make love all night to wild ass Cajun women." He took a drink of his coffee. "Something ain't right and you know it."

Reed sat silent looking at the fire. He knew Neely was right. Something was wrong, and maybe they should have stayed in the swamp country. Even still he couldn't own up to it, for two reasons. One, he didn't want to spook Neely any worse than he already was, and two, he didn't want to admit he was wrong in coming. He glanced at Devo who hadn't said a word. He just sat there staring out into the dark.

"Devo, what's on your mind? You're mighty quiet."

"Death." He slowly cast his eyes in Reed's direction. "This is it. I'll not be going back to Louisiana."

Reed straightened up from his sitting position. "Now that's foolish talk. This thing with Raff has us all on edge. The best thing you can do is get hold of yourself. I've seen this before. You'll convince yourself you can't avoid a thing and cause it yourself. We'll not be thinking or talking nonsense after tonight. We all agree?"

Neely stood up and looked over at Devo. "Maybe we ought not to of come up here in this prairie country, but we're here. And maybe Reed is right about making matters worse by worrying around and causing more problems than we have." He took a step and stopped. "I've got to empty out before I turn in. I'll be back in a minute. He left in the direction of the bluffs they were camped on top of. It was a good campsite in that no one could slip in on them but by one way.

Reed cut his eyes to Devo once Neely was out of hearing. "Look, you two boys got to hold it together. Neely is the one I worried about maybe getting the jitters. You've always been strong and up to the task no matter what it was. Why's this bothering you so much anyway?"

"A feeling, that's all."

"Hell, I get feelings all the time, don't mean nothing."

"Maybe so, but I believe you're told before it happens the dark angel is coming for you." He looked at Reed and then away. They sat silent for the next five minutes.

Finally Reed looked over at Devo. "Don't you think Neely should have been back by now?"

Devo looked up from the fire and drew his gun. "Yeah... yeah I do." He rose up and stared into the dark.

Reed stood and hollered out. "Neely! What the hell you doing out there?!"

Nothing but silence came back to them.

Neely Law stood at the edge of the bluff and relieved himself over the edge. He had always wanted to piss over the side of a bluff just to say he had peed for at least sixty feet. He chuckled as he did it. He buttoned his pants and stood staring out across the wide open at the moon and stars. He didn't belong in Kansas, but it sure was pretty. He had to give it that.

He started to turn when he felt a thud to the back of his head. He went down and out. A few minutes later he awoke from water splashing in his face. When he could focus, his eyes widened with fear. His hands were tied as well as his feet, and he was lying on the edge of the bluff. There was a gag in his mouth and tied around the back of his head.

"Your friend is right. This is it. You won't be going back to Louisiana, drinking and laying with Cajun women. You ain't Cajun

Where Outlaws Roam
Royal Wade Kimes

and don't deserve one."

He tried to speak but it was mere muffles.

"Have a nice trip."

There was nothing he could do but fall when his assailant rolled him off the cliff with a shove of the foot. He fell silently to the bottom, landing on a pile of rocks. His body was broken in several places and his head burst open. Devo had called it, 'This was it'.

Tucker may have not had time to walk down to Sisters, but they made time to see him. He was oiling a rifle when they all three walked in.

"Ladies, what can I do for you?" He put the rifle in the gun rack.

Connie answered for them. "Since you didn't have time or the courtesy to meet my sisters, I brought them to you. She introduced them quickly. Kathy was the older one and wore a ring. Billie was the younger one and obviously not married. She eyed him over like she was buying a stud horse.

"I do apologize. It's just that this is all new and I'm trying to get adjusted."

Billie spoke up. "We'll expect better from you then in the future." She had a look of hopefulness on her face.

"Yes indeed. You will see a vast improvement in my manners."

"Good, she turned, smiled and went out the door. Kathy followed and then Connie.

Tucker sat down behind his desk and took a deep breath. He felt he had lived through a possible storm that didn't quite get to storm level yet. He would try to see it didn't.

Suddenly his office began to fill up with men. They were all dressed alike. They wore wide brimmed hats, nice oiled side irons and long black dusters. They all had long thick mustaches, some black, some red and some brown. They looked impressive. Tucker felt a moment of excitement just looking at them.

"Gentlemen... can I help you?"

"You have a man here by the name of Simon Lick Tubbs?"

"I do." He glanced quickly at all of the men; and in doing so he realized his office would hold twenty men counting him, and could hold five more if they ganged in around the desk.

"We want him."

Tucker blushed at the statement. "I'm new at this, but I don't hand over my prisoners to anyone but the law. Are you men lawmen?"

"We're from Melt, Kansas, over west of here." The man talking was six foot and had a voice that commanded respect and emitted authority. "We're law there since our sheriff and deputy was killed by that scum you have locked up. We're the, Law and Order Vigilantes. Since we were voted in to take care of things, we've already put an end to cattle thieves operating in our area, and killed Big John Hanks. In case you don't know who he was, he's the bastard that raped and killed Lucy Dobbs. That don't happen again when you hang 'em."

"No, I suspect not. That is as final as it gets." He paused drew his gun and cocked it. Everyone else did too. The only thing he could compare that much hammer action to, was when he watched the Queen have a man shot by firing squad with twenty-four sharp shooters. He grinned. "Isn't this quite the scene? Where are all those newspaper men when you need them? I've dreamed of being in a standoff like this, where the law is outnumbered badly, but hasn't any intentions of backing down." He stared into the eyes of the man who did the vigilante's talking. "Now... since we know by my dream the law isn't backing down... I'm planning on shooting you dead between the eyes and the one next to you in the chest. Now all these guns may go off, and for certain they will hit and kill me, but as God is the creator, I'll kill the two of you, and more than likely will get another or two. You can damn well bet I'll be determined to." He chuckled. "Just think of the headlines. Deputy Marshal shoots it out in his office packed with vigilantes, kills ten men before he goes down in a hail of bullets."

The vigilante was stunned and confused. "You said you'd kill me and Trace here, and might get one or two more. Where did ten come from?"

"Well, you know how newspaper men are; they always make a story bigger than it is, makes for good reading." He laughed. "Just think of it, I'll be a hero and the folks back home will hear of it and be totally perplexed."

"My name is Dan Nolen and I've got to tell you, I'm pretty damned perplexed myself. I don't know who you are, or what kind of a damn lawman they have here in Dye, but you're one crazy sonofabitch… I can tell you that much."

"Well, Dan, it's a pleasure to meet you. I'm not surprised you feel that way about me, my own folks did too. The fact is they called me all those names and more."

Dan looked around at his men and slowly began to laugh. It caught on like a prairie fire. The jail was ajar with laughter. The men filed out of the jail one by one, all but Dan and one other. Dan eyeballed Tucker once more. "Now that they've left the jail… would you have gone through with that little show of bravery?"

He grinned and looked him dead in the eyes. "I would have been delighted."

"That's just what I thought." He smiled. "You know I don't know quite what to make of you, but you're crazy. I don't think you give a damn for nothing."

"I like lemon pie. Does that count?"

Dan stood staring at Tucker in disbelief. He turned for the door. "Come on, Trace, let's get us a drink." He stopped at the door. "Just so you know; we're not leaving town. We'll be over at the Dye Saloon if you get to wondering where we're at. I understand Judge Roy Maxey will be here sometime tomorrow. I figure the trial for that bastard to be the following day. If he don't get a sentence of hanging, then we'll see to it in Melt." He smiled. "One way or the other, the man will swing."

"Yes, it does seem ole Simon Lick hasn't a chance of escaping his day with the rope."

"You got that right." Dan and Trace left the jail on their way to the saloon.

Marshal Galt had ridden until nine o'clock before making camp. His two deputies were worn out and so were the horses. He was making up time lost while at the Martins conferring with his old friend Marshal Sanders. They fed the horses and made a fire. Deputy Farley was an excellent cook, so he rustled up a nice plate of beans with a chunk of pork to go in it. They drink coffee and after supper they had a shot of top grade whiskey. Marshal Galt only drank the best.

He looked at his deputies. "Have either one of you ever been to Dye, Kansas?"

Deputy Farley looked over at Nelson. "I haven't, have you?"

Deputy Nelson shook his head he hadn't either. "Why did you ask, Marshal?"

"Because we're not more than an hour or two out of Dye right now."

They looked at each other and then stared at Marshal Galt. Deputy Farley spoke up. "If that's so, why are we camped here?"

"I don't know what to expect when I ride in there. I want to see the lay of things. Also, if Reed Fletcher is following us, I don't want him riding in behind us after dark. I want to see him arrive in Dye, not wonder if he has."

"I see." Deputy Farley liked that, and he had always liked Marshal Galt. He was a thinker and a planner. "Do you think we'll have any trouble out of Tucker Shaw?"

"It's Deputy Marshal Tucker Shaw. To be honest I don't know if he'll give us trouble or not."

"Reed is going to be our trouble, ain't he?"

Marshal Galt glanced at both of them. "He could be."

Deputy Nelson yawned. "Well, it's going to be an exciting day tomorrow just about any way you look at it. I think I'll turn in."

Marshal Galt nodded to him. He glanced at Farley. "You better turn in, too."

"What about you?"

"I'm getting there. I have me some thinking to do." "About what?"

He smiled at Farley. "You never were one to hold back." He studied about his answer. "Oh... Tucker Shaw. He bothers me, but not in a bad way. I've been around and seen some characters in my time and he draws the short straw as to different. The best I can tell he's been put over a barrel by this Reed Fletcher, and there's not anything I can do about it. The law is on Fletcher's side. I don't know quite what to do."

Nelson was rolled up in his blanket but he put into the

Where Outlaws Roam
Royal Wade Kimes

conversation. "Kill the sonofabitch, that'd take care of it. Goodnight."

Reed and Devo eased ever so slowly out to the cliffs. They called to Neely but got no answer. They searched along the bluff and then went to where the horses were tied.

"Devo, something has happened. Put the fire out. We'll take turns watching the horses and camp tonight. Whoever the hell is out there, we got to kill him. He's gotten the drop on two of us, that ain't happening again."

"Reed, it seems to me we ought to have heard something. There wasn't a shot, a loud voice or anything. The sonofabitch is a hunter, a stalker." Devo was looking in all directions. "Reed, we better call this thing off and get to hell away from here. We're all going to die if we don't. In the swamps we don't get killed like this."

"Settle down. I'm not letting some damn cowboy run me back to Louisiana. I'll go back when I'm damn good and ready."

"Reed, you call the shots back home, but here someone else is."

"I said settle down. You're letting this bastard get to you."

"Hell, he's killed Raff and Neely, that's enough to get to a man."

"Things will look different come morning. Hell, Neely may have fallen and knocked his self out and we just can't see him."

"Well, if you say so. I'll take first watch."

"Okay, wake me at midnight. I'll dowse the fire."

Reed rolled up in a blanket with his pistol tucked up under his chest. Devo sat with his back against a tall red oak. He pulled his hat down just above his eyes. He was undetectable sitting there. If anyone came sneaking in he would see him first.

Chapter 14

The sun's golden rays were beaming bright over Dye, Kansas at seven in the morning. There was a dove cooing on a church house steeple and one answering down the street. Wagons were already coming in and people were stirring. Tucker was standing on the front porch of the jail taking in everything when the whiff of biscuits and bacon came across his nose. He knew Judge Maxey would arrive today and he wanted to be on hand when he did. He kept catching whiffs of the biscuits and bacon and once in a while he picked up coffee brewing.

He walked back to check on Simon Lick. "I'm going to have to leave you to your lonesome. I'm going for breakfast. I'll bring you back some, how would that be?"

"I'd be damn grateful. I've been treated like I don't exist around here."

"You won't very long."

Simon Lick stared at him. "I can't make you out. You offer to do something for me and then make a wise crack behind it."

"To be honest you don't deserve to be spoken to, so consider anything that might be said to you... something kind of special."

"Is that right?" He sneered and turned away.

Tucker chuckled. "I bet the devil is dancing and making ready for your arrival." He turned and walked out.

Simon Lick walked to the bars and stared after him, and spoke almost in a whisper. "You dumb bastard, I'm in hell now... anything after this is a piece of cake."

Tucker walked into Sisters and sat down. He was stunned. It was like he entered another world when he walked through the door. Outside was dust, wagons, noise, hammering from a blacksmith, and all the things that make up a western town. Inside Sisters it could have been London, or maybe the city of Chicago he had read of. He was taken aback when he saw an actual picture of the Queen hanging on a wall. The business was set to upper end living, yet looking at the floral framed paper menu it was obvious they catered to the poor as well as the wealthy. The prices were very reasonable and because of that all

Where Outlaws Roam
Royal Wade Kimes

walks of life were patronizing the place. It gave those who could not afford to have something a bit luxurious in their life, the chance to do so.

"May I take your order, Deputy Marshal?"

He looked up from the menu and smiled at Billie. "Yes, I would like three over easy eggs, toast, coffee, and bacon. I would also like an order to go. Oh, before you go… can you tell me why the Queen's picture?"

"Us girls thought it a nice touch. Britain is doing well and the Queen seems to be responsible for most of it."

"Yes, she's responsible for a lot of things. You do know she married her cousin?"

"No! She did not!?" Billie blushed and put her hands on her hips. "Are you telling me a story?"

"Not this time, but I can."

"Deputy Tucker, I think it will pay to watch you." She left to turn in the order and bring his coffee. There was a man sitting over from him who cleared his throat to get his attention. Tucker looked over at him and saw a very frail looking man with little round glasses on. He looked to be in his seventies.

"Young man, I couldn't help but overhear your conversation with Miss Billie. I picked up that you know the Queen?"

"I do."

"I also picked up that maybe you're not all that in love with her… I mean such as the Sisters."

"Not so much, no."

"I'm also picking up an accent. His eyes were sparkling as he spoke.

"You pick up a lot. I'm from Britain."

"I see. Well then, you might be interested in what I do."

"What would that be?" He couldn't imagine anything the little frail man could do that would be of interest to him.

"I get the news from Britain and some of it I record in my own paper. I'm the newspaper of Dye. I get the news from overseas regularly… by mail and telegraph. I am able to kind of keep folks up on what is happening in other parts of the world."

"Is that a fact?" His own eyes were sparkling now. "You mean you have news from Britain on a regular basis?"

"I do. That's also how I came by the picture of the Queen. Connie wanted it for Sisters." He paused and smiled as a twinkle came into his eyes. "I was present when you introduced yourself to the town. I wrote a piece about it and published it this morning. It's there on your table. I wrote how this new deputy had come to town, sworn in by Marshal Sanders and that your home was Great Britain." He grinned. "I didn't tell them about your headlines in the London Paper."

Tucker chuckled. "You knew the whole time who I was. Would you like to join me?"

"I most certainly would." He picked up his cup of coffee and sat down with him.

"May I ask your name?"

"Lee Paulson."

"Well, Lee Paulson, I have a question. Do you also send news to Great Britain concerning the goings on of the Wild West?"

"I indeed do. You folks love to read about the outlaws, cattle drives, and shoot outs."

Tucker smiled at his being so right. "Then, would you favor me and send your story about me to London?"

"I can." He chuckled. "Just so you know, you were found dead and they buried you over there. The family and the Queen were devastated. You can understand when you came in here yesterday as our new lawman, well, how surprised I was."

"Yes I can. And in turn you can understand how surprised I am to hear I have died and people are broken hearted about it in Britain?"

"Yes indeed, of course." He paused for a second. "Son, I mean Deputy Shaw, with your permission would you let me write and print a full blown story about you. I'll make you the best law man in the west."

"Only if you lay it on thick." He laughed. "You won't have to do much; since I arrived here it's been one unexpected thing after another." Tucker turned his head and stared out the front window. "Lee Paulson, do I have a story for you."

"Regarding?"

"The personal life of Ira Shaw, and the Queen's secret deals."

Where Outlaws Roam
Royal Wade Kimes

Lee pulled a small tablet out to write on. "Feed it to me. I'll write it down."

They went to work on the story until breakfast came. Once they had eaten they finished it. Lee was nearly hyperventilating with such a story.

Tucker had found a way to get at the Queen and Ira Shaw from thousands of miles away. He gave embarrassing details involving the goings on of both Ira Shaw and the Queen. He wouldn't have to go back to Great Britain to retaliate for his banishment. The unexpected way had come to him. What he would give to be there when Lee Paulson's story hit the streets of London.

Billie walked to his table after Lee Paulson left. "I wanted to talk to you, but Lee had all of your attention."

"He might have, but when you walk to and from this table you have all my attention. I've never seen a Billie that had so many curves."

"Here I thought you didn't even notice me."

"Oh, I noticed alright." He looked her in the eyes and she almost melted waiting for what he was about to say next. "Billie, do you have my... to go order ready?"

"Do I... I what!?" She stared at him with fire in her eyes. "I'm sure we do." She collected herself. She had raised her voice to a customer and that was a no, no, at Sisters. Not only that, it was to the new Deputy Marshal Shaw. She left in a hurry and returned with a tray of food. He barely had hold of it when she turned and left him standing there. He made her angry, but he had to go and he had to have his to go order. It couldn't be helped. He didn't seem to have much luck with the Sway girls.

He left Sisters and was walking to the jail when he saw Dan Nolen walk out of the Dye Hotel. By the time he had gotten to the jail twenty of the vigilantes were standing with him. Tucker waved to them and went inside. He took the tray to the prisoner, and then pulled two shotguns and two rifles. He loaded them and checked his pistol. The only way they were going to get his prisoner was after hell had come and gone.

He walked out on the porch and looked in their direction. Dan stepped down from the Dye Hotel porch and his men fell in behind him. They walked up to within twenty feet of the jail.

"I've thought this thing through. If Simon Lick gets off for any reason, he's to be turned over to us. We're the only law in Melt, Kansas now and it's left to us to deal out punishment."

"Why don't we cross that bridge when and if the bridge is built?"

"You talk, but you don't say anything."

Tucker's eyes went from Dan to the three men riding down the street behind them. It was Marshal Galt and two deputies. They were about to ride in beside the hitching rail at the Dye Hotel until they saw the bunch of men gathered in front of the jail. They turned and rode over to the jail instead.

"Morning, Deputy Marshal Shaw. It is a fine morning is it not?"

"Marshal Galt, good to see you. I was wondering when my help was coming."

"We're here. Do you need us for anything at the moment?"

He eyed Dan. "No, I have things handled here."

"Well, then Deputy, if we're not needed, we'll be checking in at the Dye Hotel. We need a bath and we're tired. We rode a long ways. It's been an interesting ride. We left the Martin place and for some reason our back trail seemed busy."

Tucker smiled. "It's been that way ever since I arrived to this country. You didn't smell crawfish boiling did you?"

"I think I did." He grinned and rode towards the hotel.

Reed and Devo ate before dawn and walked to the cliffs when there was good light. They walked opposite directions looking over the side. It was Devo who spotted Neely.

"Reed, come here, quick!"

Reed ran to where he was and peered over the cliff. "Holy damn!" Without looking at Devo he shouted. "Come on!"

They turned and hurried back to camp, saddled and rode down and around the cliffs to the bottom. Reed dismounted first and then Devo stepped down.

"Devo, someone tied him up. Look at this, his legs were tied. It looks like the fall busted the string holding them. His hands are still tied. I guess we know why we didn't hear anything out of him. He was gagged."

Where Outlaws Roam
Royal Wade Kimes

"Reed… this is too much. I'm telling you we got to get out of this damn country. Somebody is killing us off one at a time. We ain't so much as seen a hair of who it is. I say we quit this damn chase, let Tucker Shaw go."

"Devo, damn man, you're acting scared."

"You ain't? What the hell does it take to shake you?" Devo was looking all around him as he talked. "I bet the sonofabitch is watching us right now, probably waiting to see how we reacted when we found Neely."

Reed stood and looked all around him. It hadn't occurred to him the killer could be hiding somewhere watching. He decided to send a message. He yelled it out.

"I don't know who you are and I don't give a damn! I don't like cowards! Face me straight on and I might have a little respect for you! All I see here is a coward!"

He turned to Devo. "You get hold of yourself. Get something to dig a hole with and we'll bury him."

"Hell with that. There's a creek over yonder about fifty yards."

"This ain't the swamps. There aren't any alligators to get rid of the remains. We bury him, that's all of it."

Devo stared at him. "No it ain't all of it. All of it is us leaving here."

Reed thought about that. He needed to get Devo away from Neelys' body. He was becoming more unstable about things. He had seen panic in men before. Once it sets in, it can take over unless someone steps in to stop it.

"Devo, maybe you're right, the birds can take care of Neely."

"Let's ride, anything to get away from this place." They mounted up and rode at a lope towards Dye.

Chapter 15

Judge Maxey come riding down Front Street in a brand new buggy, being drawn by a nice stepping white horse which made the harness look even blacker. It was nearly noon and the sun was hot. He was coming from the north which put him passing by the jail before reaching the Dye Hotel. He pulled up, but stayed seated.

"You are?"

"Good day, Judge. I'm Deputy Marshal Tucker Shaw. I was sworn in by Marshal Sanders. I have all the papers in my office if you need to look at them."

"That will not be necessary. What happened to Marshal Sanders?"

"Simon Lick got the drop on him somehow and nearly killed him. I showed up in time to stop it."

"Lucky for him... is the prisoner healthy enough to stand trial?"

"He is."

"Trial starts tomorrow at nine o'clock sharp."

"I'll have him at the courthouse."

"I want him there ten minutes before proceedings. Does he have a lawyer?"

Tucker looked perplexed. "I let that get by me. I guess I better find him one. I don't see it as my job however. I'll be lucky if I can find one."

"We all do things that don't exactly fall under our titles. See Lawson and Dill. They have an office at the other end of town. One of them will take it. Tell them the State of Kansas or the United States Government will take care of them. They can send the request for payment to both places, one of them will respond with a check."

"Damn, that would never fly in Great Britain."

Judge Maxey smiled. "That's because you people from Great Britain are always afraid someone is going to get to you. That kind of thinking breeds the very thing you're afraid of."

"What makes you think I'm from there?"

"Oh come now."

The Judge drove off leaving Tucker standing on the street with

Where Outlaws Roam
Royal Wade Kimes

his mouth half open. He soon shut it and mumbled to himself. "I like him. I could have used him in Britain a time or two. But I sure need to work on this accent."

   At two o'clock in the afternoon two more riders come riding into town. As they rode towards the Dye Hotel, Tucker watched from the jail window with great interest. Marshal Galt was sitting out on the spacious hotel porch watching Reed Fletcher and one of his gunnies ride up. Tucker left the window and walked down to where he could hear the conversation. So far Reed hadn't seen him and he knew it. He leaned against the corner of Lee Paulson's Newspaper building.

   Reed was all smiles. Devo was all frown. He was eaten up with worry. "Marshal Galt, good afternoon."

   "Reed, I thought I told you to let me handle this thing. I believe I said for you not to let me catch you trying to find Tucker Shaw."

   "Oh, well, I'm not hunting Tucker Shaw. It's a free country and I'm only exercising my freedoms and taking a little ride. Besides, I haven't any way to know where the man is."

   "If you hadn't been following me you wouldn't have a damn clue. Now I suggest you stay aboard that nag you're riding and head back to Fort Smith."

   "I may do that tomorrow. I couldn't ride another mile."

   Marshal Galt stared at him. "You leave first thing in the morning. If you were to happen to find Tucker Shaw in Dye, stay away from him. If you don't, they'll be hell to pay."

   "Is that a threat?"

   "It's an order tagged with a promise." He stared at him with quiet hard eyes.

   Reed stepped down from his horse. Devo did the same. Tucker thought the man with Reed acted nervous. He had nervous eyes and kept looking around him. The two men walked past Marshal Galt and went into the lobby of the hotel to check in.

   Tucker eased back towards the jail with vital information. Marshal Galt was still trying to arrest him.

   As he eased across the street he saw a flash in one of the alley ways beside the jail. He stepped quickly to the corner of the jail and peered around it. The alley was empty, yet he was sure he saw a flash of some sort. He eased down the alley with gun drawn. When he came around to the end of the jail he saw someone dart into the alley over at the next building. He ran to the spot but no one was there. He walked down the alley into Front Street. They had vanished. A glimpse of the person was literally all he got, which made it impossible to make out anything about them. Whoever it was they were watching him. He didn't like it. Someone trying to stay that concealed would shoot a man in the back.

Doctor Bates came rushing into the jail an hour later completely out of breath. "Deputy... you better hurry to my office! All hell has broken loose! That bunch from Melt, Kansas came in and took that gang member of Simon Lick Tubbs's out of my office. They pulled him right out of his bed. They've got a rope and were headed out back of my place. There's a tree back there just right to hang a man."

Tucker pulled a rifle from the rack and took off in a run. Marshal Galt was still sitting on the porch of the Dye Hotel when he saw Tucker running. He and his deputies jumped up and followed.

Tucker rounded the doctor's office and found Dan Nolen and his men about to hang the half-awake outlaw. He was incoherent from medicine being administered to him for his wound, and wasn't responding very well.

"Halt! Take the rope off that man's neck!" The man was sitting on a black saddle bred horse which was fidgety from all the commotion. It wasn't going to take much for it to fly out from under him. It was sensing the tension and high excitement from the men around it.

One of the men with Dan stepped out away from them. "I've had about enough of you." He went for his gun. Tucker drew and fired while holding his rifle in the other hand. At the same time the black horse bolted. Tucker wasn't sure if he bolted from the shooting or someone slapped him on the rear. Before the man hit the end of the rope he fired another round and shot the rope in half. He cocked the hammer again in expectation of another one of the vigilantes pulling on him.

Where Outlaws Roam
Royal Wade Kimes

Dan held his hand up high and yelled at his men. "Stop! You fools, we don't pull on the law, we are law!"

"Dan, you're not law. You've not been sworn in as a lawman."

"The town of Melt swore us in."

"The town can elect a sheriff, and I suspect some kind of paper has to be filed to that end. They can't swear in a bunch of men to ride the country day and night bringing fear into people's lives. You can't go around being judge, jury, and executioner.

The man Tucker shot moaned and tried to move. Doctor Bates showed up about then and went to him. He had a bullet in the right side of the chest. Doctor Bates looked around at Tucker and smiled. He knew he placed the bullet so as not to kill the man. He knew because he saw the frayed rope shot in half.

"Deputy, I'll need some help getting this man to my office."

Dan motioned to some of his men to help the doctor, and then he eyed the Deputy Marshal over. "Well, where do we go from here?"

"Well, unlike what I was use to myself in my wilder days, I'm for being fair. No one was hung, so you get one free ride. If you pull anything else while you're here, you won't be happy with the consequences."

"Is that a threat?"

"That's the jolly ole truth." He let the barrel of his rifle ease towards the ground. "Dan, you and your men break it up and wait on the trial. It starts at nine o'clock tomorrow morning."

Dan nodded and left with his men. Once they were gone Marshal Galt approached Tucker.

"You handled that nicely." He smiled at Tucker and then looked at the rope. "I don't know many that could have made that shot. I know I can't."

"I was a marksman for a while for the Royal Guard. I enjoyed shooting, but there were too many rules to follow. He grinned. "You know, like rules of engagement."

Marshal Galt chuckled. "I can see how that would have gotten in your way."

"Yes, well, my whole life was in the way of my father and the dear ole Queen, different reasons mind you, but in the way just the same."

"I wonder who was the most to blame for that?" He had a humorous look on his face.

"Of course I share in the blame, but oh the secret wonder of it all." He was grinning, but then slowly the grin faded. "Marshal, why are you here?"

"You know why. You're to face charges brought against you by Reed Fletcher. He's not letting it drop as you can see. He's followed me here."

"Why are you waiting to arrest me?"

"Well, I'm waiting for Simon Lick Tubbs trial to take place. Once he's sentenced to hang, then I guess we look at bringing you back. For now, I've got to honor Marshal Sanders' act of swearing you in as Deputy Marshal."

"You must either be great friends or you follow the law down to the last letter."

"Both I guess." He turned and walked away. As he did he hollered back at Tucker. "I'll see you at the trial!"

He spoke under his breath. "That may be the last time you see me, Marshal." He then walked over and picked up the forgotten prisoner whose hands were tied behind him, and still under the influence of pain drugs. He brought him to Doctor Bates and left. It would be a day or two longer before he would be able to stand trial or be without a doctor's care.

At ten p.m. Devo Wells was asleep in his bed. He turned over on his side from his subconscious mind picking up a sound. It wasn't quite enough to wake him however. What he unknowingly heard was the window to his room raise. He was on the second floor in room seven and felt safe there. His side iron hung on the bedpost beside him while his long bladed gator knife lay on the little yellow table beside his bed. He had stopped snoring momentarily, but resumed once his mind fell once again deeper into slumber.

"Wake." There was silence. "Wake up."

Devo jumped when his eyes finally opened and he saw the image of a person standing back in the dark shadows of the room. He swung around with his right arm to retrieve his gun and

Where Outlaws Roam
Royal Wade Kimes

realized his arms were tied back, and to the headboard. His gun was gone also. He looked down at the footboard and discovered his feet tied as well. The cords were of soft leather and tied rather loosely around the ankles and wrists. Yet they were closed just enough they wouldn't slip over them. He strained to make out the person in the room with him.

"Who the hell are you?! I know you killed Raff and Neely. I guess it's my turn." There was nothing but silence. "Answer me!" Still, silence. "I could start yelling."

"I will shoot you with your own gun when you do."

"Who are you? You're not anyone I know." Fear set in. "Look, I'll give you a thousand dollars to let me go. I've got it in my pants pocket. A thousand dollars! That's a lot of cash! Anyone could use a thousand dollars!" More silence filled the room. "Okay, five thousand. I can get Fletcher to loan me four thousand! Please, I beg you, let me live!"

"Would you let me live? You and your dead friends are Reed Fletcher's hunters. You kill for money and the sport. Would you let me live?"

There was silence except for chewing. "Are you eating?"

Devo had ordered his supper brought to his room. He argued with Reed about going downstairs to eat and instead stayed in his room. He would go out in the daylight, but he didn't want to be out when darkness fell. Now it didn't seem like it mattered much. He was lying in his own bed tied up and helpless. Whoever it was that had him, they were now enjoying his supper. He had eaten very little of it, because he had lost his appetite. He hadn't told Reed, but he was leaving for Louisiana at daybreak.

"Good food... lacks spice." The shadow moved.

"Stay... stay away! Stay away from me!"

Suddenly there was a thud that sounded as if it hit a pool of water. Devo's back arched and held there for a few seconds and then fell. A long crowbar was thrust through his chest and came out between his shoulders. Four feet of the bar was sticking above him while the rest of it was through him, and deep within the bed. Blood began to drain onto the floor and soak the bed and sheets. His body shook as the nerves of life left it. Devo Wells would fear no more.

Where Outlaws Roam
Royal Wade Kimes

Chapter 16

At seven a.m. Reed Fletcher entered the Dye Jail. Tucker drew his gun immediately.

"Easy Deputy, I'm not here to confront you. I'm here to report a murder. You and I will settle our differences later. Devo Wells is lying dead in his room. It's one of the most gruesome things I've seen in a long time. Devo is the man that rode in with me. I started out with three men, I now haven't any."

"Are you saying something happened to them on your way here?"

"It did."

"Let's go take a look at this murder scene."

Marshal Galt was puzzled when he saw Tucker and Reed coming towards the hotel together. He checked his gun making sure it was loose in the holster. Something didn't add up.

Tucker smiled and shook hands with him when he entered the lobby of the hotel. "Reed here says his partner is lying dead upstairs. I thought maybe you might like to go with me to check it out."

"Lead the way."

Tucker cut his eyes to Reed. "After you... Mister Fletcher."

They went upstairs and found a gruesome sight. Tucker glanced quickly at Marshal Galt and pointed at the back corner. "Look. Whoever done this sat in this corner and ate supper. If the dead man had been the one to eat it, he would have sat at the small table across the room."

"I think you're right." Marshal Galt looked at the bedpost. "His gun rig is here, but his pistol is gone."

Reed put in. "I'd like to know how the hell they got his hands and feet tied without him knowing it, or did they get the drop on him and then tied them?"

Tucker examined the knots. "I think they done it while he was sleeping. See here how loose they are, just tight enough to not slip over, yet soft enough not to wake him. That was slow and careful work. Whoever did this is not afraid of much and can sneak around like a quiet cat."

Marshal Galt smiled. "Indian is more like it."

Where Outlaws Roam
Royal Wade Kimes

Tucker glanced at him. "You think an Indian done this?"

"No. I mean this man was quiet like an Indian. However, an Indian doesn't go around carrying a crowbar, tomahawk maybe, but not a crowbar."

Tucker chuckled. "No one else does that I've heard of."

Reed walked to the window. "They came in and exited through the window here. It's hot, so Devo had his window cracked. It made it easy to get in."

Tucker thought about that. "I'd say not all that easy. They had to get on top of this hotel someway."

"Yeah, you're right." The Marshal examined the crowbar. "I think we need to try and find out who owned this crowbar before it was used for a murder weapon."

Tucker turned and stuck his head out the window. It was a sheer drop. "Marshal, I think you're thinking the owner of the crowbar might have seen someone take it, correct?"

"I hope anyway."

"Well, whoever climbed into this window was half monkey. It's straight down."

The owner of the hotel came into the room about then. "I'm Omar Cowan, I own this place, and I." He stopped suddenly. His eyes widened and he turned pale. His hand went to his mouth and he left in a hurry. His stomach couldn't take the awful sight.

Tucker smiled at Marshal Galt. "I guess we'll have to question him later."

"It looks that way."

Tucker cut his eyes to Reed. "Well, you or Omar better find someone to remove your man. I would like Doctor Bates to examine the body before removal."

Reed turned from the window and stared at Tucker. "I'll pay for his burial and have him removed."

"As long as it gets done."

"Marshal Galt smiled at Tucker. He liked the way he handled things when they came up, and they were coming up a lot. There hadn't been very many dull moments since the arrival of Tucker Shaw. He could only imagine what the Queen went through.

Court was called in session for the trial of Simon Lick Tubbs,

Where Outlaws Roam
Royal Wade Kimes

the honorable Judge Maxey presiding. The prosecution called the first witness, an elderly man, and things were running along fairly smooth until he asked the witness to point out the man who killed Ruby Centers.

"Well, feller, I'm not sure that's him. The man I seen weighed a right smart more than that feller sitting by the Deputy Marshal. With his ears missing and his hair cut back away from his head to keep the hair out of his earholes... well, I can't be sure. He resembles the man, but like I say... I can't say with a hundred percent certainty."

"Sir... look hard."

"Mister, I can't look him to guilty. What if it ain't him?"

The next witness was the man's wife, she too wasn't certain. It was true, Simon Lick Tubbs was twenty pounds lighter and his ears and hair had changed. His face was daunted, plus his eyes had black rings around them. The last witness was a younger lady who kept staring at the prisoner.

"Ma'am, can you positively identify this man as being the man who shot Ruby Centers?"

"I can. I'll never forget those murderous eyes."

"That's all the questions I have." He turned. "Your witness."

The defense didn't bother to get up. "Ma'am, Miss April, is it?"

"Yes, April Tenkiller."

"Yes of course. Now, Miss April, the eyes, why will you not forget... those murderous eyes as you put it?"

"They're killer's eyes."

"Oh? Well, please tell the court where you got your degree in determining killer's eyes from just regular normal eyes? While you lay that out for the court, tell us, what is the distinct difference in a killer's eyes than say that of a marshal's eyes? He too is a killer. I mean his job calls for taking life when he has to."

"Well... I don't know. I guess he has mean eyes and a marshal doesn't."

"Miss April, obviously you haven't met Marshal Bass Reeves out of Fort Smith." The court erupted.

Judge Maxey came down hard with the gavel. "I'll not tolerate outburst in my courtroom! If it happens again, none of you will be allowed in here."

"Ah, Miss April, one last question. Is it true that you and Ruby Centers were best friends?"

"Oh yes, she was the best friend I had in the whole world. I miss her terribly. We did everything together. We were together the day the bank was robbed, the day she was killed."

"I see. Then would it be too horrible of me to presume you would want to see the man that killed her hanged?"

"No it would not, and yes I would like to see him hanged."

He turned on her like a mountain cat. "Yes you would! You want to see it so badly you'd point the finger at any man brought before this court accused of killing your best friend in the whole world, wouldn't you!?"

"Yes! I mean... no."

"No further questions."

Simon Lick smiled as he slowly looked over at Tucker who was cuffed to his left arm. His lawyer sat on his right side, as they sat on the left hand side of the courtroom.

Judge Maxey looked at both lawyers. "Does the prosecution have any further witnesses?"

"Not at this time, Judge."

"Does the defense have any witnesses?"

"I haven't any witnesses, Judge, but I do have a written statement from Lou Pitman, an associate of Mister Tubbs here."

"Associate hell!" Dan Nolen stood up in the back of the court and shouted at the lawyer.

Judge Maxey came down with his gavel again. "Sir, what's your name?"

"Dan Nolen, from Melt, Kansas where this scum that's on trial killed two lawmen and robbed our bank!"

"I'm sorry to hear that, nonetheless, I fine you ten dollars for contempt of court. One more outburst from you and you will go to jail."

Dan sat down though he was still angry and glaring at the way things were going.

Judge Maxey looked to the defense lawyer. "Why can this witness not be here?"

"Judge, he's a little under the weather."

Where Outlaws Roam
Royal Wade Kimes

"I see. I suppose I can allow it."

Deputy Marshal Shaw stood. Judge Maxey sighed. "This is turning into a circus, not a court proceeding. "What do you want to say, Deputy Shaw?"

"Judge, the man who is about to give absentee testimony is under the weather because he took one of my bullets in his backside. He and two others were planning to ambush me on the trail to here. You see he rides with the accused."

"I see." He cut his eyes to the defense lawyer. "Is this true, does this ghost witness have a bullet hole in his behind?"

"Ah, yes, I would probably put it like that, yes."

The lawyer would not look at the judge.

"Well, I must say, I'm of the opinion a man that would ambush another and have help doing it would not be a man to believe. So therefore his testimony will not be admitted. Now, do you have anyone else since you cannot use your absentee, and I might add... dishonorable type?"

"No Judge, I haven't anyone except the defendant."

"Do you plan to call him?"

"I do."

"Then get to it."

Simon Lick Tubbs took the stand after one side of the handcuffs were taken off Deputy Marshal Shaw and fastened around both his wrists.

The defense lawyer began. "Sir, can you tell us where you have been for the last year and two months?"

"I've been digging for gold in Colorado. I just came back when I started hearing all these tales about how Simon Lick was killing and robbing all over hell's creation. I didn't know what to do about it. I rode into Melt, Kansas just in time to hear shooting and see three men leave in a hurry on horseback. A man pointed at me and yelled I was one of them. I knew that was bad... me being a stranger and all. So I did the most logical thing, I turned my pony and run for it."

He turned his head and looked at Judge Maxey. "I don't mind telling you I was damn... dang scared. I had rode up there looking for work, but with the law chasing me for something I didn't do, well... I didn't stay around long to find any. I beat it on down to Fillmore, up the road a piece from here. I hung around there a day or two and headed southeast. I rode into Dye and stopped at the Lemon Drop Livery to have a shoe looked at, but the owner wasn't there. I tightened the shoe myself and was dead in front of the bank when two men busted out the front of it. My horse bolted sideways, they was coming so fast. Then I heard shooting and screaming inside the bank."

He stopped and took a deep breath. "Judge, my luck wasn't running any good. The chances of me being in the wrong place at the wrong time was most trying. Again I took flight. The law began to comb the country side for Simon Lick, and I hadn't even been in Kansas three good days. I'd been in Colorado until then." He looked at Tucker and faintly smiled. Then he acted as if he remembered something. "Judge, to be honest we ought to be prosecuting Deputy Marshal Shaw and Marshal Sanders for shooting my ears off. I hadn't done a damn thing and have been put through some kind of hell I tell you."

Tucker smiled. Simon Lick was one good story teller. If he hadn't known the real story he would have believed him his self.

Judge Maxey gave the prisoner a smile. "Mister Tubbs, I think you're one lying individual and I don't believe anything you say." He looked from the prisoner to the courtroom of people. "Nevertheless, if the prosecution cannot produce a witness or hard evidence to the guilt of this man, I begrudgingly will have to dismiss the charges against him. There are no witnesses to swear he is the man that shot Ruby Centers and robbed the bank, other than Miss April Tenkiller. Though she may be a good citizen, she lacks credibility because of her close relationship with Ruby Centers, and seems to be somewhat ambitious in punishing someone for it. Therefore charges against Mister Tubbs are dropped."

The court erupted into utter chaos. Judge Maxey tried to settle them down but was having little success. One of the men threw a punch and two others stepped in to hold him. Tucker drew his pistol and fired it through the ceiling. The chaos stopped as suddenly as it started.

Judge Maxey was standing up ready to draw a long barreled

Where Outlaws Roam
Royal Wade Kimes

pistol if shooting started. He waited until everyone sat back down before he himself sat. He cleared his throat.

"Before you barbarians so rudely interrupted my court, I was about to say that Mister Tubbs was to be bound over to the law in Melt, Kansas. He will be on trial there for double murder. Mister Tubbs is accused of the deaths of the town's sheriff and deputy. He is to be transported there at Deputy Marshal Shaw's earliest convenience."

Tucker was bewildered. He had never seen a guiltier man than Simon Lick Tubbs, yet he was walking away from murder. Now he questioned if he might beat the charges in Melt.

"Judge, there's not anyone to take charge of the prisoner in Melt. The State of Kansas hasn't appointed anyone, and the town hasn't elected a new sheriff."

Dan spoke up. "Let us have him. The town voted us in as a group to handle matters of the law."

Judge Maxey smiled as he gave thought to what Tucker said. He glanced at Dan. "You sir are describing vigilantes. I do not recognize that as being law." He looked back at Tucker. "The prisoner is to be kept here until a sheriff has been elected to serve Melt, or a United States Marshal is sent there. I wouldn't think it would take more than two weeks."

"Yes Judge... but I have to say, I've known prisoners that makes two weeks seem like a lifetime." He was speaking of his own actions in Great Britain.

"Are you speaking from experience, Deputy Shaw?"

"Indeed, Judge." He smiled at him and then marched Simon Lick past all the eyes of hate. He knew he better get him back in jail quickly and get off the street as soon as possible.

Suddenly a pistol shot and dust kicked up six inches in front of Simon Lick. Tucker jerked him down behind a sack of feed in front of the Morrow Feed Store. He saw three men running for cover and then heard a thud when a bullet hit the post the sack full of feed was leaning against. Another man ran into the alley by the jail. They had cut him off.

Simon Lick began to laugh. "I'm damn popular ain't I, Deputy? You know what's just real funny?"

Where Outlaws Roam
Royal Wade Kimes

Tucker glanced at him as he tried to watch the street. "No, what's real funny to you?"

"I'll tell you. It's the idea I traded a pair of ears for my neck. I'd say that was a damn good swap. I'd give a pair of ears to stay alive. My looks changed so much those dirt farmers didn't even know me."

Tucker looked at him hard. "Rooster, don't crow yet, you're feathers will be plucked in Melt, unless you catch a bullet here."

"Hell, I have all the confidence in the world in you." He cackled out.

Suddenly gunfire erupted up the street. Tucker could see the two Fort Smith Deputies shooting as they made their way towards him. Then another shot came from his left towards the jail. The man Tucker saw run into the alley beside the jail took three steps out and then fell dead in the dust. Marshal Galt appeared and motioned for him to bring his prisoner on.

"Simon Lick, if you plan to see Melt, Kansas, you better not be slow." They took off in a run. The two deputies laid down fire back towards the courthouse as Tucker ran his prisoner towards the jail. Still a bullet hit the street between his feet as he ran. He saw a puff of smoke atop the Dye Hotel. As he ran he fired three rounds at the spot where he saw the smoke. His bet was Reed Fletcher. The ones down on the street had to be Melt, Kansas Vigilantes. He hit the jail door running and shoved his prisoner inside.

Simon Lick was laughing until Tucker short jabbed him in the mouth. He went staggering backwards and fell. His hands were handcuffed which left him less balanced when falling. He lay on the floor for a few seconds feeling of his mouth.

"You loosened my front teeth you bastard."

"Get up and get in your cell."

"Go to hell!"

Tucker began to kick him in the side, then the stomach, and then the head. He tried to fend the blows off, but he wasn't doing very well. He finally rolled towards his cell.

"Stop! I got the idea!"

Tucker locked the cell and went to the front door. He peered through the crack but saw nothing. It had quietened down and

Where Outlaws Roam
Royal Wade Kimes

the street was still. After a few minutes Marshal Galt and his deputies made it to the jail. Then a voice called to Tucker. He opened the door.

"Yeah, what do you want?"

"It's Dan Nolen! I want you to know me and the most of my men had nothing to do with the little scrap that took place! A few of my boys went and done that on their own!"

"Yeah, and I'll just bet you hurried around trying to get it stopped didn't you?"

"I learned a long time ago to not mess in other people's business, and you sure don't wade into a dogfight and try to break it up! That's a good way to get hurt!" It was quiet for a few seconds. "How about it? You and me okay with one another?"

"We are if you and your men turn your guns in until you leave town."

"I don't see us getting along then. I be damned if we're the only ones in town unarmed."

"Then stay off the streets. If I see you and you have a gun on I'll take it as a threat and kill you."

Marshal Galt's head turned quickly towards Tucker and then he winked at his deputies who were smiling. They all three liked this tough Tucker Shaw.

It was quiet again until Dan walked out into the street. "I've talked it over with my men. We're going to head on back to Melt. All I ask, if anything goes wrong and that murdering bastard was to get away... you let me and the boys help you catch him."

Tucker and Marshal Galt walked out on the front porch of the jail. Tucker holstered his gun. "Seems fair to me."

Dan nodded and then left. Tucker turned and faced Marshal Galt. "Well, we settled things with Dan, where does this leave you and me?"

"Nothing's changed. Judge Maxey assigned you the job of getting Simon Lick to Melt. It's like I said, I'll not arrest you until the Simon Lick Tubbs ordeal is over and done."

"Seems fair to me." He laughed and turned for the street.

"Where the hell you going?"

"Snooping is all. Someone took a shot at me from top of the

Dye Hotel. Something tells me it wasn't one of the citizens of Melt, Kansas."

"Wait on me, I'll go with you." They were half way to the hotel when Marshal Galt cut his eyes at Tucker. "You thinking what I'm thinking?"

"If you're thinking Reed Fletcher, I'm thinking exactly what you're thinking."

They found a set of stairs that went to the roof of the hotel. They went through a small portal cut through the ceiling, and when it widened out they went through another hole in the roof its self. The last one was metal with edges that had not been turned down, leaving them sharp. They stepped out on the roof and Tucker went to the spot he saw the puff of smoke.

"Marshal, I don't see any sign anyone was ever here."

"Well Deputy, I don't either, but if you saw smoke from a gun and a bullet nearly hit you, I'd say looks is deceiving."

They went back to the portal hole and opened the lid back. Tucker started to slide through when he suddenly held up. "Marshal... blood."

"I see it. Whoever was up here cut his hand getting through the hole."

"We know what to look for now." He smiled and slid through the hole.

When they left the hotel Deputy Farley and Nelson were waiting on them at the jail. Farley had some news and was anxious to share it with Tucker.

"I spoke to Bet Price over at the Lemon Drop Livery Stable and she said her crowbar was missing. I asked her if she had any idea who might have taken it, and she for sure didn't."

Tucker was silent as he waited for more. None came. "Well... was there anything else, Farley?"

"Well, nothing but that we had us two glasses of lemonade a piece."

Tucker smiled. "Well, I guess that'd do if you don't have any tea." They all laughed and then Tucker became a little more sober.

"Marshal Galt, I'd say by the crowbar being from the Lemon Drop Livery, the man might have been staying in the hay loft at night. One thing it says. He's been here long enough to know where the crowbar was and we better be watching ourselves. Whoever is after Reed is living right here in town with us."

Chapter 17

Lord Johnathan McCray called a special meeting with certain individuals that possessed certain talents used to eliminate persistent problems. This happened after a lengthy meeting with the Queen.

Present at the meeting was Admiral Robert Fetter and his officers, Captain Ross and Major Parker. Then there was Lord McCray, Sir Sonja Peters, Sir Robert Pearl, Lord Derby, and three members with elite military background. Ben Gladstone trained in pistol and hand to hand combat, a Garret Gray, who was a tough man with great commitment when given an assignment. He was known for his fearlessness in battle.

"Walter Hobson, a planner and a hit man when contracted. His five foot and six inch height was not to be mistaken for an easy mark. He was and is the deadliest of the lot.

Lord McCray began the meeting. "Gentlemen, have any of you seen the morning paper?" They all nodded they had. "Then I do not have to tell you how the Queen feels about all this. It's outrageous and embarrassing that something like this could get into the papers. Tucker Shaw is still causing trouble and I'm afraid he must be... eliminated. It wasn't enough he was banished from Great Britain, the man has to push it further, to the point he has to go away. It seems America is not far enough. He has exposed a rather delicate situation concerning the maid and Ira Shaw. Its effects have already caused numerous problems. Mister Shaw has vacated the Shaw Estate for now. The Queen is acting as a peace keeper, a mediator you might say. She is negotiating a reconciliation of sorts. The young maid has been asked to leave, however provisions have been made for her to be well taken care of. I'm sure Ira Shaw will continue that relationship once things cool down. He's not one to beg off."

Admiral Fetter sat quietly and calmly as Lord McCray spoke. He wondered if Tucker would expose him and his mother's relationship as he had his father's, his poppa as he called him. He suspected not. Tucker dearly loved his mother and wanted her to be happy. He was smart enough to know his mother would never be with his father. He thought about Tucker and what it was that

Where Outlaws Roam
Royal Wade Kimes

drove him. It was his free spirit, his love for life and truthfulness. He was honest with himself and disliked those who weren't. He was no hypocrite and he would not let money influence his decisions. The admiral found it hard to think a man had to die for being all those things, the very thing all the hypocrites of the world claim to be, but were not.

He came out of his deep thoughts and continued to listen to what Lord McCray was saying.

"The Queen is terribly upset with the fact Tucker has exposed her dealings with India, something she had kept quiet for political purposes. The Tories are very much against easing trade agreements with India and were unaware we had any. Now she has to explain the why of it all. I think we have it worked out, but the fact is Tucker Shaw has caused us a great deal of trouble and anxiety. The possibility that he will cause more problems is a great probability." He hesitated and then continued. "There are several things the Queen of Great Britain does not want to come to light, if they were to, it would destroy all the good she has done. I'm afraid Tucker Shaw has to be stopped."

Admiral Fetter was saddened by the decision. He would carry out the order if asked, but his heart was heavy. "Lord McCray, what is the plan?"

"You are to spearhead a mission, code named Queen's Denial. You are to seek out and eliminate Tucker Shaw. You will be accompanied by Captain Ross, Major Parker, Garret Gray, Walter Hobson, and Ben Gladstone."

The three special duty men nodded to Admiral Fetter. Captain Ross cut his eyes over to Major Parker and saw the same thing on his face that he knew was on his. He too didn't like the mission. There weren't many men in the military, the Queen's Royal Guard or any other branch of service that didn't like Tucker Shaw. They would carry out their duty, but it wouldn't sit well.

"When do we leave?" Admiral Fetter was looking straight into the eyes of Lord McCray.

"Today. The ship has been made ready. You are to set sail to the place you dropped Tucker and go inland from there. Tucker is a Deputy Marshal in the state of Kansas. The village is called

Dye."

He smiled. "My Lord, they are called towns. Until I read the paper this morning I hadn't any idea he had become a lawman. That brings me to a question.

"Which is?"

"I understand United States Marshals watch out for one another. We may be walking into a den with lions in it."

Lord McCray smiled. "These western cowboys are no match for the likes of Hobson, you, Gray, and Gladstone. Captain Ross and Major Parker can hold their own as well. I wouldn't worry myself over a few tin stars."

"Begging your pardon sir, but that's what we said about a few farmers too, and we got our asses handed to us."

Lord McCray cleared his throat as he was embarrassed by the comment. "Yes, well we may have underestimated their army, but this isn't an army. Go in, eliminate the target and meet the ship at the port of New Orleans. If you aren't back within six weeks it will sail without you. It is your task to send word for additional passage if you make it back after your allotted time."

"Yes, my Lord."

They rose and left the meeting and by noon they were on their way, but not before Admiral Fetter got word to Margaret Shaw to meet him at their normal place. When she came through the door to the small room Admiral Fetter kept rented, she looked both radiant and worried.

"Robert, what is it? I know something is wrong. Does it have anything to do with the paper this morning?"

He looked her in the eyes. "Margaret, is it true you asked your maid and the impossible Ira Shaw to leave?" He was careful to avoid any talk of Tucker.

"I did. I wanted them both out. I hadn't any choice. If I let him stay and let what was exposed go on, then I would look like a weak silly woman. I had to ask him to leave. In a way it's a blessing. Tucker did me a favor. I don't have to talk to him or look at him anymore. I despise him. He is the most inconsiderate, conceited, and impossible man I know."

"I just needed to hear the why. I understand it. Maybe one day we can be together… and we can stop all this hiding around. Oh,

Where Outlaws Roam
Royal Wade Kimes

if we could be like Tucker. I envy him. He tosses all caution to the wind and lives more free than all of us. He doesn't let life get in the way."

She smiled at him. "My son is quite a man. He was exiled from here because of his stubborn will, nothing more. Oh Robert, I was so proud when I saw he was a United States Deputy Marshal. I knew he would do well once away from here." She walked from Robert to a picture sitting on the dresser. It was Tucker when he was but two years old. "I will never see my baby again." She began to weep.

He went to her and pulled her close. "Don't cry. If I know Tucker, you'll see him again."

"You think so?" She looked at him with pleading hope in her eyes.

"I'm sure of it." How could he tell her he was being sent on a mission to kill her only son, her baby? He too was part of all the hypocrites of the world. He was as dirty as her husband. He loved a woman that was married, and for the honor of Queen and Country he was going to kill her son.

Unlike Tucker Shaw, Admiral Robert Fetter had let life get in the way.

Word finally came by telegram from Melt, Kansas that Marshal Sam Talbert had been sent by the United States Marshal's Office out of Fort Smith to serve as law of Melt and the surrounding county. Tucker read the telegram sitting at his desk. He then wrote a response.

> RECEIVED TELEGRAM AND WILL BRING
> PRISONER NEXT WEEK: STOP
>
> THANKS FOR SENDING WORD: STOP
>
> TUCKER SHAW, DEPUTY MARSHAL: STOP

He gave the response to the telegraph operator and then beat it over to the Dye Hotel. Reed Fletcher was sitting in a chair on the front porch watching as he approached.

Where Outlaws Roam
Royal Wade Kimes

He stepped up on the hotel steps and stopped when he saw Fletcher reading a newspaper. All he could see of his hands were his fingers. The inside of the hand was hidden from view by the paper itself. He walked on into the porch area of the hotel.

"Reed, you remind me of a vulture sitting on a limb waiting for something to die. The problem is... it won't die."

He slowly peered over the top of the paper. "Oh, it'll get dead soon enough."

"Well, don't you change into a bird of prey... it would be a pity to lose a damn chicken hawk." He went through the door of the hotel before Reed could reply. He bounced up the stairs to room four and knocked.

Marshal Galt was all smiles when he opened the door. Tucker thought he was glad to see him, but that wasn't the case. He had a lady friend in the room keeping him company.

"Oh, well, yes, Marshal old chap, I can come back some other time."

"Nonsense! Come on in! I want you to meet Darla."

"Please to meet you, Miss." Darla was stunning. A five foot red head with blue eyes and very light freckles across the bridge of her little nose. Her shape was nearly perfect and her smile was genuine.

"Same here, and call me Darla. Marshal Galt has told me all about you."

Tucker glanced at the him. "I hope you told her how pretty I was." They all laughed and then Tucker got down to business.

"Marshal."

"Yeah?"

"I received a telegram from the town of Melt. Marshal Sam Talbert has been sent to serve as law for the town and county."

"Talbert... he's a good man, a good lawman. When are you leaving with your prisoner?"

"In three days which will be Monday. I figure it will take a day and a half to get there. I come to ask if you'd like to go along?"

"I wouldn't miss it. What time are you planning to leave?"

"One hour before daylight would be good."

"You thinking there might be someone laying for Simon Lick?"

"No, I'm thinking there might be someone laying for me."

Where Outlaws Roam
Royal Wade Kimes

Marshal Galt stopped smiling. "Reed?"

"Who else? He's hanging around this town like a vulture."

"Yeah, I've noticed. I'm of the mind he thinks I'm not going to bring you back to stand trial."

Tucker laughed. "You're not."

Marshal Galt had a solemn look on his face. "It's not going to be sweet smelling roses between us one day… is it?"

"The roses are already dying." He turned to Darla. "Indeed a pleasure, ma'am. You have good taste in men, Marshal Galt is the best." He turned and left the room.

Darla stared at the door he went through. "Men… you two like one another, yet you'd shoot it out over some kind of crazy principal deemed worthy of a friend's life."

He stared at her knowing there wasn't anything he could say. It was what it was.

Chapter 18

After Marshal Talbert read his telegram from Deputy Marshal Tucker Shaw, he threw it in the trashcan sitting in the corner of the telegraph office. What he wasn't aware of was his being watched by Dan Nolen and his men. Someone was assigned to watch him at all times. One of the men rummaged through the can and retrieved the telegram. He then ran it to the Nolen Harness Shop.

"Dan, I have what we been waiting on." He handed the telegram to him.

He quickly read it and then walked over and shut the door to his shop. "This is good. Starting Monday morning we need to be camped about ten miles down the trail. When Deputy Shaw comes riding through with that slick headed Simon Lick Tubbs, we'll blow the rest of his damn head off."

"You want me to get the word to the rest of the boys?"

"Yeah, Hank, have them come to my place tonight. We'll have a drink and discuss where we ought to set up at."

"My vote would be Eagles Ledge. Hell, a six year old kid could pick him off from there."

"Yeah, that might be the spot. One thing we don't do... is kill any law man. We make a clean shot and get the hell out."

"What if something were to... maybe go wrong?"

"It won't, like you say, it'll be easy from Eagles Ledge."

"Yeah, it will be." He took off in an enthusiastic walk.

Three days later Tucker and Marshal Galt rode out before daylight headed for Melt, Kansas with their prisoner. There wasn't any sign of Reed but Tucker kept looking back. His gut told him something was amiss.

"Tucker, what the hell are you looking at? If it's the town, don't worry on it. My deputies can handle law and order until we get back. Ole Farley is handling that Billie Sway, too. That boy is like a damn stud horse. The town's in good hands if that's worrying you."

"It's not that. I've got this funny feeling we're being followed. Let's whoa up when we make this curve in the road and see if we

Where Outlaws Roam
Royal Wade Kimes

can hear a horse behind us." He glanced very quickly at him. "You say Farley is chasing Billie Sway?"

"Yeah. He told me she had her eye on you, but you hadn't showed much interest."

"Women, it's either not enough or too much."

"Don't tell me ole Farley has shot you out of the saddle?"

"I don't think I was ever seated real well."

They stopped and waited in the dark just beyond the curve in the trail, but heard nothing. They plodded on and stopped one more time, still nothing.

Simon Lick put in. "Are all lawmen this jumpy? I didn't know you boys lived in constant fear."

Tucker dismounted and took a glove from his saddlebags and stuffed it in Simon Lick's mouth. He tied a small rope around his head and the gag to make sure it stayed.

"Damn, Deputy!" Marshal Galt began laughing as Tucker stared at him, until he too began to laugh.

"Well, damn it all I'm tired of hearing his mouth."

"I would have never guessed."

He mounted Catcher and they rode on, and every once in a while they would chuckle. Once, Marshal Galt looked back at Simon Lick and burst out laughing. It was the hysterical sight of the fingers on the glove sticking out of his mouth that made it so funny to him. They rode until nearly dark. When they came to a grove of sycamore trees with plenty of blue spring water pooled at their roots they made camp.

Tucker was unsaddling Catcher when his ears went forward and he blew through his nostrils. He drew his gun and tried to see through the trees and weeds. It was virtually impossible with darkness coming on. Catcher settled down and Tucker finally holstered his gun. He then unsaddled Marshal Galt's horse and the bronze mare Simon Lick was riding. He carried two of the saddles to camp which was forty feet from the picket line. He then went back and got the third one.

"I took care of your horse, Marshal, you better be the cook you say you are."

"Did I say that?" He was busy with a skillet and coffee pot. He had a feed sack he kept his fixings in and was moving around rather quickly preparing supper.

"This is not your first camp for sure."

"No it's not. When I was sixteen I was the Cookie's help on a trail drive once. I learned how to cook and do it fast. I also learned how to do it fast and it be good at the same time. A good cook lives off of pinches."

Tucker had a blank stare.

`He laughed at him. "A pinch of this, a pinch of that... pinches."

"Oh!"

Tucker took the dirty glove out of Simon Lick's mouth. "We're about to have supper. If you'd like to dine with us, keep your mouth shut. It will be impossible to eat if I have to gag you again."

"I'm too hungry and thirsty to be of any trouble."

"Okay. Not a peep."

They had a quiet supper and a shot of whiskey afterwards. Tucker even poured Simon Lick a shot for being quiet.

He leaned back against his saddle. "Marshal, that was a meal fit for a King."

"You ought to know. I've never known a King or Queen."

"They're like everyone else, the only difference is... they don't know it."

"Deputy Tucker."

"Yeah Marshal?"

"When we get this prisoner delivered, why don't you take ole Catcher and that good looking bronze mare, and ride away from here. Head for California or Oregon. You sure would make life easier for the both of us if you did. If you stay here, I'm bound to arrest you."

"Marshal."

Snap! A stick broke somewhere in the dark. Both Deputy Shaw and Marshal Galt hit the dirt on their bellies. Simon Lick was lying right beside them. "You two lawmen better do something." He was whispering. "They've come for me. Do something."

"We're doing it, shut up." Tucker couldn't help but chuckle.

"This ain't funny." Simon Lick wasn't afraid of much, but he was afraid of the dark. When he heard strange noises mixed with

Where Outlaws Roam
Royal Wade Kimes

darkness it sent fear through him.

Tucker looked over at Marshal Galt lying just over from him. "What do you think?"

"It could have been an animal I guess."

"I doubt it. Catcher heard something earlier. You stay here and I'll slip out the backside of camp and circle around. Maybe I'll see something."

"Go ahead." Marshal Galt eased closer to Simon Lick when Tucker backed out and vanished into the night. "You cause me any problem and I'll shoot you middle of the head, you got that?"

"You damn lawmen, you don't get nothing right. It was me told you two to do something. I damn sure ain't doing anything to get in the way."

Tucker made a wide circle and was giving up seeing anyone when suddenly he caught a glimpse of someone running. He cocked his pistol but they were gone. He ran in the direction he saw the running form. He listened but heard nothing and slowly turned for camp.

"Marshal, I'm coming in!"

"Come on."

He walked into camp and sat down. "Someone is out there, but I haven't a clue as to whom? I saw someone running away from camp, but couldn't make anything out about them."

"One lone soldier?"

"It looks that way, but there might be a whole army back the way the feller ran."

"Maybe we better take turns sleeping tonight?"

"I think so."

Simon Lick put into the conversation. "I just feel all warm inside with you two watching over me. You two can't find your asses with both hands."

Tucker right crossed him and connected with his chin. "No, but I find your chin easy enough. I hope I broke it."

Marshal Galt chuckled. "Simon Lick, you'd do well to keep your mouth shut." He turned to Tucker. "I'll take first watch if you'd like me to."

"Be my guest."

Where Outlaws Roam
Royal Wade Kimes

There wouldn't be a whole lot of sleep had. Two men were determined to watch the dark, and a third was afraid of it.

At high noon the next day Dan Nolen and his vigilantes were on Eagles Ledge watching three riders coming across the open prairie. One of the riders was handcuffed and didn't have any ears.

He turned to one of his men. "Josh, you take that buff gun of yours and get over there by that scrub oak. You lay a bullet in the center of that middle rider. That's the bastard we're after. The rest of you men lay some fire down all around those two lawmen, enough so they bail off them horses for cover. We got to buy some time to get out of here."

Josh was a tall man of about thirty years of age. He was broad and stout. He could hold a buffalo gun to his shoulder all day and shoot flies out of the air. He wouldn't have to do that today. He sat down next to the small tree and laid the big bore barrel over a small limb. He slid the barrel down the limb next to the body of the tree, which made it easy to hold the gun steady. All he had to do now was wait.

Marshal Galt was leading the way to Melt since he knew the trail. He held up for a second and looked back at Tucker. "Up ahead is Eagles Ledge. It's the highest point along this trail and a damn good place to get shot."

Tucker scanned the rocky looking ledge. "Well, I don't see anything."

"I don't either and that bothers me."

"Why's that?"

"Well, nine times out of ten you'll see an eagle sitting in one of those small trees scattered along the top there. If you don't see one of them... there's always some kind of bird sitting in them."

"What do you think?" Tucker was straining to see anything that was suspicious looking.

"I think we sit here for a few minutes." He took his hat off and wiped the sweat from the hat band. "I'm hoping if someone is up there... that he'll make a move and we'll see a flash or something." He was talking slow and deliberate. "And if there is

Where Outlaws Roam
Royal Wade Kimes

someone there, they had to get there on a horse. Maybe it'll nicker to ours."

"You two lawmen beat all. We're out here in the wide open. That little ole peak don't amount to anything. Last night was what amounted to something. I didn't sleep all night long. I was afraid you two big brave lawmen would fall asleep. I was awake to sound the alarm."

Tucker chuckled. "You were awake because you are afraid of the dark. Are all you big brave outlaws like that?" He smiled as he continued to scan Eagles Ledge. He looked over at Marshal Galt. "So far it looks alright."

"My gut says it ain't." He replaced his hat and smiled. "I think we'll sit right here in the sun for a few more minutes. Sitting out here like this will make 'em think they've been spotted. Then maybe they'll make a move. If you see riders coming in a hurry, head due south. There's an old wet weather spring over there about a quarter. It's big enough to hide us and the horses. We could make a stand there."

"You really believe someone is up there don't you, Marshal?"

"I'm not taking any chances. I've yet to see a bird light in any of those trees."

Dan backed back down off the ledge and eased over and up behind Josh. "Boy, can you hear me? Don't move or turn around. Your gun might catch the sunlight."

"I hear you."

"Do you think you could hit that bastard from here? They're out of range for these lever guns."

"Well, yeah, I think so, but they're just in range at best. It'll strain this old gun, but she can do-er."

"Well, I can't see them from back here. You'll have to tell me if they're coming on. If they don't start riding in two minutes... take the shot. I'm betting they've spotted us. Something has them spooked. Damned if I know what."

"Dan, he's a dead man."

"Good, that's real good."

Where Outlaws Roam
Royal Wade Kimes

Tucker eased Catcher in beside Marshal Galt. "You pay to be around. I've learned something from you. I wouldn't have thought about birds being on that little roost."

"Neither have they. I'm fair sure there is someone up there."

Tucker looked back at Simon Lick. He was sitting in his saddle grinning from ear hole to ear hole, which caused Tucker to grin. As he stared at him thoughts ran through his mind. Simon Lick was as worthless a man as he had ever met. He wondered how that happened. Even he had a mother and she had to have loved him. Maybe she died when he was born, what caused him to turn out to be such a wretched man only God could know.

Tucker stopped grinning at him when blood suddenly spurted forth from his chest. There was a thud and a whizzing sound like a fast flying horsefly, an instant before the blood. Simon Lick reeled in the saddle and was about to fall off when Tucker caught him. He grabbed the reins and tried to hold him in the saddle, but was losing the fight. He finally shoved him straight up and center of the seat.

"Simon Lick, you grab that saddle horn and hang on, damn you!" He whirled the horses for the spring as a bullet dug up dirt beside his horse. It didn't seem to have much left on it which meant he was nearly out of range. He looked back to see how his prisoner was doing and saw Marshal Galt coming like a runaway train. He was yelling and flapping his rifle in the air to run like hell.

They made it to the spring and dismounted. Tucker unloaded Simon Lick and leaned him against the small bank. The dirt was soft and had few rocks, unlike the springs he saw back in Arkansas. He laid his rifle up over the bank and waited as Marshal Galt joined him.

"Deputy, here is where we earn our keep."

"You think they'll be coming?"

"You damn right I do. They took their shot at Simon Lick. Since he didn't fall from his horse, they'll figure they missed and will be coming to rectify that."

Tucker crawled over to their wounded and bleeding prisoner. He had seen many wounds in battle, and this one was the death march. He turned to Marshal Galt and very faintly moved his

Where Outlaws Roam
Royal Wade Kimes

head in a gesture of a no go.

"Simon Lick, it's time to back up that tough talk. You going to wimp out or show me what you got."

His eyes opened slowly. "Deputy."

"Yeah."

"I can't show you nothing... handcuffed."

Tucker took the key to the handcuffs out of his pocket and unlocked them.

"Deputy, you have an extra gun?"

"I do." He looked over at Marshal Galt who was watching them.

"Deputy, I'm a ring tailed pole cat when hemmed in. I know I don't deserve a damn thing from you... or anyone. I've been a bad man all my disgusting life. But... when you hear horse's hooves pounding the ground our way... I'd sure like a gun."

Marshal Galt nodded to Tucker it would be alright.

"You'll have it."

Simon Lick's eyes seemed to show more life at that moment. "Maybe I'll have one proud moment in life. A man ought to have... at least... one.

Blood was oozing from his chest and bloody froth was emitting from his mouth. His eyes seemed dulled and his breathing was shorter.

Dan and his men mounted up and eased around Eagles Ledge to take chase. They thought they had missed their target. Once clear of the rocky ledge they spurred their horses into a wide open race across the prairie. Dan was in the lead for a moment, but three of the younger men passed him on fast horses. They were yelling like wild Indians, running full out after three men that were high tailing it. That changed when they saw a man walking towards them without ears and holding a pistol."

When Tucker heard horse's hooves he pulled his extra pistol out of the belt and stuck it in his prisoner's hand. "They're coming, Simon Lick."

He smiled. "Call me Simon. Mama called me Simon. You letting me do this is the only other kind thing I can remember happening in my life. Mama stealing me away on a riverboat to keep my old man from killing me was the other. I was seven then. He whipped my mama to death. When I turned fifteen I went back and done the first kind thing in my life. I rid the world of my Old Man." He smiled. "It's a funny cruel world." He turned his eyes to Tucker without moving his head. "I hated you up until now... now you turn out to be the only man to do me a good turn in my twenty-nine years."

He got up with help from Tucker and Marshal Galt. He stepped up on the bank and mostly shuffled his feet through the prairie grass while walking towards the galloping horses. When they were within fifty feet he fired the pistol at the charging riders. One of them fell from his horse. He fired two more times before a volley of bullets hit him in the chest, ribs, and head. He rolled over into a small bloody heap on the vast prairie.

Tucker came up levering his rifle. A man fell with every shot, and he had a seven shot carbine. Marshal Galt was firing rapidly but not having nearly the success ratio Tucker was.

When Tucker's rifle was empty he threw it down and drew his pistol. He dropped to one knee and held the gun with both hands. He fired three fast shots and dropped two men. He fired one more rather long shot and he too fell from his horse. He fired one last time, but they were out of range.

Marshal Galt looked at Tucker in pure disbelief and mumbled. "I've never seen anyone shoot like that."

He was stunned. Seven men lay dead every ten yards apart, and several more from Tucker's pistol shots. He himself had killed only three, and had emptied both his rifle and pistol doing it. With all the dead lying scattered across the prairie he wondered if Dan Nolen thought it worth it. They had lost at least half of their vigilante members. He walked over to a gradual rise where he could see in the distance. He could see Dan and what was left of his men loping across the prairie floor. There were several horses running with empty saddles along beside them. He shook his head and mumbled once more to himself. "What a damn stupid waste."

He was still standing looking at all the dead when Deputy Tucker come riding by him without saying a word, leading the

Where Outlaws Roam
Royal Wade Kimes

bronze mare. Simon Tubbs was tied across the saddle. Tucker was headed in the direction of Melt, Kansas.

Marshal Galt walked back to his horse and swung up in the saddle. As he eased out onto the prairie he spoke to Tucker, knowing he couldn't hear him. He was at least two hundred yards ahead. "Deputy Shaw, you're a deadly man." He pulled up. One of the men they had shot was moving. He rode over to him.

"Mister, I'm shot, shot bad."

"You ought not took law into your own damn hands."

"Too late now." He pulled hard for another breath. "Mister, water. My tongue, my mouth… feels like cotton."

He looked in the direction Tucker went. He was perplexed as to whether to give the man a drink or catch up with him. He stepped down. "I wouldn't deny a dog a drink." He took the cork from his canteen and held it up for him.

"Thanks, thanks much." He laid back and stared at the sky. "Funny, even blue sky means more when you're dying." He never said another word.

"Yeah… I reckon." He started to turn to his horse but stopped. He looked back at the dead man. He knelt beside him. There was a corner of a ten dollar bill sticking out of his vest. He looked around and saw no one anywhere. He pulled on the bill and out came two more. He looked at it long and hard and began to reason. The money wasn't the dead man's anymore. Someone would take it when they buried him. It was plain found money you could say. He's dead and hasn't anymore life than a dead tree or withered grass. It's not like I'd be stealing it. Someone might as well get some use out of it. More than likely it'd be one of those cut throat self-imposed lawmen that would take it.

He stuck the money in his pocket and again started to mount up. His eyes scanned the other bodies. He led his horse behind him and checked them over to make sure they were dead. Three more of the dead had cash and gold pieces on them. He put it away and mounted up. He looked in the direction of Tucker. He was at least a half a mile or more across the prairie. He decided to just ease along. There wasn't any reason to kill his horse trying to catch up. He rode a little further and pulled up for a second. "What the hell was that? I think someone took a shot at me."

Where Outlaws Roam
Royal Wade Kimes

Chapter 19

Reed Fletcher watched the vigilante attack play out from Eagles Ledge. He waited until the vigilantes left the rocky point before he rode up on it. He dismounted and took his high powered rifle from its case. He saw the vigilantes get annihilated and knew by that, Tucker Shaw would ride by Eagles Ledge on his way to Melt. Whether he took his dead prisoner or not, he would still have to ride there and make a report. He pulled the bolt back on the gun, ran a large caliber shell through his hair and inserted it. He did that every time he shot a man. It put an oil film on the bullet and it was part of him that hit the victim.

He chuckled at his good fortune and boasted aloud. "Today is the day you get yours Tucker Shaw. Those idiot cowboys created a diversion while I set up for the kill." He watched as Tucker lined out towards Melt. He would make a game of it and record him as his longest shot.

He heard something behind him just as he heard a thud and felt a blade go deep in his left shoulder. He fell forward on top of his gun, breaking the stock. He rolled over on his back to see who had thrown a knife nearly through him. "Who... who are you?"

"Surprised? You should have stayed on your farm in Louisiana."

"Why, for God's sake?"

"You have to ask? What a short memory. Do you think your sins stay in Louisiana, that they are forgiven and didn't follow you to Kansas? You killed a whole line of people... and you forget? The linage was no good, but my mother was a good woman, though she lived a hard tortured life. There was one thing the Cook family lived by. If you had an enemy you eliminated him. You don't wait for him to attack; you surprise him and bring the fight to his door. I am here."

"I've never heard the name Cook."

"You haven't heard the name Macie either, but you tried to run me down. Now you trail my man north to Kansas. I had to stop you."

"Your man... Tucker Shaw?"

"He and I made love."

"Love... how the hell would you know what love is?" You're a

Where Outlaws Roam
Royal Wade Kimes

Cajun bitch whore every man in camp has had at one time or another. You're the one I didn't get."

"Turns out I'm the one you should have gotten."

"I'll kill you, you bitch!" He drew his pistol but was unable to level it up. Macie rushed him and with one fast swing of a machete she severed his thumb, leaving him unable to cock the hammer back. Blood poured and ran down his wrist. Reed's eyes had horror in them. He grabbed his hand and winced in agony.

"Reed Fletcher bleeds like everyone else." She stepped away from him and watched as he looked wide eyed at his hand. "You're about to die."

"No, now look, I can make it up to you! I have more money than you could ever dream. Name it, whatever you wish, I'll make it happen for you!"

"The great Reed Fletcher begs." She heard a rock roll down the hill behind her. She jumped behind a big rock and slipped over the side of Eagles Ledge. Being from Louisiana and learning how to climb, swim, and just plain survive, she managed to slide down safely. She made her way around to where Reed had hidden his horse. She had tied hers on the same little tree, which was an offshoot of the main trail up. She mounted, untied the reins to Reed's mount and headed back towards Dye. She rode nearly a mile and heard a rifle shot. She pulled up. It came from Eagles Ledge. She knew whoever fired the shot had killed Reed Fletcher. It was a rifle report, and Fletcher's big rifle was broken. He was unable to shoot his pistol, and it wasn't a pistol shot anyway. Fletcher's saddle gun was in its scabbard, so it left only the mysterious unknown intruder. Should she go back and see?

Marshal Galt recognized imminent danger as he rode down Main Street of Melt, Kansas. He saw Tucker's horse and rode towards it. Main Street was lined shoulder to shoulder with people on both sides. One woman spat tobacco juice at the hooves of his horse as he passed by. He rode in beside the horse Simon Lick was still tied across. A sign above the door to the jail read 'Marshal Sam Talbert'. The town people left the boardwalk they were standing on and were coming straight for him with pitchforks, butcher knives, ax handles, and guns.

Where Outlaws Roam
Royal Wade Kimes

Tucker came out of the jail and stood beside Catcher. He drew his pistol and blew a hole in the ground at the feet of a tall man in suspenders and dilapidated old hat.

"If a whole bunch of you don't want to die; you better whoa up right there! When the shooting starts I won't be giving a whistle post damn if it's men, women, or children I'm killing. Your men folk are lying out on the prairie because they came against the law. They tried to kill us to get to a prisoner, plain and simple. I was determined then to kill as many as I could possibly kill, and I am now. I was trained to kill and kill I will."

The crowd now stood silently still. Dan Nolen came from an alley across the street. His leg was wrapped and his hand was bandaged. He had been shot twice. Marshal Talbert was with him.

"Marshal Galt, good to see you." He cut his eyes over to Tucker. "I suppose you're Deputy Marshal Shaw?"

"I am."

"I'm sure this unfortunate soul lying across his horse is your prisoner?"

"He was... and that is not and never was his horse."

"Well, I have Dan Nolen here under arrest for the murder of Simon Lick Tubbs, and for assault on two officers of the law. He come to me and confessed. I've just come from Doc Rose's with him. You boys shot him up fairly bad." Marshal Talbert took a moment to eye the crowd.

Marshal Galt spoke up. "I can tell you none of his wounds were from the deputy. Those would be mine." He gazed over at Tucker and smiled. Tucker had killed everyone he shot at.

"Well, regardless as to who did the shooting, he's going to jail."

Tucker spoke up. "What about the ones with him, where are they?"

"Dan here said he was the only one left. He said you two killed everyone else. Are you saying there are more?"

"Damn right I'm saying there are more."

"Well, unless you can positively identify them... there ain't."

Tucker's shoulders dropped. "Slick, slicker than pig grease, take the blame and swear be damned no one else was around. That's one trick I never got around to in the Royal Guard." He grinned at Marshal Talbert. "I guess they walk."

A man wearing a gun and sporting a nice set of clothes pushed through the town people and made his self-known. "Wait a minute, Marshal Talbert. You can't arrest Dan Nolen. It was me that was not killed. I was the last man, not Dan. I appreciate him trying to save my neck, but it just isn't so. He wasn't even there."

Then another man stepped forward. "That's a damn lie, Roy. I was the last man. Hell, I saw Henry fall and I hightailed it. I was the only one left. It was me what killed Simon Lick."

One after another stepped forward all confessing. Marshal Talbert was perplexed as to what to do. He was being outfoxed by the town. He looked up at Marshal Galt who was still mounted.

"Hell, don't look at me... I don't know what to tell you."

"You two follow me inside the jail. Dan, you come with me." Talbert looked at the other men standing in the street that had confessed. "You men stay where you are." He led Dan inside and shut the door. He then sat down at his desk and pulled out a bottle. "I normally don't drink this stuff during the day, but I need a stiff one." He turned it up and took a couple of swallows.

Marshal Galt chuckled. "You're in a pickle."

"Hell yes. I've not been in Melt, Kansas long enough to even see all its buildings and I'm in a... pickle." He corked the bottle and put it away and eyed Dan Nolen. "Dan, I think I'm going to arrest all of them. If Judge Hall can't decide which one is guilty, we'll just hang all of you."

Dan was looking at the floor in humility. He looked up when he heard that. "Now wait a minute! I confessed and I have the bullet holes to prove it was me! I was there!"

Marshal Talbert smiled. "What do you think, Deputy? Marshal Galt hasn't any nerve to say one way or another."

"I say let them all go, Dan included."

Marshal Talbert didn't expect that. "The hell you would?"

"Why not? They've paid a heavy price. The whole town has. They lost their former sheriff and deputy, and now because of ignorance, some of the women folk have lost their men." He glanced at Dan. "What gets me... Simon Lick Tubbs was going to

Where Outlaws Roam
Royal Wade Kimes

be found guilty. He was going to hang for his crimes. It was only a matter of time. Yet in foolish haste they rushed out to greet death instead of having patience and seeing justice done." He cut his eyes back to Dan. "Tell me, which one of those two ideas sounds the most noble?"

Dan ducked his eyes to the floor and didn't utter a word.

Marshal Talbert thought about it and came to the conclusion Deputy Shaw was right. He unlocked the handcuffs and told Dan to go home. He then eyed Tucker over. "I appreciate your input, Deputy."

"Marshal, if you've got a pencil and paper I'll make my report now."

"I do have some somewhere."

Tucker filled out his report and gave it to him. "Where can I get a bath?"

"Over at the Blue Blossom Hotel. I haven't been here long, but I understand a man can get some other things to go with the bath if he was so a mind."

"A bath will do." He smiled at the two marshals and left.

"Marshal Galt, that boy is a hell of a lawman. He handled that crowd outside singlehandedly. I wonder if he meant what he said?"

"Marshal, take it from me, he doesn't say a lot he doesn't mean."

"Then he's one of those all or nothing type lawmen. They say Bass Reeves is that way."

Marshal Galt had a monumental job ahead of him if he went through with trying to arrest Tucker Shaw for selling stolen property. Still, the law was the law. He glanced at Marshal Talbert and thought hard about what he was going to say before he opened his mouth.

"Marshal, I've got something bothering." He stopped.

"Yeah?" He waited for him to finish.

"Marshal Talbert, I've got to get a bath myself, maybe afterwards we can have a drink."

"Let's do that."

Something had begun to bother Marshal Galt, but he couldn't

bring himself to do anything about it. He was wishing he hadn't taken the money off the deceased vigilantes. No amount of reasoning, trying to make it right, made it right.

The following morning the two marshals rode out of Melt with the town people looking on. They rode side by side across the blue stemmed prairie grass enjoying the morning breeze. A red fox ran across in front of them on his way home. He had stayed out a little late.

Tucker pointed at him and laughed. "It looks like he's caught breakfast and taking it with him."

"Deputy, you handled things right nice yesterday."

Tucker smiled and kept his eyes straight ahead. "Well Marshal; myself I thought you could use some schooling."

"On what?" He stared at Tucker waiting for an answer.

"You ain't much of a shot. Dan Nolen looked like a sieve and not a shot one was anything to worry about." They both laughed and kept poking fun at one another until Tucker suddenly pulled Catcher up. "Whoa!"

They pulled their guns. "Tucker, check your side of the trail. I've got this one." Once they were satisfied, they rode up closer to Eagles Ledge and looked up.

"Marshal, that looks like Reed Fletcher hanging up there."

"It is."

They rode around the end of the ledge and climbed down off their horses. They made their way to the top watching for possible trouble as they climbed.

Marshal Galt took his knife out. "To be honest, I don't think the two of us can hoist him back up."

Reed was hanging from a rope tied to a small tree on top of the ledge. It looked as if his right leg was hung between two sharp thin rocks that came together.

"I'm going to cut the rope."

Tucker nodded and watched as the body hit the ground. They mounted up and rode down. Tucker stepped off first and examined Fletcher's wounds.

"Marshal, he's been stuck deep in the left shoulder. He's missing a thumb and has a bullet hole as close to between the

Where Outlaws Roam
Royal Wade Kimes

eyes as one can be put. One other thing, he has a cut on his left hand, an older cut. I guess maybe it was him that took the shot at me from top of the Dye Hotel."

"I guess so. Well, that answers one question, but his death presents another."

"Yeah... who killed him?" They both shrugged their shoulders at the same time.

Well, Deputy Shaw, let's bury him, sorry as he was, still needs burying."

"It's a nice place to be buried, Marshal. Let's put him under the edge of the ledge as much as we can."

He looked at Tucker oddly. "You ain't wanting to keep him dry are you?"

"Not at all... the closer to the edge the more the eagles can shit on him."

Marshal Galt tried not to laugh, but finally he just had to.

They got him buried and moved on out. "Deputy, I wonder where Reed's horse got off to?"

"Don't know. It's obvious he's gone."

They looked for him a few minutes and then headed out. He glanced over at Marshal Galt as they rode. "What are you smiling about?"

"Darla, I can't wait to see her again. I'm sure going to miss her when I have to go back to Fort Smith."

"Don't worry about her. After I've seen how you and your deputies work, I'll take care of her."

"Oh? You'd step in for a friend?" He laughed. "You'll think take care of her. You keep a close watch on her, make sure no bow legged rusty old men make a move on her. Shoot to kill." They both laughed and rode another five miles when Marshal Galt spoke up.

"You know I hate to see any man die, but if one had to, I'm damn glad it was Reed. It let me off the hook for taking you back. He's not around to press charges anymore. He was plain sorry anyway."

"He was sorry, but you shouldn't have been worried about taking me back... you weren't about to. There's a job comes along ever now and again above our pay scale."

"Is that a fact?" Marshal Galt put on a face of mischievous doubt. The two of them were becoming good friends.

Where Outlaws Roam
Royal Wade Kimes

Chapter 20

One week later a reluctant Marshal Galt rode out of Dye, Kansas with a red and black garter around his sleeve belonging to Darla. Tucker stood beside her as she waved goodbye to him. Like her he hated to see him leave, they had become good friends.

Deputy Farley was also looking like a lost hound with drooped eyes. Billie Sway was in tears and was being consoled by Connie. The other sister was taking care of their business and wasn't able to see the lawmen off. The only one not bothered by the farewells was Deputy Nelson. He hadn't gotten tangled up with the female side of things. He rode along beside Marshal Galt and Deputy Farley shaking his head.

Tucker had been made Marshal of Dye, Kansas and the county, and was to cover the counties that joined its four sides. It turned out Marshal Lambert of Melt, Kansas filled out his own report. His filing was regarding Deputy Shaw and the way he handled a vigilante crowd. The Kansas Governor wasted little time. He had already received a letter from Marshal Sanders asking he be relieved of duty and to put Tucker Shaw in his place as Marshal.

Tucker was living where outlaws roam and had become a part of the Wild West. It never occurred to him he would play a part in it. He turned to walk to his office when he saw someone go around the corner of the jail.

There was a barefoot track in the dust of the alley way when he bent down to examine the ground. It was a kid or woman's track. He was down on one knee looking straight ahead wondering if someone needed help, and had found him gone. Maybe they were behind the jail on First Street waiting in a wagon. He stood and walked to the back but saw no one.

"Marshal!"

He turned and walked back to Front Street. "Darla?"

"Are you looking for someone back there?"

"Well, as a matter of fact I was."

"I thought so."

"Darla, do you know something about this?"

"I might. Yesterday morning I was fixing my hair at the mirror while Marshal Galt slept. The dresser sits to the side of the window in the hotel. Well, yesterday morning I saw a young lady standing at the door of the jail. She wasn't dressed well... but Marshal, she was stunning anyway. She had long black hair, cream colored skin and a shape that was cast from an hour glass. She was barefooted and carried a rifle. She also had a pistol strapped around her. I'd say if she's still hanging around your jail, you'll not have to look for her, she'll find you."

That dark night in the Cook camp came rushing back to him. He could see her in the candlelight, her magnificent shape, and he could feel her slide across him like she did that night before he was put to sleep with some kind of powdery drug. She glistened in the candlelight and the fire danced in her eyes. His thoughts suddenly stopped at something he hadn't thought of. Since that night he hadn't wanted another woman. Why? He was a known woman chaser back home. He could have any woman he wanted, and he had. He felt a surge inside him. Why did she excite him so much?

"Marshal, Marshal, where did you go?"

"Darla." He chuckled. "On a long journey from the past."

"It must be one heck of a journey by the glow that was on your face."

"It was. Darla, I've got to get about law business. If you happen to see this woman, let her know I'm available to talk with her if she needs me."

"I'll do that." She made an expression with her eyes and lips of, you're not fooling me. "Marshal, I think I know what she needs and she's looking to you to give it to her."

He laughed. "I'll do my best." He turned and went into his office inside the jail.

Simon Lick's partner Lou Pitman had been in jail for over a week waiting papers as to where he would be tried for bank robbery. It couldn't be proved he did any shooting at any of the robberies; therefore he was being tried for robbery only. It was noon when Connie Sway came in with the prisoner's meal and sat the tray on Marshal Shaw's desk.

"Marshal, the prisoner's dinner. It's a roast with potatoes and carrots."

"That sure smells good. I've got to make tracks over there and try it out."

"You should. We have pie for desert."

"I'll feed Pitman and be over."

Connie was studying him. "Marshal, I don't believe I've ever met a man quite like you. I would have bet my part of Sisters that you would have been chasing Billie. Instead you let Deputy Farley move in. Are you sick or do you just not care for women?"

"Oh... Connie, if you only knew. I was known as an outright woman chaser in Great Britain. No daughter was safe in London or anywhere else if I heard of them."

"What changed?"

"A dark eyed beauty I can't seem to forget, but keeps appearing and disappearing like a ghost."

"In your mind?"

"Sometimes."

Connie looked at him strangely. She decided not to probe any further and left his office, inviting him over to Sisters.

She had only been gone a few seconds when Pitman sang out. "Marshal, you saved me from hanging once. I owe you. There's something I ought to tell you. I heard the lady ask you about her sister, and you saying something about a dark eyed lady. Well, I seen her."

Tucker turned instantly. "Where?"

"Standing in front of your desk. She went around to the backside of it and sat down. She opened the drawers and even had a sip of your whiskey. When she got up to leave she looked at me and smiled. Then she took her finger and put it up to her lips... you know, telling me to be quiet about her being here." He paused. "Marshal, she's the most beautiful woman I ever laid eyes on. Something else, I think she might be the most deadly woman I ever laid eyes on. Me running in the circles I have, ya get to kind of knowing who's what."

"When was she in here?"

"This morning before daylight."

Tucker went around to his desk and sat down. He pulled the

drawers out and in the bottom of the left hand bottom drawer was a folded white piece of paper. He picked it up and opened it.

"Love, this is Macie. I've traveled far and done much to see that you were safe. My family was killed by Reed Fletcher, my mother, all of them. He came after me with dogs and men. I was able to elude them. I went back to the Fletcher Farm once I was sure it was safe, and learned from the black man they called Lester that you had escaped. I also learned Reed was on your trail. I followed. I would very much like to see you tonight. I need you. I need you bad. There is a barn outside of town to the south I have stayed in the last night or two. No one comes there. I will meet you after dark.

Macie

Tucker had many emotions and thoughts running through his head. He was drawn to her and he didn't understand it. He had resisted many beautiful women in the past, played with them actually. They all came from well-to-do families having little consideration for anyone but themselves. Still they were beautiful and exceedingly willing. He replayed the night in the tent and the events that led up to it. He also wondered if she had anything to do with the deaths of Fletcher's men and Reed Fletcher himself. The note would make a good lawman wonder. He hoped that wasn't the case, though she had twice the reason to kill them. She lost her clan, and in her mind her lover was in danger.

Tucker hadn't been in America long, but he was learning you don't take anyone or anything at face value. The idea a slender well put together lady could take out men that made livings killing was almost impossible to imagine. But Macie wasn't any ordinary woman; she was at least half Cajun. From what he had seen so far they were a people that liked to eat, party, fight, make love, and continuously.

He put the note in his vest pocket and left for Sisters. He was hungry, though he had a lot on his mind.

Billie came to his table to take his order. She never looked at

Where Outlaws Roam
Royal Wade Kimes

him directly one time. "What would you like to drink?"

"A spot of tea would be fine." He smiled as he was trying to make her smile and look his way. He had been careful not to use many of the English expressions.

"We have roast or fried chicken today."

"The roast if you don't mind."

She looked him dead in the eyes. "I don't know, I must not mind, if I did I wouldn't wait on you."

"Billie, what's gotten under your blanket?"

"Well, it sure hasn't been you." She turned and left to turn in his order. When she came back with the tea he caught hold of her hand.

"I thought you and Farley were cozying up together?"

"Are all you Brits so dumb?" She jerked her hand loose and left.

He smiled and whispered. "We must be."

He ate a hot dinner with a cold waitress looking on. When he finished he paid Connie at the counter and stood staring at her. "What's the story on Farley and Billie?"

"I think she rubbed up to him to get a reaction out of you. When she didn't get it, she got angry at you."

"Well, what were all the tears about when Farley was riding out? I thought her heart had shattered into a thousand pieces the way she carried on."

"I think that was for you, too."

"Huh."

He left Sisters and went back to his office and sat down behind his desk. Pitman could see him from his cell.

"Something bothering you, Marshal?"

Pitman was somewhere in the neighborhood of thirty-five. He'd done some living in those years.

"Pitman, I'm one mixed up Marshal. I can pretty much see through anything... but women are a whole different story. I have two of them working on me at the same time. You know what I think? I think it's payback for all the times I mistreated well intentioned ladies in my past. I'd get them all worked up and thinking I was mad about them, and then drop them like a hot coal. I'm getting what I deserve."

"Ah, Marshal, when you say working on you, do you mean you're torn between the two? You don't know which one you should latch on to?"

"That pretty much sums it up."

"Well, I'm no damn Romeo, but in my truck with women I've found sitting back and doing nothing works best. It always seems to work its self out."

"Pitman, how could I put any faith in a man that uses 'truck' for a relationship with a woman?"

"Like I said, I ain't no Romeo, but my method always worked."
Pitman, do you have a woman?"

"I damn sure do. She's from the Oklahoma Territory, a fine woman. She ain't no looker, but she's mine."

"There's something to be said for that." He pulled Macie's note out again and read it. He found himself anxious for nightfall."

Macie waited until she saw Tucker go into the barn and light a lantern before she left her place of hiding beside the road. She didn't make a sound approaching the entrance. She stood silently listening for horses hooves along the road. When she was sure there were none she went in. Tucker was holding the lantern up above his head trying to see if she was in the loft.

"Tucker, I'm behind you."

He whirled with gun drawn. "Macie, never do that. I could have shot you."

She walked to him in five long strides and jumped. Her arms wrapped around his neck as she kissed him passionately on the lips. He dropped his rifle but held onto the lantern. He took his free hand and pulled her loose from him.

"Macie, give me a second to look at you! I've got to put this lantern down."

"I want you, Tucker. I want you like that night in the tent."

Now he knew. He had made love to her. Though he didn't remember, she certainly did. He had wondered all this time.

She began to undress in front of him in the lantern light. There was a stall full of hay and she backed him into it. "I need you bad."

Where Outlaws Roam
Royal Wade Kimes

"Don't you think we ought to find a safer place to be together?"

Her blouse was gone and her pants were straining to come down over her beautiful hips. Once she was completely naked in the lantern light, no man could have resisted. He began taking his clothes off and suddenly she was helping. He picked her up and threw her on the loose hay. He then walked in front of the lantern blocking out its beam of light as he slid atop her. She made a cooing sound and then fell into rhythm.

It was daylight before Tucker came out of the barn. He had Macie by the hand as he walked out to an old well. He drew a bucket of water and washed his face.

"Macie, I can't have you sleeping out here. I also can't have you walking around barefooted."

"Why not? I've walked all over creation barefooted. As for sleeping, the barn is a palace compared to what Morrell and his brothers had us in."

"You're not with Morrell now, you're with me. I'm getting you a room at the Dye Hotel."

"Are you sure?" She looked at him with her dark eyes and smiled. She was beyond beautiful; she was striking in every way imaginable.

Tucker wondered how a creature like her could have been born into what she was. There was something that drew him to her like no other woman he had ever known. Was it her animal like behavior and instincts? Was it her body? Was it the way she spoke or was it all of those things?

"Okay, Tucker, if you're sure, then I will get my horse and go into town with you. Of course you know we're going to be stared at... especially by the Sway Sisters."

"You know about them?"

"I've been in town and have seen the act the little one has put on for you. She is... how do you say... deceitful, and plays games. If you want a man, tell him you want him. Be honest with him. It is the only way to have a relationship. If it is threaded with lies it cannot survive."

Tucker looked at her and marveled. "How did you learn that

from where you come from?"

"My mother taught me things when the men folk weren't around. She said life wasn't like what she and I were enduring. I have found that to be right since I have come north."

"I see. Then you're mother wasn't born in the swamps?"

"No. she lived in a little town in Mississippi. Morrell come along and made her think he was something he wasn't. He fooled her. Once he had her in the swamp there wasn't any coming out."

Tucker shook his head in disgust. "She was a prisoner is what she was. One thing I've been wondering about. You call your father, Morrell... why?"

"He was my father by blood, but blood only. He never showed me love and for sure didn't take time being a father to me. Somehow, Morrell seemed more right than calling him father. And as for mother being a prisoner, you could say that. She and I both were until close to the end. When all the people were wiped out in the swamps we began to see the outside once in a while. We had to make quick trips to buy supplies since there were no runners to bring in things. I made notes on how we got to certain places, and what direction was what. When my family was killed by Reed Fletcher I put my knowledge to work on how to get free of the swamp." She smiled and took a deep breath. "I like this state called Kansas."

"I do too." He looked around him and then to her. "Where's your horse? You do have one?"

"I have two." She left and returned with a nice looking mare and a fine gelding. Tucker stared at the gelding. He was a well-bred boy. He saw the stock of the lever rifle sticking out from the scabbard. There were two letters in silver on it, R.F. for Reed Fletcher.

"Macie, where'd this horse come from?"

"I got him from a man that didn't need him anymore."

"Who would not need a horse like him anymore? That boy is well bred."

"A dead man doesn't need one."

"Macie, don't say anymore. I don't want to know where you got him. What I do want you to do is get rid of him and that

Where Outlaws Roam
Royal Wade Kimes

rifle."

"Why?"

"Because the horse and rifle belonged to someone that is dead, and I'm guessing it wasn't from natural causes. So leave him here. Give him to someone or sell him. While I'm making the rounds in town, you get back out here and get him gone."

"Why?" She really didn't understand.

"That horse and rifle could link you to something that would separate us forever."

Without hesitation she answered. "Okay then." She smiled and led the horses back into the woods behind the barn. She came back smiling and ready to go. "I have a makeshift corral back in the woods with water and grass for them. I will get him gone as you say tonight."

"I don't want to know how or anything about it."

She smiled and batted her dark eyes at him. "Do all lawmen worry around like you? Life is too short for much worry."

He realized Macie just took things as they came and worried about none of them. She did what she thought had to be done and that was the end of it. Where she came from there wasn't any law. The swamp people took care of their own and their own problems. He couldn't fault her for doing what she was taught and had always done from birth. He could see that, but how could he ever convince a court? How could he make them see her side of the story, her life? He couldn't. It would be an impossible task.

"Macie, do me a favor. "If anyone was to ask you about Reed Fletcher or anyone from Louisiana, you tell them nothing."

"Why?" She frowned at him.

Tucker thought she had the cutest little frown he had ever seen. Her little nose wrinkled up some when she frowned and her eyes were shining. "Because you and I both might land in jail."

"They put lawmen in jail?"

"It's been known to happen."

"That is one thing Kansas has wrong. They make things too complicated. On the Louisiana Bayou it's cut and dry. It's yes, no, guilty, not guilty, and the matter is taken care of. The law should be as such."

"I wish it were that simple. I find myself trying to conduct business with three worlds, the Queen of Great Britain, the American West, and the Louisiana Cajun. That's one hell of a mix." He began to laugh which was something he used to do all the time, but of late had stopped. It had stopped because he was accepting responsibility now, something he hadn't done in Great Britain.

He suddenly remembered a talk he had once with Admiral Robert Fetter. Robert told him that if he could just once apply himself to task at hand, he might be surprised at the harmonious outcome, and that the result of such a thing might cause him to grow up. He realized now he was speaking of responsibility. Robert had several talks with him regarding respect and leadership. He smiled. He found his becoming a United States Marshal had changed him. He was a man now, not a party boy. He saw things differently and wasn't even aware of it until this very moment.

Then an idea hit him. He wanted to see Lee Paulson the newspaper man as soon as he got back to town. He wanted him to publish a letter in the London Morning Paper signaling the Queen and his family the rival between them was over. He felt a burden lift the moment he had the thought.

"Macie, we're riding into town with you on behind me. Let them stare. I don't give a damn what anyone says or thinks. I'm getting you a room in the Dye Hotel and you will have that room until something else can be worked out. If you have anything and I mean anything that connects you with Louisiana... get rid of it, burn it, bury it, but get rid of it."

She looked at him with serious eyes. "I think I understand now. The law is different with the... the Queen where you are from than it is here, and the law is different where I am from, than it is here. Americas' west is very different, right? It has a whole set of rules and laws that are maybe stupid, but somehow abided by?"

He smiled as he thought about that. "Yeah, I guess you could say that. Maybe that's why the West breeds so many outlaws. There are too damn many laws."

"Tucker, don't worry. We will be fine." She kissed him on the lips and they mounted up. She wrapped her arms around him from behind. "Let's show them what you found."

Chapter 21

Twelve days later Tucker Shaw's father, Ira Shaw was summoned to the Queen's Palace. He was met by the Royal Guards at the entrance and shown to a large marble and gray stone room. One whole wall was filled with books nearly to the ceiling. A stepladder was at each end of the wall for use in retrieving books near the top of the twenty foot ceiling. On the wall opposite it, was hanging a large portrait of the Queen with pictures of past events surrounding it. At the end of the room was a huge desk with glass turquoise lamps laced with crystal beads sitting on each end. Two leather chairs sat in front of the desk with five foot backs on them. When Ira sat down in it to wait for the Queen he practically disappeared, giving him the feeling of being small. Maybe that was the idea. Whether it was or not he didn't like it and felt uncomfortable. He was made to wait for thirty minutes, which added to his feeling of being somewhat insignificant in the great scheme of things called life.

"I'm sorry, Ira, for keeping you waiting." The Queen walked to her desk accompanied by two pristine dressed Royal Guards and two women carrying a tray with a pure silver coffee pot and two silver cups. "Tell me, does Ira Shaw drink coffee?"

"I do. I've had coffee with you before… though it has been some time ago."

"Yes, yes, I'm sure. I have so many guests and so many things to see to, I tend to forget sometimes."

"That's quite alright. If coffee is all we forget we're in good shape." He smiled his normal fake smile.

"Ira, do you have any idea why I have called you here so early in the morning?"

"I… I guess not. I'm in hopes it is a position within the Parliament."

She didn't change expression at his comment as she waved the maid to stop pouring. The maid then dropped one tablespoon of sugar in the brew, stirred it twice very slowly and sat it in front of the Queen who had sat down at her desk. She then poured another cup two thirds full and turned to Ira. "Mister Shaw, how do you like your coffee?"

Where Outlaws Roam
Royal Wade Kimes

"Black is fine." He was looking her bottom over as he answered. "What is your name?"

The maid glanced quickly at the Queen while blushing at his question. His taking the liberty to ask a member of the Queen's personnel her name was something not allowed. The Queen had sipped her coffee and slowly sat it down. She looked at both maids with kind but directing eyes.

"That will be all."

They left and shut the large doors to the magnificent room. The Royal Guards stood like statues at each side of it and on the outside of the door stood two more. The Queen waited until the doors were closed before she addressed him.

"You married my sister and that has given you certain privileges. Trying to bed one of my maids is not one of them. Don't forget yourself while in my presence again. You are my sister's husband, and that is all that is keeping you from being removed from my presence. Your lack of respect and arrogance is exceedingly mystifying. How is it you feel you can take liberties within the confines of the Royal Palace? You and I aren't friends, Ira. Being connected to me by marriage is not something I chose... in fact I find it almost impossible to believe it is a reality... however it is... for there you sit." She sipped her coffee. "How is your coffee, Ira?"

He was so tongue lashed by the Queen he hesitated before answering. "Coffee? Oh, fine, yes fine."

"Ira, I know my sister is not happy with you; she hasn't been from day one. She and I both know you only married her to get inside the walls of the Royal Palace. You're a fool, Ira Shaw. You're married to a lovely woman who would have given her life for you in the beginning had you asked. She gave you a child that you had nothing to do with. Admiral Fetter did more with and paid more attention to your child than you did. I'm indebted to him for that. At least Tucker had the admiral as a role model for a father. Now that Tucker's name has come up, I ask again, do you know why you are here?"

"Well, no, I'm sure it's not the Parliament seat."

"Parliament? Oh Ira, you do have a rather large set don't you?

Maybe that's why my sister made the biggest mistake of her life." She stared a hole in him. "Ira, if you can forget your own aspirations for just a little while, we need to look at a situation we have. I'm trying to get in touch with Lee Paulson in the United States, in hopes he can intercept Admiral Fetter before he finds Tucker."

"Why? Are you calling him off? I don't understand. I was told Tucker's termination was crucial for the wellbeing of the country and you the Queen."

"Ira, am I to understand you would rather see your son dead?"

He sat his coffee on a small table beside his chair. "I think it would be best for all of us... yes."

"Aren't you the caring father? You are a disgrace as a father and a man." She picked the spoon up sitting beside her saucer and tapped the side of her cup in frustration and aggravation. "It might interest you to know that Tucker has published a public apology for his actions and anything he may have said in the past. He also has stated that the divisions between us are no longer there." She paused. "My heart quickened when I read the lengthy story this morning. Your son is a United States Marshal now. He has changed. If we can reverse the order regarding elimination of Tucker Shaw... we must. I know Admiral Fetter hasn't arrived there yet, but I haven't any way to reach him, that is, quickly enough to stop him from carrying out the assignment, other than Lee Paulson. He lives in the same township Tucker is the Marshal of."

Ira changed his tune suddenly. "You're right. I'm ashamed of myself. If Tucker has had a change of heart, if he's ready to make amends, then so shall I be."

The Queen smiled but was somewhat skeptical. "I'd like to believe that."

"Well... he is my blood. Maybe I need to do a little growing up myself."

She half smiled again as she was in deep thought. "Good, I'm glad to hear that, for my sister's sake."

"Have you sent the letter yet?"

"I'm not sending a letter. It would be futile. It would never get there in time. I planned to send a telegram. The problem is the

Where Outlaws Roam
Royal Wade Kimes

cable is down. I was told they are working to get it restored. Once it is useable I'll send the telegram. It could be days even weeks. I pray it's not too late."

She purposely stopped and stared at him. "If and when you see Tucker again, you are to treat him with utmost respect. You will act as if you care about him whether you do or not. You will treat his mother, your wife, the same. Do we understand one another?"

"I think that's clear. I must do my part, but does anyone fool Tucker? I think not." He smiled. "I tell you what I can do. I can start acting like a father right now and camp at the telegraph office until the cable is up and running.

She gazed across the desk at him. "I think that would be a good gesture of faith. She reached in a drawer and pulled out a paper. She folded it and addressed it herself. This goes to Dye, Kansas. Pray God's speed... that it gets there in time to stop a death."

Ira took the message, tipped his hat and hurried out of the palace. He crossed the arched stone bridge that crossed the small body of water in front of the palace. As he crossed it he dropped the message over the side. He watched as it floated downstream and finally was sucked under the water. He smiled and spoke aloud to himself. "I'm sorry Tucker, but your luck ran out." He looked back at the Queen's Palace. "It's sent." He laughed as he left the grounds of the palace.

Several weeks later Angel Hound saw three men walk into the Fort Smith Marshals Office. He slipped in behind them and listened at the door.

"Is the Marshal here?"

"Which one, we have several?"

"Any one of the officers would do. By the way, what is your capacity in this office?"

"Well, my capacity in this office is the lowly clerk, have been the lowly clerk for twenty some years. I think the question is who the hell are you?"

"I'm Admiral Fetter from Great Britain."

"Well, I'm damned impressed. We handed you boys your asses in eighteen twelve, have you come back for more?"

Where Outlaws Roam
Royal Wade Kimes

Admiral Fetter turned bright red. "I'm not here to be insulted. We're here trying to inquire of Tucker Shaw. We have been commissioned by the Queen of Great Britain herself to find him. His mother is ill and wants to see him before her passing."

"Well, if that's the case, you can find Marshal Tucker up in Dye, Kansas."

"Marshal? I thought he was a deputy." He smiled at the news. Tucker had moved up in his rank.

"He made Marshal some time ago and making a damn good one."

"I was aware he was in some village by the name of, Dye, but wasn't sure he was still there. My good man, could you tell us how to get there?"

"I sure can." The clerk told them what route to take and they left right away, but not before Angel Hound beat a trail back to the Mission.

"Mother, Immanuel!" He ran through the inner courtyard looking for Ina, his mother. She came out of a side room in a hurry when she heard his frantic call.

"Angel, here I's is!"

"Mama, I seen three men at the marshals office, and they be looking for Mister Tucker Shaw. They say they be here by the order of a Queen. They says Mister Tucker's mother bad shape. But I has a feeling that ain't true."

Ina looked hard into Angel's eyes. "Now what makes you think such?"

"Mama, I've spent the last few years learning whats to watch for when men be talking. Two of the men smiled too much and the one called Admiral Fetter was too quick to leave once he gets his information. They didn't thanks the man what told them how to get to where Mister Tucker be. A man what ain't ready to return kindness be having darkness in his heart and trouble on his mind."

Bishop Emanuel Ortega was standing back a ways listening to him. He stepped up beside him. "Ina, this young man has learned much since coming to the Mission. He has become wise in the heart and mind."

Angel smiled. "Bishop Emanuel, Mama, I have to go warn

Where Outlaws Roam
Royal Wade Kimes

Mister Tucker."

"How?"

"I can run. I was called Angel Hound by Reed Fletcher and his guards 'cause I could run so fast. I can run long too. I cuts across hills and streams and get to Dye before a horse can." He grinned. "Mama, I can do it."

The Bishop spoke then. "Ina, Angel, why not send a telegram instead?"

Angel seemed stunned. He hadn't thought of that. Ina grinned. "I's be liking that idea Bishop Ortega."

They all three went down to the telegraph office which was six blocks down the street. Bishop Ortega had the coins to pay for the telegram and Angel knew what to say. Ina was along for the excitement of it all. When they got there they were sorely disappointed.

A squint eyed little man went to shaking his head negatively. "I'm sorry, Bishop, I wish there was something I could do, but there isn't. A black cyclone blew through between here and Dye two days ago and has taken down telegraph wire for two miles. I hear-ed it would be three more days 'fore its up and telegraphing again."

Angel Hound looked at Ina and the Bishop, and then grinned. "I always knowed my gift to run might come in handy one day. I hopes it saves Mister Tucker's life."

Ina hugged him. "Son, you be careful."

"I be careful, Mama. It's those Kansas Jackrabbits that better be careful. I'll run right over them."

Once they stopped laughing they went back to the Mission and Ina packed jerky, hardtack, and filled a canteen with water. She fixed the sack where it would ride close to his lower back. It didn't weigh much and wouldn't be in the way of his shoulders when he ran. He said goodbye and left in a trot that was picking up with each step. By the time he got to the river he was striding. He ran for a half mile and caught the ferryboat and crossed to the Oklahoma Territory side of the river.

"Boy, where are you going?"

Angel Hound looked up and smiled. There was a big busted red headed woman bent down over him awaiting an answer. "I be headed to see a friend."

"Are you walking, must not be far?"

"Be far enough."

"We're headed west. That's my carriage over there."

Angel Hound looked at it and his eyes lit up. "That be the most prettiest thing I ever seen on wheels. It be red and white, and seem bigger than what I've seen. Most I see are black."

She laughed "I like big and never was much on being just one in a crowd."

She was still bent over looking at him, and Angel Hound understood what she meant, as her breast were staring him in the face. She was… big.

"Ma'am, I understands." He swallowed hard.

"How far west are you traveling, maybe we could give you a ride?"

"I be going twenty or so miles west and then I turn north. You keeps saying 'we' can give me a ride. Who we be?"

The big busted red head stood up. "Girls."

Angel Hound looked the direction the red head was looking, which was at the other end of the ferryboat. There were five girls that ranged from eighteen to twenty standing there. If all five of them had gone in together to make one dress with what they were wearing, they would have come up short.

It was then he knew the red head was a madam and those were her girls.

"Well, I don't know 'bout all that. I be in a hurry."

"Honey child, you'll have the ride of your life."

Angel Hound rode twenty of the longest fastest miles in his life in a red and white carriage. He now knew why the carriage was red, it fit. He was never so glad to be getting off of an iron wheeled carriage ride in his whole life. It was the first carriage he had ever ridden in, and one he would never forget. The girls threw kisses at him and giggled until out of sight. He felt they knew he was embarrassed and over his head with women who made their living in bed. He'd never been with a woman and they knew it. He guessed it would be a while yet before he ever was. He smiled and took off in a run.

Where Outlaws Roam
Royal Wade Kimes

He ran for four miles and was making good time. His strides were good and his breathing was smooth and steady. His heart was beating slowly like a big steam engine pushing a paddleboat up river. He had checked his heart beat once after running a three mile race and it was fifty- three seconds a minute. That gave him the ability to run long distances without tiring.

He came to a stream of water running across blue stem prairie grass. It wound around in different directions and split off in places. He drank his fill, not too much, but enough and started on. He ran until dark and found a grove of trees standing in the middle of the wide open prairie. There was a blue pool of water in the middle of them, and a coyote burst out of the timber when he came running in. He examined the trees after getting a drink, and then climbed one. He climbed to thirty feet and lay across two very large limbs. He ate a piece of jerky and hardtack and then tied himself in the tree with the rope used for his sack. He smiled and dozed off for the night. Tomorrow would be a long fast day.

At eight o'clock in the evening Tucker knocked on Macie's door at the Dye Hotel. She was staying there until something came available to rent. That hadn't happened because of a shortage of houses in Dye. Tucker was there to take her to Sisters for supper. They hadn't been to Sisters since he brought her to town. They stayed away because of the way Billie felt about her, and the town was very much aware that Billie was passed over for Macie. The town was somewhat sympathetic to Billie since she was a native to the town and Macie came out of nowhere. They walked in and were seated by a doorman in black tails and tie. Candles half way up and along the walls lit the whole place, and two candles were placed at each table. A fragrance filled the air that was of a flower scent. A three piece band was playing softly in the far corner, which added to an already romantic mood.

They were in luck. Billie was off for the night. They were waited on by Kathy and the night was almost magical. Tucker had never been serious about a woman in his life, and to fall in love was out of the question. But as he stared across the table at the most beautiful creature his eyes had ever looked upon, he thought he just might be. Her lips curved up and around to perfection, her eyes always danced in any kind of light, and her shape drove him insane. Over the last seven or eight weeks he had grown to understand her even more. He found that her heart was the biggest asset of all and she was honest to a fault. There wasn't any foolishness and she spoke her mind plain. Macie Cook could one day be Macie Shaw.

Kathy came back after supper was had and brought them desert. It was apple pie served with coffee. Tucker could not take his eyes off of Macie. He felt like he was in a dream. She smiled and the light picked up the shine on her lips. "Tucker, you are in for a long evening, treating me to such a... a night."

"It's called 'romantic night'."

She smiled as she softly blew on a bite of her pie. Her lips were inviting and she knew it. She had Tucker Shaw where she wanted him... in her heart and around her finger. In a little while she would have him in her bed. The night would go from candlelight and wine to wild passionate out of control love, two lovers glistening in moonbeams of light flooding through a hotel window.

Marshal Galt and Deputy Farley were on their way to Fort Smith from the Oklahoma Territory after apprehending a horse thief. They were on the ferryboat crossing to the Arkansas side when Marshal Galt saw something familiar. He walked over to a man holding the reins to a fine looking horse.

"Mister, where are you from?"

"I'm not one to give out information, especially on my person."

"I promise it'll be okay. I'm a United States Marshal out of Fort Smith. Do I need to ask you again where you're from?"

"I guess not. I'm from Kansas." He ducked his head down and wouldn't look at Marshal Galt after that exchange.

"What are you doing down here?"

"Well, the horse and mule auction is this weekend. I'm figuring maybe to sell one and buy a couple."

"I take it you're a trader?"

"I am."

"Mind me asking where you picked up this gelding you're

Where Outlaws Roam
Royal Wade Kimes

holding here?"

"I bought him from an old man in Sota, Kansas."

"Where's that at from Dye?"

"Twenty miles north." He eyed the marshal. "Why do you ask?"

"How old is this old man you bought him from?"

"Eighty-five, maybe ninety. He's gone down a lot in the last year. I've bought a many a team off that old man."

"I see. Ah, did he happen to say where he come on to this fine gelding?"

The man seemed reluctant to speak. Finally he did. "Is this here horse of mine stoled or something?"

"He was, but not anymore. The man that originally owned him is dead. That horse came from Louisiana."

"Well, all I can tell you; he said a young lady sold him the horse rigging and all. I bought the whole shooting match. I even got this lever gun in the deal. Hell of a rifle. Do these letters on the stock here match up to the man you think owned this ole boy?"

The letters R.F. were inlayed in silver on the stock. "They do for a fact."

"What was the man's name?"

"Reed Fletcher, he wasn't much."

"Bad one was he?"

"Bad enough."

Marshal Galt went back and stood beside Deputy Farley and the gruff looking horse thief."

"What's up, Marshal?"

"Well Deputy, I think we need to take a ride to Dye, Kansas."

Deputy Farley's eyes got big and sparkled in the moonlight. "When do we leave?"

He laughed. "Farley, that Billie Sway girl is out there ain't she? I forgot about that. I think maybe tomorrow." He paused and rubbed his chin. "Farley, Marshal Shaw is seeing a gal out there ain't he?"

"Yeah, according to Billie's letters she's a dark eyed rather pretty lady. Said she's a stranger in town, said she came out of nowhere. It seems Marshal Shaw came riding in with her back of his saddle one day, and they've been together since."

"Yeah, I bet her and that horse yonder have something in common."

Farley raised one eye brow as he looked at him. "What's that, Marshal?"

"I bet they're both from Louisiana."

Where Outlaws Roam
Royal Wade Kimes

Chapter 22

Tucker and Macie were breathing heavily lying beside one another in the darkness of her room. She was smiling but he didn't know it.

"Are you okay, Tucker?"

"Honey, I've not been okay since I met you. I've been out of my head."

Suddenly he heard shots being fired out in the street somewhere. He jumped from the bed and hurriedly got dressed. "I hope those shots are just some drunk blowing off steam."

"Be careful."

He ran out of her room and down the stairs. He stopped at the hotel entrance and carefully looked out at the street. There was a man standing in front of the jail. He stepped out and walked towards him.

"Mister, what's your problem?"

An elderly but tough looking cowboy whirled around to face Tucker with a gun already in his hand. "Are you the marshal?"

"I am."

"Well, you've had my boy Lou Pitman locked up in your jail for a damned eternity. I've come to get him out. If the law ain't going to try him, then he needs to be let go."

"I agree, Mister Pitman."

The elderly Pitman looked surprised. "You do?"

"I surely do. However, I am not the one who makes that decision."

"Well I be damned, you're powerless? Like me?"

"Seems so. I tell you what we can do, I can write a letter to the Governor of Kansas and ask Lou be released until trial if they're not going to do anything. I'm sure he will be given credit for time served."

"Like hell. My boy is innocent!"

"I'm sure he is." He felt it better not to argue the fact.

"You don't believe me?"

"I didn't say that."

Lou was in Dawson, Kansas with me and my cowpunchers the week all those bank robberies went down. Yeah, he rode with

Where Outlaws Roam
Royal Wade Kimes

Tubbs a few times, Simon Lick I think they call him, but he wasn't with him when Dye and Melt was robbed."

"Then why hasn't he said something?"

"Lou is a funny boy. He figures he's done enough he ought to pay for some of it. I don't see it that way. I say if you get away with it, stay away with it."

Tucker chuckled. "Makes sense to me." He studied Mister Pitman for a moment. "Sir, what's your name?"

"Ray Pitman."

"Well Ray, what you say we go in and have a talk with Lou?"

Ray eyed the marshal with skepticism. "This some kind of trick? I mean, are you arresting me for disturbing the peace or something?"

"Nah, I just want the facts and maybe get to the truth."

They went inside and Tucker unlocked Lou Pitman's door. He made some coffee and had him and his father sit down.

"Lou, your father says you were in Dawson the week of the robberies in Dye and Melt, is that true?"

"I guess so."

"Look, Lou, it'd be one thing to go to jail for something you did, but it's a whole 'nother for something you didn't. But of course there is the little incident where you and your gang were setting up to ambush me, to spring Simon Lick."

Lou tilted his head down toward the floor. "Yeah... but I'd say I paid for that. I took a rifle slug in my left cheek and I've been in jail for quite a spell. That ole sawbones doctor poked and jabbed until I felt like a pincushion. I paid dearly for it already."

Ray eyed his son over. "What kind of a damn son are you? Us Pitman's don't ambush or back shoot no one."

"Lou glanced at his father but avoided eye contact. "Wasn't my idea. I was just there."

Tucker smiled at the two men. "How is it you came to be with them if you weren't in on the holdups?"

"When Simon Lick was caught, the boys come looking for me to help break him out of jail. It happened we didn't get to Fort Smith in time to break him out. Marshal Sanders had left with him heading for Dye. Naturally we figured it would be no trick a tall to break him loose from a lone marshal. To be honest, we

Where Outlaws Roam
Royal Wade Kimes

thought it was going to be easy after we saw Marshal Sanders was out of the picture. We watched you for a while and decided you were a tenderfoot... but it didn't turn out to be so." He coked his head side ways to Tucker. "You're a damn good shot with that rifle of yours."

"Ray, do you have any other witnesses that would swear Lou was in Dawson with you and the hands, other than your own men?"

"Sally Couch. She works at Dawson. They had a big square dance one night and she danced with me, Lou, and two or three others. She's a type setter for the paper there."

"I tell you what you do. You get me a sworn affidavit from her, signed, and a lawyer or law officer to give signature as witness to her testimony, and I'll turn Lou here loose. Now they'll be one condition, if the law wants him back in jail regardless... until trial, then it'll have to be."

Ray smiled and shook his hand. "You're a good man, Marshal."

"Ray, I didn't ask, but where is your ranch? I mean how far is it from here?"

"It's a day's ride, maybe a little less. I live in Oxford, used to be called Napawalla, named after the Osage Chief. I live on the other side of the Ninnescha River."

"Sounds like a nice place."

"It is. I have a good operation there. I run cattle and a few horses."

"Maybe I'll get over that way sometime."

"You're welcome anytime... no matter how this turns out. I'm getting on up in years. I can't get this right leg over the cantle like I used to. Lou here is going to have to take over one of these days. You can see why I need this to go right." He smiled at his son.

"I won't be able to if I keep taking bullets in the backside."

Ray's smile left him. "If you'd been where you were supposed to be you wouldn't have taken one." Ray looked at Lou with displeasure in knowing he was old enough to know better.

An interesting thing took place at the grove of trees Angel Hound was sleeping in. Admiral Fetters and his men rode into them before good light. They had no idea Angel Hound was in the trees above them.

The admiral was upset. "Captain Ross, I told you we should have waited until daylight to travel. We have strayed off the trail twice. We will delay here until daylight."

"Yes sir... if the stars were visible I could navigate and surely put us on course."

Garret Gray spoke up. "It is apparent none of us are Kansas Plains Cowboys." He laughed at his joke.

Ben Gladstone and Walter Hobson didn't find it funny. In fact they were not happy with much of anything. They wanted to be there already. Major Parker was the only one that stayed quiet.

Admiral Fetter sat his horse and observed the men with him. Garret Gray was about half crazy in his opinion. He had been involved in too many bloody campaigns. Walter Hobson never smiled, talked little and when he did, it was a complaint. He wasn't a whiner, he just wanted things perfect at all times. Most precision killers were like that. He believed in exactness and strictness in preparing to eliminate a target. To the admiral, he was the one to fear and respect even among themselves. He was the tool of death. The mission 'Queen's Denial' had the perfect man to kill a man that might be hard to kill.

He looked over at Ben Gladstone. He too was deadly when he had to be. He was also loyal, something he didn't think Garret Gray was. Walter Hobson would be loyal to the Queen, but that would be the extent of it.

Captain Ross and Major Parker were good men and loyal to a flaw towards him. He smiled at that. They were good men.

Hobson turned his horse to face the admiral. "We should be there today, right?"

"I believe so, yes."

"Good. I've had enough of this chasing around all over the country back of a horse. Let's get to this spot in the road they call Dye and kill Tucker Shaw. We can have him killed and be having tea by afternoon if we can find the blasted road again." Hobson wasn't happy at all.

Admiral Fetter thought about what Hobson said. The man didn't know Tucker and didn't care to. Maybe if they had been

Where Outlaws Roam
Royal Wade Kimes

around him a few times but that doesn't constitute knowing a man. His life meant nothing more to him than an inconvenience, a delay in afternoon tea.

He smiled as he thought of Tucker. He had a lot of memories of him as a small child, baby in fact. He was a brilliant boy and would have gone far but for his father making life miserable for him and his mother. He'd tried to step in as much as he could. He took him fishing and taught him how to ride and shoot.

He glanced over at Garret Gray. He was a killer for hire and had little feelings for anyone, and Gladstone was basically numb from brain to heart. He simply didn't appear to have emotional feelings. Then he thought about himself. He didn't have the wolf like instinct these men had. He had feelings. His heart wasn't black and cold like they were, but then, that's why they were picked. They were cold hearted killers. It wouldn't matter to them if it was a woman or a child they were to eliminate, they would kill them same as a man. Without realizing it he mumbled to himself.

"What am I doing with these men? What am I doing here?"

"Did you say something, Admiral?"

"No Captain... talking to myself is all." He smiled. "I'll be okay."

Angel Hound was listening to them talk and heard one of the men confirm his suspicion that they were up to no good. He must beat them to Dye. He had cut across several hills yesterday and had gotten in front of them. He could do it again. He was well rested and he felt he could run like the wind after hearing what they were up to. He was thinking about all of that when he heard another horse coming. The grove of trees was becoming crowded.

The rider pulled his horse up in the growth of timber slow like when he saw the other riders. "Morning, I'm Marshal Sanders." He looked them over well and kept his hand on his holstered gun.

"I'm Admiral Fetter, from Great Britain. These men are servants of the Queen. We're on a mission. My dear fellow, did you say you are a United States Marshal?"

"I did say that, yes. Ah... what kind of a mission, Admiral? I hope you don't mind me asking?"

He smiled. "The Queen wants us to find Marshal Tucker Shaw and let him know his mother is deathly ill. We are to bring him back with us."

"What if he don't want to go?" Marshal Sanders kept looking at Hobson as he listened to Admiral Fetter. He figured him to be a deadly man.

"Surely my dear man he will want to see his dear departing mother before she passes?"

"Yeah. Yeah you'd think so."

"I'm a bit confused, Marshal."

"Tucker marches to his own drum. If you know him, Admiral, you probably know that." He observed the other riders for a short second. "By there being so many of you... I'm sure you do."

Garret stepped in. "Marshal, why don't you stick to law and drop out of the mind reading business. We'll take care of Tucker Shaw."

"You got a name?" Marshal Sander's voice had suddenly changed.

"Garret Gray, if it is anything to you."

"Well, Garret Gray, out here in Kansas a man doesn't talk to another man with disrespect. It can get his ass shot off."

"Are you challenging me?"

"No sir, just stating a fact."

"Well, I demand satisfaction. I'll not have a barbarian talking to me in such a manner."

Marshal Sanders smiled as he pulled his hands from the saddle horn. "You demand satisfaction? Feller... is demanding satisfaction the same thing as calling a man out for a gunfight here in the West?"

"It certainly is."

Marshal Sanders took a deep breath and sighed. "Well, I guess if I have to honor your custom... how would pistols be a straddle horses?"

"My choice of weapon exactly. Explain... straddle."

"We draw and shoot while mounted on our horses. I just don't feel like trying to get off my horse, pace ten steps and go to shooting at each other. Getting back on is a chore in its self for

Where Outlaws Roam
Royal Wade Kimes

me right now. I'm still a little sore from a run in I had a while back."

Garrett was amused. "On the ground or on a horse the end result will be the same."

Marshal Sanders cut his eyes to the admiral. "It sure will be. I'm sorry you're going to lose a man, Admiral. Keep in mind I didn't pick this fight. Would you mind counting to three?"

Admiral Fetter was stunned at the sudden exchange of events. "Might we try to keep cooler heads? There's really no call for hot tempers. After all, we're strangers... the fact we're not from America we may not understand your ways."

Marshal Sanders chuckled. "It's up to your friend. I just stopped to water my horse."

Garrett was puffed up like a red rooster sitting on an early morning fence post. "Admiral, I will be disgraced if you do not commence to count."

Admiral Fetter nodded and prepared to count once he was out of the line of fire.

Angel Hound was above them and his eyes were large with the aspect of a shooting.

"One, two, three!"

Marshal Sanders drew and shot Garret Gray through the throat. He went sprawling backwards off his horse as blood sprayed up in the air and then towards the ground. His gun had just cleared the holster when Marshal Sander's bullet hit him. He waited to see if anyone else had any ideas of pulling on him, when they didn't he holstered his gun.

"I'm going to tell you men straight. If you've come for any other reason than what you said regarding Tucker Shaw, we'll send your Queen a note as to where she can find your graves." He clucked to his horse and rode out in the direction of Dye.

Angel Hound could hardly contain his self but stayed quiet despite his excitement.

Admiral Fetter looked around at the rest of the men. "Well, the Queens' Merry Men are certainly doing well so far."

Gladstone spoke up. "Gray always was a fool."

"That may be. We must get about burying him... fool or not."

Where Outlaws Roam
Royal Wade Kimes

Hobson spurred his horse. "You bury him, Admiral. I'm going on. I'm keeping that fast marshal in sight. He's headed to Dye and so am I." He left in a jog.

Admiral Fetter turned to Captain Ross. "We will give this man a decent burial; after all he was loyal to the Queen." He paused and then looked straight at Gladstone. "If anyone else strikes out on his own I will have him hanged. Walter Hobson will be dealt with when we get to Dye. I will not have high minded men who can't take orders."

Gladstone stared at him. "Admiral, if I were you I'd shoot Hobson and then tell him why you did. Otherwise, you'll be a dead man."

They buried Garett Gray in a shallow grave and rode out. Angel Hound slid down the tree and took off due west while the men riding horses rode north and would turn west after a mile or two. He would be ahead of them if he could keep his stride, and he knew he could do that. He had seen enough by gray dawn to keep him excited all day.

Where Outlaws Roam
Royal Wade Kimes

Chapter 23

Tucker was standing on the porch of the jail talking to a farmer who was missing a cow when he saw Angel Hound coming at the other end of the street. He was running and looked to be about spent.

"Excuse me, Mister Meadows." He left the man standing on the porch as he ran towards Angel Hound. He caught him in his arms as he started to fall. As long as he was going forward he was alright, but when he tried to stop he started down.

"Mister Tucker! I shore be glad to see you!" He was heaving so hard Tucker could barely make out his words.

"Son... give yourself a minute to catch your breath."

People were gathering in small groups here and there on the boardwalk and street. They stayed back a ways as they didn't know what was happening and for sure didn't know the Negro boy. Dye, Kansas had never had any colored folks living in it.

"Mister Tucker... they's a coming! They be here in maybe an hour, two at the most I figure."

"Who's coming, Angel Hound?"

Man called Admiral Fetter and hired killers I thinks. They bad men. Marshal Sanders on his way here too. He already had a run in with them... killed one dead as a swatted fly."

Tucker looked down the street in the direction Angel Hound had come. His mind was racing. Why was Admiral Fetter here? If Marshal Sanders had a run in with him and his party, then they weren't coming as friends. Were they here bringing a message? Why would it take more than Robert... Admiral Fetter?

"Angel Hound, did you happen to hear any names?"

"The one be killed was called Garrett... Gray."

"Are you sure?" Tucker knew who he was, an assassin. He then figured it. His publication exposing the Shaw family and the Queen had provoked a reaction. He was sure Robert Fetter; Admiral Fetter as he was called in rank had not seen or heard of his apology letter.

"Mister Tucker, I remembers another one that was real anxious to gets here, his name be Walter Hobson. He left the admiral and chased after Marshal Sanders. I don't mean he try to catch him, but was staying in sight of him, whiles the others buried the dead one."

Tucker stood straight up and stared down the street. "Walter." He smiled. "They sent their best." He looked at Angel Hound. "You've done well. You've probably saved my life. Walter Hobson would have set up somewhere and shot me from a window. With him not knowing I know he's coming, the advantage is mine. He'll have to face me instead of shoot me from a distance."

"I knowed you was in trouble. I had to gets here."

"You ran all the way?"

"Most the way. I catches a ride with a red headed lady for a little ways." He wasn't daring to speak of the rest of it.

"Let's get you some water and food." He took him to Sisters and ordered him a nice plate and a gallon of water. He then took him over to the jail and let him lie down on a cot. He was exhausted and would be asleep in no time. He went to his rifle rack and pulled one of the lever guns. He loaded it and then checked his pistol. If the British were coming, he was going to be ready. He walked out on the porch and waited.

Marshal Sanders pulled up a mile outside of town. He knew he was being followed by one of the men from the grove of trees. It concerned him when he realized the man was suddenly gaining on him rather fast. What if those men didn't want him to get to Dye before them?

The rider raced by him and swung brutally hard with his pistol. It took him by surprise and he was caught in the side of the face with the blow. He blocked part of the attack with his elbow as he realized just in time what was happening. He went tumbling from his horse and hit the ground on his back. It knocked the air out of him, and when he tried to rise up the rider ran his horse into him. He went sprawling forward on his chest.

"Stay down! I could have killed you had I wanted. We're not here to kill American Lawmen, only British ones."

The man dismounted while holding a gun on him. "Stay on your stomach."

"What for?" Marshal Sanders knew what for, but why comply so easily.

Where Outlaws Roam
Royal Wade Kimes

"I've got to tie you up." He stepped towards him with a rope. "My good fellow, are we doing this easy or shall it be done the hard way?"

Hobson finished tying the marshal up and then turned his horse loose. He left him tied up in tall grass alongside the road. Eventually someone would see him, but it might be awhile.

Tucker saw a stranger to Dye, Kansas riding into town, but he wasn't any stranger to him. The two of them had worked a case together that entailed spying on their own superiors. One of those being secretly watched was found to be a traitor. Hobson didn't bother to have the man arrested, he cut his throat instead. A lot of men die from having their throats cut, but not while they are sleeping beside their wives, and the wife only discovers it when she awakes the next morning.

When Hobson was fifty yards away he stepped into the street. "That's far enough."

The surprise look on his face could not be denied. He was sure he would slip into town, get a room at a hotel and kill Marshal Tucker Shaw from the window.

"Step down off your horse."

"Dear Tucker, you must have some notion I am here to do you harm. Nothing could be further from the truth."

"Hobson, you travel nowhere unless it is to do harm to someone. Since you're in Dye, and since I'm in Dye, and since we both know what your title is, all else we could talk about would be foolishness at best." He chuckled. "And since we're not really friends, I see nothing else to do but take care of business. You being here is a threat in its self. That means you have a choice. You pull that pistol or I pull mine... because you're not leaving here."

Hobson stepped down from his horse and walked over away from him. "Is this the way the law is handled in the Wild West?" Would I not have to pull my pistol first in order for it to be a legal kill on your part, my dear boy? I'm sure I read in one of those dime novels telling of the west, that the man who draws first is the man who hangs for killing the other. How would it look, a marshal pulling on an innocent stranger?"

Where Outlaws Roam
Royal Wade Kimes

"I'm not concerning myself with code of behavior when it comes to a snake like you. The chips fall where they fall. So... if you would like any kind of advantage at all... you best be pulling that hip high pistol."

Hobson smiled, but only to hide what he was thinking and feeling. He wasn't behind a window. He was out in the open facing a younger man than himself, and a known marksman. This wasn't the time to play fair or wait around. This was a time for suddenness. His gray eyes zeroed in on Tucker's heart. He made his move and the report of two pistols was heard by the crowd gathered on both sides of the street. Then a third shot.

Hobson drew his gun and fired at the exact same time as Tucker. His draw wasn't smooth enough, he jerked hard and roughly instead of coming smoothly up and out. Tucker's bullet hit him in the chest. He fell backwards three steps and fired a second shot into the blue sky as he was falling backwards.

Macie was sewing a button on one of Tucker's shirts when she heard the shots. She jumped up and ran to the window. She saw Tucker walking over to a man lying in the street digging his heels into the dust.

Tucker looked down at Hobson. "Where are the others and where is Marshal Sanders?"

Hobson had the oddest look on his face. "How... how could you know about... us... and Marshal Sand." His eyes stared at Tucker but he was gone.

Angel Hound came running out of the jail and slid to a halt a few feet from Tucker and the dead man. "That be the one called Hobson."

"Yeah... that's him. The rest will be coming. Angel Hound, I need you to do something for me, think you can?"

"I will try."

"Head back down the south route and see if you can find Marshal Sanders. He should have been here before Walter Hobson. I fear he's lying wounded or dead."

Before Tucker could say more he was off to the races. By the time he had gotten to the end of the street the whole town was taking notice. They had never seen anyone run like that.

Where Outlaws Roam
Royal Wade Kimes

Angel Hound slowed his pace once out of town. He trotted along and watched the tracks for blood. Then he saw a horse standing out in the middle of prairie grass waving in the breeze. It made him think of the waves he used to see in the gulf. He eased up to the horse and caught hold of his mane. He still had a saddle on, but the bridle was missing. He managed to open the saddlebags and was in luck. It was the side with grain in it. He got it off and poured the feed on the ground. He then searched the other side of the bag while the horse ate.

"You stays right here big boy till I gets something to ride you with." He felt in the bag and pulled out a small rope. He grinned real big at his good fortune. He figured a good marshal would always have some extra rope to tie prisoners up with in case handcuffs weren't enough. He took the rope and made a half hitch in it and made himself a halter. Once the horse ate he mounted and headed down the road. He rode for about a quarter when he saw what looked like a place where confrontation took place. Hoof tracks and scuff marks didn't match the rest of the tracks in the road. He looked to his left out in the tall grass and saw something red. He eased the horse towards it. He bailed off and ran to Marshal Sanders.

"Marshal! You be dead?" He removed a gag from his mouth and untied his hands and feet.

"I'm not dead. I hurt and ache too much to be dead. You didn't just stumble on to me, did you?"

"Mister Tucker sent me. I was laid up high in one of those trees you and those men was having a talk in. I knowed Mister Tucker be in trouble if I don't gets word to him. He was waiting on Walter Hobson... killed him dead."

"Good, he needed killing. You say you were in a tree while we was jawing this morning?"

"I was. That be how Mister Tucker knowed you be in trouble. He says you should have made it to Dye before Hobson."

"Well, let's mount up and beat the rest of them there. They should be coming along real soon. I figure they buried the one I shot. Dead men can slow you up some."

"You rides the horse, me, I'll run along beside you."

"You'll what?" He eyed the boy over.

"I run where I go. I ran near all the way from Fort Smith to warn Mister Tucker about these men that were looking for him."

"You ran from Fort Smith?"

"I did. It was a nice little run." He grinned. "They call me Angel Hound."

"I'm pleased to meet you." He stuck his hand out and they shook hands. Then he scrounged around in the grass until he found his bridle. He tightened the cinch and mounted up. "Well, I'm ready if you are."

"I be ready, leads off.

Where Outlaws Roam
Royal Wade Kimes

Chapter 24

Marshal Galt and Deputy Farley left Fort Smith in the afternoon. They took the ferryboat across the river and headed west. He figured to make Dye by late the next day if he rode until nine or ten o'clock at night. He knew the trail so it shouldn't be any problem.

"Marshal."

"Yeah Deputy?"

"You and Marshal Tucker are good friends aren't you?"

"We are."

"Well… why are you doing this? I mean, what if that girl of his is the one that sold the Fletcher horse and rig? That doesn't mean she stoled him. It also could drive a wedge between you and Tucker if you arrest her. Hell, it could cause some real trouble. Love for a woman can cloud a man's thinking. I've been in a rain ever since I met Billie. Then there's the question of who killed Reed Fletcher and his men. You said the horse was gone when you found Fletcher. Maybe the men who killed him took the horse and she came by him honestly. I mean, that's a tall order killing a man the way he was, his thumb gone, a knife in his back and a bullet between the eyes. If a woman done all that, I'm staying way further than just downwind of her. Think about it. That's some kind of hate if after you kill a man; you hang him out for everyone to see. Another thing, what about the man with the crowbar sticking through him? What kind of woman did all that?"

"It'd have to be one full of hate… and you're right, I doubt a jury would believe it could be done by a woman. Keep in mind this lady may be from Louisiana, and they are tougher than most. Hell, they had 'em fighting alligators by the time they were five."

Deputy Farley cut his eyes over to Marshal Galt. "No kidding?"

"No kidding."

Marshal Galt hid his smile and they rode the next thirty minutes in silence. He enjoyed putting one over on his somewhat gullible deputy once in a while.

Admiral Fetter rode to the edge of town and stopped. His heart sped up. He wanted to see Tucker, not kill him. But the mission wasn't for Old Home Day. It was to eliminate a problem, a man who knows enough that if he so wanted to, he could blackmail the Lord's and Queen of Great Britain and be a very wealthy man. For they would pay his asking to keep what he had in his head, in his head, and not out to the public.

Major Parker was sitting his horse beside the admiral. "Sir, why have we stopped?"

He looked at the major. "Should not the question be; why have we come?"

"Sir?" He glanced at Captain Ross, and then returned to the admiral. "Orders sir."

"Oh yes, those God damned orders. God save the Queen and to hell with everyone else. Let the world be damned and all who partook in playing its fool. Major, you haven't any idea how many times I've wanted to tell the Royal Ass Parliament to shove their orders. This is another one of those times. None of you here with me today know anything about Tucker Shaw. I can sum it up for you in one sentence. He's more honest about life than all of us put together, and not afraid to buck the damn world." The admiral was looking down the street and then turned to Major Parker. "You see, Major... Tucker Shaw is his own man and doesn't let status or titles influence his decisions. I may be to blame for that. I'm the one that taught him all those things, the very things I can't live up to myself." A small tear appeared at the bottom of his left eye. He wiped it away quickly. "Let's ride before I do something unthinkable and resend the order."

Ben Gladstone broke his silence. "Admiral, if you did that... I'd have to kill you."

"I know that, Ben. If I did that, I wouldn't give a damn."

Captain Ross spoke up. "Ben, you'd die in the process." He faced him with a very sober face. The major sided with him. "That's right, Ben. You'd have to kill us all. One of us will get you."

Admiral Fetter smiled. "That'll do. We came here on a mission and we're not going to be the Queen's Denial. We will obey orders regardless of how we feel."

They rode down the street four abreast. The admiral didn't

Where Outlaws Roam
Royal Wade Kimes

know what to expect. Walter Hobson could have already killed Tucker, though not likely. He worked slower and created a greater percentage in making the kill. Then there was Marshal Sanders they met at the grove of trees. He surely told Tucker of their coming. The element of surprise was gone. That was why he elected to ride in four abreast. They would ride in and face him head on.

Marshal Tucker Shaw and Marshal Sanders were waiting on the porch of the jail. The jail its self was made from rock and clay. The porch was added after the jail was built.

"Well, here they come." Tucker pulled the hammer back on his rifle. Marshal Sanders did the same.

"You know something Marshal Shaw... saying goodbye to this business has come hard. I wanted to retire and call it a day. I'm on my way to Pueblo for goodness sakes."

Tucker chuckled. "Why don't we take off like a couple of these Kansas Jackrabbits around here and go? I will if you will. I'll not look back."

Marshal Sanders looked around at him like a blowing mule. "You wouldn't run right now if you knew you was going to split hell wide open. You ain't fooling me."

"Well, since you talked me out of it, let's don't be late for the party."

Together the two lawmen stepped out into the street and began walking towards the four riders. Tucker watched Admiral Fetter for a few seconds and then took in the other three.

"Marshal, I know the man to your right at the end. His name is Ben Gladstone. He's a man of iron will. He's the one to be throwing lead at if we can't talk them down. The one over from him is Admiral Robert Fetter. He's a close friend of the Queen and my mother."

He looked over at Tucker. "Will that give us an edge on talking him out of all this?"

"I couldn't say. I kind of doubt it... as for those other two... their seamen and good ones. They know what they're doing."

"I feel like I'm standing off the Red Coats without the coats."

"Trust me, you are."

Where Outlaws Roam
Royal Wade Kimes

Admiral Fetter pulled up. The four riders stopped and sat silent. He looked around at the stores and shops along the street.

"Good day, Marshal Tucker Shaw."

"Admiral Fetter. I'd like to say it's good to see you… but I don't know that to be the case just yet."

"You have an attractive little village here."

"They're called towns."

"Yes of course. I made that same correction to Lord McCray before we left."

Tucker eyed Gladstone. "I see they sent some of their best. Garret Gray, Walter Hobson, and here we have Ben Gladstone. Ben, what in the world did you do to get promoted."

"Promoted? I don't know what you're talking about."

"The last I knew of you, they had you knocking off widow women for housing space."

"Tucker, you talk a lot. All the time I knew you I never saw anything out of you that impressed me. That goes for your mouth, your family, and your attitude."

Marshal Sanders whispered to Tucker. "Maybe you ought to let me do the talking… your approach is having the wrong affect."

Tucker smiled and cut his eyes to Admiral Fetter. "My, Ben's in a bad mood is he not?"

"Tucker, we've been sent by the Queen." He looked at him with sad eyes, for he loved his mother and had strong feelings for Tucker too.

Tucker smiled "I figured as much. Admiral, I'm thinking you left the homeland well before the news of mine and the Queen's agreement of peace. You know nothing about the publication of apology that has ended the rival, do you?"

Admiral Fetter looked stunned. "Go on."

I gave the Queen my word she was not to worry over misguided fools like me. She has since confirmed and agreed to the peace between us." He glanced at Marshal Sanders and looked straight at Admiral Fetter. "Robert, I'm dispensing with the Admiral… and calling you Robert as I always have. With that said I have someone I want you to meet." He motioned for the person standing in the doorway of the jail to come out on the porch. "Meet Lee Paulson. He owns the newspaper here and is

Where Outlaws Roam
Royal Wade Kimes

the one with the contacts for publication in the Morning News of London."

Lee came out two steps further. "That's right, Admiral. I own the Dye Paper. It's true that Marshal Shaw has made amends with the Queen and she responded favorably. The rift between them and everyone else has ended."

Admiral Robert Fetter slowly and quietly began to laugh. He grew louder as he did. "We came all this way and." He laughed more. "And the mission has been aborted?"

Ben Gladstone bellowed out over the admiral. "The hell it's aborted! The Queen's Denial is not turning on me! I'll not be denied killing this man that made a mockery of the Imperial Army! He slanders his own family, disrespects the Queen herself! She forgives this dog eating peasant?"

He whirled his horse sideways to the two marshals and dismounted at the same time. When the horse bolted forward Ben was already shooting. His first bullet hit Marshal Sanders left thigh. His next bullet grazed Tucker's right shoulder. It wasn't deep and caused little damage. Tucker fired once, twice, and a third time. He hit Ben twice, but he was a big man and didn't go down. Instead he fell behind a wagon and rolled to the boardwalk. Marshal Sanders fired two times at him, but none of the shots were clear ones.

Admiral Fetter was ordering Ben to cease fire but he was having none of it. Finally he pulled his own gun. He, Captain Ross, and Major Parker were the only ones that could see him. He had made it to the corner of the dry goods store and was leaning up against the wall. He was breathing heavy and bleeding badly. He reloaded his empties and took a deep breath.

"Tucker, let's end this, just you and me! What do you say?"

"I see no reason why not."

He cut his eyes to Marshal Sanders to see how he was. He smiled when he saw it was a flesh wound.

Ben Gladstone stepped out into the open. Then something unexpected happened. Admiral Fetter stepped in.

"Benjamin Gladstone, I was and still am the commander of this mission. You have disobeyed direct orders and furthermore you took matters into your own hands. You overrode the wishes of the Queen in which you boast being righteous in protecting her honor. You haven't any honor, Mister Gladstone. Drop your weapon or I will have no choice but to shoot you down where you stand."

Ben looked wild eyed at him. "Admiral, you can go to hell!" He raised his pistol to shoot at him, but was met with three bullets. The Admiral, Major Parker, and Captain Ross fired at the same time. All three bullets hit Ben Gladstone in the heart. He was driven backwards off of his feet. He hit the dirt hard and rolled over in a twisted heap. He never moved again.

Where Outlaws Roam
Royal Wade Kimes

Chapter 25

That night Admiral Robert Fetter and his two officers dined at Sisters with Marshal Shaw, Macie, Marshal Sanders, and Angel Hound. They all got a big kick out of Angel Hound as he told how he lay high above them in the grove of trees and listened to the talk. He said he nearly fell out of the tree when Marshal Sanders shot Garret Gray.

Billie and Connie came to their table with two large trays. There was expensive wine and steaks for everyone served with potatoes and green beans.

Admiral Fetter was taken with Macie. She had a certain feeling of mysteriousness about her, an air that spelled tough when she needed to be. He was satisfied no one knew all there was to her, except maybe Tucker. If he knew anything about women, Macie was dedicated to Tucker. She was his and his only.

When supper was over everyone said goodnight and went to their rooms, except Macie, Tucker, and the admiral. That was when things became more serious.

"Tucker, may I speak freely?"

"Of course you can."

Macie smiled. "Before you do; I think man talk is taking over and you two don't need me around for it."

"Why... my dear lady, you are most welcome to stay."

"Admiral, you are a perfect gentleman, something I've begun to enjoy, but I know when it is time to move along." Then she did something that tickled the admiral. She bent down and took her shoes off. She smiled. "I didn't learn how to wear these things until I came here. Goodnight, Admiral."

He kissed her hand and then she turned to Tucker. "I will see you in a little while." She tiptoed, kissed him and then turned. She left them both standing there mesmerized.

"You have something special there, Tucker."

"I know."

At dawn the next morning Admiral Fetter was down at the Dye Newspaper. He walked in and shut the door behind him.

Lee Paulson looked up in surprise. "Good morning. This is quite the surprise. Tell me, what do I owe this visit to?"

"My good man, I'll get right to the point. I understand you're able to get articles of news published in Great Britain. I've seen that first hand." He stopped and seemed to be searching for words.

"Yes, Admiral?" Lee was puzzled and anxious to hear what he was about to say.

"Is it at all possible for you to get a direct message to someone there?"

"It might be. Who may I ask?"

"Tucker Shaw's mother, Margaret Shaw."

"Oh?" He removed his little round glasses as he gave that thought. "Admiral, I might get Charles Letts, the owner of the Morning News of London to take a message to her."

"I'll pay you handsomely if you can get it done. Here is the message. One other thing; is there a way to get it done today?"

"Well... I don't know that answer."

"Then do what you can, but I pray for speediness."

"The telegraph has been down. If it is up and running it is possible. I will tell Charles it is of utmost importance and urgent."

The admiral gave Lee a letter. "Send this to Margaret Shaw and have her send word back one way or another. Can we trust Charles Letts to be a good chap and keep his mouth shut?"

"Well, I don't know that answer either. I've not known him a great long time. What dealings I've had with him thus far have shown him trustworthy."

"Then send it." He smiled. "I must go. I don't want the captain and major to start a campaign looking for me."

Lee laughed and showed him to the door. He then opened the letter and read it.

"Oh my!"

He hurried to his office and took some change from his desk. He would need it to send the telegram. He hoped it was up and running, because this letter needed sent.

The telegraph had been back up and running since midnight, giving Lee the ability to send the letter to Charles Letts. He laid the letter down in front of Homer Suggs who ran the telegraph office.

"Homer, I need you to send this to Charles Letts in London. Tell him I need this delivered immediately."

Homer read the letter and then quickly went to work on it. He glanced at Lee. "This is quite something."

> DEAREST MARGARET: STOP
>
> I'M SURE YOU ARE SICK WITH WORRY ABOUT TUCKER, AND ME AS WELL: STOP
>
> I WOULD LIKE TO INFORM YOU THAT YOUR SON IS FINE, AND I TOO AM OKAY: STOP
>
> HE HAS FOUND A LADY THAT I DEARLY HOPE HE HOLDS ONTO, YOU WILL LIKE HER: STOP
>
> MARGARET, I'VE MADE A DECISION: STOP
>
> I'M NOT COMING BACK TO BRITIAN: STOP
>
> I AM GOING TO MAKE AMERICA MY HOME: STOP
>
> IT IS MY HOPE YOU WILL COME TO ME HERE: STOP
>
> YOUR TUCKER IS ALREADY HERE AND I SUSPECT YOUR GRANDCHILDREN WILL BE: STOP
>
> YOUR FUTURE HUSBAND WILL BE TOO, IF IRA SHAW HAS BEEN MADE THE PAST: STOP
>
> WE ALL AWAIT YOU HERE IN THIS BEAUTIFUL PLACE, AMERICA: STOP
>
> GO SEE WATTS AND WATTS AT THE SEADOG HARBOR: STOP
>
> HE HAS A SHIP CALLED THE LONDON QUEEN THAT HE LIVES ON: STOP

> TELL HIM TO STOW YOU AWAY ON BOARD AND BRING YOU AT SHIPS TOP SPEED: STOP
>
> HE IS TO BRING YOU TO NEW ORLEANS AND BE PAID THEN: STOP
>
> HE SERVERD WITH ME ON MY SHIP SO HE KNOWS AND TRUSTS ME: STOP
>
> LET ME KNOW WHAT YOU DECIDE, AS I AWAIT YOU ALREADY WITH GREAT ANTICIPATION: STOP
>
> I WILL MEET YOU IN NEW ORLEANS IF YOU CHOOSE TO COME: STOP
>
> WITH DEEP RESPECT, ROBERT FETTER: STOP

Lee was leaning over Homer the whole time he was sending the letter. He straightened up once it was sent and wiped his forehead.

Homer had tobacco juice running down one side of his mouth. He was a fat little man with a face full of white whiskers. "Lee, there's going to be fireworks in Britain. What do you think ole Margret will do?"

"Well, the admiral made a mighty good case for his bid to her. I mean, her son, her future daughter-in-law, and a passel of grandkids could all be here. All she seems to have there is Ira Shaw. It seems Admiral Fetter and ole Margaret have been making whoopee under cover." He laughed. "I made a joke there, Homer."

"I'll laugh when one of your jokes is funny."

"You do that, Homer." He paid him and left for his office with anxiousness of a reply. The next day or two was going to be exciting.

Marshal Galt and Deputy Farley rode into Dye slow and easy at two o'clock. They pulled up in front of the jail. Deputy Farley kept looking towards Sisters hoping to see Billie. He wasn't so lucky, but Marshal Galt on the other hand was. Darla spotted him from

Where Outlaws Roam
Royal Wade Kimes

her window at the second floor of the saloon. She put her shoes on and beat it over to the jail.

Marshal Galt had just stepped upon the porch to the jail when Darla walked up. "Marshal, I thought you'd never come back."

He turned and smiled at her. "Well Darla, it's like this... I wanted to come but wasn't able to make up a good enough lie to make the trip. Fort Smith Marshals are hard to fool."

"Well, whatever the reason, you're here and I'm glad."

He stared at her for a second. He wondered if she would feel that way when she found out why he was in Dye. He bet not. "Darla, I got to get freshened up, get a bath and such. I have a little business and then maybe we can have a little fun."

"Marshal, my toes are curled already."

He turned a shade of red and wasn't about to look over at Deputy Farley.

"Do you want me to come to the hotel, or meet at the saloon?"

"It's quieter at the hotel."

"See you in an hour?" She looked up under his hat into his eyes.

"Yeah, an hour."

She left humming as she went.

Deputy Farley chuckled. "Marshal, her toes is curled already. How sweet is that? Marshal, would you tell this old dumb deputy what it is you do that curls their toes. Or is it just the one there you affect that way? I don't think I've ever known a toe curler before."

"You're about to not know nothing you keep prodding." He smiled as Farley dismounted laughing the whole time.

Marshal Shaw came to the door to see who was doing all the talking and laughing outside. "Marshal Galt, Deputy Farley! I can't believe it! Come in, I've got a bottle in here someplace! You can wash the dust down."

They went in and sat down. Tucker gave them each a cup and they all three had a drink of good Kentucky Whiskey.

"Ah, Marshal Shaw, me and Deputy Farley would like to check in at the Dye Hotel and get us a bath. Darla done spied me, and she, well, we're going to see each other in an hour and I got to get around. Once I get freed up I'd like to sit down and talk to you."

Tucker laughed at him. "I use to have a hard time getting freed up myself."

Deputy Farley kicked in. "Marshal Tucker, you have no idea. Marshal Galt curls her toes."

Tucker cut his eyes to Deputy Farley. "He does what?"

"Curls their toes. At least he's curling Darla's, she said so."

Tucker started laughing and Farley joined him. It was about then Marshal Sanders walked in.

"What's so funny?"

Marshal Galt saw the bandaged leg. "What happened to you?"

"I keep trying to retire, and I think it's going to kill me."

Tucker took it up. "We had a visit from some old friends back home."

"The hell you did?" He glanced at Marshal Sanders.

"He's telling you right, Galt. I killed one of them, and got shot when I sided up with Marshal Shaw here."

"You boys will have to give me the whole story later. I've got to get going."

Marshal Sanders stared at him for a second. "What's the hurry?"

Tucker chuckled. "Oh, he's going to go curl some toes."

Marshal Galt stood up from his chair and looked from Tucker to Marshal Sanders. "You two kiss my you know what." He turned to leave, but Tucker stopped him.

"When do you want to see me?"

He grinned. "I'll be a while."

"Well, if I'm not here, I'll be at the Dye Hotel in Macie's room."

Marshal Galt's smile pulled in some. "Macie?"

"Yeah, Macie Cook. She and I have been seeing one another for a spell. She's staying there for now." He paused and smiled. "Marshal, I guess my wild chasing days are over. I'm looking to settle down."

"Is that right? Well... I sure hope it works out for you." He glanced quickly over to Deputy Farley who had a frown on his face. He then cut his eyes back to Tucker. "I'd like to meet her

Where Outlaws Roam
Royal Wade Kimes

sometime. She must be quite the gal... one of those mysterious types."

Tucker was grinning, but it faded away. "What do you mean by that?" He assumed it was a teasing comment, but it also sounded like a probing law man question without the question.

Tucker had already been worrying about Marshal Galt's bloodhound nose sniffing around when he discovered Macie. She was from Louisiana, and he might naturally zero in on her as a suspect in the killing of Reed Fletcher and his men.

Marshal Galt grinned. "Oh, you know, the kind that keeps a man guessing. That's all."

Tucker felt close to Marshal Galt and Marshal Sanders, but he was guarded of Marshal Galt when it came to Macie. He was strictly by the book, where Sanders seemed to have heart mixed in with his job.

"Marshal, just make sure it's keeping 'a man' guessing... and not a law man."

Marshal Galt's smile left him. "Well now, Marshal Shaw, I sure didn't mean anything."

That was the first time he felt Marshal Galt lied to him. If so, it was the first chink in the weakening of a friendship's foundation.

"Good, that's good. Us marshals always seem to be watching for things, don't we?" He observed his expression and body movement as he started to answer. He saw he had made his friend nervous.

"I guess maybe, but I'm too tired right now to worry with much. I'm going for my bath and then... we'll see how things work out with me and Darla."

Deputy Farley put in at that point. "Hell, you two can talk about your women all you want, but I'm not playing second fiddle to any of you. I'm sprucing up and beating it over to Sisters. I figure me and Billie got some catching up to do."

Tucker eyed both of them over as he was now growing suspicious. He didn't want Marshal Galt to know that, so he changed the subject.

"I tell you what, you and Farley go on and get your rooms. I'll take your horses down to the livery. I'll have them rubbed down, fed and watered, how's that sound?"

"It sounds damn good! You have a deal. I appreciate it."

"Maybe we can have supper tomorrow night say six-thirty. I'll bring Macie. I know she'd love to meet you."

"Yeah… that'd be real good… that'd be just real good." They left for the hotel and Tucker stared at the door they went through.

Then, forgotten Marshal Sanders grunted. Tucker turned his head in his direction and looked at him with a blank stare.

Marshal Sanders was an old lawman that didn't miss much. "What the hell was that all about? He left here without saying so long, goodbye, kiss my ass, or anything to me. He forgot I was even in the room. I noticed a thickness to the air when the conversation got on Macie. Is there something I don't know and maybe ought to?"

Tucker walked to the door. "I think so, but right now I've got two tired horses that need the saddles off of them. I'll be back shortly."

"Hold on. I'll go with you. I may be a little lame but I can lead one and help with the rubbing down."

Marshal Sanders had become fond of Tucker. He thought a lot of him, but he was worried. He had known Marshal Galt a long time and they was good friends. There was something in the wind. He just hoped it didn't smell so bad he had to make a choice of some kind. He was an old law man and his nose was seldom wrong. He'd wait and watch.

Where Outlaws Roam
Royal Wade Kimes

Chapter 26

Charles Letts delivered Lee Paulson's telegram to Margaret Shaw as he was asked. He wasted little time, as he had read the letter and was excited at the reaction it would have. He wanted to see what kind of ripple it made in the quiet but deep waters within the Shaw family and the Queen. Margaret being the Queen's sister, it might possibly cause her to get involved. If she did, Ira Shaw would become what he always was... a commoner.

Margaret read the telegram sitting in a plush red and white flowery chair. Her hands trembled when she saw who it was from and her heart sped up to a runner's speed when she read the contents.

"Oh Robert." She walked to the Victorian style window looking out onto the street in front of the house. Fine stepping horses and beautiful carriages were passing by in both directions. She loved her Country, but she loved Robert and Tucker more. She then thought of Ira. She felt nothing for him. He had killed her love many years ago. In fact, after the first year she began to feel nothing for him. He had shown her in his every action he had only married her to be part of the fabric in politics. His being the Queen of Great Britain's brother-in-law allowed him certain powers, but nothing like he wanted. He lusted for a position in Parliament, and he might have been given one but for her letting the Queen know not to.

She put the letter in a bag and called for her butler. "Porter, you have been with me many years."

"I have, madam."

"What would you do if I left here?"

He was standing straight and tall, but his head suddenly turned to her. "Madam, I, I don't know. I haven't anyone but you... and once... Master Tucker."

"How would you feel about America?"

His smile took the place of worry. "I hear it is grand... and would be grander if you were there. I will be happy wherever you are."

"Then make arrangements to leave here at once. I will have my funds sent to Dye, Kansas in America, and will see my sister regarding everything else. I can't think at the moment. I'm too excited. I must see the Queen immediately."

"I will have one of the stable boys hitch a fine team to the carriage at once."

"Thank you, Porter."

He left with excitement and urgency in his step.

An hour later Margaret walked into the Royal Palace and was greeted by her sister the Queen. They kissed each other on the cheek and went directly to her private part of the palace. They sat down and tea was brought in on an elaborate tray of silver and brass.

"Margaret, I'm glad you have come. I've missed seeing you. I know you have worried terribly over Tucker. I hope the news of our differences being settled and his full apology to Great Britain has helped ease all that."

"It has." She took a sip of her tea.

The Queen suddenly smiled. "I used to see that twinkle in your eyes when we were children. What is up with you my dear Margaret?"

"I'm in need of your help... and this is something you're going to enjoy."

"Oh?" She actually giggled. "I suddenly remember those days when you and I would get into trouble. It was always after you would say... 'we're about to do something you are very much going to enjoy'. Do you remember?"

Margaret laughed and put her hand on her sister's arm. "I do! Isn't it grand?" She stopped and looked into her eyes. "I love you my sister."

She stared at Margaret. "I haven't heard that word in years... love. I love you too, my sister." She lifted her hand and patted away a tear. "Now, what is this mischievous thing you are talking me into?"

"I'm leaving Great Britain and Ira Shaw."

"You are what?" She nearly spilled her tea as she sipped from the tiny cup.

Robert is not coming back to Great Britain. Tucker is there, he

Where Outlaws Roam
Royal Wade Kimes

has someone he is very fond of. My life is there now, not here. Robert and I will be married." She smiled. "I need a divorce from Ira. I also need the house and stables sold. Ira gets one fourth of the sale of the house, one horse, one saddle and... he can have all his women. That was what was agreed to in writing when we married, well, except for the part about the women." They stared at one another and then burst into laughter.

The Queen gathered her composure. "Yes, it was what he signed." She studied Margaret for a moment. "I have a question."

"Yes."

"Will you tell Robert now?" She gazed at her with caring eyes.

"Yes, it's time."

"Good. I've been afraid you might rather let things go. Sometimes it's easier to not cause the waters to be restless. I feel it proper and right, and I am relieved."

"What if he were to be bitter over it? What would I do?"

"You have a way about you, and the right words will come. Robert loves you. If he could be your lover all these years while putting up with Ira, I think he will welcome the news."

"I will tell him as soon as I see him."

The Queen stared off in another direction. "Margaret, not that anything will happen on your voyage to America, but I think it wiser to tell him now. I would put it in a telegram."

"A thing like that? I would be taking an awful chance. If I was there and he became angry, at least I would have a chance to try and make him understand. I just don't know about that, Sis."

"Well, he's your man. All I can say is... it's what I would do. Everyone treats things differently."

Margaret stared out a small window in thought. "I'll think about it." She stood. "I must be going."

They hugged, shutting their eyes as they held one another.

"Margaret, don't you worry about things here. I'll take care of Ira and your possessions. They will be sent to you when and where you say send them." She looked at her one more time. "Margaret, do you think we will ever see each other again?"

Margaret hadn't even thought of such a thing. It struck her hard as she realized this could possibly be the last time she would see her sister. "I'm sure we will. We must."

"Yes, we must."

They walked to the wide stone hallway leading to the entrance of the Palace. Two members of the Royal Guard were summoned to escort Margaret to her carriage. She stepped up in the carriage and sat in the back seat. Porter took the drive lines and waited for her to tell him to move out. She took one last look at the Royal Palace and waved to the second floor when she saw the Queen of Great Britain, her lovely sister standing there with hand forward.

"Porter."

"Yes madam. Get up there team, we're going to America." The carriage and team lunged forward, taking her and Porter to a new world and a new life.

Admiral Fetter could not stay away from the telegraph office. He was standing there when the telegram came from Margaret. Homer Suggs had a stunned look when he slowly handed the telegram to him.

> DEAREST ROBERT: STOP
>
> YES, I AM COMING TO AMERICA TO BEWITHYOU AND OUR SON: STOP

Admiral Fetter read the line again. He looked up at Homer who was gawking at him and grinning.

"Admiral, I didn't know Tucker was your boy. I guess Marshal Tucker Shaw is who she's referring to ain't it?"

He continued to read.

> I SPOKE WITH MY SISTER AS TO TELLING YOU ABOUT TUCKER AND SHE THOUGHT IT TIME: STOP
>
> I'VE ALWAYS WANTED YOU TO KNOW, BUT THE FAMILY COULD NOT AFFORD THE SCANDAL: STOP
>
> I COULD HAVE WAITED UNTIL I ARRIVED IN AMERICA TO TELL YOU: STOP

Where Outlaws Roam
Royal Wade Kimes

MY SISTER REASONED OTHERWISE IN THAT SOMETHING COULD HAPPEN ON MY TRAVEL ABROAD: STOP

SHE COULD HAVE TOLD YOU ABOUT TUCKER IF SOMETHING HAPPENED TO ME, HOWEVER SHE AND I FELT IT BETTER COME FROM ME:STOP

YOU WERE ALWAYS PLACED IN A POSITION TO BE AROUND TUCKER WHEN POSSIBLE: STOP

IRA KNEW TUCKER WASN'T HIS SON AND THEREFORE HE HATED HIM: STOP

HE WAS NEVER TOLD YOU WERE THE FATHER AND HE DIDN'T MUCH CARE WHO WAS: STOP

HE WAS WARNED THAT IF HE SPOKE OF THE MATTER PUBLICALLY HE WOULD BE QUIETLY EXECUTED: STOP

MY SISTER WAS BEING READIED TO BE THE QUEEN OF GREAT BRITAIN: STOP

A MAN LIKE IRA SHAW WOULD NOT BE PERMITTED TO BE A PROBLEM: STOP

I LOVE YOU ROBERT FETTER AND I HOPE THIS HASN'T CHANGED ANYTHING: STOP

IF IT HAS AND I ARRIVE UNWANTED, I WILL UNDERSTAND: STOP

I WILL MAKE A DECISION THEN AS TO WHAT I SHALL DO: STOP

MORE THAN LIKELY I WILL STAY NEAR WHERE TUCKER IS AND LIVE OUT MY LIFE: STOP

I PRAY YOU STILL WANT ME FOR I CAN'T IMAGINE NOT HAVING YOU IN MY LIFE: STOP

> I'M TAKING A GAMBLE YOU LOVE ME DESPITE MY FAILURE TO TELL YOU ABOUT YOUR SON, AND AM BOARDING THE VESSEL YOU ASKED ME TO: STOP
>
> I WILL NOT BE TRAVELING ALONE AS I AM BRINGING PORTER WITH ME: STOP
>
> ROBERT, I LOVE YOU, NO OTHER MAN CAN TAKE YOUR PLACE: STOP
>
> I COME TO YOU ANXIOUSLY, BELIEVING OUR LOVE CAN STAND UP TO PAST MISTAKES: STOP
>
> MARGARET E TORRES: STOP
>
> I'VE USED MY MAIDEN NAME AS I WILL BE DIVORCED BY THE TIME I SEE YOU: STOP

Admiral Fetter looked up from the letter with tears streaming from his eyes. He turned to Homer. "I'm a father and I have a lady who loves me, who believes in me, who is willing to bet on our love. A woman brave enough to board a ship and travel three thousand miles to me." He paced back and forth thinking things through. He stopped. "Mister Suggs, is it?"

"Yes, Suggs." Homer was bugged eyed watching and listening to Admiral Fetter.

"Mister Suggs, send a message. Send it to the Queen of Great Britain. Tell her I thank her for all she is doing on Margaret's and my behalf. Tell her there will be one hell of an after party for a wedding here, and that she is invited. I will let her know when. Sign it Admiral Robert Fetter."

"I'll do-er." He had a wide grin on his face when he looked up from the message he had finished writing down. He was looking at a happy man.

The admiral went back to the hotel and called his officers to his room. "Let's dispense with the Royal Service for now men. I'm speaking to you as one man to another."

They looked at each other with a blank sort of stare. Captain

Where Outlaws Roam
Royal Wade Kimes

Ross then turned to the admiral. "Sir, what's this all about?"

"I'm leaving the Royal Navy and plan to start a new life here in America. I've notified the Queen of Great Britain. Not only that, but Margaret Shaw who is getting a divorce is coming here to be with me."

Major Parker broke into a big smile and Captain Ross followed. "Sir, may I speak?"

"Major Parker, I told you this is a man to man talk. Be my guest."

"Congratulations on starting a new life." He shook his hand as did Captain Ross. The major suddenly stopped. "I'll be right back!" He sprinted out of the room and came back within seconds with a small bottle. "We must toast to the new chapter in your life, in all of our lives. With you gone who knows who our new admiral will be, or if we will even have our positions aboard ship."

He gave the bottle to Admiral Fetter, and then he passed it to Captain Ross, who passed it on to Major Parker. He eyed the two officers hastily.

"Boys, what about starting a new life in America with me? I doubt I'll have a ship, but I plan to have a ranch. That's what they do here in Kansas, is ranch, raise cattle. I guess we could be wild west outlaws, or United States Marshals." They all laughed and had one more shot from the bottle.

Major Parker looked around the room at Captain Ross and Admiral Fetter. "God save the Queen, I'm staying!"

Captain Ross looked wide eyed at the two of them. "I'll be coming with you!" They all grabbed one another and danced in a little round circle in the room holding each other around the shoulders, laughing and crying.

Chapter 27

Tucker was sitting at a table in Sisters at eleven-forty-five a.m. having dinner with Macie, when Deputy Farley walked in. He spotted Tucker and came to his table.

"Good morning, Marshal, Miss." Farley acknowledged Macie right away.

"Sit down, Deputy."

He sat down and kept looking towards the kitchen. Tucker smiled.

"Well, normally I say a man is real hungry when he's eyeing the kitchen, but I have an idea it's not the stomach bothering you, but more the heart."

He grinned. "Marshal, you're a smart dude. Well, I don't mean you're a dude, you're shore as hell not. Anyone that could do what you done with Simon Lick and those ole boys in Melt, Kansas, well, he ain't no damn dude." He blushed. Pardon me, Miss, I didn't mean to spew out such talk in front of you."

"I've heard worse."

"Deputy Farley, this lady is my sweetheart, Macie Cook."

"I thought that's who you were. I hope the two of you don't think me out of line saying so, but you're a beautiful lady."

Macie smiled and practically lit up the room. "That is very nice of you." She batted her eyes at Tucker. "You better be careful or I'll have me another man."

The three of them laughed. Billie walked up to the table unnoticed by Deputy Farley.

"Good morning, Deputy."

He stood up from the table and removed his hat. "Good morning. I'm a few minutes early."

"That's okay. I'll bring you a nice glass of tea while you wait on me. I'm a little late myself. I've a peach cobbler in the oven and it's taking its time being done." She left for the tea as the deputy looked on like a lonesome hound.

Tucker was amused. "She'll be back, Deputy."

"Oh, I know. It's just... she's so darn beautiful."

"That she is."

Macie looked at Tucker and smiled. She saw Deputy Farley was

Where Outlaws Roam
Royal Wade Kimes

in love.

Tucker saw the same thing. "When you two getting married?"

"Married!? Hell... I ain't that far along."

"Could have fooled me. Say, where's your boss at?"

"Marshal Galt is Galting around at the Dye Hotel with Darla. The two of them are like two turtles. I've not seen it mind you, but when it takes that long to get it done, you're bound to be moving around like turtles." He glanced at Macie. "I'm sorry, Macie. I'm not use to talking much around ladies. I'm always around some old sweaty marshal somewhere." He smiled and looked back towards the kitchen.

"Deputy Farley, Marshal Galt never did say why you two rode out here."

"He didn't?" He turned red around the neck and ears. "I really don't know. I wanted to see Billie so I asked to tag along."

Tucker knew something was wrong. "What's bothering you, Farley?" He left the deputy part off; for he was sitting with someone he suddenly didn't know. Why would a lawman dodge a question when he was supposed to be a friend? Tucker's eyes darted over to Macie and back. She caught his signal that Deputy Farley was being less than honest and was nervous suddenly.

"There's nothing bothering me, Marshal. I'm just waiting on Billie. We're going down to the creek for a little while."

"Well, Deputy Farley, one of the first things I was taught in the Royal Guard was to know when a man was lying, and you my dear friend are lying."

He suddenly became quiet and stared at Tucker. "I've never had a man call me a liar before. Marshal or not, you need to take that back."

"Farley, you prove to me you're not lying and I will apologize to you, the state of Arkansas from which you reside, swim the ocean and kiss the Queen's ass."

Deputy Farley suddenly felt way over his head. He already knew Tucker was a tough man, and he also knew he would not back up. He thought about his options. If he made a play on him, he most likely would be killed. If he let it go, he would most likely have to explain what they were doing here. Neither option set well.

"Look, Marshal, I'd tell you why we're here, but it ain't my place. Marshal Galt needs to do that. All I can say is I'm hoping this trip turns out good, you and Marshal Galt being good friends and all."

"Well now, Farley, I can't think of a reason in the world why we wouldn't remain friends. Can you think of a reason? Now before you answer that, remember the Good Book. 'No liar shall enter the Kingdom of Heaven'."

He glanced at Macie who was looking at him with calm eyes. He looked back at Tucker. "Look, the deal is, Marshal Galt is up here on a hunch. He's trying to figure out who killed Reed Fletcher and all of his men. Since Macie here is maybe from Louisiana, I think the marshal thinks she might be able to tell him who might have done the killings." He waited for Tucker to speak.

Billie walked up about then. "I'm ready." She was bubbling over with the prospect of spending time with young Deputy Farley down by the creek.

Tucker smiled. "Well Deputy, your date is just in time." His eyes went from Deputy Farley to Billie. "You two have a good time." Billie didn't know what was going on, but she felt the tension.

When they left Tucker looked at Macie. "Something had to have happened for Marshal Galt to ride here. He may know about you and me seeing one another, but that's not what brought him here. Farley said, 'you maybe being from Louisiana', means Marshal Galt has had contact with someone that has caused him to come snooping around. I don't like it. Is he here to see what you know, or is he after you? Either way, old bloodhounds don't give up easily."

"What should I do, kill him?"

Tucker was taken aback by that. "No we don't kill him! Macie, this isn't the swamp where you kill to end problems."

"I wish it were. It's much easier and simpler." She smiled across the table at him.

"You worry me some. There's a part of you that has your families swamp ways. Those ways don't work with law."

Where Outlaws Roam
Royal Wade Kimes

"I know, you've told me a hundred times. But the inland people make life so complicated when it can be so simple."

"Well, in a society there's more to it than trapping alligators and shooting people."

Macie stared at him with fire dancing around in her eyes. He had made her angry. "You talked down to me then. You slandered my upbringing. Maybe I didn't grow up in the Queen's Palace and ride white horses in parades like you. Maybe I didn't have pretty clothes and wasn't draped in jewels and come from conquerors of nations. But I done something you haven't. I survived hell, Tucker Shaw! I watched a whole people die in agony one at a time from a plague. I lived with the fear I was next while listening to the cries at night. I survived a mean old daddy and uncles that were born with no chance, and too stupid to realize there was anything more. I watched a mother die a little every day from the sadness of not being able to get me away from all of it. You may think all they did was hunt alligators, breed, and kill folks, but they had feelings, and they had thoughts. There were good people in that swamp same as there were the kind I was born into. If one was in trouble, so were they all. Maybe my daddy and his brothers weren't that way, but for the most part the swamp people were. They took care of their own. A friend was a friend. He didn't go around behind your back trying to get dirt on you. At least the swamp men were men. I don't know what you would call Marshal Galt, and those like him."

That was the first chewing out Tucker Shaw had ever gotten, and for sure the first one he had ever taken. He looked at her in awe. She won his respect in a different way. He loved and respected her as a lady, but what she just did made him respect her for her principals, though they might be a little off center from his, she stood up for them. She was all woman.

"Macie, I don't ever remember saying I was wrong in my life, though I have been a lot of the time. I'm saying it to you, I'm truly sorry and I deserved that chewing. I feel you left very little of my behind though." They laughed and then stood to leave.

"Where are you two going?" It was Marshal Sanders and Angel

Hound.

"I'm walking Macie to her room and then I'll be at the jail." He smiled. "You know Marshal Sanders... I'm about ready to hand this job back to you."

"Oh no you don't. I only have to wear this badge one more month and I'm gone. You're the Marshal of Dye and the surrounding counties, me, I'm marshal where they send me. Since I'm retiring I think they're letting me run my time out here in Dye."

"Well, don't get too comfortable. I may slip off and you end up with it again."

"I'd make it my top priority to track you down and bring you back." He laughed and slapped Tucker on the shoulder. He held Macie's hand and looked her in the eyes. "Lord girl... what I'd give to be twenty-five again. You're prettier every time I see you."

"You are such a flirt, Marshal Sanders."

"Oh, Tucker. I saw Marshal Galt a little bit ago. He asked me if we could all maybe have supper tonight here at Sisters at around seven o'clock instead of six-thirty. I told him I'd try and get it together. Does that work for you?"

"I suppose." Tucker's eyes casually went to Macie. She was already looking at him. He now felt Marshal Galt was using his supper invitation to get a look at Macie, and maybe question her some.

They turned to leave but were stopped again by Marshal Sanders. "Are you ever going to tell me what it is you think I ought to know, but can't find out from you?" He grinned and winked at Macie.

"I'm getting closer to telling you all the time." They turned and left with Tucker laughing.

Where Outlaws Roam
Royal Wade Kimes

Chapter 28

Tucker was sitting out on the porch of the jail near two in the afternoon when Admiral Fetter came up and sat down.

"Robert, I'm sorry I haven't been to see you today. I've been somewhat busy. Can you believe Tucker Shaw just said that? You used to tell me if I would apply myself I might like the results. I'm doing it and the results work a man to death." They laughed together and then Robert became serious.

"Tucker, I'm no longer an admiral. I resigned."

Tucker practically fell out of the small wooden chair he was sitting in. He looked around too fast and was leaning back against the wall.

"You resigned the Royal Navy? Why? What happened?"

"Several things in a row I guess. One was when they gave me orders to eliminate you. I took the assignment just so I could keep an eye on things… and maybe figure out a way to get you away. I didn't have to do that once it got down to just one man, Ben Gladstone. I knew he wasn't close to a match for you. I had an extreme piece of luck, Marshal Sanders coming along and killing Garret Gray like he did. Walter Hobson was who worried me the most, but then he got a surprise. You were waiting on him. He was sure he would ride into town, set up and kill you from a distance. I bet he was sweating when he realized he was going to have to face you close range."

"He wasn't as sure of himself, I can say that."

"Tucker, I'm staying here. I'm going to buy a ranch here close by and become an American. What do you think?"

Tucker jumped up from his chair and pulled Robert to his feet. "I can't believe it! You're staying here in Kansas?!"

"I am."

"You wait until I tell Macie! She'll be pleased. Hell, you'd think you were my dad as much as I have talked about you to her. I told her you taught me to ride, shoot, play chess, and manners when I took a notion to use them." He laughed, but Robert chuckled rather halfheartedly.

"Yeah, we did a lot of things together. You were the son I didn't have." As he said that to Tucker, he thought how true a statement it was. Tucker was truly the son he didn't have, for he was his son, but he didn't have him.

Suddenly gunfire was coming from down the street. Tucker took off in a run with Robert trying to stay up. Two more shots were fired and they came from inside the saloon. He eased up to the door and peered in. He saw a man hunkered down behind a table and another across the room. He started to yell at them when gunfire broke out again. He stepped through the batwings.

"Hold your fire!"

"Go to hell!" A tough looking cowboy that hadn't shaved in a week spun around from the table he was at and fired at Tucker. The bullet whizzed by his ear as he drew and fired. The cowboy jumped sideways after he fired his first bullet, which caused Tucker to miss. He was astonished he had missed him. It was the first miss in years. He came out of his stunned moment and dived for the end of the bar. He heard a bullet make a thud in the floor by him. He knew by that the other man joined in with his partner. He sat quietly behind the end of the bar.

"Boys, this here is Marshal Tucker! Like it is now, all that will happen to you is a week in jail and loss of firearms for the week. This thing goes any further and someone is going to get killed. You call it, jail or boot hill?"

"We didn't start this damn fight!"

"What's it all about?" Tucker waited.

"Well, those two across the way over there hiding behind the roulette wheel, called us damn Yanks. They ain't nobody calling a southern boy a Yank. Hell, we're from South Texas. We came up with a cattle drive. We're riding around looking for work."

Tucker called to the other two. "Is that true what this cowboy said?"

"It most certainly is. The British has always called you Americans, Yanks."

Tucker laughed. "I be damn. Is that you Captain Ross, Major Parker?"

"It is me, Major Parker, tis us, Sir Tucker Shaw."

"Hey, you cowboys! Throw your guns out, you two British do the same!" He waited until he heard four guns hit the floor and then he stood. Robert Fetter was standing just outside the

Where Outlaws Roam
Royal Wade Kimes

batwings. He came in when Tucker stood up.

Tucker laughed at the four of them. "I'm afraid there's been a big misunderstanding."

The stocky built cowboy was frowning and still not happy. "What kind of misunderstanding?"

"Well, these two men are British. It is true the British call us Yanks, but they use the term Yank for all Americans. It hasn't anything to do with the war."

Parker smiled. "I see now why they were angry." He cut his eyes to the two cowboys. "I'm afraid we have a lot to learn as cowboys. We just arrived here and plan to stay. We're going to work for Admiral Fetter here. He is retiring and buying a jot of land. I think you boys call it sections."

"Sections?" The cowboy was shocked and at the same time was very interested in hearing more. "Why don't I buy us all a drink?"

Parker grinned. "No, it was the two of us that made the mistake and caused all the trouble, it's only fitting we buy."

The cowboy fuzzed up. "Look, us boys down south call to buy a drink, it'll not be set aside. We're buying. Now if you would like to buy the next round... well, that there's a different story." Laughter took over as the four of them bellied up to the bar.

Robert looked torn in what to do suddenly. "Ah, Tucker, I need to talk with you on a personal matter as soon as I can. That said... I would like to meet these two chaps looking for work before they get away and hire on to some brand. If I buy a ranch I'm going to need some men who know what they're doing. God knows I know nothing about herding little fork footed cows around."

Tucker laughed at him. After that statement he was inclined to believe him. Cattle were anything but little. "When you want to talk I'll be at the jail." He left the saloon with Robert buying the next round.

Ray and Lou Pitman along with a room full of cowboys were in seeing Marshal Tucker Shaw at the time Robert came by. He realized he would have to wait. Tucker was reading a document and didn't see Robert stick his head in. When he read it over he looked up and smiled.

"Well, it looks in order. Lou, I'm turning you loose. I'll be turning this paper into Judge Maxey. If there are any outstanding warrants I don't know about... I'll have to come see you."

Lou swallowed kind of hard. "Unless me slapping around Mavis Jones for mistreating a horse... I reckon not."

"That's not quite what I'm talking about." He smiled at him and started to say something, but Ray put in.

"He's talking about any other holdups. They by damn better not be." He looked his son over with disapproving eyes. Then he smiled. "Say ya slapped ole Mavis around did ya? I hadn't heared that." He slapped his leg and the whole jail shook from laughter when Pitman and his men turned it loose. "I bet ole Mavis pissed his pants when you called him on that. He always did treat a horse too rough."

Lou took it from there. "Yeah, I told him I was going to show him what his horse was going through. I slapped his face a couple times, kicked him in the side once or twice and then kicked his ass about once." They all bellowed out as the whole bunch went out the door and mounted up. Ray looked over at Lou. "Did the sonofabitch apologize for his actions?"

Tucker realized those happy go lucky cowboys had forgotten him. They had taken care of a matter... and then it didn't matter.

"Hell, ole Mavis not only apologized to me, I had him apologize to his horse. He kissed him right on the end of the muzzle." They bellowed out again.

"By damn, Lou, Boys, this day calls for a round of drinks... I'm buying." They all whooped, whirled their horses and headed for the saloon in a lope.

Tucker was grinning until he saw Macie coming down the boardwalk on the other side of the street. She crossed and hurried to him.

"Something wrong?" She had a grave look on her face.

"Yes, I just saw a man in the lobby of the hotel. He's an old broken down horse trader from Sota, Kansas. Tucker, he's the man I let have the Fletcher horse and gear. There was a man with him, a younger and taller man. He had the old coon point me out to him and then he approached me. He said a Fort Smith Marshal

Where Outlaws Roam
Royal Wade Kimes

questioned him about the horse and asked to see the rifle. He said the letters on the stock was initials for a Reed Fletcher. Then he said the old man and himself didn't much cotton to the Fort Smith Marshal, and could be persuaded to say they never saw me before. She turned her eyes to the floor. "Tucker, I paid the man five hundred dollars for silence and asked him to ride on. He said they would once he had a few drinks."

"Macie, honey, you can't fix a wrong with another wrong... with damn crooks anyway." He remembered his wild days in Britain. He had fixed many wrongs with more wrongs. The problem with that was; he never knew if the fix was going to stay fixed. He processed the current events through his mind and smiled.

"Macie, those two don't even know Marshal Galt is up here. Now we know Marshal Galt isn't here to find out if you have any information that would lead him to the stolen horse, and the demise of Fletcher. He's here to arrest you if he can, but there lies the hitch. He doesn't quite have all he needs to do so. He needs proof you took the horse and didn't get him from someone. He needs a bill of sale and the old man from Sota to testify you were the one he got the horse from. As for Fletcher's departure, he hasn't any proof at all you had anything to do with it... and I can't think of a way he can get any."

"Tucker, you've never let me tell you why Reed Fletcher was hanging from Eagles Ledge. Please let me speak it. I have to."

He didn't want to hear it, but he saw the pleading in her eyes. "Turning you down isn't in the cards is it?"

She smiled and then became sincere as she began. "Reed Fletcher was setting up his long range rifle. You were riding towards the town of Melt leading your dead prisoner's horse. He could kill at great distances with that gun. I knew you were a dead man. I came up from behind and threw a knife in him. He fell and broke the big bore rifle, that was when he tried to pull his pistol but I was too quick. I stopped him." She hesitated and then went on. "I whacked his thumb off and disabled him from pulling the hammer back on the gun. I kept him from shooting you in the back. You wouldn't have survived a hit from that big gun. Tucker, I followed him to Kansas and watched his every move. I felt sure he would try one of his long range alligator shots on you."

"Alligator shots?"

"Men like him bet big dollars on who can make the longest and best shot on a gator. He hunted them and brought rich people from the cities to hunt them as well. He shoots for the fun, not the meat."

"I see." He looked her in the eyes. "Here's what I'm not seeing. I don't understand, Macie, if you had Fletcher disabled, why in the world did you kill him?"

She looked at him in disbelief and surprise. "Tucker, I didn't kill Fletcher! Someone was coming up the back of Eagles Ledge and I scaled down the front side. I didn't get a look at who it was. I made off with Fletcher's horse and my own. I rode for a distance and heard a rifle shot. I knew whoever was up there had shot Fletcher because his saddle rifle was in its scabbard. I waited a little while and decided to ride back. I found him shot in the forehead. It was me that hung him out over the ledge. I knew you would be riding passed Eagles Ledge on your way back to Dye and would see him.

Tucker now knew Macie had saved his life. He pulled her to him and kissed her. He was also relieved to find out she hadn't killed Fletcher… but who did? "You stay here. When I come back I will personally walk you to your room. If Marshal Galt even says boo to me, I'll put him to sleep."

He turned and headed for the saloon. He would do whatever it took to protect Macie, even if it meant going from Marshal Tucker Shaw to Outlaw Tucker Shaw of the Wild West. As he walked towards the saloon he had one other thought. The Wild West is a lot more complicated than one might think. It isn't so colorful if you're the one doing the coloring. It's dangerous and dirty at times.

Robert Fetter was sitting out on the porch of the Dye Hotel when he spotted Tucker stepping fast towards the saloon. He had seen that walk before and it always without fail meant action. He jumped to his feet and ran out in the street beside

Where Outlaws Roam
Royal Wade Kimes

him. He said nothing as Tucker smiled. They never broke stride as they approached the saloon. Robert flipped the leather cord loose holding his pistol in its holster.

Marshal Sanders was coming out of Sisters after having coffee and saw Tucker and Robert heading towards the saloon. He didn't miss Robert flipping his hammer cord loose either. He started hot stepping it in their direction and checking the loads in the cylinder of his gun as he went. He was still favoring the one leg but his adrenalin was high and he hardly noticed it.

Tucker entered the saloon with Robert beside him. The two cowboys Robert had hired were sitting over in a corner sipping on beer. They immediately recognized trouble and got up from the table. They made their way over beside Robert and Marshal Shaw. They faced the bar where five men stood. Two of those men were Captain Ross and Major Parker. They turned and realized what was taking place. They too gathered around beside Tucker and Robert. The other man who wasn't with anyone, stepped away from the bar immediately.

"Mister, turn around."

Robert rolled his eyes when he saw an old stove up man turn around.

Tucker glanced at Robert and smiled. "Not you, your friend there."

The younger much taller man turned to face him. "What's this all about?"

Marshal Sanders walked in and realized there wasn't a spot for him, so he took a seat over to the left at a table. Ray and Lou Pitman and their hands were sitting around tables at the far end of the room. Lou tapped Ray on the shoulder and jerked his head in the direction of possible action. They all turned their chairs to where they could watch.

"I'm Marshal Tucker Shaw, but for the next little while I'm just plain Tucker Shaw." He pulled his badge off and laid it on a table. "We welcome folks to Dye, Kansas that come here to be good citizens and act right. Them that don't, we show those the road. I've not any use for a blackmailing, lying, crook that puts upon women. Normally you'd do time for something like that.

However, I'm just going to teach you a lesson. I will warn you before you take the schooling... it's a hard damn class."

"Well, now look I didn't mean to get the Marshal of Dye all riled up. Don't tell me you're sweet on that little dark eyed hellcat?"

Tucker glanced at the old man. "Sir, you're old enough to be a wise man. Get on your horse and leave Dye, and distance yourself from this criminal."

He turned up the last of his beer and sat it down. "I believe I'll do that, Marshal." He squinted his eyes at the taller man as he looked up at him. "Mister, I wasn't sure I liked you, I don't guess I do." He cut his eyes hard at the men standing with Marshal Shaw. He grinned through stubby white whiskers and showed no teeth at all. He looked back up at the tall man. "It looks to me, you're being asked to dance." The old man took feeble slow steps leaving the saloon. He had to walk through the men lined up in front of him. They parted and let him go past.

Tucker took four fast steps and connected with the chin of the tall man. His head went backwards, and caught another punch in the same place when it came forward again. He grabbed him and slung him towards the batwings. He fell and quickly stumbled to his feet. Tucker landed a long straight right that everyone in the saloon winced at. It sent the tall man right out into the street. A wagon was passing by and the team of black horses shied swiftly sideways to avoid the commotion.

Marshal Galt was up in his hotel room enjoying another round with Darla when he heard yelling outside. He rolled the beautiful naked Darla off of him and went to the window completely nude himself. He watched for only a few seconds. He turned and frantically started slipping clothes on.

"Where are you going?" Darla was surprised by his getting dressed.

"Business." He left in a hurry carrying his boots.

Meanwhile the tall man stood up and looked around him. He had lost Tucker. He turned a full three hundred and sixty degrees before he found him again. Tucker connected one more time. The tall man went backwards and fell flat of his back. A cloud of dust had plumed in the street from his hitting the ground.

Where Outlaws Roam
Royal Wade Kimes

Robert was observing the old broken down man getting ready to leave on his horse while the fight was going on. He led a bay colored horse over to a hitching rail and dropped the reins around the rail. He then walked over to Robert leading another bay and handed him the reins.

"Sir, I'm guessing this horse belongs to the tall man."

"It shore does. From what I can see, he'll be ready for him right soon. Funny ain't it, your come uppin's gets around to you sooner or later." He tee heed for several seconds while leaving town.

Robert took the horse and led him to an open spot, where the man taking the beating could see him. He got to his hands and knees and crawled to the horse. The four men who now were on payroll for Robert Fetters, tossed him aboard and slapped the horse on the rump with their hats. They were all laughing as they watched him go, swaying from one side to the other out of sight.

The Pitman crew was standing in front of the saloon. When the fight was over they went back in for more drinks. A good fight always calls for more drinks.

Marshal Galt slipped out of the livery and went down a backstreet undetected while leaving town.

Marshal Sanders walked in beside Tucker. "Son, you can fight."

"Compliments of the Royal Guard."

He put his hand on Tucker's shoulder. "I'm purely speculating mind you, but did that fight have anything to do with what I ought to know, but don't yet know?"

Tucker's eyes looked towards the jail and he saw Macie standing there waiting for him.

She smiled at him. She felt safe with Tucker. After witnessing the exhibition he put on in the street, she felt very safe. She now knew he would do whatever it took to keep her from harm.

Marshal Sanders looked in the direction he saw Tucker looking. He smiled and then mumbled. "Yeah." He glanced very quickly at him. "I think I'll have a drink." He turned knowing Tucker didn't even hear him. He understood it. He had the same thing waiting for him in Pueblo. It didn't matter... he would see him at Sisters for supper.

Chapter 29

Tucker spent an hour in Macie's room making sure she didn't have a need not taken care of. He was on his way back to the jail and ran into Marshal Galt riding into town. Tucker instantly knew something was up. He was supposed to be with Darla. Where had he been? Fort Smith was in the opposite direction, and there's nothing in the direction he was coming from except prairie grass, and more prairie grass.

"Marshal, Tucker Shaw!"

"Hello there, Marshal Galt. You finally came out of hiding?"

He sheepishly smiled at him. "I'm plain sorry I haven't been around. I've been busier than I had previously thought I would be... if you know what I mean?"

"Well, I thought I did until you come riding into town, instead of being in town. How is Darla anyway?"

"She's the best." He chuckled. "You didn't mean in bed did you?"

Tucker stared silently for a moment. "Is this your way of cooling down?"

"I'm not following you."

"Well, you and Darla been at it awhile up there in your room, at least I thought you were... maybe not. If you were, then I was wondering if you take a ride afterwards to cool down. I'll say this, you don't look worse for wear.

He reared back in the saddle and laughed. "I'm eating good. We play and then go eat, play and go eat. I've caught up on sleep, too." He leaned up in the saddle and took a peppermint stick from his mouth. "Truth is... I thought my ole horse might need a little exercise."

Tucker again stared at him. He knew his friend was lying. By that alone he knew he and Macie had trouble. Marshal Galt wasn't going to go away or let anything drop. Though Reed Fletcher had been out to kill him, and Macie stopped him, it wouldn't make any difference to Marshal Galt. Proving she did or didn't do it wouldn't be easy.

"Well, I guess I better put my horse up. I'm sure Darla's waiting on me."

Where Outlaws Roam
Royal Wade Kimes

"You know Galt... maybe you ought to think about getting married?"

That was the first time Tucker had used an unfriendly tone of voice and left 'marshal' off his name. He caught it and tried to pass it off.

"I use to say, 'not me', to marrying, but Darla has me wondering about the future. I'd never say that to anyone else... just my close friends." He waited to see if there was a reaction of any kind when calling him a close friend. There wasn't.

"Well, if you're thinking it, might as well do it." Tucker stood staring.

It was getting harder for them to talk. There was a for certain strain between them now. "I might just do it." He managed a smile. "I guess we could get by on marshal's pay."

"Macie and I plan to."

"You planning to marry that girl? Well... let me be the first to wish you the best... you'll need it."

A coolness ran down Tucker's back. "Why would I need it?"

"You know... Kansas, it's a tough place to raise a family is all."

Tucker was sure the statement had a deceptive meaning. "Galt, if there's one thing I'm not, it's afraid of work, or anything else that might be tough."

Marshal Galt had been forcing a smile, but finally decided to dispense with it. "Yeah Tucker, if there's one thing you've proved since coming here, you're not afraid of much and you're a stayer. I'll see you at supper. I'm looking forward to seeing what it is in a woman you like."

He didn't respond, and he too caught what Galt said. He left off 'marshal', when he said his name. Things had definitely cooled between the two of them. He also didn't like his comment about what kind of woman he liked. He watched him mosey on towards the livery and then he headed towards the saloon. He wanted to say goodbye to Ray and Lou before they left. Then he would head back to the jail.

"Tucker."

"Robert, I'm sorry I wasn't here. I ran into Marshal Galt and had a drink with Ray and Lou Pitman."

"Don't worry about it. That was quite the show you put on in the street." He handed him a wad of bills. "The tall man left his saddlebags in the saloon. It wasn't like he had a chance to get them. There's five hundred and ten dollars there. I guess you can keep it or send it to him by mail… if you know where he lives."

"Ten dollars is all that's his. The rest is mine and Macie's. She and I share a bank account."

Ray and Lou Pitman rode by the jail leaving town and waved to them. Ray hollered back. "You ever get up my way you've got a place to stay!"

Tucker grinned and waved.

Robert half waved until an odd look appeared on his face. "Tucker, what are they doing leading Catcher and your bronze colored mare?"

"I sold them to Ray."

"Why? I didn't think you'd part with those two."

"He asked me if I'd sell them. I set a price and he bought them. I learned a lesson, don't price your stuff around ranching cowboys."

"I'll buy them back for you!" He made an effort to get up and Tucker put his arm in front of him.

"Let it go. I appreciate it, but I live by my decisions."

"Well, okay, but it don't set well you losing those two beauties."

"Don't worry about it, Robert, there are other horses. Who knows, I might just get up that way and buy them back one day."

Robert stared at him for a minute and decided to drop it. He had a more pressing issue to discuss. "Ah, Tucker, I need to speak with you on a very important and delicate matter that involves you greatly."

He instantly felt and heard the difference in Robert's voice. He stared at him very intently. "You have my attention. Talk out, I'm listening."

"Well, I'm making a journey. I will be gone for a little while, maybe a couple of months. I'm planning to leave in a week or so. I first have to close on a ranch I have looked at already. I'm excited about it. Ross, Parker, and the two cowboys I hired will watch the ranch. I hope they are able to fix it up some. It's been

Where Outlaws Roam
Royal Wade Kimes

let go a little. I'm buying two sections. That should be a nice enough spot of ground, don't you think?"

"Yeah... that's one hell of a spot." Tucker was shocked by his oldest friend buying such a large piece of ground. He would have never thought him a rancher. He guessed it wasn't too late. "Where are you taking this journey to?" He cocked his head to one side and looked Robert in the eyes.

"New Orleans."

"New Orleans!? What is in New Orleans that has anything to do with your ranch in Kansas?"

He looked at him for the longest of time and then smiled. "Your mother."

"My mother is." He stopped and stared at him. "Robert, my mother is coming here?"

"She is. We're to be married. I have already let the Queen know there will be one hell of a party after the wedding, and she is invited."

"What happened to Poppa Ira?"

"He is being made to go along with whatever the Queen and your mother's wishes are."

"You are full of surprises, Robert Fetter. I'm proud for you... and mother."

"Yes, well, I have one more surprise that will checkmate all others."

"What could possibly checkmate such news as grand as mother coming to America, and the two of you being married? I'm damn near in tears now."

"Well, grand as that is, this is better." Suddenly tears began to fall down his cheeks as he looked at his son.

Tucker began to choke up. A tremendous lump had shown up in his throat unannounced. He had never seen Robert cry before. Whatever this news was, it was dear to the heart.

"Tucker, I've been informed by your mother and the Queen that you... well, you're my son. You haven't one ounce of Ira Shaw's blood in you. You are a Fetter."

Tucker was standing by one of the chairs on the porch of the jail and grabbed hold of it to sit. He said nothing for a minute while staring at the floor of the porch. He finally looked at Robert.

"Why did they not tell us? When I think back of my childhood it was you that was always there, you were the one that taught me, loved me, and disciplined me, not Ira." We've been played for two simpletons. I suppose it looks worse on you than I... after all I was but a small tyke to start with."

When Tucker stopped talking they stood staring at one another. Robert reached for him but was so overcome with emotion he stumbled from weakness. Tucker grabbed on to him as if life would suddenly end if he let go. The world was right except for Marshal Galt and his quest to arrest someone for the murder of Reed Fletcher, and the stealing of his horse.

Marshal Galt sat down on the bed beside Darla staring out the window of the hotel. He was slowly getting undressed while she poured him a drink of whiskey. She could see he was in a somber mood from what he had been since arriving in Dye.

"What's wrong with my Marshal Galt?"

"I've got myself a big damn problem."

She handed him the drink. He turned it up and gulped it down with one swallow. "I'm at a place I've never been before. I've got to make a decision between the law and a friend. The problem is... I'm not sure I have the proof to make it stick on the law side of things... and if I don't... I lose the case and the friend."

Darla scooted up behind him and pressed her bare breast to his now shirtless back. "If you haven't proof, why pursue it?"

"I guess I've been a law man too long. A man was brutally murdered and if that wasn't enough, the bastard that done it hung the victim out over a cliff for the world to see. Unsolved cases bother me... and I'm real damn curious as to who went to the trouble to hang the man over a cliff. Right now all I have is my suspicions, but they're strong. I did just get a little information, but not enough."

"That sounds awful, but given time it'll probably work its self out." She kissed his shoulder. "You think a friend of yours was involved in something like that?"

"I do."

Where Outlaws Roam
Royal Wade Kimes

"Well, if he is, he needs to pay for it... but if all you have is a hunch, that's kind of thin. Instead of causing a problem with your friend, why not lay back and see what happens? Your friend might make a mistake and give himself away."

"I can't chance that. The longer it goes without being solved the harder it'll be to catch or prove who done it. I already don't know where the man's horse ended up. I had the horse in my hands and stupid like, I let him get away."

He turned his head somewhat around towards Darla as her face lay on the back of his shoulder. "No, the law needs to solve this case. Whoever killed the man, he needs to be brought to justice. A crime like that doesn't need to be let go. Not only that, but this man had others that worked for him. They're dead too. "It's a hard decision, but friend or no friend I guess I have to do my duty. It makes me a little sad to have to be the one to bring them in, and if they're guilty... well, I'll feel damn bad about it all."

"Sometimes a person has to make decisions with the heart, not the book."

He turned to her. "What do you mean?"

"You have described a hideous crime, but you might want to give your friend the benefit of the doubt. If he is truly a friend, then use your heart until he proves otherwise. If it turns out he is guilty... then go by the book."

"Darla, I swore an oath to uphold the law. The day I stop is the day I need to turn in my badge. I can't let friends influence me on the way I go about my job."

"I know. You are strong willed. Galt, there's not much about you that isn't strong." She tickled his ears and ran her hand through his hair. "Marshal, have you still got enough steam left to take care of this naked woman you have in your room?"

He turned. "Let me see what I can do."

Chapter 30

Sisters was packed when Tucker and Macie walked in. The place would seat sixty people and every table was full. Macie was wearing a new dress she bought for the occasion of dining at Sisters with guests. The front of the powder blue dress swept low in the front revealing her firm womanhood, and the backside daringly dipped down to the palm of her back. She was breathtakingly beautiful. Tucker was proud to be seen with her. He dressed in a new black hat and frock coat for the occasion.

Marshal Galt stood up so Tucker could see where they were setting. He gently and softly touched Macie on the back to proceed to the table. He held her chair and slid it forward perfectly for her seating. He smiled at everyone and sat beside her. Marshal Galt, Darla, Deputy Farley, Marshal Sanders, Robert Fetter, and Angel Hound were all seated at the table.

Tucker looked over at Angel Hound dressed in a white shirt and bowtie. "I've not seen you around, where have you been the last day or two?"

"I be running a lot. I got me a letter from my mama says there is a foot race going to take place in Fort Smith. They be running five mile and the winner wins a hundred dollars. I be training for it."

"All ages running?"

"I reckon. It don't make me any difference who be running, he be left setting."

"Can side bets be made on this race?"

"I reckon. I heard tell they bets on races like that. Mama wouldn't prove of me betting. I ain't got money anyhow."

"I do." He took five hundred dollars out of his pocketbook he pulled from a very classy black vest. "You lay this down on you to win. Tell one of the Fort Smith Marshals that Marshal Tucker Shaw asked that they oversee the bet." He paused and smiled. "If you're going to run, you should make some real money. I'll split the winnings with you."

"You means it?"

"I most certainly do."

Angel Hound put the money away and thanked him for his

Where Outlaws Roam
Royal Wade Kimes

support.

Marshal Sanders was all smiles. He had been slipping away and timing Angel Hound. He liked the young man and wanted to see him succeed in whatever he did.

Marshal Galt was eyeing Macie. In fact he hadn't taken his eyes off her since she sat down. Darla noticed that and was becoming frustrated with it. She was misreading him, thinking he was being somewhat flirtatious. She kicked under the table causing a sudden jump from him. He cut his eyes at her and then glanced around the table to see who saw him get kicked. He realized everyone but Marshal Sanders and Angel Hound saw the event.

Tucker smiled at him. "Did you bump your knee there, Marshal?"

He didn't answer, but instead asked if everyone was ready to order. He then turned to Macie. "How did you happen to land this wild Marshal of Dye, Kansas? I understand you're not from here."

"I didn't land him. I met him and we were attracted to each other. Where on earth did you hear I wasn't from here?"

He looked confused. "Well, I don't know come to think of it, but are you?"

She smiled. "I thought everyone was from Dye, Kansas."

That answer caused the table to burst with laughter.

Robert Fetter raised his glass of wine. "A toast to new beginnings."

Tucker responded. "Hear, hear." He was staring at Galt.

Deputy Farley was sitting at the table, but he was far from being there in heart and mind. He watched Billie serving tables and was consumed with her until a man reached up and pulled her down close to him. He stood, threw his napkin on the table and marched over to the man.

"You let go of her, or I'll make you wish you'd never been born."

He turned her loose and then stood. "I've turned her loose, now how are you going to make me wish I wasn't born?"

He suddenly grabbed the man between the legs. His grip was like a vise, causing him to bend his knees and speak in a low desperate tone.

"Please, Mister, I'm sorry. I was out of line. Please, I can't take much more."

"You mess with me again and you'll not be having offspring. We understand one another?"

"We do."

"What's your name?"

"Boyd Smith."

"Well, Boyd Smith, I'm Deputy Farley. If I have any further trouble with you, I'll throw you in jail for a month, after I've beat the hell out of you."

"They'll be no trouble. "Please, just turn me loose. Why didn't you say you were a deputy? This could have been avoided."

"It has turned out alright. Enjoy the rest of the night." He turned him loose and went back to his table with everyone looking on.

Billie was quite taken by the occurrence. That was the moment she knew Deputy Farley was hers for life.

Marshal Galt was pleased with Deputy Farley, but that didn't detour him from his reason for having supper with Tucker and Macie. He kept looking at her hoping to maybe get a reaction to cause an invite for a question. So far it wasn't working.

They had supper and were having dessert when Marshal Galt asked another question. "Macie, have you ever been to Sota, Kansas?"

She smiled. "Why on earth would you ask that?"

"Well, I spoke to a man that said he bought a horse in Sota that originally belonged to you."

"Who is this man?"

"A horse trader I met."

"Well, Marshal, I don't know any horse traders. Did the man say he knew me?"

"Well, no, I don't reckon he knows you personal, but knows of you."

Marshal Sanders was looking at Marshal Galt with very stern and disapproving eyes. He knew how Marshal Galt was... when he was after someone he could be relentless. For some reason he was after Macie.

Where Outlaws Roam
Royal Wade Kimes

"Marshal Galt, this isn't the place or time."

He cut his eyes from Macie to Marshal Sanders and immediately dropped the questions.

Tucker's eyes darted from Marshal Sanders, to Marshal Galt, and then to Robert Fetter, his newly found father. He raised his glass. "To good Marshals, loving family, and better friends."

Everyone drank but Marshal Galt. He was looking back and forth to Macie and Marshal Sanders. He finally glanced at Tucker. "Marshal Sanders is right. Maybe we should talk about some things tomorrow."

"Here's one we can talk about right now." Tucker came with a fast crossing right that caught him dead on the chin. He went sprawling backwards in his chair. He crashed into the table behind him and never moved.

All three of the Sway Sisters came rushing out to see what the commotion was. Billie had fire in her eyes when she saw what had happened. "Marshal Tucker Shaw, this is not a saloon!"

Connie stepped in. "Billie, that's enough." She glanced at Tucker. "I don't know what this is about, surely you had good reason, but I am afraid I must ask you to leave."

"Reason enough... if you would be so kind as to except my apology." He smiled at everyone and took Macie by the hand. "Let's be going. I do believe supper is over." They tuned and left.

Marshal Sanders was looking on wondering what it was all about. Something was in the air and he planned to find out what."

Robert smiled. He didn't know why Tucker decked Marshal Galt, but it was alright. That was his son.

The following morning before daylight, Tucker rode a rented horse from the livery out to the ranch Robert Fetter was buying. He had Macie with him. He was met at the yard gate by Robert, Ross and Parker. The two hired hands rode up on horses from the corral and barn.

Robert was all smiles. "What a wonderful surprise! Get down and come in!" He was excited his son had come to see him and brought his significant other. He turned to his ranch hands. "Men, I have an announcement to make." They all waited as

Tucker and Macie walked in beside him. "Men, Tucker and I have been sent word by his mother Margaret and the Queen of Britain herself that Tucker is... well... he's my son."

At first there was processing silence, and then Ross and Parker began clapping their hands. The two hired hands joined in. Once congratulations were had by all, Tucker, Macie, and Robert went inside. The interior of the house was okay, but would need some fixing up in places and a woman's touch for sure. There weren't any curtains and other niceties that a female brings to a home.

Robert poured them a cup of coffee and they sat down. "I'm glad you came out. I have a question for you, but I already know you've come to answer it."

Tucker chuckled at him. He knew Robert well enough to know he would be curious about the decking of Marshal Galt. "I figured when I decked Marshal Galt last night you knew something was wrong."

"I know you, Tucker. Yes I knew."

"Well, here it is. Marshal Galt is trying to pin a murder, and maybe more than one on Macie."

"What? Why, the sonofabitch must be eliminated! What kind of a friend is he?" He glanced at Macie and put his hand over hers at the kitchen table.

"I'm afraid friendship doesn't come into play here. There was a man by the name of Reed Fletcher that followed me up from Louisiana. He brought with him some men. They're all dead. Fletcher was found dead hanging from a cliff. Macie stopped him from shooting me in the back with a long range rifle."

"That's justified."

"Except for the fact she wasn't the one that killed him. She stopped him with a knife, but he was shot dead in the forehead with a rifle. Macie heard someone coming and beat it away from there." He paused for a minute. "Robert, I've got to try and find the real killer. I'm a marshal, it's my duty. I've also got to protect Macie. Because Marshal Galt suspects her and won't let the Fletcher murder go. To get him off Macie's trail I've got to know who else was on Eagles Ledge. I might ride back up to Melt and see Marshal Lambert. He may know something, or have seen something that would be a clue." He looked at Robert with sober eyes. "I'm here to tell you, Macie and I are going to disappear for a while. You understand if I tell you I can't divulge where I'm going?"

"Most certainly, it will keep anyone from beating the, 'whereabouts' of you out of me. They couldn't anyway... you're my son."

"Yeah, and speaking of that. I can't tell you how proud of that I am, but would it be alright with you that I continue to call you Robert?"

He laughed. "No problem. It's enough just knowing we're father and son."

Chapter 31

Back in the southwest a tremendous bank of black clouds was building. It looked bad. They had a green cast underneath and in a few places they were green looking in the middle. It had been a while since Kansas had seen any bad weather, in fact it had been fairly dry and rain was needed. This looked like something not needed. The clouds might have lots of rain in them, but to anyone who lived in Kansas for very long knew by looking the clouds were packing wind and hail. Tucker had seen storms before, but he wasn't familiar with Kansas twisters. His saving grace was Macie. Her being from Louisiana she had seen it all and lots of it.

They had bought two worn out older horses to leave Dye on. They would have to do until Tucker could put better mounts under them. They had been gone from the Fetter Ranch for a couple hours when Macie pulled up. Birds were flying low to the ground and lots of them.

"Tucker, when birds do that it's certain we have a bad storm coming. It will be here in an hour or less. We need shelter."

"Well, we neither one know this country." He looked far into the distance. There were rolling hills with yellow flowers and bluestem prairie grass. "Honey, we're pretty much out in the open. Let's kick these old nags into a lope. I don't know how much they can stand, but we need to cover some ground."

Macie looked back one more time as they hit a long stride across the prairie floor. She was worried. They might not have to worry about Marshal Galt if they were caught in the open with the storm she could see approaching.

Marshal Sanders had breakfast early and walked over to the jail. He wanted to see Tucker and ask him what the hell was going on. His decking Marshal Galt and Galt's questions to Macie last night told him there was a storm brewing. It wasn't the one building in the southwest either. He walked in and called for Tucker but received no answer. He then walked around behind his desk and sat down. There was a letter lying center of it with his name written across it. He picked it up and walked to the door of the jail. The wind was picking up and it was growing dark. He watched as a man drove his team and wagon at a fast trot to the Lemon Drop Livery. The street was clear of people and then a bolt of lightning streaked from cloud to ground, followed by a loud clap of thunder.

He went back to the desk, sat down, turned the lamp up and stared at the envelope. Marshal Sanders, inside is the something you need to know.

Marshal Sanders,

You're the only lawman at present I feel I can trust. I said to you the other day I might hand this job back to you, though I didn't mean it, I'm doing just that until I find some answers to a killing. I'm asking you to take over Dye for me until I get this thing cleared up. I'm not turning in my badge, but I need your help. Marshal Galt has it in his head that Macie killed a man by the name of Reed Fletcher. I can't take a chance on him arresting her without proof. She didn't kill the man and I have to find who did. Maybe my disappearing will shake the real killer up. I'm hoping to bring him out into the open… make him make a mistake. I want Macie left alone, and she won't be as long as Marshal Galt is hounding her. I hope you understand and can play along. Keep your eyes and ears open and suspect everyone.
Ridin' away,
Marshal Tucker Shaw

Just as he finished the letter rain began to fall in buckets as the wind picked up. Then a few pieces of hail hit the roof. He walked to the window and looked out. The wind was blowing hard and the rain was coming down in sheets. He could hardly see the Dye Hotel. He looked down the street and saw a covered wagon tumble over. The horses had been unhooked and taken to the livery. He guessed the Lemon Drop Livery was full of horses and mules.

His thoughts went back to the letter and Tucker. He didn't approve of his way of handling the situation he faced, but he knew Marshal Galt. Tucker was right about him. He would hound

Macie until something happened. It would be harder to search and concentrate on finding a possible suspect if you were watching your back all the time.

Suddenly the door swung open. It was Marshal Galt. He came in and removed his slicker. He looked surprised to see Marshal Sanders.

"Morning, Marshal Galt."

"Morning. Ain't this weather something? Bad as it is here, I pity the poor devils northwest of here. It looks worse that direction." He looked around the office of the jail. "Where's Marshal Shaw? I told him we might talk this morning." He cut his eyes at Marshal Sanders and locked on him. "No coffee?"

"I just got here. The marshal isn't here and there doesn't seem to be any coffee made. I've had plenty though. I ate over at the Dye Hotel."

"Reckon where the marshal is this morning?"

"Maybe he's sleeping in with Macie." Marshal Sanders eyed him over.

"Yeah... maybe." He walked to the window and looked out. "This looks like it may set in and be here awhile." He turned and faced Marshal Sanders, water still dripping from his hat. "Marshal, me and you been friends a long time haven't we?"

"We have. We've seen some times chasing outlaws across the Oklahoma Territory and half of Kansas."

"In all that time, have I ever caused you to doubt me?"

"No, I don't think you ever have."

"Well old friend, I have something to tell you." He walked over and opened a cabinet door. "Marshal Shaw has a lot to learn. No jail should be without coffee." He turned and sat down in front of the desk. Marshal Sanders sat down behind it.

"Okay, what is it you have to tell me?"

"Well, it's about Macie. Marshal Shaw being in love with her is making it hard for me." His eyes darted from the floor to Marshal Sanders a couple times nervously. "You see I'm fair sure she killed a man by the name of Reed Fletcher out of Louisiana. It's obvious she's from there, a born Cajun if I ever laid eyes on one. She dodged my questions last night and was damn crafty at it. I think, bad as I hate to say it, Marshal Tucker knows she did it.

Where Outlaws Roam
Royal Wade Kimes

You see Fletcher was after Marshal Shaw for stealing his steamboat and selling it. I think he was out to kill him, but he didn't get it done... because I believe Macie killed him. I think she followed the man and hunted him down. I all but know she sold, traded, or got rid of his horse and gear to that broken down old man that was here the other day. I ran the man down Marshal Shaw beat half to death and tried to get him to tell me what he knew. He was so damn scared to talk he just sat on his horse clamped down tighter than a snapping turtle on a finger. I finally caught up with the old man. He said he didn't have any recollection of buying a horse from any girl. I know damn well he was lying."

"Well, so far Marshal Galt, all I've heard is a bunch of suspicion, accusing, and a lot of unfounded information. What you've laid out to me is not built on any proof, but a heightened cynicism of the girl. I sit here wondering where that comes from. For certain it is not the kind of thing a lawman works from. You're right, we've known one another a long time, and this is not the kind of thinking the Marshal Galt I know is a party to." He studied him closely for a moment. "This is not like you. It's like you to run a person until they cave in, but it's not like you to run them with little to no proof of wrong doing."

Marshal Galt stared at him for a minute. "I know Tucker Shaw saved your life once and brought your prisoner in. You put him in office. I can see that being enough to take his side and be short sighted on this thing. I see that, but be damned if the two of them get away with pure damn murder." He stood, turned and walked to the door. He hesitated for a moment like he wanted to say something more. Then he turned the doorknob and left. He walked back to the Dye Hotel in the blinding rain while Marshal Sanders watched him.

He pulled the letter from inside his vest and whispered. "Marshal Shaw, you may have done the right thing. One thing you have done, you've bought yourself some time. Good luck old boy. I'll hold the fort until you get back."

Tucker and Macie were riding as fast as their worn out horses could take them. The wind was picking up from behind them and it was cool air coming off of rain. They topped over a small rolling hill and Tucker spotted something to his left. They turned and made for it. When they pulled up there were two wagons parked by a big mouthed cave. They rode their horses inside and immediately raised their hands.

"That's right, Mister, get 'em up. You see this here big bore rifle of mine... it's a hair trigger. I can part ya damn hair with it too." He looked over at another dirty looking unshaven man and grinned. "Abe, what you think 'bout her?"

"I think I want to see what's under those garments myself. Little gal, get down and get those damn clothes off. Let's have us a look see. I bet you got a pair that... that'd make a man go boar hog crazy."

Tucker cut his eyes over to the other side of the cave. There were two men and three women. They looked as if they had been treated badly.

Macie glanced at Tucker and then looked back at the man who did the talking. "I know Abe's name, what's yours? I like to know who it is I'm about to get naked with."

"Amos!" His eyes widened and the whites could be seen through his dirty rusty face. "Damn, Abe, we got us a live one!"

"Watch her, Amos, some of these she males can be hellcats."

Tucker spoke up. "Amos, Abe, you two boys interested in women... or gold?"

Amos was eyeing Macie, but promptly turned his attention to Tucker. "What'd you say?"

"You boys like women or gold?"

Amos looked nervously at Abe and quickly turned back to Tucker. "Where's any gold at? You got gold?"

"I do for a fact. I just robbed the Dye Bank and I made off with four sacks of the stuff. You let me and my lady go... you can have it."

Abe put in. "Amos and me don't believe in fairytales."

"Oh it ain't no tale. I saw that terrible damn cloud building back in the west for two days. I made my move before it hit. I knew my tracks would be washed out and I could get out of the country free as a bird. I just didn't plan on running into you jaspers."

Where Outlaws Roam
Royal Wade Kimes

Abe had lowered his rifle just enough to look over the barrel. "You talk too much, and we ain't damn jaspers. If'n you got gold like you say you do. Let's be havin' us a look see."

Tucker lowered his hands and twisted to his right as if to open the bags. That move put his hand closer to his pistol. He drew and fired four times before the two rust coated men could fire their rifles. Abe was hit twice in the head and Amos caught two slugs in the chest, causing him to fire his gun into the top of the cave while falling backwards. Tucker sat searching the cave for anyone else who might be hidden.

One of the men hovering in the corner stood up from his squatted position. "Mister, that was some shooting! We're shore glad to see you. We're indebted to you."

"You folks okay?" Tucker was looking at a slender built man wearing a worn out hat and clothes to match.

"Yeah. We wouldn't have been had you not come along when you did. They got the drop on us. We were hunting a hole to get in and ran smack dab into them like you did. The difference was... Tom and I aren't handy with a gun like you are. I'm Jim Wilson. They was about to do unthinkable things to my daughter, but you saved her... and us."

"Well, I'm glad you're okay."

Macie dismounted and looked about the women. She came back to where Tucker was sitting on a rock watching the storm rage outside.

"Tucker, I love you." She sat on his lap and kissed him. He looked at her with great pride. He knew he had done the right thing leaving Dye and getting away from Marshal Galt. He knew when he looked into her eyes.

Chapter 32

The rain let up at noon and Marshal Galt came down to the lobby of the hotel. He stopped at the front desk and summoned the clerk. "Can you tell me if Macie Cook is in her room?"

The clerk looked at his badge. "She is not."

"Do you happen to know where she went?"

"I do not."

"How long has she been gone? Do you know that?" He was irritated with the clerk's short answers with no information in them.

"She left before daylight."

"She what?"

"Yes, she and Marshal Tucker Shaw left before daylight."

"Well, which way did they go, what direction?" He was upset and nearly frantic.

"That's funny... I failed to see which way they left town. It's a policy of mine to always see which way my guests go when they leave. I sometimes watch from which way they arrive too." He smiled and left the marshal standing there perplexed.

He bounced up the stairs and knocked on Deputy Farley's door. When it opened he pushed him backwards by entering so fast.

"What's wrong, Marshal?"

"Tucker Shaw is running! Farley, the sonofabitch is running! I knew it, I knew it! He's guilty, that damn Cajun he's sweet on is guilty as sin and he knows it." He paced back and forth in front of Deputy Farley as he thought things over.

"What are you talking about, Marshal?" Farley had a confused look on his face.

He stopped pacing and stared Farley in the eyes. "I'm telling you Marshal Tucker Shaw has fled in the night with his damn murdering girlfriend."

"No... No way. Marshal Shaw doesn't strike me as the type to run from anything. There has to be more to it."

"Hell boy, they'll all run when they see the boogie man law closing in. He doesn't want to see that damn Cajun bitch he's saddled with get her neck snapped any more than anyone else

Where Outlaws Roam
Royal Wade Kimes

would."

He walked to the door. "Look, I'm going down to let Marshal Sanders know what happened. You get the horses saddled, we're riding. I've got an idea he's headed to Sota. I made the remark at the table last night that I had gotten some information, and Marshal Tucker saw me ride into town yesterday afternoon. I bet he put it together I caught up with the two he run out of town. I'd say he's riding to Sota to find out just what I know."

Deputy Farley reluctantly began putting his boots on to go saddle horses after Marshal Galt left the room. He strapped on his gun and just touched the doorknob when he heard a light knock. He opened it to a sober faced Billie Sway.

"Deputy Farley, what's going on?"

"What do you mean?"

"The clerk downstairs just told me that Macie and Marshal Shaw left before daylight this morning. I was looking for him and Macie to apologize for my sarcastic remark last night. Then Marshal Galt comes bouncing down the stairs like there is a fire somewhere."

"Yeah, well, it seems Marshal Shaw has taken Macie and fled."

"Fled... from what?"

"Well, Marshal Galt thinks Macie may have murdered a man, and that Marshal Shaw is protecting her."

Billie laughed. "Oh my, this is funny."

"What is?"

"The idea he thinks Marshal Shaw would run from anything. That tells me he doesn't know him at all. If there is one thing as a woman I know, neither him nor Macie run. They may have created some space and give themselves some time, but trust me, my woman's intuitions are not wrong. I'd bet my part in Sisters he's not running... he's chasing."

Farley smiled at her. "Billie, the more I'm around you, the more I want to be."

She walked right up in his face and looked him in the eyes. She was only two inches shorter at five foot and five inches. "That's good, because I plan on you and me growing old together." She kissed him. "Now, what is that Marshal Galt up to?"

"Well, we're going after them I guess." He had a blank look about him.

"You don't want to... do you?"

"No I don't. I'm like you; Marshal Shaw is not the running kind. I think Marshal Galt has it all wrong, though he truly believes he's right."

Billie answered him matter of fact. "Deputy Farley, you watch yourself out there. Marshal Galt may think he's right, but don't let his overzealous belief get you into trouble. Some people can become obsessed with their jobs and being right. Be careful."

"I will." They left the room knowing danger was very imminent.

Marshal Sanders saw Marshal Galt crossing the street in a hurry. He opened the door for him as he reached for the knob. "Come in out of the rain, Marshal."

He had a profound look on his face. "You knew I was coming?"

"I knew."

"Then you know Marshal Shaw has lit out?"

"Lit out? No, but I do know he's taken a leave of absence. He left me in charge with a letter to that end."

"Our talk this morning... you already knew? I see now where you stand sure enough. What reason did he give for leaving?"

"He said he had some things that needed sorted out and attended to... and that he couldn't do those things from the confines of the jail."

"Why did he take Macie with him?"

"He said he might be gone for a while, which makes sense to take her."

Marshal Galt stared hard at him. "Well, you may buy into his leave of absence bullshit, but I don't. I'm going after him. I'm bringing that Cajun whore he's with back to Fort Smith to stand trial for the murder of Reed Fletcher."

"I'd be careful about jumping to conclusions... and I'd use a little prudence when trailing Marshal Shaw. I was talking to Lee Paulson last night and he told me Tucker outsmarted the whole damn Royal Guard. He's not your run of the mill runner."

Marshal Galt flew angry. "I'm going after the sonofabitch with

Where Outlaws Roam
Royal Wade Kimes

or without your confidence or blessing."

Marshal Sanders stared at him. I'd rethink what you're about to do."

He smiled at Marshal Sanders. "You know, maybe it is time you retired. You've gotten old and worn-out. That's what's wrong with most the lawmen today. They can't make decisions and most are about half cowards." He turned for the door. "Marshal, you just sit here behind your desk and let the real lawmen run down the outlaws."

"Marshal Galt, don't say things you'll regret later. One other thing, reframe from calling Macie a whore. I like her, so show a little respect."

He slammed the door as he went out.

Marshal Sanders watched him as he headed for the livery in the drizzling rain. He had foregone the friendships of both him and Marshal Shaw. He felt Galt had let pride and stubbornness get in the way of good judgment. He was going after them in what he believed to be 'in the name of the law'. He saw it as a man setting out to prove he was right. Vindicating one's self can sometimes blind a person to the real truth. He hoped Marshal Galt came to his senses. He had been a good lawman in the past. It would be a shame to lose him. The good ones were hard to come by.

Where Outlaws Roam
Royal Wade Kimes

Chapter 33

Marshal Galt hadn't any real idea where to look for Marshal Shaw and his lover. He did however think his hunch to ride to Sota was a place to start. He headed that direction and had ridden an hour and half when he met two wagons.

"Mister, whoa up there!"

The lead wagon pulled up. The ground was soggy causing the team of black, white nosed mules to slide a little when stopping. The driver was sitting on the seat by himself. A young curly headed blond girl stuck her head out from the covered wagon to see who had stopped them.

"Mister... oh, I see you're a lawman." He smiled and looked relieved.

"Yeah, name's Galt, this here is Deputy Farley." Farley smiled and tipped his hat.

"What can I do for you, Marshal Galt?"

"We're looking for a friend of ours, Marshal Shaw, would you have seen him?"

"Shore did. He saved our lives is what he done."

Deputy Farley perked up and smiled at the fact Marshal Shaw had saved them from certain death. Marshal Galt showed little emotion.

"Where was this at, which direction? It's damned important we find him."

"Back yonder a piece. There's a cave kind of down on the side of a rolling hill. When that storm came in we held up there. What we didn't know was, so were a couple road agents. Then Marshal Shaw showed up with his woman and took care of them in short fashion. I never seen a man so good with a six shooter."

"Ya say due north?"

"Straight up this trail about two miles past the fork heading west."

"Did they happen to say where they were going?" "Not that I recall."

"Well, we're much obliged." They clucked to their horses and rode on. It was now obvious to Marshal Galt they weren't headed to Sota. They would have turned at the fork in the trail

Where Outlaws Roam
Royal Wade Kimes

that was only a mile up.

"Deputy, let's pick it up a little. The storm has delayed our friend Tucker Shaw."

The Ninnescha River was one mile ahead of Tucker and Macie. On the other side of it was the Pitman Ranch. A beautiful house sat on a long sloping hill. Cattle dotted the prairie all around it. Horses were running in big bunches here and there. They had finally ridden out of the heavy rain and were very content to deal with the mist.

"Macie, that looks like quite a place."

"It is beautiful." She grinned when she looked over at him. "Maybe one day you and I can have such a place."

"There's no maybe to it." He laughed as his eyes looked for a place to cross the river. The road seemed to be gone. It was obvious the hard rains had been here too. The river was up and very muddy.

"Tucker, this is angry water. We can't cross this."

"Yeah... it looks scary alright." He turned and rode northeast a ways, and then turned and came back. "That's no good, maybe southwest a ways."

"Maybe so." Macie kept looking at the raging river. She was no stranger to water. She lived and grew up on it. She learned at an early age to respect it and how to make it work for you. There were times to leave it alone. This one was one of them. They rode a mile downstream. There was only one place that offered any kind of crossing opportunity, and that was two miles back up stream. They rode back and dismounted to look it over.

"Tucker, this is dangerous water. She looked out across it and noticed the canebrakes all along the banks on both sides. They were thick and beautiful, but held water back when a river or creek came out over its banks.

Tucker had a concerned look on his face. "Well, I guess we could make a campfire and wait for the water to go down. There doesn't appear to be much else we can do. It'll be dark in a little while."

She looked around her. "Even that may be hard to do. There is little wood around and what there may be will be wet."

"Yeah. You're right." He walked over to the edge of the water and noticed back up on the bank an old hollow drift log. He peered inside it and was pleasantly surprised. He pulled out a bunch of dry leaves with twigs and stems of other trees that had gathered up inside the hollow cavity. He gathered an arm load and brought it back to Macie.

"Tucker, you found a miracle."

He gazed at her. "I sure did." He dropped the dry leaves and pulled her to him. He kissed her and pulled her tighter to him by the bottom side of her hips.

"You stop that or I'll light another fire right here in the mud."

He laughed and pushed her back. "Tonight you are mine."

"Promise me." She laughed and then suddenly froze. "Tucker... riders."

He saw them and could tell they were tracking at nearly a lope. The rain made their tracks very visible. "Macie, take the horses down around the side of the bank. He pulled his rifle.

Marshal Galt wasn't having any trouble following the deep tracks in the mud. He was closing in fast on the unsuspecting Marshal Tucker Shaw. Deputy Farley didn't like it. The further they rode the less he felt good about it. He began to lag behind a little. He had been lagging for the last half mile when Marshal Galt pulled up.

"What's wrong with you? Is that horse lame or something?"

"No, but we could pull a tendon in this mud if we don't slow down some."

"Yeah, you could be right." He looked up from the tracks and was astonished. "Hell, there he is big as life right out in the open!"

Farley strained to see. He hoped it wasn't him, but he was sure it was. "Marshal, are you sure about this? He's been your friend. Maybe we should give him some time, at least let him tell you what he's doing."

"Hell boy, I know what he's doing. He's running."

"Well, he helped those two wagon loads of folks in the doing. I'd say he ain't running too hard."

"Yeah, well, I'd say by looking at that river yonder he's run far

Where Outlaws Roam
Royal Wade Kimes

as he can."

"Yeah, looks so… and when a cat or a wolf is hemmed in, he's ready to fight to the death."

"A guilty man will do that. That heifer he's tied to is going to be the death of him. She ain't nothing but trouble. The way she butchered up Reed Fletcher and that poor devil in the hotel. The bitch is plain mean. Her good looks didn't fool me."

"Nothing fools you, does it Marshal?"

He looked around at Farley with anger in his face. "What the hell does that mean?"

"It means you're never wrong. Do you think maybe you could be wrong just once?"

"I could be, but not likely. Now get your head out of your ass and pull that rifle. We're going to take those two back."

Suddenly Marshal Galt heard a rifle lever a shell in a chamber. He turned and was staring at the end of Farley's rifle barrel. "Marshal, you can give me orders, but you can't order me around, there's a difference. You're not talking down to me either."

He thought about that for a minute. "Farley, you're right. I'm sorry, I was out of line. I just don't want those two to get away is all."

"Funny, I don't want to catch them." He stuck his rifle back in the scabbard.

"You what?"

"I don't. I don't want to catch them. I've been a lawman long enough now my gut tells me when something ain't right and doesn't add up. I'd think you would know before me. Marshal, I've got to say it… you're blind in this deal. You're not giving the benefit of the doubt."

Marshal Galt had heard that from Darla. Maybe he wasn't, but law was law. "Deputy, I'm going in after those two with or without you." He shot him a quick glance. "What say ye?"

Deputy Farley picked the reins up to his horse. "I'm here, lead off."

Marshal Galt clucked to his horse to hit a lope.

Tucker squeezed off a round when Marshal Galt

came into range. The bullet whizzed by his ear. It startled him just a little. The idea Tucker could get that close so far away. He fired back at him, but the bullet wasn't anywhere near him. He wasn't the best shot anyway.

"Marshal Galt, go back! I could have killed you with that shot! The next one will bring blood!"

Marshal Galt slowed to a walk and then pulled up. "I'm taking Macie in Marshal Shaw! I'm taking her in for the murder of Reed Fletcher!"

"You've taken on more than you can get done!" There was a moment of silence and then Tucker spoke again. "It's a shame about you! You're a great lawman! You know the law and dedicated your life to it! The problem is you've hardened your heart! You lost the ability to be fair in your dealings with people!"

"Law is law! Emotions don't enter into it!"

"Then come a shooting! Hell's angels are waiting on one of us!"

Macie was down by the water's edge. "Tucker."

He turned his head and saw her holding two cane sticks in her hand. "Around this canebrake the water makes a swirling pool caused by the thick cane. If we dive under the water we can use this cane to breathe through."

He turned and saw Marshal Galt kick his horse into a full gallop. He fired twice as he was running and both bullets dug mud up twenty yards out in front of him. Tucker grinned and levered five rounds in his direction, and then dived into the water. He swam around the thick canes and dropped under the water with Macie, holding the tall cane for breathing tubes.

Marshal Galt had held up a minute when the bullets from Marshal Shaw's gun splattered mud at him and his horse. He raced on and slid to a stop along the raging river bank. He scanned the river as Deputy Farley arrived. There wasn't a sign of them anywhere. No one could have survived such a raging river. They might have possibly made it on a horse, and even that was plenty doubtful. He kept looking, but saw nothing.

Deputy Farley stepped down from his horse and walked to the edge of the treacherous water. He stared out into the river and

Where Outlaws Roam
Royal Wade Kimes

half choked up. "Marshal, they died together. They had rather be dead than be separated. I hope it was enough for you."

Marshal Galt looked around at Farley with a stunned stare. "I never figured on this. Marshal Shaw loving that Cajun gal enough to die with her... never figured it."

Deputy Farley shook his head in sadness. "I guess I would have. He was all the way with whatever he took on. He loved Macie. I know just how he felt. I feel the same about Billie."

Marshal Galt studied about that. He thought a lot of Darla, but was it enough to die for her... he reckoned not. He turned and mounted his horse and then rode over and collected the reins to the two wore out plugs Marshal Shaw and Macie were riding.

"Well, I guess we can head back, ride as far as we can before dark." He took one last look across the river. It was some mean flood water going down the river, and no human being could be alive that was caught out in it. He turned and headed for Dye. It wasn't the outcome he wanted and he might be looked upon in a bad way by some. He knew Farley was upset with him already.

Deputy Farley started to turn and happened to see a cane stick move suddenly. The water was whirling, but it was an odd movement. He stood bent forward trying to look around the canebrake. He glanced quickly back the direction of Marshal Galt. He looked again at the cane. He was excited when he saw Marshal Shaw and Macie come to the top. They realized too late Deputy Farley was still there. He grinned at them and looked back again at the marshal. He signaled with his hand to go back under.

Tucker grinned and slowly sank under the water as a happy Deputy Farley mounted up. He clucked to his horse and caught up to Marshal Galt.

"You know Deputy, I can't figure Marshal Shaw getting rid of his mare and gelding. He didn't make many mistakes, but riding these crow baits was sure a bad one."

"Well Marshal, I guess he needed some money if he was going to be on the run. I can't see him holding up a bank or anything."

"Yeah, I guess you're right." They rode in silence until night fall.

It took another day for the water to recede enough for Tucker and Macie to cross the river. They walked to the Pitman Ranch and were greeted by Ray Pitman himself. Lou and most of the hands were gone with a fair sized cattle drive to Kansas City.

"You two look like the worse room in hell."

"Well Ray, we've had hell. We're soaked to the bone, and have been chased and shot at."

"I thought I heared shots. I walked out on the porch and listened, didn't hear anything and went back in. It was raining and when the river gets on a high horse I can't hear much. One noise mixed in with another and I ain't any good. I guess it's from all the shooting I've done over the years. It's good to see you anyway. I've got Catcher and the bronze mare in the dry waiting for you like you asked. I've treated them so well they may not want to go with you." He laughed and brought them into the house. "Your saddlebags are on the entry table." He smiled. "That's a fancy pistol you've got in the bag."

"It was given to me by the Royal Guard for best pistol shot. It has a nice balance and I can put them where I point with it."

"Yeah, I never seen one like it, all that engraved scribble."

"Yeah, that sums it up. It has my initials on it and the date, along with a picture of the Queen of Great Britain. Oh and of course 'Great Britain's Royal Guard Elite'. I have never carried it. I took it to the range, tested it and put it away. I had left it behind and thought it gone for good. My father, Robert Fetter brought it to me."

"Fetter? I thought your name was Shaw?"

"So did I, so did I. It's a long story. I'll fill you in later."

"Well, you two have the run of the house. There's a tub in both bedrooms. Take your pick. There are clothes for both of you. My wife is going to be upset she wasn't here to meet you. She's on the drive. She rides some and cooks some. I normally go, but she asked to go this year. She has some shopping to do she said. I bet I don't make a nickel on those cows." Macie laughed and so did Ray.

Where Outlaws Roam
Royal Wade Kimes

Chapter 34

Marshal Galt and Deputy Farley rode into Dye on two worn out horses. One of the horses pulled a tendon like Farley was afraid of, and caused them to have to camp on the prairie for a day. It was slow going leading a lame horse.

Robert Fetter was at the dry goods store getting supplies for his trip to New Orleans as well as for the newly acquired ranch. He put his keg of nails down and had his two hired hands finish loading the wagon. He made his way to the jail to see what he could learn.

Marshal Sanders was sitting behind his desk when the two lawmen walked in. "Hello, Marshal, Deputy."

"Good day." Marshal Galt sat down in the chair in front of the desk. Deputy Farley leaned up against the wall. He didn't plan to stay long.

Marshal Sanders eyed them over. "Where are Marshal Shaw and Macie?"

Reluctantly Marshal Galt looked up. "I'm sorry to report that their dead. He drowned in a flooded river. Macie had already dove in I guess."

"You mean to say, they purposely drowned themselves?"
"Looks so. I never figured Marshal Shaw to do such a thing, but I seen him go under."

Deputy Farley put in. "I guess he didn't want to live without Macie."

Marshal Sanders was visibly shaken. "I just wonder what the man must have been thinking."

Marshal Galt looked up again. "I don't think he was. A man that would die over a bitch like her... he can't be thinking right."

Before Marshal Galt knew what was happening his head was stretched backwards as far as it could be stretched and a long bladed knife was at his throat. Robert Fetter had been standing at the door and heard what was said.

Marshal Sanders jumped to his feet and drew his gun. "Robert, don't do it! Let him go. Think about this thing."

Robert's eyes darted frantically from Marshal Sanders to Galt. "A man that speaks of the dead like they are insignificant doesn't deserve to live! He's less than a vulture looking for dead flesh." The blade was cutting the skin. A trickle of blood beaded up and ran down his neck.

"I understand how you feel, but if you kill this man you'll hang. What's Tucker's mother going to do if she loses both her men?"

Deputy Farley was in a tight spot. He could tell Robert that Tucker was alive and give him away, or he could let it play out. If it went wrong he would have caused Robert to be hung. He decided to go for another option. He would lie.

"Robert, this is Deputy Farley behind you. Tucker left me a letter. He said it was something he wanted you to know, and for me to express how important it was."

"You're lying! I saw my son before he left here. He would have told me."

"No, no he wouldn't have. Turn Marshal Galt loose and I'll give you the letter."

He looked around at Farley with bloodshot eyes from stinging tears. "If you're lying to me, you and this man here are dead men." He slowly let off the knife and backed away. Marshal Galt leant forward grabbing his neck and then turned.

"You sonofabitch!"

Robert kicked him dead in the face. He peeled out of the chair and slammed against the desk. Marshal Sanders looked at Robert and smiled. "Like son, like father. The both of you have knocked him out."

"Robert, you and Deputy Farley need to get on out of here. I'll take care of Galt when he wakes."

Deputy Farley motioned for Robert to follow him. He waited for him out on the porch while Marshal Sanders poured a pitcher of water on Marshal Galt's face.

Farley looked back at the door of the jail. "Let's walk across the street. I don't want anyone hearing what I have to say." Once they were in the middle of the street Farley began. "Tucker is alive. He and Macie got away. Marshal Galt is convinced they're dead."

"They're alive?"

"Yes, they dived off in a swollen river and didn't come up. That was because they didn't have to. They had two cane sticks fixed

Where Outlaws Roam
Royal Wade Kimes

to breathe through. Cane is hollow. It makes a natural air pipe. I saw them and motioned for them to stay down. They're just fine. I can't say that about me. You near gave me a heart attack in there. If you had killed Marshal Galt, well, I don't know what I would have done. The only thing I could think of was lie to you."

Robert started to hug him and remembered someone might be watching them. "Deputy, that's the best news I've heard in days. You are a gentleman and a damn good officer."

"I appreciate that. Well, I guess if there isn't anything else, I'm going to get a bath and see Billie."

"One minute. Why is Galt so driven to arrest Macie? What kind of man speaks of someone he thinks dead the way he did?"

"Marshal Galt has always been a good man. I don't know why he won't let go. Truthfully, I think he's under paid and overworked. He's changed some of late, no denying it, but he's a good man."

"Son, I was an admiral aboard one of the finest ships ever sailed. In that time I commanded and was under command of many men. I've seen power, authority, long tours at sea, and plain loneliness change men. When that happens, nearly one hundred percent of the time the man has to be relieved of command or booted from the ship and service. I think Marshal Galt needs booted."

Deputy Farley stood contemplating what Robert Fetter said to him, as he watched him walk to his wagon.

Four days later Tucker was standing on top of Eagles Ledge. He walked out to the small tree Fletcher was hanging from. He looked out across the plains and smiled. He felt free up here. It was where the eagle roosted. He guessed it felt free also. He came back to have another look at the place Reed Fletcher was killed. He wanted to examine the ground and search the area for some kind of clue, any kind. He was desperate to find something to prove Macie's innocence. With Marshal Galt not hunting him, he felt free to search without worrying he was close by. He left Macie at the Pitman Ranch until he returned for her. No one would take her from Ray.

He peered over the side of the ledge and shook his head at the thoughts of Macie going down it. He wasn't afraid of anything, but that bothered him to look down towards the ground. He examined the ground and found the broken stock to the big game rifle Fletcher was using.

"What's this?" He was talking to his self. He picked up a sheath made from alligator. It was well made and unusual. Cowboys didn't have such fancy sheaths to carry their blades in. This must have belonged to Fletcher. He tucked it away and kept looking for evidence. He was sure he would fine a shell casing but none turned up.

He turned and went down the trail slowly to where they had tied the horses. He came back up and just before he entered the area where Fletcher was murdered, he noticed a dim trail leading off northeast. He followed it down and found it came out to an open and level spot on the prairie floor. He stood in the middle of the area and looked completely around him. He spotted a tree where a horse had been tied. He could see where it had gnawed bark off of the small tree. He walked to it and stood looking at the grass and sand. He took a step and then another. He was about to take the third when he saw something white. He walked to it and saw ants everywhere. Whatever it was it was all but gone. There were three dim white spots in the dirt. He talked to the ants like they could hear him.

"You guys have to eat, but I sure wish you could have left whatever this was alone." He stood up and turned to walk away when a reflection caught his eye. Two steps over was a thin tin can three inches wide and four inches long. He opened it. Inside the can was one stick of peppermint candy. He looked over at the spot where the ants were. The candy must have spilled. The owner of the candy cleaned up the most of it and left the candy dust and smaller pieces for the bugs. But when he went to mount up he must have lost the can from his pocket.

Tucker began to mumble to himself. "Marshal Galt tied his horse to the tree and slipped up Eagles Ledge from a different angle. That's why he was so long getting to Melt. In his hurry to catch up to me he spilled his peppermint. I wonder when he missed his candy can. Now I know why it was so important to arrest and convict Macie for the murder. It's a funny thing, it wasn't murder to start out with, but killing a man that is helpless... makes it something else besides stopping a criminal act, and it makes it anything but an act of law.

He stood and walked back to Catcher. "Ole partner, we found what we came for. It looks like Marshal Galt has taken the law into his own hands. He's become judge, jury, and executioner." He stepped up into the saddle and headed for the Pitman Ranch.

Chapter 35

Marshal Galt left Dye, Kansas the day before a surprised Marshal Sanders saw Tucker and Macie riding in. He was standing on the porch of the jail and his jaw nearly hit his knee.

"Can't be. By God it is!" He stepped down from the porch and met him in the middle of the street. "You no good, rotten, sorry excuse of a lawman! You left me here all this time thinking I'd be here for the rest of my days, doomed to be without my darling and ranch in Pueblo?" He slapped him on the leg and nearly dragged him off his horse. "I'm so damn glad to see you. I had given into the idea of you being dead. Now I have to get use to you being alive all over again. You have any idea what that'll be like? Hell, I've been shot, beat up, tied up, and a thousand other things since you've been around." He shook his hand, then walked around and helped Macie off her horse and hugged her for the longest of time. "You two go to the Dye Hotel, get a room and baths. I'll take care of the horses."

Tucker hesitated. "Marshal, before you go... where is Marshal Galt?"

"He left yesterday." He looked Tucker in the eyes. "We'll talk."

"I'll be over."

They left for the hotel and found Deputy Farley waiting for them on the hotel porch. "I see you made it. I'm guessing you are here because you have a suspect other than Macie." He looked at her and smiled. "You two sure put a lump in my throat when I thought you had drowned."

"Yes, I have a suspect... in fact I have proof of who it was killed Fletcher. As for drowning in the river, I thank you for not giving us away."

"Well, I knew you needed a chance. My gut told me to let you have it. I've heard lawmen that listens to their gut make the best lawmen. Maybe that means I might make one."

"You'll do already." They shook hands and parted, but only a step or two before an afterthought came to Tucker. "Hold on a minute. What are you doing here? I was told Marshal Galt left yesterday."

"He did, but that don't mean I have to. Billie and I are getting

Where Outlaws Roam
Royal Wade Kimes

real serious about things. I'm thinking Dye may be my home, or one nearby."

"You've made a good choice. See you later."

"I'll be at Sisters a lot." They laughed and went their separate ways.

Tucker checked them in while Macie went up to the room ahead of him. She was looking forward to a hot bath.

Macie opened the door to her hotel room and froze immediately. She looked around her and saw no one or anything unusual. The hallway was empty, but it felt cold and ghostly. She turned the knob slowly and stepped back inside her room. She pulled a thirty-two pistol Tucker had given her from the bag she was carrying. She walked back out into the hallway and proceeded to the stairs. She looked down into the lobby and saw a business man in a suit holding a smoking cigar. He wore a round hat and had a rather large stomach. He was joined by a lady and they left. She looked back up the hallway the other direction. It was dark at the other end making it impossible to see anything or anyone if they were there.

"Macie."

She whirled and cocked the pistol at the same time.

"Whoa up!" Tucker held his hands in the air. "What's going on? Are you okay?"

"No... I'm not okay." She took a deep long breath. She hadn't realized it but she was breathing hard. "Tucker, I had the realist, strangest feeling someone was watching me."

He walked to the end of the hall and checked the exit door. He came back to her and held her to him. "There isn't anyone. You haven't anything to worry about." He could tell she was very unsettled. "What do you say we forget about the room and go see Marshal Sanders? Maybe we'll head on down to Fort Smith?"

"Yes, I'm ready." She was almost trembling. She looked over her shoulder one time as she and Tucker walked to the stairs. Her swamp ways had kicked in back there in the hallway. She had the same feeling she would get when an alligator was in deep water traveling close to the bottom, approaching for a kill. She gave thought to that. Maybe that was all it was, a flashback to a time gone by.

"Marshal, I think Macie and me know why Marshal Galt wanted her arrested so badly." He laid the tin can out on the desk in front of Marshal Sanders. "Does this look familiar?"

"Marshal Sanders looked at it, and with sad eyes he looked up at Tucker. "It's Marshal Galt's candy tin. Where'd you find it?" His face had turned pale, for he was afraid of what Tucker was about to say.

"Eagles Ledge."

"Could it be he lost it when you and him cut Fletcher down?"

"I'm afraid not. I found this where he tied his horse up, which happened to be a different place than the one he and I used. He was at Eagles Ledge before we went there together."

He looked at Tucker and then Macie. "I'm sick of heart. Macie, I'm sorry for what Marshal Galt has put you through... and I'm sad for him. I don't know what went wrong with him. He's been one hell of a law man. I don't understand it. Me and him been friends for two decades. He was the best of the best."

"Men change sometimes." Tucker felt bad for Marshal Sanders. He could see how badly it hurt him to know his old friend had murdered a man.

"Well, normally I'd let the officer in charge take care of his case, but if you don't mind, I'd like to ride to Fort Smith with you. Once this is settled, I'm turning in my badge. I'm not finishing out the week or two I have left. I've had it with the whole damn mess."

"I don't mind, fact is I left you in charge."

"Of the town... not your case. We'll leave in the morning if that's okay. We can get Deputy Farley to watch things. He needn't know about this for now."

"I agree." He looked at Macie. "Well, I guess then we leave in the morning... you alright with that, Macie?" He was thinking about the earlier incident at the room.

"That's fine. I think I might like to stay the night anyway."

He heard something different in her tone of voice. It was like she was ready for a fight or was on the hunt. She looked at him

Where Outlaws Roam
Royal Wade Kimes

and smiled slightly. She had gotten over her scare.

"Then I'll see you kids in the morning, say six o'clock?"

Tucker smiled and stood with Macie. "Six it is."

They left and walked as far as the boardwalk in front of the Dye Hotel. "Macie, what is going on?"

She spoke low and precisely. "I don't know. Do you believe in the Boogie Man, or super naturals, or feelings of something sinister?"

He thought hard about that before he answered. "I guess I do, yes."

"Then find another hole for the cinch you're using, the ride could get a little rough."

"Dang it Macie, you're not making sense."

She looked at him and then reached up and touched his cheek. "My love, Marshal Galt, or something more is watching. Don't be so sure he rode to Fort Smith. I'm not and I'm keeping this gun in my little bag close to me."

This was a side of Macie he hadn't seen. She was a Cajun, unafraid of anything. He looked towards the jail and then into her eyes when he lifted her chin with his hand.

"Macie, are you spooked by some ghost or something. I'm not saying this to offend, so don't take it wrong. The Cajun people practiced and partook in a lot of spirit world mumbo jumbo didn't they?"

"Some did. Mom was a Christian and read me the Bible."

"Then what is it?"

"I'm not sure. I believe in ghost, and maybe that's what I felt in the hallway."

"Don't tell me you think Reed Fletcher's ghost is in the hotel. Is that why you want to spend another night here?"

"Not exactly, but it will be interesting to see what happens."

He chuckled. "What will happen is... I'll make love to you, it will be so powerful I'll be asleep two minutes after, and the ghost will all have to wait to spook me." He laughed and then picked her up off her feet and carried her into the hotel.

Chapter 36

Angel Hound won his foot race. It wasn't even a contest for him, as he finished well ahead of the pack. Ina, Bishop Ortega, and Angel Hound's half-sister Pixy were cheering him on. Bishop Ortega did however frown at the large amount of money Angel Hound got for a certain five hundred dollar bet that was placed. The Fort Smith favorite caused the odds to be at five to one. Tucker and Angel Hound cleaned up, plus he received his one hundred dollars winning purse. The Bishop's frown left him and was replaced with a smile when he was given five hundred dollars of the winnings.

The two Marshals, Sanders and Shaw along with Macie rode into Fort Smith at near dark three days later. They got rooms at the Boss Hotel on Fourth Street. Not a lot of words had passed between them on the ride down. Tucker and Marshal Sanders were in sober moods because of their reason for making the ride, and Macie was still uneasy about her feeling. She was taught from her childhood to listen to her apprehensions. She rode behind Marshal Sanders and Tucker, and kept looking back. When she got to the hotel room she placed the Bible near the front door.

"Macie, what are you doing?"

"I'm moving this little table by the door and putting this Bible on it. Do you have something to say?"

He wanted to laugh but knew better. "No, I guess not."

She put her hands on her hips. "I could have put one of those witch doctor dolls on the front of the door if I was into dark spirits. I don't see anything wrong with having the Good Lord watching the door."

"Well I don't either, but he'll do that anyway if you ask him."

"Well... ask then. Tucker, something is lurking out there, in here, somewhere. I'm not wrong. I can feel it and I feel it strong."

Tucker pulled his pistol and checked the rounds. "Well, I'm ready for it."

"What if it's something you can't shoot?"

"That's enough of that." He looked at her. "Look Macie, have a

Where Outlaws Roam
Royal Wade Kimes

little faith. Whatever it is, we'll handle it."

She stood staring at him and slowly a smile appeared. "Okay then. Take me to eat, I'm hungry."

"That's my girl!"

They met Marshal Sanders at the Kitchen Emporium on Garrison Avenue. It was considered one of the best eating establishments in town. The coconut pie had a lot to do with that assumption.

The night went without event. There wasn't any visit by ghost or any knock on the door, or windows being raised. Macie was witness to that as she tossed and turned beside Tucker all night long while he slept, which irritated her. The idea he could sleep while she fretted. At near two in the morning she fell asleep and didn't awake until six-thirty.

She went to a small dresser with a mirror and a small gray wash bowl. Tucker had gone down stairs for coffee. She took a small washcloth and wet it. She looked into the mirror to wash her face and jumped sideways.

"Oh!" She whirled and ran to the window. She was sure she saw am image outside her window through the mirror. She picked up her pistol by the bed and walked back to the window and raised it. She peered outside in all directions but saw no one. She left the room and went down the hallway to the end opposite the lobby. There was a stairway to a third floor. She went up and took the stairs to the roof. She cocked the pistol and went out. She fired as a man bailed over the side of the building. The bullet knocked a hole in the side of the twelve inch heightened edge. She ran to where he disappeared and looked over. She saw someone slide through a window on the floor she had just come from. She hurried back down but he was gone, no trace of him anywhere.

Tucker showed up with two cups of coffee and found Macie outside their room with gun in hand. "What's going on?" He had a concerned look on his face and looked past her to the end of the hall. He didn't see anyone lying dead, so he looked back at her waiting for an answer.

"That feeling I had manifested its self to a live image today. I saw someone looking in our window a minute ago. Whoever it was, he was watching me. I saw him on the roof and I took a shot."

"What? What did he look like?"

"I only glimpsed him. I don't know."

"Okay, well, let's have our coffee and then go see Marshal Sanders and let him know. He might get a visit too. Then we have to see Marshal Galt and arrest him. I'll be watching for anyone acting suspicious."

She tried to smile as she took a sip of her coffee.

Marshal Galt left the Kitchen Emporium a couple hours later walking east between the Fort Smith Courthouse and Garrison Avenue. He walked past a corner and stopped dead in his tracks. He was staring at a man holding a six gun, grinning as he pointed it at him.

"Mornin' Marshal."

"Who the hell are you?"

"It's not who, but what. I'd be what you'd call a vindicator. I've got a message for you, Marshal. You got yourself a damn surprise comin' today. Marshal Sanders and Tucker Shaw are in town to arrest you for murder. Tucker found your candy box at the place where Fletcher died."

"Marshal Shaw is dead."

"Nah, nah he's not, neither is Macie, no thanks to you. She came with them. Macie grew up on swamps and water. That little high water river couldn't outdo her." He stared at the marshal. "What kind a man tries to pin a murder on a girl like Macie? Fletcher was a no good bastard and deserved to die. I don't see how it is, you bein' law, you would try to hang her for savin' the world from him."

"Law is law. I was doing my job is all."

"You do poor work." He grinned through dark stained teeth. "I figure you got maybe an hour 'fore they come for you. I'm gonna be close by watchin' you hang for what you put Macie and her man through."

"Mister, what's all this to you?"

"Like I said, I'm a vindicator... and I'm vindicatin'." He stopped

Where Outlaws Roam
Royal Wade Kimes

suddenly. "Oops, I was wrong. I see your marshal friends comin' now." He turned down the alley and disappeared before Marshal Galt could turn back and see where he went.

"Marshal Galt!"

"Hello, Marshal Shaw... morning Marshal Sanders."

"You don't seem surprised to see us." Tucker kept his hand low to his gun.

"I would be, but I was just told you were alive, and that the two of you are here to arrest me for the murder of Reed Fletcher."

Marshal Sanders put in. "We're doing what you'd do if the role was reversed. It doesn't look good. The evidence points to you." He paused when a question came to him. "Who told you Marshal Shaw was alive and that we were coming to arrest you?"

"To be truthful I don't know who the messenger was, but he was just here. And as for evidence pointing to me... it pointed to Macie to start with. I'm beginning to think I might have been wrong about that, but it sure as hell wasn't me that killed Fletcher. I'm at a loss as to who did... unless." He turned his head ever so slightly towards the alley.

Tucker smiled. "We all make mistakes... and maybe that's what this will be, but like you say... law is law. We got to go by the book. Just because we're friends... law is law and overrides all that... doesn't it?" Tucker was throwing back to Marshal Galt what he had always lived by. He was making a point that sometimes commonsense and empathy can and should play a part in the job.

"I guess I had that coming. I can kind of see it, now that I'm on the other side." He stared at them for a minute. "Well, where are we at here? Do we try to find the real killer and forget arresting me, or do we fight it out here in the street?"

Tucker laughed. "You mean you're not coming peaceably? Are you going to make a run for it? Pray it doesn't rain and flood the rivers."

Marshal Galt didn't know what to say and didn't have to, Marshal Sanders took it up.

"Marshal, I've known you a long time. I'm willing to give you the benefit of the doubt if you'll give me your word you won't run."

"Marshal Sanders, you know damn well I won't run. You got my word."

"Let's shake on it."

They walked to within arms distance and shook hands. Marshal Galt looked over at Tucker. "I should have done this with you and Macie." He glanced at Marshal Sanders and smiled just as a loud shot from a rifle went off and the bullet from the gun knocked him off his feet.

Marshal Sanders and Tucker ran for cover. A bullet whined off the road brick as Marshal Sanders ran behind a rain barrel by the hat and boot shop. Tucker saw a puff of smoke across the street on top of one of the buildings. He fired three times to give Marshal Sanders time to find better cover, otherwise the shooter would have gotten off a couple more rounds.

Tucker had taken cover at the corner of a bakery. "You okay, Marshal?"

"Outside of my sore leg from my last gunfight, yeah, I'm tolerable."

"Tolerable?" Tucker waited for an answer as to what that was.

He laughed. "Yeah, Marshal Tucker Shaw, tolerable, means fair to middling."

He wasn't real sure about fair to middling either, but played along. "Oh, I see. I've still got a ways to go on this western lingo." He fired a round towards the top of the building which happened to be the Fort Smith Hide Rendering Company. Nothing happened. He reloaded and fired three more rounds as he made his way to Marshal Galt.

"Damn... damn Tucker. I'm, I'm hit bad." He was right, blood was coming out front and back.

"Lie still." He looked in the direction of Marshal Sanders. "Go for a doctor and a wagon!"

"I'll try." He holstered his gun and took two steps when bullets bounced off the brick beside him. He fell back to his position.

Tucker had his gun pointed in the direction of the rooftop, but he was also out in the open. He couldn't figure it. Why hadn't the shooter taken a shot? He sure was free with his shots at Marshal

Where Outlaws Roam
Royal Wade Kimes

Sanders. He cut his eyes quickly at Marshal Galt. He wasn't going to last long if he didn't get help.

"Tucker!"

He turned and saw Macie up the street. "Stay back! I need a doctor... and fast!"

She turned to leave when Angel Hound showed up. "You stays here! I gets us a doctor." He took off like he was shot from a gun. He probably never ran that fast in his prize winning foot race. Macie followed him for a ways and quickly realized her effort wasn't needed.

Tucker fired another round at the top of the building. Nothing happened. He began to wonder if he was still up there. He didn't have to wonder but a few seconds longer.

"Tucker Shaw! Why the hell you trying to save that damned old marshal? He's the one what was after Macie, and he wanted to arrest you for taking Reed Fletcher's boat! Tell you, Tucker, it's a confused world out here!"

"Out here?" Tucker surmised he was a convict or escaped prisoner. But then it hit him... Lou Pitman. Was Lou trying to help him in some crazy way? It's for sure he would know about Marshal Galt running him and Macie into the river, Ray would have told him. Lou would be that kind of a friend. He would try to return the favor for someone helping clear him of the Simon Lick holdups.

"Tucker, finish that old trap bait off and that'll be all of them what done us bad turns?"

Macie had hurried back to the corner where she was when Angel Hound went for the doctor. When she heard the voice calling out to Tucker, her heart sped up as she froze in her tracks. Under her breath she whispered. "Hon." Had he survived someway?

She called to him. "Hon, is that you?"

"In the flesh! I've been takin' care of business girly. I was damn near shot to death by Reed Fletcher. My wife was eat by a gator tryin' to get away from him and his damn hounds. I was left for dead, and would have been had that nigger Lester not come back to see if'n I was. He told me Reed Fletcher done left Louisiana on the trail of Tucker Shaw. He said he had enough Reed Fletcher's killin' and abuse of folks. He got me on my feet and then left the farm. I was terrible weak, but I lit out after Fletcher!"

"Hon, come down where we can talk."

"Macie, ole Hon ain't that damn dumb. I come down and they'll put their law upon me, and try and arrest me. I say we finish it. Kill the damn marshal laying there. He's the last that has come agin us. I follered Fletcher and his men, killed 'em off one at a time. I made 'em sweat like me and my woman did. You stopped ole Fletcher with that knife. He'd a killed your man shore. Your uncles taught you well on knife work. I was coming to help you finish the bastard, but you went rabbit on me and run."

He laughed. "You should have heard the bastard beg when he seen me. He saw me through his rifle sights afore. I took a bullet high enough in the shoulder to live. He damn near tore my head off with his second shot. I fell and laid still as a sullen opossum.

Fletcher knew why I was at Eagles Ledge. He knew the end had come. He'd run people and shoot 'em down for pure pleasure of it. Well, he was on the other end when he saw me. I made him beg. He offered me gold, money, all kinds of pretties. You know what I told him, Macie?"

"No, I guess not." She knew Hon. All she could do was listen, for there would be no giving up or turning back. He was committed to what he was doing.

"I told him if'n he could bring back my wife, I'd not shoot him. He couldn't do it. So I gave him another chance, Macie! I said if'n you can bring back my brothers and their wives... I'll not shoot you! He couldn't do that either. That's when I told him he wasn't so damn powerful after all. I shot the sonofabitch dead center between the eyes."

"Hon, that's good, but don't you think the killing needs to end there?"

"No, hell no! That Marshal Galt... he run you like Fletcher did us. He has to die! Know something Macie, if'n he hadn't come slipping up Eagles Ledge I would have skinned ole Fletch out. I had to hot foot it off of there. He heard me shoot old Fletch and surmised I took a shot at him. Tucker was already gone... but ole Marshal Galt was checking all the dead vigilantes. He trailed me

Where Outlaws Roam
Royal Wade Kimes

around the backside of Eagles Ledge. I gave the bastard the slip and headed for Melt. Him being the good, run you to death marshal he was, he got his horse and followed me. He reckoned I was one of the Melt Vigilantes. Reed and all these marshals are dumb, Macie. They wouldn't last two days in the swamp." He paused for a second. "That was a real nice touch, you hanging ole Fletch out over the ledge to dry. Marshal Galt would have found him shore if'n he hadn't followed me off Eagles Ledge."

Tucker heard it all. He now knew Marshal Galt was innocent. He shook his head and looked at Galt. "I be damn."

"Marshal Galt managed a smile. "Yeah... me too."

The both of them had been wrong about who killed Reed Fletcher. Tucker took a deep breath. "Hon, a doctor will be here any second. I want your word you'll not harm him. Let him come to me."

"Are you drinkin' gator juice? No way in hell does that tin star badge see a doctor."

While he was answering, Tucker checked the loads in his gun. He cocked it and glanced at Marshal Galt. "I've got to kill that crazy Cajun or you're going to die. I'll be right back."

He looked at Tucker with weak eyes. "Go get him. I'm not going anywhere."

Tucker signaled Marshal Sanders to put as many rounds as he could in the direction of Hon. He let him know to start shooting on three. He held up one finger, then two, and then three. He broke into a dead run across the street to the side Hon was on. Marshal Sanders fired six rounds into the top of the wall near the roof. Tucker fired three rounds of his own and made it to a canvas covered front to the rendering building. The owner was hunkered down and pointed to the stairs.

Tucker saw the door at the end of the stairs and knew on the other side lay death, but for whom, him or Hon.

Where Outlaws Roam
Royal Wade Kimes

Chapter 37

Macie ran through the ally to the backside of the rendering building and saw what she thought would be there. An iron stationary stepladder was attached to the two story building. The Cooks never went into anything they didn't have a way out. Beside the ladder was a small four by four roof extending out from the main building. It was the backdoor entrance and was used for the workers to take breaks. There were a couple small chairs under the petite porch. She sat down and waited.

When Hon came down the ladder he was in a hurry. He knew Tucker was right behind him. When his feet hit the ground he stopped suddenly. He sensed Macie and half turned.

"Hon."

"Macie." He grinned and turned to face her. "Can't fool a Cook."

"It's done." She had her gun in her hand and he saw it.

"You wouldn't shoot your old uncle would you?"

"I will if I have to. I don't want to. Hon, go back to Louisiana and get lost in the bayou. Go home, let Marshal Galt live. He was doing what he was hired to do... catch criminals and solve crimes."

"What crime? Fletcher was a murdering bastard. He killed our whole family except me and you. I'm all that's left to carry on the Cook name."

Though she didn't have a lot of good feelings regarding the name, she had sadness for him. "You're right, he was no good, but the Cooks did things that weren't good too." She looked him in the eyes. "Fletcher needed punished for his crimes, but by law. I stopped him from killing my man, but you shot and killed him when he had nothing to defend himself with. You executed him."

"I did for a fact." He grinned. "Macie, you and Tucker come with me and I'll let that damned old man chaser live."

Tucker saw Hon talking with someone underneath the small roof at the bottom of the ladder. He figured it to be Macie. He hurried back the way he came and out the front of the rendering business. He walked around to the corner of the backside of the

Where Outlaws Roam
Royal Wade Kimes

business and listened. He stepped out.

"Hon, its Tucker."

He whirled around. "Did you hear our talk?"

"Some. I can't go to Louisiana. I'm a marshal and belong here. Macie and me plan to start a family one day."

He looked at her and then back at Tucker. He had the oddest look about him. "That puts me lonesome. I have no one. Hell, Macie, Tucker, I did Fletcher and his men for you... so we could live our lives knowing we took care of those what caused us great harm."

Macie shook her head slowly. "No Hon, you did what you did for yourself. I'm sure you thought about your brothers and your wife every time you killed one of them, but you didn't really do it for me."

He stood there for the longest time it seemed. Then a slow grin formed on his dirty rusted up face. Realization set in. He wasn't leaving Arkansas. They had a set of laws up in the inlands not known in the swamps. He turned to Tucker. "To hell with it, I've set things right. I'm leaving."

Tucker glanced at Macie. "Hon, I can't let you leave."

"Hell, Tucker, you can't keep me from it." He drew his pistol and was met with a bullet as he fired his gun. He stumbled backwards and fired again. Tucker shot him again. He still didn't fall and managed to fire one more harmless shot into the ground. He dropped to his knees right in front of Macie. "See ya... girly." He fell face down. His life had ended.

Tucker stared at Hon's lifeless body and realized he wasn't meaning he was leaving Arkansas. He was cashing in. Tucker walked to Macie who had kneeled down beside him. She looked up at him.

"A people and a time past."

One week later Tucker and Macie were sitting on Catcher and the bronze mare about to leave Fort Smith for Dye, Kansas. Marshal Sanders was saddled and heading for Pueblo, Colorado. Marshal Galt was standing with the help of a crutch alongside Angel Hound, Pixy, Ina, and Bishop Ortega. They were seeing them off. The Bishop was very happy. Five thousand dollars cash showed up in the offering box in the Cathedral. He surmised, but hadn't any real way of knowing if it was steamboat money.

Angel Hound stepped closer to Catcher and touched Tucker on the boot. "Mister Tucker, I wants you to know you be my best friend. I'll never forget you. It was you freed me and Pixy and the others from a bad time. I has a powerful feeling inside me right now, Mister Tucker. I can't hardly takes you leaving, though I know it gots to be. Don't forget ole Angel Hound."

"I could never forget you, Angel. You're my friend. You saved my life. You know, you were my Guardian Angel then. Fletcher called you Angel Hound. I think he got that wrong. I'm with your Mother Ina. Just plain Angel works real well." He paused for an instant. "Angel, you once asked if I ever needed a good man sometime, well, I plan to keep being a marshal, but I also plan to have a ranch of some kind. Be figuring on coming to Kansas... say in a year."

He grinned as tears ran down his cheeks. Mr. Tucker hadn't forgotten.

Tucker looked over at Marshal Galt. "Come see me when you get better."

"I plan to. I owe you, Marshal, Tucker Shaw." He said his full name and title with a certain amount of respect.

"All you owe me is a supper. As I recall Macie and I didn't get to finish the last one."

"Yeah, come to think of it I guess you didn't, but I really wouldn't know. Best I remember I was out." They all laughed at the stab of humor. "I'll be to see you. I've got to ride up to Melt when I'm back on my feet good. I failed to give them something I found while we were there. I guess I could keep it, but it belongs to them really. So I'll take it to them."

"Melt's not that far from me compared to Fort Smith... you want me to take it to them?"

"No, no, this is something I need to do... and I'd like to do."

Tucker smiled. He understood then. Marshal Galt was rectifying a matter of some sort within himself. He nodded to him ever so slightly letting him know he understood.

He then looked at Pixy. "You're becoming a beautiful lady, watch after Angel and your mother."

Where Outlaws Roam
Royal Wade Kimes

"I will, I promise."

Tucker remembered how she saw to his comfort the night he was brought to the Fletcher Farm. She was living in misery and still looked to him. That was who she was. She saw to people.

"Ina, God bless."

"He be blessing this old woman every day." She beamed with her joyful smile.

Marshal Sanders and Macie said their goodbyes and rode out. They traveled together until it was time to say goodbye.

"Tucker, Macie, I guess this is it." He looked away and grabbed a breath. A gentle tear rolled down his old cheek. "Lived my whole life and never felt about anyone the way I do you two. It's kind of like you're my kids or something. Damn it, I don't like this a bit. I'm giving you one last order before I go. The both of you got to come see me."

Macie was sitting on the bronze mare beside Marshal Sanders. She leaned over and kissed him on the cheek and then wiped away the tear. "We will come see you, we love you."

Tucker rode around on the other side of him and leaned out of his saddle and grabbed him. He held on for the longest of time. Tears blurred his vision as emotion burst from his being.

"Funny, I was made to come to the Wild West for punishment. It's turned out to be anything but. I owe it all to you."

"Tucker, you are part of the Wild West." He laughed. "It hasn't been quite the same since you showed up."

They parted and waved to one another as they went out of sight. He and Macie rode another five minutes or so when he pulled up.

"What's wrong, Tucker?"

He looked at her and grinned. "You're going to meet my mother before too long. I suspect Robert is either in New Orleans or on his way by now. I'm fairly sure you'll meet the Queen of Great Britain as well." He laughed at that. "Anything can happen where outlaws roam."

The End

Where Outlaws Roam
Royal Wade Kimes

www.ingramcontent.com/pod-product-compliance
Ingram Content Group UK Ltd.
Pitfield, Milton Keynes, MK11 3LW, UK
UKHW041945230426
12048UKWH00008B/152